Michelle Boule

Storm
in the
Mountains

Turning Creek
Book 2

For my grandmothers,
wonderful women who knew how to break the rules

for Rita Boule, who was the first adult I knew who read more than I did

for Alice Sauser, who never leaves me doubting that I am loved

ACKNOWLEDGMENTS

Heartfelt thanks and the best hugs I can give go to: My editor, Brenda Errichiello, who is amazing at many things, but mostly at knowing what is needed where. My copy editor, Stephanie Petersen, who acts like she knows it all, because she does, in fact, know it all. D'Ann Ederhoff, who generously supported this book in so many beautiful ways. Katy Ernst and Jennifer Murrell, who read my drafts and love me in spite of my flaws. My family, for their unyielding support and love. My husband, Ries, my own hero, who charms me when I need it most. The Lord, my God, who never lets me be and always calls me towards greater things.

CHAPTER 1

Colorado Territory, 1860

Marina was bored. She was bored, and, for once, she wanted to do something other than playing cards and drinking. She needed another form of entertainment this morning. She had no real reason to go visit Petra, but she had nothing better to do, and she knew Petra would put her to work.

The flight to Petra's alone was enough to begin to calm her. The summer wind was full of the smell of grass, pine, and flowers as Marina soared high above the peaks of the Turning Creek valley. There were few things she loved more than flying. The sky was so blue it hurt to look at it, but Marina could not peel her eyes away until the ground was only feet away from her talons. She landed with a graceful hop on her harpy talons and changed back into her mortal form in the open area between the buildings of James and Petra's dairy farm.

Marina Ocypete was one of the three Remnant harpies of this generation, descended from the original three harpies from the old myths: Celaeno, Ocypete, and Aello. The world was full of Remnants, descendants of the Greek gods and their creatures, with various degrees of power retained from their ancestors' blood flowing in their veins. Last year, when Zeus had tried to rebuild Olympus, many Remnants had been drawn to the tiny valley. Most of them had stayed after the battle that had followed, and they had built new homes and new lives in the shadow of the beautiful mountains in the Turning Creek valley, deep in Colorado Territory.

It was midmorning, so Marina knew to go straight to the milking barn, the largest building on the Lloyd farm. Petra Celaeno had married James Lloyd – a dairy farmer from England who made excellent cheese – just last season. Marina ran her fingers through her tangled brown curls and dug into her pants pocket for a length of twine. When her hair was as controlled as she could make it, Marina pushed open the door of the milking barn.

The air inside was warm and full of the smell of animals and cream. Marina noticed Petra sitting on a milking stool and headed in her direction. Petra's deep olive skin shone with the sweat of work. She looked up as Marina approached, and smiled.

Petra's hands did not falter in their movements. "Good morning. You've arrived just in time to miss most of the work. James and I are finishing up the last cows now."

At the sound of his name, James's head, topped with dark, wavy hair, popped over the backside of the cow behind Petra. "Nice to see you, Marina. Petra is not telling the entire truth. There is always work to be had on a farm."

Marina smiled. "I was hoping you'd have something that required an extra hand. I've been rattling around my mountain too long and wanted some company."

"What qualifies as too long? One day?" Petra asked.

Marina crossed her arms. "Three days."

"Three entire days. Gods, no wonder you came here. I can't imagine you spending one day in idleness, let alone three." Petra sighed dramatically. "I suppose I'd rather have you here than getting into trouble elsewhere." Marina stuck her tongue out at Petra and the two women laughed.

There were three harpies in every generation, one daughter born to each mother. Normally, the harpies lived separate, lonely lives, but this generation was different. Petra, Marina, and Dora had each come to live in the tiny mountain town of Turning Creek many years ago. Over time, their bonds had grown, and they had become family. Marina would give her life for her sisters.

A head poked around the door leading to the storage area. "Do I hear Marina out there?" Robert asked.

"Depends on why you want to know?" Marina quipped.

"Oh, no reason. Things are just never dull when she's around, and today was turnin' out to be mighty boring." Robert's blue eyes twinkled at Marina. Robert Mullins and his older brother, Adam, worked as ranch hands on James's farm. They were more like family members than employees to James. In Marina's mind, they were part of her family now too.

"I'm glad to know I'm useful to you at least." Marina looked meaningfully at Petra after grinning cheekily in Robert's direction.

"You can be useful." James cut in. "Drive the cows in the corral next to the barn out into the pasture. Petra and I will finish up here and send these two out shortly." He patted the rump of the cow in front of him. "Robert, you and Adam take the milk to the cheese house and dump it in the vat. I'm going to be working on a batch later today."

Everyone dispersed to perform their duties. Marina opened the gate to the pasture. Two cows wandered slowly through the opening. The rest just looked dolefully at her. She puffed out a breath of air and walked around to the back of the corral. Marina pulled on her harpy and allowed her vocal cords to change.

A harpy's true voice was harsh, like sound traveling through ground glass. Marina yelled loudly at the cows. The ones closest to her leapt into the air. Their fellows bellowed in terror as they all rushed to escape the fiend in their midst. Marina cackled and clapped her hands. This was the fun she had been missing.

Petra burst from the barn. "Styx and fire, Marina. What're you doing?"

Marina spoke between bursts of laughter. "They wouldn't move after I opened the gate. You're right. They are hilarious when they're scared."

Petra stomped over to where Marina was wiping mirthful tears from her eyes. "They could've hurt each other trying to run away from you."

"Smooth your feathers down. They're all fine. Besides, it's not like you've never done it before." Marina stepped into Petra's space. Marina could see the anger on Petra's face, but she was having too much fun pushing her buttons to back down.

Petra leaned into her. "That was different."

Marina laughed. "I don't really see how."

James cleared his throat and walked over to the two women. Marina had not even heard him enter the room. "Ladies, I know how much you like to argue, but I'd appreciate if you shook hands instead of trading blows."

"I'd rather fight," Marina said.

Petra backed down. "I don't want to get into a fight today."

A little flare of disappointment rose up within her. Marina and Petra were evenly matched, and they always ended up laughing, apologizing, or both in the end. Marina sighed inwardly. Petra was not always as willing to engage in a good brawl these last few months. Marriage was taming Petra, and Marina was not sure she approved.

James waved towards the table sitting under a large tree in the yard. "I'll get some drinks. You two go sit down and cool off."

Petra and Marina, acting properly chastised, sat down in amicable silence until they were joined by James, who carried a pitcher of water and a pitcher of light Kölsch.

Marina took a sip of the beer. "Did Vine give you this? It tastes just like what he's been serving at the saloon lately." Daniel Vine, the proprietor of the local saloon, was the Remnant of Dionysus.

James clinked his cup against Petra's. "I traded some wheels of cheese for a barrel. It's been nice to have on hand during the hot afternoons. We don't get into town as much as you do."

Adam and Robert came out of the cheese house, a tidy white building sitting to the right of the milking barn. Marina slid over so that she was sitting in the middle of the bench and patted the bench on both sides.

"Come join me, boys."

Adam took off his wide-brimmed hat, wiped his brow, and replaced it on his head before sitting. "I've always been taught to say yes when a lady offers you an invitation."

Petra snorted. "He called you a lady."

Marina winked at Adam. "I've always been taught to take what compliments I can get."

"Very wise," Adam said.

Marina sat opposite of Petra and James, and she watched them as the group discussed the tasks that needed to be completed before the end of the day. Petra and James sat with the sides of their bodies touching. Marina hid her smile with another drink from her cup. Petra and James were always touching. A hand there. A shoulder leaning in. The light touch of fingers. She wondered if they even realized they were doing it. Petra was happy, and that made Marina happy – mostly.

Marina turned to face Robert, who maintained an appropriate distance between them. "You and Adam are talented with the horses and the cattle. What're your plans? Long term, I mean."

Robert shared a look with his brother and then graced her with his boyish smile. "We're going to stay here for a spell. We're almost finished with the new bunkhouse, and we'll be hiring a couple more men when James expands the herd. Can't leave now. Things are just pickin' up."

"So being beaten half to death by the Aegis on Zeus's orders hasn't changed your mind?" Marina's lips quirked up in a smile, but she meant the question to be serious. Zeus had taken over James's body in an effort to rebuild his kingdom and tear their lives apart.

Robert put down his cup and looked at James. "I thought I would die that day, but I know it wasn't you. Adam and I made a commitment to you and this place. We'll stay to see it through."

James's responded to Robert's confession in a quiet voice. "Your loyalty is humbling, and I am grateful for it every day."

Adam broke the tension with a wink at Marina. "We've worked too hard to leave just yet. Besides, we know you, Petra, and Dora sent them all to hell — or wherever Remnants go when they die."

Petra's lips thinned. "Hell is close enough to the truth."

"You will both always have a place here, but I've told you before, I will be happy to loan you money to buy your own ranch. I have plenty to spare." James still had a sizable fortune left from what he'd brought over with him from England.

"Not yet." Adam was firm. James nodded his head in understanding.

"I'm glad you're both here. You play a decent game of cards, and Petra and Dora are no good at such idle diversions. I was worried, though, when you first found out about us. You weren't too keen on the idea." Marina jabbed Robert in the ribs.

Adam laughed. "He sat still as a rock for two hours together. I thought those monsters had bashed his head in for good."

Robert leaned around Marina to glare at his brother. "They did bash my head in. At least I didn't cry when Iris showed us her wings."

Adam looked up into the sky. "She's like an angel come to earth, golden feathers and all."

"Don't work too hard on that crush, older brother. I think she's much too old for you."

"Twenty-five is not young, but I would never presume, not with Miss Iris." Adam stopped speaking abruptly and drained his cup. Marina and Robert laughed.

Petra caught Marina's attention. "So why are you really here today?"

Marina shrugged. "I told you. I was bored. At least with Zeus causing problems last year something was always happening."

Petra slammed a hand on the table, making the cups rattle. "Styx, Marina. Just enjoy being still and having peace for two minutes together."

Marina drew her brows together. "Does being still involve another cup of ale?"

Petra rolled her eyes. "I'm serious. You need to find something to do besides play cards at the saloon. You cause trouble when you're idle."

Marina thought Petra was too cautious these days. She expected that of Dora, but not from Petra. "Not my fault if it finds me."

Petra threw up her hands. "I surrender. You're an idiot."

Marina raised her glass in a salute. "Agreed. I might go into town to see Iris. There's plenty of light left in the day. Got anything that needs to go?"

Adam stood. "I've a letter for you to take. Let me fetch it from the house."

Marina took the letter and said her goodbyes. She released her hold on her harpy and let it roll through her. She changed and leapt into the air before the others could even register her movements. As a Remnant of Ocypete, the power of her line was speed, and Marina called on it now to tear through the sky. The wind made her eyes burn, but the delight in her surroundings far surpassed everything else. The afternoon sun traveled towards the western peaks and bathed everything in warmth.

She was careful to land to the west of town and change before walking the rest of the way in. While many of the residents of Turning Creek were Remnants, most were not. Those who were, hid the truth from the mortals, who did not always take kindly to the news that long-forgotten myths and monsters were alive and living on the homestead next door.

Marina went to the mail depot first to drop off Adam's letter. She was surprised to find the depot empty except for Iris, who stood behind the counter. After Zeus's defeat, the mail depot had become the unofficial place where the new Remnants came to announce their presence and let it be known they meant no harm. Mortals ended up there too, eventually. Everyone needed Iris's services.

Iris was the Remnant of the original goddess of that name, The Messenger and the prophetess of the gods. Now she was the postmistress of Turning Creek and the protector and chronicler of Marina's generation of harpies. Adam had been right about Iris; she did look like a mortal's idea of an angel with her petite frame, blonde hair, and blue eyes.

The open room was dominated by a counter on the left. At first glance, it looked as if half a downed tree had been left where it fell. Stools sat like sentinels on the outside of the counter. The wall behind the counter was filled with bird-hole slots and larger openings towards the floor. About half were filled with envelopes and packages of various sizes and colors. A pot-bellied stove rested in the back right corner, surrounded by four small, round tables with chairs. The tables were empty, and Iris was sorting letters.

"Where is everyone?" Marina asked as the door slammed shut behind her.

"Good afternoon to you too. It's too nice out for everyone to be cooped up inside. Even L.A. and Johnny abandoned their checker game to go enjoy the sunshine." L.A. and Johnny were two much-older gentleman who spent the better part of each day playing checkers in the depot.

Marina handed the letter to Iris. "I went to see Petra, and Adam gave me this."

Iris took the sealed envelope and put it into one of the slots behind her. "How are things on the farm?"

"Good. The same as every day on the farm. Gods, I don't know how Petra stands it." Marina flopped onto a stool.

Iris raised a pale blonde eyebrow at her. "Don't you?"

A general feeling of frustration rose in her gut. "Yes, I understand. True love *changed* her, and so on, but she's still a harpy. Still a monster." It felt petty to give her frustration a name. She was glad Petra was content. *No,* Marina amended, *Petra is happy.*

"My bird, you are more than a monster." Iris patted Marina's hand.

Marina huffed. "Well, of course, but that is what I am first and," she waved her hand in dismissal, "everything else just seems, well, boring and useless."

Iris laughed. "You are single minded."

"At least I'm easy to figure out." Marina rubbed her hands together. She could go to Vine's and have a drink before flying home.

"When are you planning on leaving town today?" Iris asked.

"Soon. I don't have anything to keep me here for now. Why?"

Iris pulled a letter from a slot. "This came on the delivery coach today. It's for Reed, and I believe it is not good news. Bad news is not the kind that improves with age. I think he'll want this. I was going to deliver it myself, but since you are here, you can take it. If I don't give you something useful to do, you'll end up drinking and playing cards all night." Iris had an affinity for the written word and could often glean emotions from the paper on which they were written, especially if the feelings that inspired the words were strong.

Marina eyed Iris. "How did you know I was considering a night of cards? Can you read my mind? Maybe you forgot to tell us you could do that?"

Iris rolled her eyes. "I know you, silly bird."

"I forgot it was delivery day. No wonder everyone is outside." Turning Creek was an isolated town. The nearest railway stop was many valleys over. Deliveries came from Leadville, the largest town to the east, only once a month. Sometimes less frequently in the winter.

Marina took the letter from where Iris had laid it on the counter. The address was written in a feminine curl. "I'll take it."

"Thank you," Iris said. Marina paused at the door when Iris called to her again. "Try to stay out of trouble. If you really need something to do, go on rounds with Thomas tomorrow." Thomas was an orphan, and Iris had taken him in after the battle with Zeus. He was the Remnant of Achilles. In the myths, Achilles had possessed sandals with wings that allowed him to fly. The real Achilles did in fact have wings, but they were attached directly to his feet. The Remnants of Achilles could run faster and farther without tiring, a remnant of the abilities the wings had provided their ancestor. One that Thomas found handy when delivering the mail.

Marina agreed and left. Even though the depot had plenty of windows, she had to blink a few times to adjust to the bright sun. She walked north along the wooden boardwalk of Main Street. A year ago, Main Street had been the only street, but with the number of miners lured by the mineral strikes to the east, Remnants, and just people in general moving into the valley, Turning Creek now boasted two additional streets. On top of that, delivery day meant there were more people in town today than usual, as the arrival of the coach was not just about a new variety of supplies to be had; it also meant catching up with neighbors who lived in other parts of the valley.

Marina wound her way around the people gathered in the street. She walked by the mercantile and waved to Simon, who was busy stacking some of his new acquisitions for maximum effect in one of his large front windows. When she got to the sheriff's office, she poked her head in the door, but the one-room jail and office space was empty. Marina went back outside and searched the street for signs of Reed. The sheriff was a tall man and generally easy to find in a crowd, but she did not see him.

She did spy two brown-headed girls huddled against the wall of the building next door, arguing. They were identical twins and belonged to Paul and Lily Hughes, who owned the tailor shop.

Marina walked until she stood next to the girls. "What're you arguing about?"

The girl with the larger gap between her two front teeth hastily put a slingshot behind her back. "Nothing, Miss Marina."

Marina crouched down next to the girls. "Now, Agnes, I saw the slingshot that is now behind your back. Why are you arguing?"

Amy balled up her fists. "Agnes won't let me have a turn."

Marina rubbed her chin and looked over her shoulder. "What were you shooting at? There are a lot of people and horses walking down the street. This isn't the best place for practicing."

Agnes mumbled something incoherent.

Marina continued. "You know, if you're going to shoot a weapon in town, you need to make sure that you don't cause more damage than you mean to and that you don't get caught." Identical smiles broke out on their small faces. "Hand it over, and I'll show you what I mean."

Agnes pulled the slingshot from behind her back and gave it to Marina. "Please don't tell Mother. She'll be furious."

Marina winked. "It's our secret. Now go find me five rocks each that are only the size of the top of your pinkies."

The girls ran off laughing and in minutes had a small pile of rocks at Marina's feet. Marina took in the targets within easy distance and picked up one of the small pebbles.

"Now, what you have to do first is find a target. Widow Finch's boarding house across the street is just right." Marina put the pebble in the pocket of the pouch, pulled back, aimed, and let the rock fly. It plinked against the nearest window of the boarding house. The girls cheered.

Marina hushed them. "We have to be stealthy or we'll get caught. One more, I think." Marina let another pebble fly. A moment later, Widow Finch opened the door and looked around the street. With a shrug, she went back inside. Marina and the girls collapsed in laughter.

"Unless you have practiced often, it's too easy to make mistakes when there are people around that you might hit on accident," Marina cautioned. "If you accidentally hit the flank of a horse, it could throw its rider or kick someone. If you send a rock too hard or too big into a window, it could break. I would advise that you practice out back until your aim is better before venturing onto Main Street again."

Agnes and Amy nodded. "We promise," they chorused.

A commotion two buildings down snagged Marina's attention away from the girls. Katherine Johnson sat on the bench of a wagon with her eyes staring, unfocused, straight ahead. Her husband, Andy, was throwing stuff into the back of the wagon while he yelled at his wife. Marina did not have to strain her ears to hear his tirade. She was sure everyone in the entire valley could hear him. His harsh words were not limited to a list of his wife's failings. He included Simon and a few others in his diatribe for good measure.

With each word, Katherine's head sunk lower into her shoulders. Marina was almost positive that Andy had never actually hit his wife, but words were a powerful weapon on their own. Anger, sure and swift, filled her. Marina enjoyed its warmth as it raced through her blood.

Anger was the easiest of all emotions for Marina. In her mind it was clean and familiar. She bent down and selected the largest rock from the pile, took aim, and watched with pleasure as the rock hit Andy squarely between his eyes. Marina tucked the slingshot into the back of her pants.

Andy roared in anger and looked for the culprit. A small line of blood ran from his forehead down his nose. He turned his hawkish nose in all directions until he spotted Marina and stomped over to where she stood. Agnes and Amy shifted until they stood behind her.

Andy pointed an angry finger at Marina. "Something hit me."

Marina shrugged and let her anger and power seep from her. "I didn't see anything." Marina flexed her hand. She had two knives, both weighted for throwing, on her. One in her boot and one at her waist. She had excellent aim, and she knew she was faster than Andy.

Andy tried to peer around Marina at the girls. "Maybe it was one of them."

Violence throbbed through her blood, and she made no effort to rein in the power leaking from her. Marina grabbed his arm and brought his face level with hers. She let her harpy slip into her eyes and she felt her teeth grow pointy. Andy's skin paled as she spoke. "They had nothing to do with anything. Don't even look in their direction, or it's the last thing you'll use your eyes for." Marina let her power leak into her voice as she persuaded him. "Go home. And be nice to your wife for a change." Marina did not like using her powers of suggestion on others unless it was necessary. It was like cheating. But this was a good cause, so she didn't hold herself back.

Andy was foolish, but he was not an idiot. Most Remnants could hide what exactly they were from other Remnants, but the nature of harpies gave them away. Few things were powerful enough to face a harpy, and Andy Johnson definitely was not one of them. He scowled and stalked back to his wagon. Marina kept the girls behind her until his wagon was out of town. She relaxed and reigned in her harpy before giving the girls back their slingshot.

"One more thing. Never pick a fight you can't finish." Marina tousled each brown head.

The doors opened behind them, and Lily Hughes stepped out. She was a modest woman and a Remnant of Medusa. Her straight brown hair was pulled into a bun, which would have looked severe on anyone else, but only served to enhance her large brown eyes. They narrowed when she spied the girls next to the building. "I thought you two were supposed to be sweeping the boardwalk."

"I'm sorry, Mrs. Hughes. I stopped and was talking to them." Marina smiled with what she hoped looked like innocence. Marina knew Lily Hughes was powerful in her own way, and Marina respected her.

Mrs. Hughes eyed the three of them, considering. "You two run along and go finish your chores before dinner."

"Bye, Miss Marina," they yelled as they ran, relieved, through the front door of the tailor shop.

When the girls were out of earshot, Mrs. Hughes turned to Marina. "I saw what happened with Mr. Johnson. Katherine's not powerless. I don't know why she doesn't just stand up to him. I also know you kept the girls from causing some serious damage with their new slingshot. Thanks for that too."

"I can't stand bullies." Marina sighed, allowing the residual anger to ebb away. "The girls need some practice with the slingshot. I informed them Main Street was not necessarily the place to do that." Marina shifted her weight. From the corner of her eye, she saw Reed Brant cross the street towards them. "If you'll excuse me, I've got a letter for the sheriff."

"Of course, and thanks again."

"Anytime." Marina walked towards Reed. She noticed the grace in his stride and the easy way he held his tall frame. Marina was taller than most women and some men, but Reed still stood over her. He was a handsome-looking man, if one cared for such things. Marina did not know why she had never noticed this about him before. Their paths converged in front of the sheriff's office.

"Afternoon, Marina. That was a bit of commotion with Andy. Care to share some details?" Reed lifted up his hat, smoothed his hair from his forehead, and replaced it.

"Just Andy Johnson being his usual, charming self." Marina leaned against the front wall of the sheriff's office and faced the street.

Reed grunted. "His redeeming qualities are few and far between." Reed angled himself so that he could see Marina and most of Main Street.

"I agree. How're you doing this afternoon?" Marina watched his face as he talked. He looked at her, but his eyes moved often, taking in the people moving up and down the street, going about their business. He noticed everything. Marina approved.

"Top of the world, today, as always. It wasn't only Andy I saw you talking with. You saved me from giving the Hughes twins a lecture on weapons on the street."

"I know idleness causes problems."

Reed looked down his straight nose at her. "You must have an overabundance of time, then, judging from the amount of effort you spend on questionable pursuits."

Marina shrugged. "Nothing wrong with a few card games and rounds of ale."

Reed smiled, but it faded before he spoke. "Nothing at all, if you spend a portion of time also doing something useful. My offer stands. I could use help. Especially on the occasion when there's a Remnant problem I'm not equipped to handle."

Reed was a mortal, and he knew his limitations. He had issued an open invitation to all three harpies to assist him when he needed more muscle for a job. He moved and stepped closer to her. He had not shaved in a day or two, and brown hair covered his tanned face. Marina had to look up to meet his eyes. She shifted her weight.

Reed's voice dropped so that he would not be overheard. "Never would've thought you'd have a soft spot for youngsters. That was a kindness to help them. And, while I don't approve of the method, Andy deserved what you gave him."

Marina smiled. "I do have a soft spot for kids." Marina dug into her pocket and pulled out the letter. "That's not the only useful thing I'm doing today. Iris asked me to deliver this. She said it might be bad news."

Reed's brows drew down. "It's from my sister, Claire." He opened the letter and started reading. Marina watched his face. His eyes, the color of clear whiskey, darkened. Something tugged within her. She put her hands into her pockets. "I hope the news isn't bad."

Reed's lips thinned as he folded the letter up and tucked it into the pocket of his duster. "It is. There's been a death in the family. Claire's husband."

Marina thought of the other harpies, thought of Iris, James, Adam, and Robert. She thought of losing the people in her life that she had come to call friends, including Reed. Her heart ached in a way that was new.

"I'm sorry." Marina laid a hand on his arm. He was warmer than she expected. She pulled her hand back and rubbed it on her leg.

Reed looked at her, but his eyes slipped from her face and focused on something over her shoulder. "Thanks. I'm going to head in for the night. Afraid I won't be good company at the moment. Have a good evening, Marina." He went inside and Marina stood there, staring at the closed door.

Marina hesitated. If she were in mourning, she would want a good drink or a fight to take her mind off things. Perhaps she should follow Reed and drag him to Vine's for a drink. Her hand was on the latch of his door when she decided against it. She enjoyed his company, but she did not think that Reed's idea of letting loose was the same as hers. She remembered the warmth of his arm, and her hand tingled. It was best to leave him be on his own, Marina thought.

Marina left the boardwalk and crossed the street to Vine's saloon. She wanted a drink, a good game of cards, and some laughter. Vine might have something new on tap. More than anything, though, she needed something to chase away the memory of the sadness she had seen in Reed's eyes.

CHAPTER 2

Marina came back to town the next day and headed straight for the depot. Iris tried to put her to work sorting mail, but Marina kept putting the letters in the wrong places. Marina tried reading a book instead, and she soon grew restless. She walked the length of the mail depot, turned at the front door, and swung around towards the back table, where a serious game of checkers was being waged.

Johnny and L.A. had been best friends for as long as Turning Creek had been a town. As far as Marina knew, they were the oldest residents of the valley. Johnny's voice rose as he waved a finger in L.A.'s face. Without breaking stride, Marina pulled a knife from her boot and threw it into the wall beside the men's heads. L.A. dropped the black disc he was holding, and Johnny bumped the table, sending checkers sliding from their squares.

"Miss Marina, I almost had him beat," Johnny wailed.

"Stop cheating, or I'll tell your wife where you spend your afternoons." Marina strode over and pulled her knife from the wall.

"Won't bother me none. She thinks I'm at Vine's having a pint to escape her nagging." Johnny smoothed non-existent hair over his balding head.

Marina leaned over the checker table to retrieve her knife. "She's can't be that much a fool. It's barely past breakfast. Too early for a pint or a glass of whiskey."

L.A. scooped up checkers and re-laid the board. "It's never too early for a proper drink."

"If I tell her where you really go, she'll know where to find you." Marina winked.

Johnny sputtered. "You wouldn't ruin my fun, now would you, Miss Marina?"

She laughed and slapped the poor man on the back. "I wouldn't tell on

you. I know your wife, and even I would think twice before crossing her."
In truth, Johnny's wife was the Remnant of a harmless water nymph and no
danger to a harpy, but Marina did not create trouble for herself, even if that
was the popular opinion. She just never said no when it came calling—and
it seemed to find her often.

Harpies tended to be a violent, territorial lot, and Marina had no
problem with those particular tendencies. She went back to pacing, flipping
the knife that was still in her hand.

She made two more circuits across the room before Iris slammed her
book on the counter. "Really, Marina. Could you please be still for two
minutes together? It's too early for your restlessness." Iris pinched the
bridge of her delicate nose.

Marina placed her elbows on the counter, rubbed smooth by years of
visitors, and leaned close to Iris so the men in the back would not hear.
"I'm bored. Come fly with me today. We can walk out far enough and no
one will see us change."

It was low of her to play on Iris's newfound love of flying, but if she
did not find something to placate her days-old boredom, Marina would pull
her own feathers out. The creation of Iris's wings was the only good thing
Zeus had done for them before they'd sent him back to the underworld
where he belonged.

Iris had worked hard to build up the muscles in her back. It had taken
her months to have enough endurance to keep up with the harpies for even
a couple of hours. She loved to fly, and Marina loved to watch the joy on
her face when she did.

"I went with Dora two days ago, and I'm still sore. Maybe tomorrow.
There's plenty of mail to deliver today, if you would like to lend a hand. I'm
sure Thomas would appreciate the help." Iris smoothed her corn silk hair
back, though not a strand was out of place.

Marina looked down at her faded work pants and scuffed boots. "I'll
take some mail today."

"You have to ride a horse. No flying in the daylight."

Marina snorted. "You take all the fun out of everything."

Iris narrowed her eyes at her. "Not all the letters are for Remnant
families. Just how would you explain to a mortal how you happened to be
halfway up the mountain with a bag of letters and no horse in sight?"

"Divine providence?"

It would be better if she could deliver the mail in her harpy form with
the letters clutched in her clawed hands. The look on the mortals' faces
would be hilarious.

"You never take anything seriously." Iris put her book under the
counter and turned to sort packets and packages into the bird-holes on the
wall behind the counter, using a system only she knew.

"I take lots of things seriously. Hunting, drinking, and avoiding boredom are serious endeavors," Marina said. Iris shook her head and continued sorting.

Despite her bluster, Marina knew she needed something to occupy her time. One could only hunt and drink so often. Her sister harpies had not been as entertaining recently, and Marina had been left alone more than she preferred. Petra's happiness over her recent marriage and her surge of domesticity made Marina's teeth ache. And Dora, never the liveliest of the three, had been even more laconic than usual, spending time in her new herb garden.

Iris turned from her task and pointed to a stool at the end of the counter. Marina obeyed the unspoken command. "Why are you so twitchy and restless lately?

Marina picked at an indention on the counter. "Everyone's busy."

Iris put her hand over Marina's to still her movement. "You need something useful to do."

Marina snorted. "You sound like Reed. He said everyone needs something useful to do."

"I agree with him. He sometimes needs help with things. I know he has asked for your help." Iris paused, studying Marina's face. "You can't pace in here all day, every day."

L.A. looked up from his table and interjected. "Plus, if you stay around here, you'll keep messing up our board and throwing knives into Miss Iris's nice walls."

Marina slumped on her stool. "I appear to be outnumbered."

As if summoned, Reed walked through the door of the depot with a firm set to his broad shoulders and determination in his whiskey-colored eyes. Sandy brown hair curled over his ears and from underneath the wide brimmed hat on his head. An empty coffee mug dangled from the fingers of his right hand. He stopped short when he saw Marina.

"Morning, Sheriff. You look purposeful. Anything going on I can help with?" Marina rubbed her hands together. Her day was looking up.

"As a matter of fact, I was just coming to send a message to you, or rather one of you." Reed looked at the men in the back, took a step closer to Marina and Iris, and dropped his voice. "I think Reggie Miller spied a chimera up in the valley on Pikus Peak, by his farm."

"No need to whisper," Marina said, pointing to L.A. and Johnny. "Those two are married to nymphs."

Johnny and L.A. waved at Reed then went back to their game.

"A chimera? Sounds like my day is getting better." Marina rubbed her hands together.

"Nasty piece of work, a chimera," Johnny said as he jumped one of his pieces across the board. L.A. cursed.

Reed frowned at Marina. "You needn't look so gleeful about it. I've read chimeras aren't exactly the friendliest sort."

Iris ducked below the counter and came back up with a large, green, leather book whose binding was cracked in several places. "You sure it was a chimera?"

"Only have Reggie's description, which involved a good bit of babbling about how he wasn't crazy. It had a snake tail, a lion front, and was as large as a man. He admitted he saw it from across the valley, but whatever he saw spooked him. I sent him to the boarding house for breakfast. Thought I would get one of the harpies to go up Pikus with me. See what we find." Reggie was a mortal, so if he saw something strange in the trees, he would likely try to quantify it with some known animal.

Marina stood and belatedly realized her movement had brought her almost flush with Reed. "Iris was lecturing me on the merits of being useful before you came in. I'm available."

Reed blinked at her slowly and cleared his throat. "I'd be grateful for the help. This isn't something I'd want to come across alone." He did not move away from her, and Marina could feel the heat coming off his body. It was both disconcerting and exhilarating.

Iris flipped through the book she had grabbed and pointed to a page featuring a black and white drawing of a chimera. "I guess you have found some time to read those books you've been borrowing from me. Your reading has paid off. I think you're right. Two things you should know before you go. A chimera is often an omen of disaster to come, and they can breathe fire."

Reed rubbed the back of his neck. "Sounds lovely. Why are things never boring in this town?"

"Last time we had omens in Turning Creek, things did not go well." A line of anxiety appeared between Iris's eyes and her mouth turned down. Before Zeus had taken over the body of Petra's now-husband, Iris had channeled a prophecy of impending doom.

"Let me go grab my stuff." Marina took the stairs two at a time. Finally, something else to do besides deliver letters. Hunting a chimera would be a sight better than hunting game.

Marina went into the small room Iris kept for the harpies when they were in town and looked at the weapons she had on hand. She dithered, trying to decide which to take. A harpy was a weapon all to herself, but Marina loved the feel of a sword in her hand. Her mother had been an excellent teacher, and Marina had been a talented pupil. Months ago, she would have kept all her weapons hidden, but she had stopped hiding what she was, even in her mortal form: a deadly predator.

A Remnant's aura, or soul, had a different feel to it, and they could usually sense each other. For most, the sense of otherness was all they gave off to other Remnants, but for the Remnants who were powerful, like the harpies or Iris, their individual natures were hard to conceal. When meeting for the first time, many Remnants knew they were speaking to a harpy and acted appropriately deferential. Even mortals who had no knowledge of Remnants sometimes used caution around the harpies. A predator has a way of giving off a vibe that says stay back or you might become dinner.

In the past, she had worked harder to hide what she was. After the battle with Zeus, Marina wanted to be prepared for anything. She had realized that being in a small mountain town made people more forgiving of her choice to wear pants and an array of weapons. Marina took the sword and three knives from the chest.

Reed took one look at her when she came down the stairs and laughed. "Think you left some of your weapons upstairs."

Johnny and L.A. whistled at her.

Marina made a show of rolling her eyes. "A lady can never be too prepared."

Reed flashed a wicked grin at her, and Marina's heart skipped. "Sparrow, you ain't no lady."

She hated that nickname. He only used it to get a reaction from her. Marina ignored it and returned the smile. "A fact for which you'll thank the gods after I save your scrawny hide from the big, bad chimera."

"By all means, big, bad harpy. Lead the way."

CHAPTER 3

For the first half of the day, Marina flew in large circles over Reggie's land, looking for signs of the chimera. It was a perfect day to feel the heat on her feathers while flying through the blue sky, and Marina had enjoyed the hunt from the air. The tracks of the chimera were easy to discern; the creature crushed the grass as it dragged the snake half of its body through the valley.

After locating the trail, she dropped down to the ground and joined Reed on foot. They followed its trail to a small stream, where all evidence of the creature disappeared. Marina took back to the air to backtrack, but the trail only led back to the stream. Marina followed the trail a third time, this time in her mortal form, hoping she would see something new. The trail only went one place. Nowhere.

Marina changed and walked beside Reed. She wrapped her hair into an untidy bun and shed her duster in the heat of the afternoon. Marina straightened and rubbed her back.

Though her mortal form seemed to indicate she was in her mid-twenties, Marina was much older. At sixty-two, she was young for a harpy—they often lived to the ripe old age of three hundred—but bending over and peering at the ground for hours tied her back into knots. She would have to change later and fly. The change would ease her soreness, and flying would work out the kinks in her muscles.

"You look like you're hundreds of miles away. Bored already?" Reed's even tenor punctured her daydream.

"I was thinking I'm too old to spend half the day hunched over. That and I think we may have lost the trail in this stream." Marina blew the air out of her lungs in a puff of frustration.

Reed's gaze appraised her, traveling over her scuffed boots, sturdy pants, and sensible work shirt. To her surprise, she found herself wondering what he did think of her. Marina thought she had too many curves, her hair was a tad too curly, and she opened her mouth more often than most men preferred. It was a good thing harpies did not take permanent mates, or she would be in danger of becoming an old maid one day. Petra and James were the exception to the rule. The only exception in the history of the harpies.

Reed looked away from her and pointed to the far bank of the stream. "I'll take that side. You take this one. We'll walk upstream and look for an exit. If we don't find one, we'll turn around and try downstream."

It was as good a plan as any, so Marina obeyed and hopped over some rocks to reach the other side. She kept her eyes down to the ground, searching for flattened grass and lion paw prints.

"You don't look old enough for back problems." Reed picked up their conversation after they had walked a few yards.

"I'm sixty-two years old." Marina paused and looked across the stream to gauge Reed's reaction.

He jerked to a stop. "What?" His easy smile from moments ago faltered, and lines appeared between his eyes as he squinted at her.

"I am sixty-two years old. Are you sure you aren't getting up there in years? Your hearing seems to be going. How old are you?" Marina cast her eyes back down and continued her search.

She heard his footsteps continue on the rocky gravel of the stream bank a moment later. Due to the altercation with Zeus, he knew some of the Remnants' secrets and he had been reading Iris's books, but there was much he still did not know.

"Thirty-three. How old is Petra?" Reed asked.

Petra was the oldest of the harpies. "She is seventy-one this year," Marina said, thinking of Petra's domesticity and grinding her teeth together.

A pause in his step. "And Dora?"

Dora, whose freckles only added to her air of innocence, brought out all the protective tendencies in Marina. Petra had her darkness of soul to protect her, and Marina had a love of violence and speed. Dora was something different. Marina could not name it, but there was some bit of humanity in Dora that the other two harpies lacked. It was an elusive something Marina would give her life to defend. "Sixty-eight."

"How long do harpies live, then?" Reed spoke without looking at her, intent on their prey.

"We come of age at fifty. That's when our loving mothers boot us from the house and we have to spread our wings in the world. Harpies live for about three hundred years, unless Iris is correct. She thinks Petra's marriage has shortened her lifespan some, but we won't know if Iris is right until Petra dies. If my mother is still alive, she's about one forty-two now."

Marina's mother had told her that failing to remove a daughter from her house or taking a mate for life would cause her own death. It was the curse the gods had given the original harpies. To the gods, who were immortal, a shorter life was the worst punishment they could imagine. Iris estimated Petra would age similarly to a mortal, starting from the point when the harpy had fallen for James. From what Marina understood, it had something to do with love evolving the violent nature of the harpy into something…different. Iris had been vague on the last bit, and Marina had not pressed for details.

Reed turned towards her and stopped. "Your mother kicked you out?"

Marina shrugged but kept walking. "It's our way."

"You said if she's alive. Don't you keep in touch?"

Marina stopped and turned around. "Why would I?"

Reed opened his mouth, then closed it. He shook his head then resumed walking. Marina turned back around and kept walking. Harpies were creatures of violence first. Marina knew what she was: a weapon. Violence and happy families were not things that Marina could imagine existing in the same space.

"I come from a large family. I'm fifth of ten. My father is a judge, and all my brothers followed suit in one way or the other. Can't imagine not living in a house bursting with noise and people who would give their right arm to make you grin. Or put frogs in your bed, depending on the day."

A thread of longing pulled through her, and Marina snipped it off before it made a stitch in her heart. Petra had found some version of the domesticity that Reed described, but Petra always had been less than comfortable with her darker nature. Where Petra avoided it, Marina embraced it.

"Sounds messy."

Reed laughed. "Worth every moment."

Marina looked around at the area around the creek. They had been walking upstream long enough. "There are no signs of an exit here. Let's go back and move downstream."

They passed the spot where they had turned north and kept going. The sun was arcing towards the mountain peaks, and the decent light would be gone soon. Pressure to find some trace of the chimera, if that was actually what they were looking for, ate at Marina.

"What was your mother like?" Reed asked.

Marina tried not to think of her mother often. "I think she cared for me in her own way. Harpies are not the best of mothers. She taught me what she thought I needed to know to survive."

Reed paused on his side of the creek and moved his gaze from the gravel to Marina's face. "And what does a harpy need to know?"

"How to fight in my mortal form. How to use a knife and a sword. She was an old-fashioned sort, so I had to teach myself how to use a firearm. She taught me how to use my harpy skill of speed, how to be a weapon, and to love what I am." Marina felt her harpy preen with pride at the list.

Reed chuckled and walked on. "I can see your pride shining from here. I'll admit you're the fastest thing I've ever seen. Don't get too full of yourself."

Marina grinned in delight. "That's the best compliment I've had all day, Sheriff."

The sun sunk lower until the bottom of the orange orb touched the peaks to the west. If they were going to find something, it needed to be now. It would soon be too dark to do any tracking.

Marina listened to Reed's measured steps on the other bank. "What are we going to do if we find the chimera or whatever it is?"

Reed looked at the coming sunset then turned to Marina. "I know how you like to swing first and maybe ask questions at a later date. I'd like to talk to it first and see if he means harm. Most of the people around here don't know a thing about Remnants, and I think we'd all like to keep it that way for now. So we talk first."

Marina put her hands on her hips. "I'm the model of peace and patience. I'd never start a fight unprovoked."

Reed snorted. "Unless you were restless."

Marina laughed and kept walking. "Best way to shake out the boredom of a day. Followed by a stiff drink."

The sound of Reed's footsteps slowed, and Marina turned to ask him if he had found something. The hair on her neck rose seconds before a tan and black blur bounded from the trees and knocked Reed from his feet and into the water of the creek.

The change exploded over her in a flurry of feathers. Her harpy screamed in outrage as she dove for the chimera holding Reed under the water in the stream as he struggled. *That slinking piece of filth is not going to drown him*, she thought. Reed was hers to protect. Hers.

Marina dug her talons deep behind the mane of the lion's head. In her harpy form, Marina was the size of a cow with the body of a bird of prey, and she leveraged that weight to toss the chimera onto the bank of the stream. Marina landed on the chimera and pressed her talons into its flesh. She used the claws on the ends of her wings to keep the snapping jaws from doing any damage.

The smell of warm blood roared through her, and the chimera twisted, sending small puffs of fire from its mouth. The fire licked at her feathers. Marina barely felt it over the rage throbbing in her head. They had not come here with the intention to harm, but the chimera would be lucky to escape the harpy's wrath now that it was running freely. It had *dared* to attack Reed, to attack her. She chanced a glance at Reed. He was alive, dripping and sputtering. He looked pale under his tanned skin, but he was breathing. Relief hit her square in her feathered chest.

Marina narrowed her eyes and bared her teeth at the chimera while she pushed his face into the rocky bank. A renewed rage at the danger Reed had been in throbbed through her. The thrill of the fight was nectar on Marina's tongue, and she drank it with greed.

This was so much more fun than delivering mail.

Marina laughed, her voice deep and broken. It was a harpy's voice, full of savagery. "Poor cub. Didn't your momma tell you never to play with your food?"

The chimera rolled onto its back, forcing Marina to let go or be crushed. Marina never took her eyes off the creature.

"Reed, you still breathing?"

He coughed up some water. "Takes more than that to kill me."

"Good." She turned her full attention to the chimera. The snake body slithered behind the majestic forefront of a sleek lion whose mane now dripped pink as its own blood mixed with the water from the stream. It looked like a grotesque drowned rodent.

"What're you doing here?" Marina's voice rasped over her harpy vocal cords.

The chimera's voice was low. It had trouble forming the words with its lion jaws. "Whadoyo care?"

Possessiveness flared. "This is my territory. You're trespassing."

"There'rrre other Remnantsss here." Its voice improved with use, though it spoke with a lisp. A snake tongue whipped out between the lion's teeth and Marina shuddered.

Though she had an angular female face and the body of a bird of prey in her harpy form, she'd never considered herself grotesque. "None of them are as ugly as you."

"I beg to differ. You're not much to look on yoursssself."

"Why are you here?" The call to commit violence was a burning need in her blood, but Marina could rein it in if the chimera meant no harm. It might have attacked Reed out of fear. If it did mean to cause trouble, Marina would happily divest the creature of its head.

The chimera coughed and a puff of fire escaped its mouth. "Sssame reassson asss anyone elssse, I sssupose. To live free."

Marina looked at Reed again. He had his gun out and the hammer cocked back. "That man over there is the sheriff of Turning Creek. We don't take too kindly to people causing trouble in the region. Remnants causing trouble do not get the benefit of a mortal trial. They get a claw in their neck." She waved one of her wings for emphasis. "Or my teeth in their throat."

The chimera's tongue darted out and licked the tip of its wide lion nose. For a moment, Marina thought it was going to fight back, and excitement raced through her. Disappointment followed when the chimera said, "I undersssstand."

Reed spoke up. "Funny way to come in peace, by attacking us."

"You were tracking me. I thought to act firssst before giving you a chanssse to find me."

Reed said, "We just wanted to verify a story. The man who lives in this valley is human and doesn't know a Remnant from a hole in the ground. If you mean to settle here, go across the valley to Aspen Peak. No one living on the valley side of that mountain." Aspen Peak was next to Jolly's Folly, where Marina's small cabin stood. If the chimera settled there, she could keep an eye on it. "Don't make trouble and you'll get none from me." The chimera nodded. "Don't attack first next time." The chimera nodded again. "Can you change into human form?" The chimera nodded but did not change. Reed continued, "Good. Don't come into town like that. You'll get shot."

"Or worse," Marina accentuated her words by flashing her pointed teeth. The chimera was now behaving like an overgrown lapdog. Irritation scrubbed against her, and she clenched her claws, imagining the chimera's head crushing between them.

The chimera shifted its gaze from Reed to Marina. It knew who the real threat was. "I will not encroach on your territory or causssse trouble again, Mistress Harpy."

Marina grinned, showing all of her pointed teeth to her advantage, even the back ones. "Should you decide to cross me, know that I'm not the only harpy here. You'll have more than me to contend with should you cross the line and harm a mortal or Remnant." Marina took a step back.

The chimera inclined its head and gave a mock bow. "I undersssstand, missstresss." It turned and half walked, half slithered into the trees.

Reed walked fifteen feet down the stream and snatched his hat from a tangle of branches on the side of the stream. Steady drops of water fell from the rim after he put it on his head. His wet shirt clung to his broad chest and Marina dragged her eyes away, the violence from moments before morphing into something altogether more dangerous.

"Well, that went south faster than expected." Reed sat on a patch of ground in the sun and removed his boots. He upended them and water sloshed onto the rocks.

Marina hopped over to him on taloned bird feet. Harpies were made to fly and glide, not walk. Careful to keep her claws away from his skin, she ran a finger over a set of small puncture marks on his shoulder. Reed stilled at her touch. The shirt around the area was pink. "You're bleeding."

"Just a scratch."

Marina had to make sure. "Take off your shirt. Let me see." The throatiness of her harpy vocal cords made the request sound more suggestive than it was. Heat flooded her face and Marina was grateful her skin was darker in this form, making a blush hard to detect.

Reed hesitated and Marina flashed her teeth at him. He rolled his eyes. "Don't get all scary monster on me. I think you would've gladly crushed the chimera to hear its head pop, but you won't hurt me."

Marina laughed, the sound like sand over wood. "Then you've never seen me really scary. I guess I need to try harder."

Reed looked at her face for a long time. Marina wondered what he saw. "Thanks for saving me."

Marina lifted her shoulders in a ghost of a shrug, the best she could do with wings. "It would've been too hard to carry your wet, dead body back to town. Now, let me see your shoulder."

Reed laughed, unbuttoned his shirt, and pulled it down to reveal four puncture wounds where the chimera had held him down. Marina's claw clenched at the remembered image of Reed under the water, unable to breathe. The wound no longer bled, but it would need to be cleaned so it would not fester. "They don't look too bad, but you should have Doc look at them when we get back."

"Yes, ma'am."

"I'm serious. Who knows where that kitten's claws have been." If that chimera ever laid one tiny claw on Reed or anyone else again, Marina would make it beg for death.

Reed buttoned up his shirt. "I'll go. No need to glare. Want to escort me there to make sure?"

"If I stay a harpy and chase you through town until we get there, we'd give everyone something to talk about for weeks." Marina shifted out of her harpy form and sat in the sun next to Reed.

Reed's eyes traveled over her. "You make out all right? Thought I saw you get singed around the edges."

The side of her body where the chimera's fire had burned her was hot and itched like a sunburn. "Just a touch. Tomorrow, I'll be as good as new. One of the benefits of being a big, scary monster. I heal fast." Marina let the feral light slide into her eyes as she smiled at him.

Reed cleared his throat and shifted his eyes across the river. "Mind if I ask you something?"

A light blush crept up his neck. *Interesting,* she thought. "Ask away."

The blush crept higher. "As a harpy, you never have clothes on, but when you change back, you have clothes again. How does that work?"

Marina smothered a laugh. She would not have guessed that Reed would blush over her being unclothed. "Magic."

"Magic? That's a sorry explanation."

Marina rolled words around in her head, searching for the ones that would make sense to him. "My harpy is me but it isn't. When I become the harpy, my mortal self is sort of pushed to another place. When I'm mortal, the harpy is always in me because that is my true self, my essence, but the harpy has no use for my mortal form and it pushes it...elsewhere, along with whatever is attached to that form. Or at least most of it. It doesn't work on big things, like my sword. That's why as a human, we're still violent, but as a harpy, we lose some of our compassion." It was the best she could do to explain.

"Elsewhere?" he pushed.

"That's the best I can explain. It's just not here."

The last warmth of the day seeped into her bones and dried Reed's clothes. The traveling sun moved their patch of light until they sat in shadow. Reed stood and offered her his hand. The warmth of his hand over hers traveled up her arm and lodged in her stomach. Reed seemed unaffected and dropped her hand once she had gained her feet. Marina rubbed her tingling hand over the roughness of her pants.

They walked in silence to where they had left their horses. The sun was fading, and Marina put her duster on before swinging into the saddle. It would be full dark by the time they reached town, and the saloon would be in full swing by the time they returned. She could have a pint before flying home.

"I've been thinking." Reed slowed his horse so they could ride side by side.

"Somehow that sounds like the beginning of a bad idea."

Reed's mouth quirked up. "Since more Remnants have been moving into the valley, being sheriff is not as simple as it used to be. If I'd have come up here alone today, I'd be dead."

Short, tight pain lashed around her chest. "I think you would've made a decent showing in the fight, given more time."

"Maybe, but I'm glad I didn't have to find out. I could use your help on a more regular basis."

"Sheriff Brant, are you propositioning me?"

Reed touched the brim of his hat and suppressed the smile tugging at his mouth. "If by propositioning, you mean offering you a job as a deputy, you'd be correct. Colorado isn't an official territory yet, so it wouldn't be official, exactly. I hold office because the people asked me to, and I'm asking you with that authority to help me out. I know the town would approve. Simon and Henry already suggested I get some help after more Remnants started coming in. Plus, it would keep me from being dead."

The idea had merit. She would spend less time aimlessly wandering around the depot or flying around the mountain and more days in Reed's company. The idea both thrilled her and sent a tinge of fear through her. "I'm not sure the town would accept me as a deputy."

"Because you're a harpy?"

He saw so much of her and yet missed the glaring details. "Because I'm a woman."

Reed's gaze was piercing. "Sparrow, this is the west, and we live in a town full of half-gods and monsters. They'll get over it."

Marina gripped the reins tight. "If I say yes, you have to stop calling me that. I'm not a songbird. I'm a bird of prey."

"Sweetest songbird I ever heard." Reed winked at her and then kicked his horse into a canter.

She should have let the chimera eat him for dinner.

CHAPTER 4

As Marina had predicted, the sound of men laughing and talking over the slightly off-key piano poured out of the saloon and onto Main Street. She sent a longing look towards the entryway.

Reed chuckled as he swung down from his horse. He favored his hurt shoulder. "Hang around long enough, and I'll buy you a drink."

Lines of pain bracketed his mouth, and Marina remembered him under the chimera again. She did not think she would forget that image anytime soon. "Doc's first, then drinks. And I'll buy you a round of the good whiskey too. None of that rot gut Vine sells to the miners when they're already drunk."

Reed handed her the reins of his horse. "Take them over to Henry's stable and wipe them down. I'll head to Doc's, get patched up. Meet me there."

Marina nodded her assent and then walked the horses down the road to Henry Foster's blacksmith shop. Due to the increased population of Turning Creek, Henry had expanded his small smithy to include a larger forge area, a corral, and a barn. Henry Foster was not just any blacksmith. He was the Remnant of Hephaestus and had many hidden talents when it came to shaping metal. Marina put the horses in two empty stalls, removed their saddles, wiped them down, and fed them. It was almost an hour before she made it back down the street to Doc's.

Lee Williams, known as Doc to most of Turning Creek, was the resident physician. He was a Remnant and follower of Asclepius who treated everyone, Remnant and mortal, with the same care. He also had the power to bring people back from the dead. It was a handy talent to have, unless some crazy people decided you were cavorting with the devil and made the sheriff put you on trial. Lucky for the town, Doc Williams had found allies in the local harpies and the sheriff when that nightmare had come to pass a few months ago, and now everyone left well enough alone.

Marina knocked on the door to Doc's office, then lifted the latch to go in. There was a sitting room at the front of the office with a couch and two chairs placed around a small stove. It looked like any other waiting room except for the glass tank of brown and yellow snakes against one wall. They were the symbol of Asclepius and nonvenomous. *Still unsettling though,* Marina thought as she walked through the room. A light shone underneath the closed door on the back wall. She knocked on the door.

"Come in," Doc said.

Reed sat in a chair next to a table. An oil lamp sat next to his shoulder, shining light on the row of puncture marks there. Doc's dark-haired head was bent over Reed's shoulder. Doc dipped his fingers into a bowl of paste and rubbed the mixture over the puncture wounds. Reed did not flinch, but his mouth thinned into a fine line.

"I had to put a stitch in two of the deeper wounds. I'll remove them in a couple days, provided you don't do anything stupid to rip them out yourself." Doc picked up a roll of linen from the table and started wrapping it around Reed's shoulder.

The pain lines still stood out around Reed's eyes and mouth. Marina put her hand into her duster pocket and pulled out a flask. She held it out to Reed. "Something to tide you over until we get to Vine's."

Reed grabbed the flask and moved his arm to unscrew the cap. Doc snapped at him. Marina grabbed the flask, twisted off the cap, and handed it back. Reed took two sips from it before giving it to Marina. She took a drink and returned the flask to her pocket.

"Will he live, Doc?"

Doc frowned at her. "Of course. A chimera did this?"

Reed nodded. "Marina made him pay for it while I tried not to drown."

Doc tied up the end of the linen. "Chimeras are bad pieces of work. You're both lucky to have escaped so easily." He turned to Marina. "The sheriff tells me you were burned."

Marina crossed her arms and glared at Reed. "Nothing much. It feels fine now."

Doc straightened and looked Marina in the eye. With a start she realized he was the same height as she was. "I know you heal fast, but you're not invincible. If the burns bother you, please let me look at them."

Marina nodded with a sigh. "You know I will, if it's bad enough." The doctor patched her up often. She wanted to stay on his good side.

Doc made a noise in his throat. "What concerns me most is your definition of bad enough."

"Still alive, aren't I?" Marina winked at Doc.

Reed stood and pulled his shirt off the back of the chair he had been sitting in. He winced as he put his left arm through the sleeve. "Ready for that drink, Sparrow?"

Marina smiled. "Always."

The warmth and noise enveloped them when they walked through the open doors of the saloon. A long bar covered the left side of the room, behind which Daniel Vine, purveyor of fine spirits and the Remnant of Dionysus, stood chatting with a patron. Round tables with chairs occupied the middle of the room. Longer tables with benches lined the back wall. An almost-out-of-tune piano was being played in the corner by one of Vine's serving girls.

Marina pointed Reed towards the bar. "You buy the first round and I'll get a table in the back."

She weaved her way through the tables, greeting people as she went. There were only a couple of patrons she did not know. The silver and gold boom was in full swing in the eastern parts of the range and, while it was out of the way, Turning Creek still got its share of miners drifting through. Marina sent out small tendrils of power, feeling out the crowd while she walked.

One or two men turned in her direction and tipped their hats in greeting. She nodded and acknowledged them. The men she did not know were mortals, which did not mean they did not have the potential to be trouble. It just meant she could handle them easily if it came to it. Marina thought this would be a quiet night.

Marina sat at a bench against the wall, giving her an unobstructed view of them room. Reed carried over two pints of dark brown ale and sat next to her on the bench. There was a small distance between them. He leaned back with a sigh.

Marina picked up her glass and clinked it against Reed's. "Here's to not getting killed today." She raised the glass and breathed in the malty sweetness of the ale before drinking.

"Not my usual toast, but today it'll do." Reed drank from his cup. Marina watched him out of the side of her eyes.

They enjoyed the first half of their drinks in silence. "What trouble do you have planned for tomorrow?" Reed turned his body, opening himself up to her.

Marina mirrored his movement. "How come you always assume I'm going to get into trouble?"

"I know you."

Marina took another drink. "Aspens will be changing soon. Petra, Dora, and I are going to do the first of the fall hunting."

"It means a lot to folks that you do that. I'll start making the rounds through the valley soon and we'll have a list of who'll need help come winter."

Marina ran her thumb over her glass. "Winters here can be hard, and hunting is easy for us as harpies. With the three of us working together, we can hunt and smoke enough meat for those that need extra when the winter is long. Besides, this valley is ours and the people are part of it. By default they belong to us too."

Reed watched her for a beat. "It means something to people that you look out for them. It means something to me."

Marina jabbed her elbow into his side. "Don't get sentimental on me. Honestly, we'd go hunting regardless. We don't need all the meat we take down. I just love the kill. Someone's got to eat it."

Reed chuckled. "Very practical of you."

Marina responded with a smirk, and the conversation lapsed into companionable silence. After a long pull on her drink, Marina spoke again. "Why did you become a sheriff?"

"My dad was a judge. Always taught us to respect authority and the law. We all went into some kind of law enforcement. Service to others is a noble calling. You're very possessive of this town. So am I. I came west to make my own way. Hard to find yourself when you're overburdened by an abundance of family." A smile played at the corners of his mouth.

"Do you miss them? I know they write to you often."

"Growing up, I thought I'd never want to live in a house that crowded again, and then I came here. Distance has a way of clarifying things. I want to live in a house with that kind of fullness. Bursting with love and laughter." Reed drained the last of his drink.

She could see him in a house full of children and a wife who waited at home for him. Marina finished hers and stood to put some distance between herself and Reed. "I'll get the next round."

Marina carried their empty glasses to the smooth top of the bar. Vine saw her and walked over to the corner where she stood. Daniel Vine was an average man, average height and average brown hair. He could have easily faded into the background anywhere—except for his eyes, which were green like summer grass.

"Evening, Marina. What can I get for you?" Vine had the easy manner of a bartender, which made most people want to trust him. Marina knew he could only be trusted to look out for himself, even to the detriment of others.

"Do you have any more of the whiskey with honey?"

Vine put two tumblers on the bar. "I do. I saved a bottle for you."

Marina narrowed her eyes at him. "Just when I try to dislike you, you butter me up. Pour the glasses."

Vine smiled and poured a generous amount in each glass. "I keep thinking that if I keep the good stuff for you, you'll come around and tolerate me at least."

Marina lifted the glasses off the bar. "This is me tolerating you, but keep it up, and I might like you one day. Your drinks are too good for me to hate you outright."

"Well, I guess that's better than nothing." He moved on to the next patron.

Marina returned to the table—and to Reed. "If you haven't tried this yet, you're in for something fine."

Reed's fingers brushed hers as he took the glass. He touched the rims of the glasses together. "To good whiskey and good health."

Marina sipped the whiskey. It burned a sweet trail through her mouth and down to her belly. She closed her eyes and breathed deep. "Mmm, that is delicious. Gods, that man knows his spirits." She opened her eyes to see Reed watching her with a queer expression on his face. "What?"

He cleared his throat and spoke into his glass. "Nothing." He sipped it and closed his eyes. "This is good."

"I'd never lie to you, especially not about whiskey."

Reed swirled the amber liquid in his glass. When he raised it to his lips, Marina thought his eyes matched the whiskey perfectly. He caught her eyes and smiled. "You going to take me up on my offer? Come be my partner?"

"I haven't decided."

"I can't ask Petra now that she's tied down, and Dora doesn't seem like she'd be inclined to help."

Like a pebble in her shoe, irritation over Petra's domesticity burned in her. Marina swallowed it down. "You're right about Dora. She's the peacemaker. Dora has been spending her time with Doc. She has a substantial herb garden and has been following him on rounds. She'll be a regular nurse in no time. Odd occupation for a harpy, but I think she's happy."

"Seems like you're my only option."

"Don't sound so thrilled about it."

"Just being practical."

Marina finished her whiskey. "I'll be back in town in three days. I'll give you an answer one way or the other then."

"Sounds fair to me."

Marina stood and paused on the other side of the table. Marina put her hands flat on the surface and leaned over towards Reed. "One thing though. I like coffee in the mornings."

Reed grinned and his face turned up to hers. "Good, 'cause that's what I make. Night, Sparrow."

Marina left the saloon. She had not been back to her cabin for a couple of days, and suddenly all she wanted was her own bed. She took to the night air and laughed. A glass of whiskey and Reed's company was a great way to end a long day, and now she was headed home.

CHAPTER 5

It had been Dora's idea to do extra hunting last year when the snow was deep. Long winters in the mountains were hard on many. This year, they had resolved to start hunting earlier in the fall, when the animals were getting fat on the bounty of the harvest season and the harpies had no problem hunting big game. They had set out before the sun and had returned to Dora's cabin laden with meat for the smokehouse.

Marina's arms were red up to her elbows. The coppery warmth of the blood was on the air and mixed with the smell of meat already curing in the smokehouse. It made her mouth water. Between the three of them, they had brought back three deer and an assortment of rabbits. Dora staked down the hides for scraping, Petra carried armfuls of meat to the smokehouse, and Marina finished stripping the last carcass of its meat. Everything they could use would be cured or smoked. What few things they could not utilize, they would fly deep into the woods and leave for the scavengers.

Sweat threatened to run into her eyes, and Marina ran her forearm over her the side of her face, leaving a red streak in its wake. The blood had already started to dry on her arm, cracking and pulling at her skin with every move. Marina walked around the side of the house, where a small creek offered a place to wash the worst of the mess from her skin. When all the work was done, they would brave the coldness of the water and take full baths, but for now, a quick washing would do.

Petra came out of the smokehouse, bringing the smell of meat and burning wood with her. Her tightly curled black hair was pulled back with a scarf to keep it out of the blood. "Tell us about the chimera you and Reed found."

"Not much to tell." Marina helped Petra carry the last load of meat into the smoke house. The heat and smoke smothered her while she dug the hook into the haunch of venison. Marina took a lungful of clear air as soon as she stepped out into the open again. The sense of being confined eased.

"James was in town yesterday, and Iris told him. She told us to keep our eyes open." A smile bloomed across Petra face when she said James's name. It happened every time. Marina wondered if Petra was even aware of it.

A mixture of envy and irritation swirled through her. "It wasn't much of a fight, and in the end, we let it go."

"That's not the story I heard." Dora looked up from her work. "Dr. Williams said Reed had some nasty puncture wounds in his shoulder. Doc also said you had some burns."

"The burns are already gone. Doc put a couple stitches in Reed's shoulder. They weren't too bad. Doc says they'll be fine in a week." Marina said.

"From what I know, I heard you saved his life." Dora pulled the knife across the hide in front of her, scraping off excess fat and meat.

Marina shrugged, knelt beside Dora, and started scraping one of the other hides. "He would've been fine without me. Would've gotten a bit more water in his lungs though."

Petra joined the work on the hides. "A chimera is a forewarning of doom." Petra frowned as she scraped. "We've had enough doom around here in the last year. I think the gods owe us some peace."

Last summer, they had almost lost James. Petra, believing James was dead, had disappeared for months. As much as Marina craved diversion, she did not want it at the cost of those she loved.

"I don't think the chimera will be a problem. I let it know what waits for it should it cause trouble in our valley." The harpies looked at each other and smiled. Marina let her teeth grow pointy.

Dora laughed. "One day you're going to have to teach me to do that." Marina could change parts of her body while keeping the rest of her mortal. It gave her the ability to surprise the Hades out of people.

Marina flashed her teeth once more before allowing them to return to normal. "You're too nice to go around scaring people for fun."

"Maybe, but sometimes I wish I scared people more." Dora frowned as she worked.

Marina stopped and looked at Dora. "Your problem is that you're always nice and nice is how you look, all pale skin and freckles. No one looking at your big blue eyes would think you were something scary underneath."

Dora looked up from her work and ran her eyes over Marina. Then she looked at Petra. "You're nice, Marina, but there's a wildness about you, even in your mortal form."

Marina grinned. "Your dresses always have flowers on them. You could try wearing pants. For some reason, a woman wearing pants is very off-putting for men," Marina suggested. "I've also found multiple weapons in plain sight to be intimidating."

Petra coughed and rubbed her hands over her skirt, which was really two very wide-cut pant legs. "James said some men have trouble thinking around women in pants because they can see too much of their legs."

Marina looked at her faded grey pants. "My legs are completely covered."

Petra giggled. "I said the same thing. He said it was the shape of them, not the skin itself." A blush splashed across her face, and she averted her eyes.

"Men are ridiculous." Marina went back to work.

"One of these days you may not think so." Petra chuckled.

Marina snorted. "Doubtful."

"Just because you found something different doesn't mean we all will." Dora's voice was laced with melancholy.

"You don't know that," Petra insisted.

A flash of anger at Petra and her happy life flared in Marina. "I'm a harpy. A monster. A weapon. A monster isn't meant for commitment and families." Petra started to protest, but Marina cut her off. "James is different. I'm happy for you, but what're the chances of that happening again?"

"Iris thinks it's possible." Marina saw Petra's harpy looking at her through Petra's eyes.

Marina felt her own harpy feed off Petra, and her anger grew. "Who says I even want to be tied down with the same routine day in and out? I'd die from the monotony. It's not natural. The time will come for me to have a daughter, but it is not now. "

Petra stood and towered over Marina. "You think all you are is a monster. We're more than that."

Marina stood. Fury made her voice shake. "No, I'm not. You're not. We are monsters, made for violence and torture. I accept that. I am not made for domestic life, so stop acting like we can all just choose to be something else one morning because a man has caught our fancy."

Petra took one step closer to her. "Do you think I am no longer myself? That I traded being a monster for being something unnatural?"

Dora stepped between them. "That's enough. Your anger is just feeding each other. Both of you go get some air."

Marina hesitated. The need to finish this fight beat a tattoo in her mind. Dora faced her. "Take a walk."

Marina turned and stalked off into the woods. The air cooled the heat of her cheeks. As soon as she was surrounded by the quiet of the trees, she was ashamed of her words. She loved Petra and did not begrudge her the new life she was building. She just was not sure where she fit into it.

Marina sat on a fallen log covered in green moss. It was soft and cool under her fingers. She would not begrudge Petra an ending she could not see for herself. Petra had clawed her way out of the violence to find love and peace. Now that Petra lived with James on the farm, Marina knew her sister's loyalties were divided. Marina felt her own loyalties stretching to include James, Robert, and Adam. Adding people to their family meant complications.

Years ago, when the harpies first settled in Turning Creek, they'd taken their time getting to know each other. Raised in different cities, by different mothers, they were sisters of purpose and heritage, not blood. It had taken months for their friendships to form and for the threads of loyalty to bind them tight. Iris was always there, pulling them together and reminding them of their humanity.

One night around a campfire, under a sea of pines, the four of them had sat and shared stories of growing up. Some of the stories brought laughter, and others tears. That night, their histories had become entwined. Marina had looked into the face of each of her sisters, and she had known that she'd finally found a home and a family. That night had chased away many of the demons Marina had carried with her to the New World.

And now, things were shifting again for the harpies. Marina lifted her head and looked for an answer in the clouds overhead. They floated by, shaped like pillows, and the sun shone warm. Marina would do what she needed to do to mend the damage of her words. Petra deserved better than her bile. It would not be the first time Marina had begged forgiveness from Petra, nor Petra from her.

Marina trudged back to the clearing beside Dora's cabin. Petra and Dora had finished scraping the hides and were stretching and re-staking them to the ground. Petra narrowed her eyes and stood.

"Please forgive my harsh words." Marina bit her bottom lip and then plunged ahead before she decided humility was overrated. "I know what I am. Your new life has been an adjustment. You've found a middle ground between what we are and something else. I can only see the violence in front of me, and I'm all right with that. I've been wrestling with the worry that you won't need us now that you have James. All I have is the two of you and Iris and I'm not good at sharing." Marina crossed her arms over her chest and waited.

Dora's face grew soft. Petra stepped around the deer hide and pulled Marina into an embrace. "Silly harpy. Nobody could replace my sisters. I need you to remind me of what I am by taking me on bloodthirsty hunts."

Dora wrapped her arms around both of them. "No matter what happens, we'll always be a family."

Peace replaced the darkness in Marina. "Don't tell anyone how soft we're getting. It'll ruin my reputation."

The three of them laughed together. Dora pushed away and said, "Let's wash up and then have some tea and biscuits."

***

Marina sucked in a breath when the full force of the cold creek hit her body. Dora tossed her a bar of soap, and Marina scrubbed quickly over the goose flesh on her skin. She threw the chunk of soap at Petra's head when she was done with it. Petra caught it before it hit her face, lost her balance, and flopped like a fish into the water. Marina then scooted out of the creek before Petra could retaliate.

Dora's cabin was as simple as Marina's, but with feminine touches that hers lacked. A pair of blue-flowered curtains blew in the afternoon breeze. A tablecloth of yellow flowed over the round table in the kitchen and a quilt of bonneted ladies graced the bed. Marina's bed was covered in a simple blanket of blue and her bed was rarely made.

"Reed offered me a job," Marina said after Dora poured the first round of tea.

Petra's eyebrows went into her hairline. "Doing what?"

"Being a deputy."

Dora choked on her tea, and Petra burst out laughing.

"I'm not joking. Not all the Remnants moving in are peaceful, and he needs back-up with claws." Marina's fingernails elongated into brown claws that she waved at Petra and Dora.

"You're the least responsible of all of us, but I suppose using your brute force to keep the peace does not require much finesse." Petra took a dainty sip of tea.

"Being a brute is what I do best. It's why I always win when we fight." Marina clenched her clawed hand and imagined Petra's smile fading as she scratched it off her.

"I win often enough." Petra winked at her, and Marina stuck out her tongue in retaliation.

"You two are worse than children." Dora rolled her eyes.

"I think if Reed can put up with your behavior, he'll find you quite useful. It's a good job for you. There aren't many alternatives. Of course, you could always become a soiled dove and work in Vine's. This town does have a shocking lack of prostitutes." Petra grinned.

Marina gave up her irritation to laughter. "I'd definitely never be bored if I started that kind of business. It would save me the trouble of finding a mate. Men don't expect much of their paid women. With no other competition, I might even have some regulars who wouldn't care about my looks."

Dora leveled serious eyes at Marina. "You must realize how beautiful you are."

Marina ran a hand over unruly curls. "I'll agree to pretty, but the loudness of my mouth overcomes whatever goodwill my looks win me."

"At least you know your own faults." Petra saluted her with a tip of her teacup.

Marina returned the salute. "If I don't admit their existence, I can't use them to my advantage."

Dora slumped in her chair. "Honestly, you two are impossible."

"By Styx, I hope so." Marina sipped her tea and thought of all the fun she was going to have being a deputy in Turning Creek.

"Let's fly before I have to go." Petra returned her empty teacup to the sink. "You two can escort me home. I know James and the boys would be happy to see you."

Though large and deadly, harpies were graceful fliers. Marina soared over Petra and Dora as they raced through a cloudless sky, keeping the setting sun on their left. In her mortal form, Petra's skin was the color of barely creamed coffee, rich and smooth. As a harpy, Petra was ink black, but now the relentless darkness of her feathers was broken here and there by grey.

Dora and Petra landed in the yard in front of the main house. James walked out of the cabin, followed by Adam and Robert. Marina dove down, stopped just before crashing into the ground, and executed a flip before landing.

"Show off," Petra muttered before changing and planting a kiss on the lips of her husband. Marina pulled her harpy form into herself and then curtsied when she had mortal legs once more.

"Welcome, ladies. You're just in time for coffee or tea. There's some dinner left if you're hungry." James handed his half-full teacup to his wife. Petra thanked him with a knowing smile.

Marina sidled up to Adam. "Got any more of that coffee for me?"

Adam gave Marina the boyish grin the younger women of Turning Creek fawned over him to see. "Of course, Miss Marina. For you, anything."

"See, this is a gentleman who knows how to treat a lady." Marina linked arms with Adam and turned them towards the cabin.

"Pardon, Miss Marina, but it's mostly because I know you'll rip me to shreds if I refuse." Adam emphasized his statement with mock wide eyes.

Marina elbowed him in the side and he had to jostle to keep from spilling his mug of coffee. "I take back all the nice thoughts I was just having about you. Now, tell me you have some whiskey for that coffee and I'll forgive you."

Adam laughed as he walked through the door alone and returned a short time later with coffee for Marina and tea for Dora and Petra. He flipped Marina a flask. She caught it and poured some into her coffee. The group sat under the tree in the yard. Without the sun, the air raced lines of cold down her skin, but the coffee mug was warm, and Marina was surrounded by her family. Contentment, smooth like silk, filled her. Only Iris was missing.

James lifted his arm and Petra slid into the spot next to him. "How was the hunting?"

Petra laid her hand on James's thigh and molded herself to him. "Decent. We'll go a few more times before the first snow comes. There's still some room in Dora's smokehouse. There'll be plenty for the winter with extra in case anyone in the valley has need of it."

Thunderclouds loomed, and the small party broke up as the sun disappeared. That night, a late summer storm washed over the mountains in a torrent of rain and thunder.

CHAPTER 6

Two days later, Marina stood in the morning sun on the boardwalk in front of the sheriff's office and waited. She fingered the knife at her waist and shifted her weight. She wondered, again, if this was wise, agreeing to work with Reed. There were reasons to say no, but there was one glaring reason to say yes that had propelled her to this place. Marina knew she needed something to do with her time.

The door opened and Reed stepped outside. He did not have his hat on yet and his hair was wet. "Morning," he said and handed her the cup of coffee in his hand. "Hold on." He went back inside.

Marina sipped the coffee. It was unsweetened and black. The bitterness burst over her tongue and kicked her mind into wakefulness. She rolled it around her tongue and turned her face towards the sun.

The door creaked behind her and Marina turned. "Thanks for the coffee."

Reed came to stand next to her at the railing. "I recall you telling me it was required."

Marina smiled into her cup and took another sip. "Keep listening to me, and this is going to work out fine."

"I might listen, but I'm not promising to act on the words that come out of your mouth," he said.

Marina put a hand on her hip. "And here I thought we were going to get along fine."

Reed leaned into her. "Oh, we'll be right as rain, as long as you don't go half-cocked into every situation, and on occasion take my advice instead."

Marina lifted her cup to put some space between them. "I'm not sure I like your tone."

Reed laughed. "You came here to say yes. We both know what we're getting into. You're stubborn as a mule, but you have the skills I need."

"What do I get out of this?"

"Being useful to others on a more regular basis."

Marina rolled her eyes. "I think you've got the better deal."

Reed grinned. "Never said the bargain was fair, Sparrow."

Marina narrowed her eyes at him. "Against my better judgment, I'm saying yes."

Reed's smile widened and the worry lines around his eyes eased. "Thank you."

Marina wondered how long he had worried over her answer. "What's first?"

"When nothing else is doing, I make the rounds about town, check in on folks. Today seems like a good day for that." Reed finished his coffee and extended his hand for her cup.

Marina handed hers over. "Sounds fine. Where do we start?"

"We'll start on the other side of the street. Henry, Widow Finch, and Vine's first. We'll do Simon's and Doc last." Reed went into his office and came back out a few minutes later with his hat in place.

"Lead the way." Marina waved her arm wide.

Marina followed Reed as he crossed the street. The windows and shutters of the boarding house opened as they walked past. The round face of Widow Finch appeared in a window and she waved at them. Reed waved back. Marina slowed and a beat later realized she should have waved too. She shrugged and jogged to catch up.

The fire in the forge was roaring when they walked into the blacksmith's shop. The fire that lit Henry's forge was taken from the original forge of Hephaestus on Mount Olympus. The smell of the wood fire and hot metal permeated everything. Henry's back was to them when they walked in. Henry was tall, wide-shouldered, and defined physical strength. Marina knew he had a heart as soft as pure gold.

Henry looked over his shoulder. "Mornin' to you both. I'll be with you in a minute."

Marina walked over and peered around Henry's shoulder. "What're you working on?"

Henry lifted a pot with a broken handle. "Nothing you'd find interesting, Miss Marina. Smithin' ain't all knives and pointy things."

Marina ran a finger down the pot. "More's the pity."

Henry smiled at her, then said, "How's the day so far, Sheriff?"

Reed shook Henry's hand. "Fair to middle, I think, but looking up." He looked at Marina.

"Does this mean you've taken Sheriff Brant up on his offer? Are you going to be Turning Creek's new deputy?" Henry pulled a thick apron from a peg and tied it on.

Marina looked at the other projects laid out on Henry's bench. None of them looked like weapons and her interest waned. "I am, at least until Reed decides I'm more trouble than I'm worth."

"Miss Marina, you may be trouble, but you are worth some effort at the end of the day." Henry started his statement by looking at Marina but then shifted his gaze to Reed as he spoke. He had the uncanny ability, like Iris, to dispense needed advice when it was not sought.

"Duly noted." Reed smiled at Henry.

"Just so," the blacksmith replied.

"I think I missed something." Marina looked at the two of them.

Reed spread his hands palm up. "Henry was just reminding me that even though you're likely to be a pain in my hide, you're a good partner to have around."

Marina pointed at Reed. "It's not like you're without your thorns."

"I'm a prince most days, except around you, it seems."

Marina crossed her arms with a slow smile. "I'm a good influence then."

Reed laughed at her. To Henry, he said, "Any news?"

Henry pumped the bellows. Marina felt the heat on her face, though she was standing some feet away. "That was some storm we had two nights ago. No damage that I've heard of though. It's been quiet."

"Let us know if you hear anything." Reed turned to go.

Henry called Marina's name. "I'm glad you've joined the sheriff. The Remnants of the valley will feel a sense of safety they have lacked."

"Thanks." Marina walked beside Reed. A frown played over her face.

When they were in front of Widow Finch's boardinghouse, Reed stopped. "What's wrong?"

"Will the Remnants of the valley actually feel safer with me as a deputy? Will that sense of safety come because they think I can protect them or because I am scary enough to ward off almost everything else that might harm them?"

"Does it matter?"

Marina looked around the street. People were starting to conduct their business on Main Street. Simon was setting out wares in from of the mercantile. Amy and Agnes Hughes were in a huddle whispering in front of their door. When Agnes saw her, her face lit up and she waved. Marina smiled and waved back.

"I don't know. I don't want everyone to be scared of me," she nodded in the direction of the twins, "but if scary keeps them safe, then I'm not sure it matters. Sometimes being scary has its uses."

Reed looked at her with respect. "You're going to do just fine. If you'll accept a consolation, I know those girls adore you."

Warmth and satisfaction filled her. Before she could reply, a rider barreled down Main Street from the north. Marina's mouth pressed into a tight line when she saw who it was.

"What's got Andy Johnson in such a lather?" Reed walked into the street to intercept the speeding horse.

Andy jerked on the reins harshly and the horse jolted to an uneven stop. "Sheriff," he wheezed. "My wife. She's gone. Need help finding her."

Reed patted the neck of the heaving horse. "Take a few breaths and tell me what happened."

"I woke up yesterday morning, and Katherine was gone. She was just gone. Someone's taken her."

"Why don't you get on down from the horse and give her a rest. Come sit down in my office and tell us what happened." Reed's voice was even and controlled.

At the word 'us', Andy looked at Marina as if he had just realized she was there. His eyes narrowed. "What's she doing here?"

Marina gave him a bright smile and stepped closer. "I'm the new deputy. Morning to you."

Andy swung off his horse and yanked the reins in the direction of the saloon. "I need a drink."

"Day's still young, Mr. Johnson." Reed fell into step beside the man. Marina followed them, her anger beginning to bubble under the surface.

"Didn't you hear? Something took my wife. I've got a right to mourn." Andy reached the double doors of the saloon and pulled the handle. The doors rattled but remained locked and closed. "Dammit. What am I gonna do?" He started pounding on the door.

Reed grabbed his shoulder and spun him around. "The saloon is closed. Come to my office, and we can talk. I need to know what happened."

"She's gone. What more can I say?" Over-sized tears started to flow down Andy Johnson's face. Before Marina could feel sorry for him, he added. "Who's going to make my dinner? I'll starve to death. Katherine was a good wife. Always fed me and darned my socks. I can't do those things. I'm hungry." He grabbed the front of Reed's shirt. "You have to get her back."

The combination of Andy's selfishness and his laying a hand on Reed brought down the barriers keeping Marina's irritation and anger at bay. Marina let her power flow over her and crash out into the two men. "Get your hands off the sheriff, and stop your blubbering, you fool."

Shocked by the power in her voice, Andy yanked his hand off Reed. The door opened behind him and Daniel Vine, crumpled with sleep, stood in the doorway. He took in the wrathful harpy on his doorstep, the irritated sheriff, and the crying man and opened the door wide without a word. Marina was the last one in the building. She fumed as Reed led Andy to a front table and Vine poured a round of whiskey for everyone.

"I know it's early, but if you are going to interrupt my sleep, I might as well make it worth my while." Vine poured four glasses and, without waiting for them, downed his portion. "I'm going back to bed. Close the door on your way out. And Sheriff, don't let Marina behind the bar."

Marina smiled despite her cooling anger. "Sweet dreams, Vine. Thanks for the morning constitutional."

Marina did not think she could be still enough to sit down. She stood to the left of Reed and watched him ask Andy questions.

"Tell us what happened," Reed said.

"We went to bed like normal, night before last, but when I woke up, Katherine was gone."

"Just like that?" Reed asked.

"Just gone," Andy repeated.

"Did she take any clothes? Was there anything missing from the house, barn, or storeroom? Were all your horses in the barn?" Reed continued to ask questions in a calm voice. Marina wanted to yell at him. *Of course his wife left,* she thought. *He is an insufferable lout.*

"What're you implying, Sheriff? My Katherine did not leave me of her own free will." Marina snorted at Andy's comment.

"Answer the question." Reed leaned closer to Andy and his voice lost some of its gentleness.

Andy leaned back in his chair. "Nothing was missing. All her clothes and things were just where she'd left them. We only have one horse, and you saw it when I rode in this morning. Something took her."

Marina stopped her pacing and stalked over to stand next to Andy. He craned his neck to look at her. "You keep saying something, not someone. Why?" Marina sent out tendrils of power in his direction to check her first impressions. Andy was not a Remnant.

"There's no one around for miles and miles by our farm, but there're plenty of bear and wolves. Maybe some animal got her."

Some animal, like the voice of reason, Marina thought. Watching Andy, Marina could not think of one reason Katherine would not want to have been eaten by wolves. Reed looked up at her with a question in his eyes. Marina shook her head. "If she had been attacked by an animal, there would be blood, a body, something. Did you look around before heading into town?"

Andy scratched his head. "Well, I waited for her to make breakfast, but it was noon before I realized she was wasn't coming."

Renewed anger crashed over her, and she clenched her fist in an effort to keep herself from clobbering him over the head. Marina walked away from the table and leaned on the bar.

"What did you do then?" Reed prompted.

"I checked the barn and the garden by the house. She wasn't there, so I went back in to wait. When she didn't come home by this morning, I knew something was wrong." Andy put his face in his hands. "Who's going to cook my supper?"

It was too much. Marina's anger flowed into her words. "You'll have to learn how to do for yourself, you worthless..."

"Marina." The note of censure was plain in his voice. Reed turned his attention back to Andy. "Marina and I will look into it. If your wife can be found, we'll find her."

"Thank you, Sheriff. Got any more whiskey?" Andy shook his glass.

Marina made a fist to punch him in the face. Reed grabbed her arm and moved her away from Andy. She let her harpy look out from her eyes, but she stayed where Reed put her. Reed gave her a warning look before he went behind the bar. Andy perked up when he saw where Reed was headed.

When he walked back to the table, Reed held a small bottle of what Marina knew to be one of the cheapest drinks in the house. He handed the bottle to Andy, who took it with a shaking hand.

"Why don't you go sit a spell in the garden out back until Vine opens for the day? Marina and I'll have a look around and come talk to you later."

Reed pulled Andy up and steered him through the back door, which led to a small garden and sitting area. Marina glared holes in the back of Andy's head as he walked away. She would have preferred breaking his nose, giving him something to really cry about. Instead of living out that particular fantasy, she took a deep breath and quelled the violence.

Reed came back inside and walked past her. "C'mon."

When they were off the street and behind the closed door of the sheriff's office, Marina spoke. "You know she just left him. He's a selfish bully on a good day and worse the more he drinks. Hells, I'd leave him too, except I'd probably beat the life out of him first."

Reed rubbed the back of his neck. "You're right, but we'll have to have a look around to make sure. You're a fast flier, right?"

Marina chuckled. It was not a comforting sound. "The fastest. Speed is my gift."

"Good. I want you to fly over to the Johnson's cabin and have a look around."

"It's a waste of time. She's long gone."

"He said she didn't take the horse," Reed pointed out.

"Maybe someone helped her."

"Fly out and check for signs of something odd, blood or tracks or similar. Come back, let me know. If there's nothing to see, we'll wait a few days, see if she turns up."

"Waste of time," Marina said.

"Be that as it may, I want you to go." Reed's voice was firm. He was asking without demanding. Marina appreciated the effort.

She hesitated before leaving. "Back in the bar, when I let my harpy show through, you never blinked."

Reed winked at her. "I've seen you scary. That wasn't it."

Marina dug for the thing that was really bothering her. "I want to do a good job at this." She waved her hand in the air.

Reed moved closer to her. "You'll be fine. Getting people to obey rules isn't just about intimidating them, though you can do that in spades. It's more. You'll figure it out."

Marina hoped he was right. "Guess it's a good day for flying. I'll be back before noon."

"Fly safe, Sparrow."

***

Three days of standing outside the sheriff's office, waiting for Reed in the mornings, had burned the routine of Turning Creek into Marina's brain. She knew she could wait inside, but the morning sun was glorious in the mountains. The rough planks of the building poked her shoulder blades, but Marina did not move. Through half-lidded eyes, she watched the curtains of Widow Finch's boarding house being opened to the morning sun. In less than five minutes, a young girl, still in braids, exited the front door of the boarding house and began sweeping a rush broom over the boarded walkway. The swish of her movements and her quiet whistling were the only sounds on the street.

School would start in two weeks, all the students in the valley and surrounding mountains crowding into the new one-room schoolhouse and church on the other end of Main Street, but until then, Shelly emerged every morning at this time to sweep and whistle. She whistled the same simple song every day, a tune Marina did not recognize, but to her dismay, caught herself humming later on. When the job was done, Shelly went inside to help Widow Finch serve breakfast and clean the rooms. Shelly looked mortal, but Marina knew Shelly was a Remnant of some lesser god. Marina had begun to lose track of who was descended from whom.

Marina shifted her shoulders and continued to watch the daily, predictable movements of Turning Creek waking up from her vantage point in front of the sheriff's office. On cue, the door next to her opened and the smell of Reed, a tangle of soap, gun oil, and leather, assaulted her. The man in question stepped across the threshold and handed her one of the cups of coffee he was carrying. She held the cup to her nose and breathed in its bitter smell, trying to banish Reed from her senses. Unfortunately, the coffee did not keep her eyes from noticing his shaved jawline or the casual way he leaned one hip against the railing in front of the building.

"Morning." His voice was rusty.

"Thanks for the coffee. How are you today?"

45

Reed's eyes swept the street. "Top of the world."

They drank in silence for some time, but it was a comfortable one. It was the same routine they had fallen into the first day and now, even after a handful of days, it seemed this morning cup of coffee was a ritual. Neither spoke until their cups were empty.

Reed broke the silence. "I've got something for you, something to make your job more official." Reed pulled a flat leather disk out of his pocket and dropped it in Marina's outstretched hand.

The object still held the warmth from Reed's body. Marina turned it over. Hard leather was stretched over a three-inch metal disk. The words "Turning Creek Deputy" were stamped on the front over a picture of Atlas's Peak with an eagle flying over them. Marina held the disk closer to her face. The eagle had claws on the end of its wings. A harpy. She laughed.

"I had Henry make it. Thought you might like something official to flash around."

Marina flipped the disk in the air. "Besides my scary face, you mean?"

Reed took her empty cup. "Besides that. I'll get more coffee and we can discuss the day. You want to come in?"

"It's too nice to be inside," she said. With a nod, he went into the building. Marina ran her thumb over the leather disk, thrilled to have it and touched that Reed had taken such care to have it made for her.

He returned and gave Marina her cup back.

"What exciting adventures will we be embarking upon today?" Marina made sure to lay the sarcasm on thick. They had, of course, found nothing at the Johnson farm, nor had Katherine Johnson reappeared. Nothing had happened in the last three days except one bar fight, which Marina had broken up with zeal.

Reed's eyes scanned the street, which had acquired some additional foot traffic while they drank their coffee. "Thought I might go on up to Johnson's farm and take another look around. Andy's wife is probably in Utah or Texas by now, but I'd like to look again."

Marina snorted. "Andy's only upset because he doesn't have her to yell at anymore. Besides, I already flew around. There's nothing to find because if she has any brains at all, she's gone for good."

"Be that as it may, I'd better go have a look see. Something might've happened and we just haven't found a body yet."

Marina rubbed her hands together. "I'll saddle up." The thrill of the hunt and something to do hummed through her veins.

"No, I want you here." Reed directed a pointed look her way. The firm set of his jaw told her he knew she wanted to argue.

She hated to disappoint him. "What in the name of the gods am I going to do here?"

"Do the job I hired you for. Keep an eye on the town and ask around.

See if Katherine talked to anyone before she left. Try Simon's, Vine's, and Henry. They handle people passing through and might've heard something."

Marina groaned.

"I'm a better tracker than you." She pouted.

Reed chuckled. "You look like a spoiled child with that face." Marina stuck out her tongue. "You are better than me at tracking," he said. Marina preened as he continued. "But you're also better at telling when people are lying, so I want you asking around. Doubt we'll find a thing, but we'll do our diligence, and Andy will have to live with himself for being a drunk bastard of a husband."

"You said I was better than you." Marina grinned.

"At tracking. I'd tell you not to let it go to your head, but I see that advice is too late. I'll be back by dinner. Widow Finch made me some stew yesterday. I still have some if you want to trade findings over a meal. That is, if you're staying in town tonight."

Marina had not been home for a couple of days, and she wanted to go flying. She was going to refuse when she thought of something else. "How come everyone calls Harriet Finch 'Widow Finch', but no one calls me 'Widow Ocypete'?" Single women were not commonly accepted, so the harpies pretended to be widows whenever they were introduced to new people. It saved them from questions and allowed them to live alone.

"Because no one believes you're a widow." Reed's face broke into a wide grin. "No one believes any man in his right mind would marry you."

"Then it's a good thing harpies are not the marrying kind."

"Of course, any man married to you would probably kill himself."

Marina threw her cup at him, and he caught it in one graceful motion. "At least I wouldn't have to put up with him long."

Reed laughed and ducked back into his office. "See you tonight, Sparrow."

It was too early to go snooping around town, so Marina walked to the depot instead. Iris would be awake, and she always had information to share.

"Good morning, my bird," Iris said without looking up from her book.

"What is it with people calling me names related to birds? I have a proper Greek name. Marina Ocypete." She over-enunciated the syllables. Marina plopped down on a stool.

A low chuckle sounded from Iris. "Reed getting under your skin already? The day is early yet."

Marina sniffed, annoyed Iris was so close to the mark, though not precisely in the way Iris imagined. The man was rugged, smelled delicious, and he made her want to box his ears in.

Iris looked up. "I'll take that as a yes. Did you have breakfast yet? You were gone when I woke."

"I had coffee with Reed, but nothing to eat yet."

"Thomas," Iris called.

His head popped around the corner of the back storage room. "Yes, Miss Iris?"

"Will you go bring down some apples and cheese for Marina?"

"Of course. Howdy, Marina. Caught any bandits today?" Thomas was addicted to dime novels, and in his imagination, Marina and Reed were on the cusp of saving the town from marauding bandits every day.

"There's been a sad lack of bandits lately. I could use a good fight. Let me know if you see any."

Thomas laughed and raced up the stairs at double a mortal's speed. He quickly returned with the food and went back to the storage room.

"Where's Reed this morning?" Iris asked.

Marina crunched into an apple. She chewed through the shock of sweetness in the back of her mouth. "He's going up to the base of Folly to look over Johnson's farm."

"Can't blame her for leaving."

"Exactly, but Reed wants to make sure nothing carried her off."

"Like what? Man-eating bear?"

"There are worse animals in this valley now." Marina let a glint come into her eyes. Her harpy begged to be let out. She really needed to go flying tonight.

Iris rolled her eyes at Marina. "A harpy who enjoys upheaval more than she should being the worst of all."

"I am what I am." Marina polished off the apple and stretched her arms above her head. "Have you heard anything recently? Beyond the usual strange things?"

Marina's senses screamed *danger*, and the door to the depot opened. The urge to let her harpy loose in the enclosed space screeched in her ears. Marina was up on the balls of her feet and crouched low within a single breath. Iris stood pale behind the counter, a long knife clutched in her hand. *She must keep the weapon hidden under the counter,* Marina thought. She was glad her friend would not be helpless, but it was not as if The Messenger had anything to fear with a harpy to defend her. No matter what kind of trouble it would cause, Marina was prepared to change in the middle of town to defend Iris.

The lithe form of an ordinary girl walked through the door. Her hair was a tarnished brown and her overlarge brown eyes went wide when she saw Iris. Her wide, but delicate, nose flared and then she found Marina in the back of the room and froze. Marina let the violence of her harpy seep from her pores and fill the room. The girl's eyes swept down, and a second later, her body dropped into a crouch; she ducked her head almost to the ground. Marina tried to see past the urge to draw blood first and ask questions later when her senses told her the girl in front of her was submissive, feline, and young, but still dangerous and still powerful.

Marina let her teeth elongate and she flashed a pointy smile at the cowering girl. She knew what effect they had on most people. "You're not mortal."

The girl trembled, and Marina almost felt sorry for her. "No."

Iris clutched the knife tighter. "You're new here."

If possible, the girl moved lower to the ground. "Yes."

"What are you?" Marina's voice had changed timbre, incorporating the quality of nails on glass. This dance would be easier if Marina could sense what kind of Remnant the girl was. Unfortunately, it did not work that way.

"Sphinx."

That explained the impression Marina had of a feline. The girl exuded a kind of wild power that beat in the back of Marina's head. Submissive pose or not, the girl had the ability to be dangerous, or would be when she was fully-grown. The sphinx in the old myths had the body of a lion and the head of a woman and tended to eat whomever gave the wrong answer to the questions it asked. Not someone you would want to invite home to dinner.

"What's your purpose here?" Iris asked.

"My family moved here recently. We're building a place on Shaker's Way." The mountain was south of town, opposite of Jolly's Folly. "I'm in town with my brother. My father asked me to find The Messenger and ask permission to remain in this territory."

The use of Iris's title slowed the speed of Marina's racing heart.

"Your father was right to send you, but he sent you to the wrong Remnant." Marina's voice was all harpy now. She wrapped steel bands around the violence inside her to keep her human form intact. This young one was no threat now, but she might be later, and Marina wanted to scare her into remembering. "This territory belongs to the harpies. Others are allowed to stay, but if they seek to do harm to other Remnants in this area or the mortals living here, they answer to us. We're not a merciful race."

"I understand, mistress." The words were a whisper.

The harpy in Marina reveled in bringing another to heel, but the rest of her saw the girl was still wet behind the ears. Marina would be better served by using this time to create an ally, not an enemy.

She lightened her voice to more a more mortal timbre. "I'll not eat you. Please, stand up." Marina pulled her harpy back and ran her tongue along her now-flat teeth. The girl obeyed and her wary eyes flashed back and forth between Marina and Iris. "You startled us is all. I'm sorry if we did the same to you."

The girl inclined her head again, accepting the words while showing she was still submissive. A nice trick. "I also apologize. It wasn't my intention to get off on the wrong foot."

Marina extended her hand to the sphinx. "My name is Marina Ocypete. I live on Jolly's Folly, north of town. This is Iris, The Messenger."

The girl's handshake was firm. "My name is Pearl Nasso."

Iris slid the knife back into its hiding place behind the counter. She ran her empty hands over its well-worn work surface. "Would you like some tea while you wait on your brother?" Pearl nodded and Iris went up the back stairs.

Marina shifted her weight and watched Pearl. "Where's your family originally from?"

"A little nothing town on the edge of the Blue Ridge Mountains."

"What brought you to a little nothing town in the heart of the Colorado Rockies?"

Pearl's shoulders went up in a shrug. "Father said it was getting too crowded there."

Iris returned, placing the teapot on the counter. Iris, who was much better at manners, poured the tea and made small talk with Pearl. Marina used the opportunity to watch the girl and listen. Pearl was the only girl in a family of six. Both of her parents were still living and were farmers by trade.

Pearl sighed. "Mother thinks I need to learn needlework. She says learning to shoot and run around the hills is not what proper ladies do. She said she only has one girl, and she'll be damned if I turn out like my brothers." Pearl cringed. "Pardon my language. Mother also says I must stop cussing."

Marina patted the girl on the back. "Shooting guns and running around the hills is fun. Maybe if you spend enough time on the needlework to be passable, you can escape to the outside and find more interesting pursuits."

Iris narrowed her eyes at Marina. "No need to lead the young astray."

"Just some friendly advice is all." Marina and Pearl shared a grin.

The itching on the back of Marina's neck started again moments before the door opened, bringing in a blast of summer air and a man with shoulders so wide it was a small miracle he fit through the door. His head, rather than being dwarfed by the span of his body, was equal in size and covered in brown disheveled hair. Marina's harpy once again screeched to be let out, but she held herself in check. Jumping to conclusions had not done her much good the first time. She did a mental check of the weapons she had on her; four knives and a gun. Careful did not mean stupid.

"There you are," the man growled.

Pearl's reaction was immediate. She slipped from the stool in front of Iris and lowered her head. "I'm sorry."

"Sorry? I've been waiting for twenty minutes wondering where you got off to, and you're in here drinking tea like you're some kind of fancy lady."

Pearl's chin twitched up, but her eyes stayed downcast. "Father gave me an errand. I was doing as I was told." Her eyes did sweep up at the end, but immediately flicked down again.

The sphinx was not as submissive as she let on. "You must be one of her brothers." Marina offered her hand to the man. "I'm Marina Ocypete, the deputy of Turning Creek. Pleased to meet you."

He looked like he would rather bite her than touch her, but he eventually put his huge paw in her hand and squeezed harder than was necessary. Marina gave him her most saccharine smile. She could smell a bully a mile away. She squeezed back.

"Claude Nasso." He huffed out the name and released Marina's hand to wag a finger at Pearl. "Time to go. Say goodbye to your friends."

Pearl mumbled her goodbyes and walked out. Claude followed her, letting the door smack closed against the frame.

"That was interesting. He must have learned those fine manners in a barn," Marina observed. It would be amusing to follow them home, as a harpy, and swoop over a few times. If Claude got worked up enough, he might change, and then she would know what kind of scary monster he was.

"No." Iris's voice was firm.

"What?"

"You're not to go flying after that man and his poor sister. Don't you think you scared her enough for one day?"

Iris knew her too well. Marina flopped down in the seat vacated by Pearl. "He needs to be scared. You always assume the worst."

"But I'm right, aren't I?"

Marina crossed her arms. "Maybe."

Iris cleared her throat, ignoring the comment and picking up the dishes from their tea. "Stay here. I have a message for Reed before you leave."

Every two weeks without fail, Reed received a letter from his father. His brothers and sisters wrote regularly, so it was rare a week would go by without Reed having some new mail. Iris pulled a thick paper with an official seal from the rows of bird-hole slots behind the counter. It did not look like a family letter.

Iris handed over the envelope and pointed to the seal. "There is a committee in Denver petitioning the United States to accept Colorado as an official territory. They want each town or region to draft a list of resources and take a census for their proposal. As the town's postmistress, I would normally be the best candidate for the job, but they've asked Reed to assist me. He's the only person besides myself holding anything similar to an official office here, so we've been asked to write the report for Turning Creek."

"And you need Reed to help because the report can't come from a woman."

"I see you have found the meat of the matter." Iris sighed and smoothed her hands over the expensive vellum.

Both she and Iris were descended from generations of women filled with the power of myths and history. Besides her official title as The Messenger and her ability to gather and disperse information, Iris also held the gift of prophecy. Unfortunately, mortals did not typically measure power through history and abilities. They measured it through gender.

"I'll tell him tonight. He asked that I stay in town to have dinner so we could exchange information on our findings for the day. I'm going back up to my mountain tonight. I miss my own bed."

"Petra seems content in her new path." Iris spoke with her back to Marina. Her hands moved over the letters, touching each one before going on the next. Iris had once admitted to the harpies that the act of delivering letters was so ingrained into her psyche that she felt compelled to do it.

Marina ground her teeth audibly. "I'm happy for my sister, but her life now is a miracle. It's not the life we were created for, and miracles are seldom repeated."

"How do you know Petra's path could not also be your own?" Iris turned to face Marina.

"There are no other men as forbearing as James Lloyd in the entire world. No man wants a woman stronger than he is and a monster to boot."

Iris's vibrant blue eyes clouded with melancholy. "Poor bird. You're not a monster."

"You only think the best of us, and that's why you're the one who guards us. No one else wants the job. I like being a monster most days. It's useful." Marina walked around the counter and wrapped Iris in a rib-breaking hug. Marina towered over the petite woman. In the time of old myths, the original Iris had saved the harpies from Zeus's wrath, and afterwards, she and her descendants had never stopped saving them, even from themselves. "I'll follow the path of my line and have a daughter, but I will do as my mother did and her mother before her. I'll find a sire for my daughter, not a mate for life. I have plenty of fertile years left. I'm a weapon, not a housewife. I know my place in the scheme of things."

Iris gave her one last squeeze. "Go, then. I know Reed didn't task you with sitting here all day, drinking tea, and eating my biscuits."

With a nod, Marina stepped through the door, letting it swing shut behind her.

CHAPTER 7

Marina headed to the mercantile first. If she were lucky, Simon would be too busy to talk. The man could hold a conversation with a rock for hours. She paused outside the door and prayed to the gods for fortitude, then pushed open the door. The bell above the door announced her entrance. The mercantile was empty, save for the dust motes flipping in the early morning light that was streaming through the large front windows. Orderly rows of household goods occupied the right side of the store. Barrels and bags of foodstuffs had been labeled in a neat hand. Bolts of brightly colored cloth were piled on shelves against the wall. The left side of the store was just as neat, but occupied with tackle, mining equipment, saddles, tack, nails, and other hardware.

A woman, as orderly as the store she ran with her husband, walked out from behind a curtain that separated the family living quarters from the store front. "Good morning, Miss Ocypete. How are you this morning?"

Marina smiled. "I am doing just fine, Mrs. Kramer. You?"

Beth Kramer folded the towel in her hands and placed it under the counter. "None of that, Miss Ocypete. After what you three have done for this town and for my family in particular, you are welcome to call me Beth."

Last year, Simon had been kidnapped by Cyrene and Atlanta, Remnants of huntresses. Dora and Petra had tracked down the huntresses and retrieved Simon before he could come to serious harm.

"Please, then, call me Marina. Where's Simon this morning?"

Beth's smile faded and she shook her head. "He's feeling under the weather. Just a touch of a cold I think, but you know how men are sometimes when they're sick. I tucked him back into bed with some warm broth and told him to rest for a bit. He'll be fine tomorrow."

"I'm sorry to hear that." Marina was sorry Simon was under the weather, but not sorry she was going to be able to ask her questions of Beth instead. "I'm here on official business, actually."

"Oh, yes. Please let me congratulate you on becoming the deputy. Simon and I were so pleased to learn that you had accepted the position. With all the people and Remnants moving in, we know you won't put up with any funny business."

"Thank you for your vote of confidence. I'm still learning the ropes." Marina paused for a second, reveling in the strange pleasure that accompanied Beth's words of support before she continued to the task at hand. "I want to ask you some questions about Katherine Johnson. Mr. Johnson has asked us to look for her." Marina knew, after three days, that everyone in the valley would know that Katherine Johnson was missing. Even as spread out as most of the inhabitants were, word traveled faster than water after a spring storm.

Beth shook her head. "I heard that she left poor Mr. Johnson, though I'm not sure he didn't deserve it."

"I know you spoke to her whenever she came into town. Can you tell me anything that might help?"

"I know Mr. Johnson was not the best husband. I don't think he ever actually hit her, but he was not a nice man." Marina thought Beth was being a little too lenient. "I know everyone is saying he deserved what he got. I just don't think she would have run away into the night without a word."

While people did disappear into the mountains with some frequency, there was often some warning beforehand, gathering of supplies and the like. "Is there anything else about Mrs. Johnson in particular that might help?" The mercantile was empty except for the two of them. Marina still looked around out of habit before asking, "I never had occasion to be in close proximity to Mrs. Johnson. Do you know if she was a Remnant? I know Mr. Johnson is not."

If the Johnsons had moved to Turning Creek before or during the affair with Zeus, Marina would have already known the answer to this question. But Andy and Katherine Johnson had moved to the valley a month after Zeus had been defeated.

Beth was the Remnant of a nymph with little power of her own, but Marina was hoping Mrs. Johnson had confided in her. She nodded. "Indeed, yes. Katherine was the Remnant of Scylla."

Marina could not recall a single thing about Scylla. "I'm not sure I remember that one."

"Depending on the myth, Scylla was a serpent with a dog or a bird head. Katherine said her family history indicated that the dog version was closer to the truth."

Marina committed the details to memory so she could later relay them to Iris, who would be able to do some sleuthing in the archives. "Do you know if Mrs. Johnson had any powers or abilities?"

Beth rubbed her fingers over her lips as she thought. "She never said."

Marina nodded. "Thank you, Beth. That was very helpful."

The door opened and Paul Hughes, the tailor, came into the mercantile. "Good day, ladies." He was a tidy man. His clothes were ironed and his hair had been smoothed into place. His stitching was as precise as his appearance.

"What can I do for you today?" Beth asked.

"Lily asked me to stop by and get some oats, sugar, and tea," he said.

Beth walked around the counter and pulled some large tins from a shelf. "I will get those for you right now."

Mr. Hughes looked at Marina. "My girls have been diligently applying themselves to become proficient with their slingshot. They informed me that you advised them to practice often and away from the street. Thank you for that intervention."

"It was no problem at all. Glad to hear that they've been practicing." She turned to Beth. "I'd best be going."

"Do you need anything else today?" Beth asked her as she scooped oats into a sack.

"That'll do for now. Tell Simon to get better soon. Goodbye, Mr. Hughes."

"I will. Good luck in your search. Katherine is a nice person. I hope you find out what happened to her."

Marina left the mercantile and headed north up Main Street to the blacksmith shop. A small cottage stood behind the smithy, with red flowers lining the boxes hanging from the windows.

Though it was still early, Henry stood before the forge, his face red from the heat of the fire. His mop of curly dark hair was damp with sweat. On any other man, his hair would lend a boyish air, but Henry was too solidly built for that. The hammer clanked in a steady, even rhythm. Marina walked into his line of sight, leaned against the wall, and waited.

Henry worked for a handful of minutes, then put the metal he was working on into the cooling vat, where it hissed and created a cloud of steam. He wiped a forearm over his face and walked in an uneven gait towards Marina. Henry had been born with a clubfoot, the mark of his line, and he limped when he walked. Though the long hours he spent in front of the forge were painful, the power of the forge was his to wield and to bear.

Henry wiped his hands on a rag hanging from a peg on the wall. "Mornin' Miss Marina—or should I say Deputy Marina?"

Marina waved him off. "None of that now, though I'm here on official business."

Henry straightened up. "Care to sit and tell me about it?" He motioned her over to a bench by the corral. Marina sat.

Henry joined her with a sigh. "How're you likin' the new job? It seems to suit you."

Marina leaned against the post at her back. "Fine, so far, though I did think the job would be a tad more exciting."

Henry chuckled. "Life is not always an adventure. Sometimes the day-to-day has to be adventure enough."

Marina snorted. "Petra has warned me that you have a habit of being brutally honest."

Henry shrugged. "Don't see a reason to be otherwise. So, what is this official business?"

"You heard Katherine Johnson is missing?" Henry nodded and Marina continued. "Sheriff Brant and I are looking into it. Andy is convinced something happened to her. I think she woke up one morning and realized she was married to a worthless man."

A cool breeze nudged them, and Henry turned his face into it. "Oh, I think she realized that long ago. Why does Mrs. Johnson's disappearance bring you to the forge?"

"You get passers through here. Have you heard anything odd from people traveling through or seen anything strange in the past week?"

Henry thought before answering. "Nothing unusual that I recall. It's been a slow week. I shod the horses of the new family, Nasso, I think their name was, earlier in the week. They are Remnants, but he was a civil man and seemed all right. He had a lot of questions about the town. Word's spreading. This is a decent place for Remnants to be.

"I met two of his kids, Pearl, and her older brother, Claude, this morning. I don't know what he is, something powerful. She's a sphinx. She'll be a force to be reckoned with one day, but she's young now. Pearl was nice enough. Her brother was decidedly less friendly."

Henry shifted again to face Marina. "Mr. Nasso didn't offer much information regarding his family or himself. Experience has taught us to hold most things close. He was polite, but other than that, I didn't get a sense, one way or the other, from him."

"Claude's behavior didn't sit well with me, but being rude and overbearing is not an indication of anything other than a tendency to be a jerk or an idiot or both. Anything else?"

Henry rubbed a hand along the stubble of his jaw. "Not that I recall."

Marina stood. "Thanks, Henry. If you think of anything else or hear anything, let us know."

Henry stood and shook her hand. "Of course. Have a good one."

"You too." Marina had one more stop to go. It was nearing the noon hour. Perfect timing for a pint at Vine's and a hand or two of cards.

***

Marina tapped the top of her cards and eyed the pair of fives in her hand, trying to will them into face cards. The rest of the cards in her hand were junk, and she was not going to be able to improve them. She watched Roger, who sat across from her at the table. He had a glass half full of whiskey in front of him, and his hand was steady. That meant he had a great hand, which was more than she could offer this round. She looked at the other man at the table.

It was Reggie's turn to bid or call. "I fold."

Marina threw some coins in the pile. "I call." She winked at Roger. "Show me your cards."

He laid his cards down with a soft flourish. "Two pairs."

"Damn." Marina showed her fives.

Roger turned his head to call to Daniel Vine, who was standing behind the bar. "Vine, a round for the table if you please. Marina likes to lose her money. Least I can do is buy her a pint."

"I think that was my last round." Marina sat back in her chair.

Roger gathered the cards into a pile and started shuffling them with efficiency. Later on in the day, his hands would not be so sure. "One more hand."

Marina shook her head. "I know when to stop."

"Reggie?" Roger asked.

"You've already taken all the extra money I brought to town today. Good thing I went to the mercantile before coming in here." Reggie frowned into his drink.

Vine placed a pint of brown ale in front of each of them. Marina took a sip of the malty liquid and sighed. "Reggie, have you seen anything strange on your property lately?"

"You mean since I saw the monster?"

Marina nodded, and Roger perked up. "Monster? What monster?"

Marina looked between Roger, who was a Remnant, and Reggie, who was mortal; he did not know the people playing cards with him were something other than human. "Reggie saw something on his property last week, and Reed and I went to check it out."

Reggie, never one to turn down a good audience, launched into his story. "I was out in the upper field last week, when I saw something by the creek. At first, I thought it was a bear. It looked like it had a shaggy head, but it was golden in color. I stood there, unable to look away, and suddenly the thing turned and looked at me. I was far away, but I'm telling you, my blood froze in my veins. I saw an illustration once of one of those African lions, and its face looked just like that. I couldn't see its body because it was in the trees, but then it moved."

Reggie paused and pulled a long pull from his glass. "I swear its body slithered away into the bushes." Reggie leaned in and dropped his voice. "Like a snake." He sat back and took another long pull from his half-full pint.

"This is one of your jokes," Roger said. Reggie was notorious for his jokes.

"No. I swear on my mother's grave. That's what I saw." Reggie met Roger's eyes.

Roger smiled. "Did you have some of your wife's coffee before going out there?"

Reggie smiled. "Yes, Lord, but that woman can't make coffee or cook much for that matter. It's a good thing everything else she does is fantastic." Reggie made a crude gesture with his hands.

Marina's beer went down the wrong pipe, and she coughed. Reggie looked at her. "Sorry, Marina. Sometimes I forget you're a woman."

Marina coughed again, more embarrassed that she was embarrassed than anything else. "Well, that just makes me feel wanted. We never found the thing you saw, but let us know if you see it again." It was better if Reggie did not know what kinds of things lurked in the dark corners of the valley. Reggie nodded.

A man with greasy hair and a badly wrinkled shirt walked over to their table. Art Turner owned a farm at the base of Baldy and Shaker's Way, on the south side of the valley. He was as short on stature as he was on brains. "Mind if I sit?"

Reggie pointed to the empty chair at the table. "Want to play a hand?"

Turner ran his thumb over his glass. "No. I heard you talking about that thing you saw. I've seen something strange too. I saw a lion up on Baldy."

Roger leaned back in his chair with a sound of disgust. "Seein' a mountain lion in the mountains is nothing to tell stories of."

Turner shook his head vigorously. "No, not a mountain lion. A real lion. Like they have on the dark continent."

Marina squinted at Turner. "Are you telling us you saw an African lion on Baldy?" Mount Baldy was a short, squat mountain pocked with caves, caverns, and canyons. It was a favorite hiding spot for bears, wolves, bighorn sheep, and those who did not care to be found.

Turner nodded. "Yes, ma'am. I did indeed."

Marina would have sooner believed him if he had seen a minotaur. "That seems unlikely," Marina said.

Turner put his glass down hard enough to make the ale slosh over the side. "I know what I saw."

"All right. I'll go up and have a look when I get a chance. If it is a big lion of some kind, it'll leave scat or other marks." Marina was certain she would find nothing, but she would look anyway. A hunt was a hunt—and she needed something to do. Marina stood and picked up her glass. "If you gentleman will excuse me, I need to talk to Vine before I leave."

Marina put her glass down on the side of the bar nearest the door.

"Afternoon, Vine."

Vine stopped wiping glasses and approached her with a wariness she appreciated. "Afternoon yourself. What can I do for you?"

Marina explained her errand. "Have you heard any talk lately? Anything strange that might be related?"

Vine rubbed his hands over the bar top. "Nothing of note. For sure, nothing to do with Mrs. Johnson being missing. If you ask me, she moved on to better pastures. Andy was in here often enough."

"You don't sound too fond of him. I thought bartenders liked everyone."

"We're just careful not to show our distaste. He was in here often enough for me to take his measure." Daniel gave her a wan smile.

Marina recognized that if Daniel Vine found you wanting, you were a sorry soul indeed. She kept her thoughts to herself for once, and congratulated herself instead. "I, for once, agree with you, may the gods help me. Just doing due diligence, as Reed says." Marina drained her glass. "Thanks for the ale."

She left the saloon and headed back to the depot to wait until it was time to join Reed for dinner. It had turned out to be an exciting day, and Marina found she was looking forward to sharing her adventures with Reed.

CHAPTER 8

Later that day, Marina fiddled with the end of her braid as she walked
to Reed's. While waiting at the depot, she had allowed Iris to braid her hair,
and it was more elaborate than the simple braid she preferred. Iris's deft
fingers had woven a braid around the crown of her head that left the curls
in the back loose. Marina had also, at Iris's insistence, changed into cleaner
clothes. Marina distantly noted that Iris had been bossier than normal this
afternoon. It was definitely time to spend some time away from town.

Marina turned to go down the alley between the mercantile and the
sheriff's office. She intended to go through the back door and up the stairs,
but she heard splashing and slowed her steps before coming out of the
alley. The glare of the setting sun was in her eyes when she came around the
corner. Her feet ground to a halt after her eyes adjusted.

Reed stood at the hand pump behind his building, naked to the waist.
The glow of the late sun lit his skin like fire. Rivulets of water ran down his
muscled shoulders. Goosebumps covered all the skin she could see. Reed
was making too much noise to hear her approach and did not look up.

Marina was not interested in finding a mate, but that did not mean she
did not appreciate the options available. She placed a careful step on the
porch behind the building, then another step, and leaned over the railing.
Reed, still oblivious to her, stuck his head under the pump and lifted the
handle to release a stream of water. He stood and slicked his wet hair back
from his face. He was going to turn around in a moment, and then she
would be caught flap-jawed and gaping. Better to expose herself first, she
thought.

Marina cleared her throat. "Nice of you to clean up for me."

Reed swiveled, and Marina kept her eyes locked firmly on his face. She
felt the heat of a blush spread on her cheeks and hoped the sunset would
mask it.

Reed picked up a rag on the side of the basin under the pump and rubbed his hair dry. It stuck up in light brown spikes. "I smelled more of horse and dust than anything else. Didn't want to ruin dinner." Reed grabbed the shirt he had laid over the back railing.

"Don't get dressed on my account." Marina leaned over, placing two elbows on the railing and settling in for the show. "Please continue. The view is quite nice."

Reed rolled his eyes at her as he shoved his arms into the shirt. "Mother taught me a gentleman comes to the table fully clothed and clean."

"Fully clothed?"

"She started out telling us we were to wear shirts at dinner. My oldest brother tested the rule by coming to the table with only a shirt. Nothing else. Made sure to choose one that was a bit too small. Didn't cover all it should've," Reed laughed.

Marina's elbow slipped off the railing, and she just missed banging her chin on the wood as she collapsed in laughter. Reed laughed harder at her slip. Marina straightened from the near fall and asked, "What did your mother do?"

"She amended the rule to include the words fully clothed. Matthew had to do the dishes for a week." Reed finished buttoning his shirt and picked up his gun belt from where he had left it on the porch.

Marina wondered what a house that lively would be like and laughed again. "Your mother kept you and your siblings in line. If they were all like you, she must have been a singular woman to have kept you going in the right direction." Marina wiped tears from her eyes.

Reed leaned against the railing next to her. "My brothers were much worse than me."

Marina cocked an eyebrow at that falsehood and made a sound in the back of her throat.

Reed turned to her, his smile relaxed. "I was better, most days. My mother would've liked you."

Marina highly doubted that. "I met a sphinx today."

Reed's gaze sharpened. "A sphinx? As in a lion who asks riddles and eats people?"

"You really have been spending your nights reading. Yes, that sort of sphinx, but she's still practically a baby, so no riddles and no eating people – yet."

His lips thinned. "You sound disappointed."

"She's the daughter of a new family, the Nassos, who've moved in on the base of Shaker's Way. I'd guess she's no more than eighteen, but it's hard to tell with Remnants. I could," Marina paused and rolled her tongue around in her mouth, "taste her power. It was raw and young. I could take her now in a fair fight, but when she is mature, she might get the better of me." Marina put a hand over the knife on her belt.

Reed's eyes followed her movement and then he shifted to put his shoulder next to hers. He faced the last of the glowing sunset and said, "I'd always bet on you, no matter how powerful the opposition. I've come to view you, and the other harpies, as some kind of indestructible warriors. I've been witness to you holding an angry mob in check. You defeated Zeus. Just the other day, you held a chimera at bay with one clawed hand. If I start believing you aren't the scariest thing out there, I'll never get a wink of sleep."

His praise warmed her. "I do love a vote of confidence."

"Don't go getting a big head. Come on up. Stew's on. I want to hear more about the Nassos." Reed held the door open and motioned Marina inside.

The smell of stew hit her as soon as she stepped indoors. She headed up the stairs and felt his eyes on her back as she climbed. "How was your day? Did you find any traces of Katherine?"

"Nothing. She's long gone and better off. Only thing that bothers me is she didn't take a horse or borrow one from any of the farms close. No one has a horse missing. I checked."

"She could have easily walked this time of year. The weather is wonderful, except Johnson did say she disappeared the night of the storm last week. Of course, he could've been so drunk he did not know what day it was." Marina's stomach growled.

Reed motioned her to the table. "Agreed. We'll just have to wait and see. May never know more. Tell me about the Nassos." He pulled two bowls from a shelf in the kitchen and began ladling stew.

Marina cut two slices from the loaf of bread on the table. "There are multiple siblings, though Pearl was somewhat vague when Iris pressed her. She came to town with an older brother, Claude, who is the definition of a bully. Pearl acted submissive, but there was rebellion in her eyes. They'll have trouble with that one." Marina chuckled.

"Most young girls are trouble. Especially for their older brothers." He placed a steaming bowl of soup in front of Marina.

"I wouldn't know. I never had an older brother to bother," Marina remarked without sadness. Even if she had been a lonely child, she had her sister harpies and Iris now.

"Anything else?"

Marina blew on the stew and took a bite. It was rich and filled with the sweetness of carrots and beef. She chewed slowly. "Widow Finch is a wonderful cook. Nothing else about the Nassos, really. Henry reshod some of their horses when they first came to town. Mr. Nasso asked questions about the town and if it was a safe place for Remnants. Nothing out of the ordinary. They seem normal enough."

"For Remnants," Reed added.

His comment gave Marina pause. "Does it bother you? The Remnants moving in?"

Reed lowered his spoon and met her gaze square on. "I don't care one way or the other, but I do care that Remnants are an unknown quantity. Hard to keep peace and protect people when you don't know what you might be facing around the next corner. Just makes my job harder is all. Seems to me most Remnants are like anyone else. They just want to live their lives."

"More people means more trouble, but it also means there is a greater chance of things being interesting. I just don't like being taken unawares by other big, bad things. I do like interesting, though," Marina said.

"You're more crotchety than a trapper in the city some days."

"It's my territory. I used to know everyone in the valley, but now there are more and more new people." Marina frowned into her stew.

Reed laughed at her. "You act like you own the whole Rocky Mountains. They don't need to ask your permission. You aren't the land office. Besides, I know you're only upset because you've been in town for a few days too many. You've been here helping me instead of out there." He waved his spoon to the northwest, where Jolly's Folly sat.

Marina gripped the spoon until her knuckles shone white. She missed her mountain. He saw through her so clearly. "They're my damn mountains." Her voice had dropped an octave, and Marina felt her teeth grow sharp.

Reed stilled and spoke in a soothing tone. He was not scared, but relaxed. "Don't pull your harpy tricks on me. I'm not scared of you."

Marina shook herself and shoved a chunk of bread in her mouth. She chewed while she pulled her harpy back. She really needed a night outside of town. "You're right. I'm restless. Meeting Pearl Nasso did not help. I need to go flying, or hunting, or find a good fight, or all three together would do it. Speaking of which," Marina's eyes gained a particular gleam that made Reed groan. It was a sparkle that said she was about to get into trouble. "I was in Vine's today, and there's a rumor going around about a lion seen in some caves on Baldy."

"A mountain lion?" he asked.

Marina rubbed her hands together. "No, a real lion. An African lion."

Reed swallowed then coughed when the bite lodged in his windpipe. "According to who?" he wheezed out.

"Art Turner."

"Turner is an idiot. Probably doesn't even know what a lion is, let alone where Africa is located. An ocean away. In case you're forgetful."

Marina grinned, showing her mortal teeth, but she knew the harpy was in her eyes. "I'm going to kill it, and then we'll see who laughs when I walk down the street with it around my shoulders."

"You'll cause a riot."

"I'll never have to buy another drink in the saloon again." It would be glorious, she thought, and the look on everyone's faces would be worth the risk.

Reed rolled his eyes. "Don't go searching for every trouble out there. Enough seems to find you on its own. You'll get yourself killed."

Marina gave the barest hint of a shrug. "A harpy has to do something for entertainment around here."

"Your sisters aren't as bloodthirsty as you seem to be."

"They're not as comfortable with our more violent tendencies. Petra was always afraid her darkness would swallow her, so she pushed it away. Dora covers up hers by being the peacemaker, even if she has to do so by force." Marina twirled her spoon between her fingers. Her sisters dealt with their harpies in their own way, but her approach was more direct.

As if reading her thoughts, Reed asked, "What about you?"

"It's better to just embrace the truth of what I am than spend time pining for what I'm not."

"What are you?" he prodded.

"A monster, of course." She grinned with a mouth full of pointed teeth. Marina let her eyes darken and thoughts of blood and violence danced through her mind like thunder.

Reed stilled again, but this time a trickle of fear emanated from him. Marina knew he trusted her, but harpies were not something you snuggled up next to at night. They were the things you ran from in terror. It was best that he not forget what she was and think she was like other women he knew. She never forgot.

"Fool woman. You're set on going, at least take Petra or Dora with you." Reed gripped his spoon tighter than he needed to.

"Why? I'm a predator, not a town lady. I don't need help. I know my way around a gun. I can shoot a moving target at over a hundred yards. I can throw a knife better than anyone else in town. I do not intend to use my gun or my knife. I want to hunt it down in my harpy form." Marina wanted to feel it beneath her talons. She imagined the warmth of its blood on her skin, and she sighed.

Reed gave her a disapproving look. "Killing for killing's sake isn't any way to go about things."

Marina put her spoon down in her empty bowl and crossed her arms. "The blood is not the point, though I won't lie, I do like the kill. I'm a predator, and no predator likes another predator in their territory. This valley belongs to the harpies. To me."

A vein in Reed's neck started to throb. "You're going to get yourself killed." His hands clenched and unclenched. Marina wondered if he was imagining her neck between them.

If she wanted to keep her job, she knew she should probably spend less time finding ways to irritate the sheriff. Unfortunately for him, the progression of his anger made her laugh even as she met him flame for flame.

Marina opened her eyes wide and tried to look innocent. "I'll be extra careful, and I promise not to die."

Reed's anger deflated, but a line of worry remained between his eyes. "If you do make it back to town with your fool head intact, I'll buy you a drink."

"The good stuff," she insisted.

"As you insist." He took their bowls and laid them on the counter by the water basin.

Most of the day Marina had longed for this moment, when she would leave town and fly home in the cool night air. Now that the moment was here, she was reluctant to go.

Marina stood. "I should be going."

Reed turned to face her. "I'll walk you out."

He gestured for her to go down the stairs first, so she did. She could feel his eyes boring into the back of her as she made her way down. When they reached the landing, he reached around her to open the door. His arm brushed her side and she felt the contact like a spark of recognition. She walked through the doorway and onto the back porch, blinking and trying to catch her bearings.

She could feel Reed walking behind her. He paused on the top step and she kept going until her feet were on dirt. Her side burned where he had touched her. Marina took a breath before turning around to face him.

The lamp from inside was behind him and she could not see his face clearly. His posture was relaxed, but intent.

When he spoke his voice was low. "Should I bring down two cups of coffee in the morning or will you be off trying to get yourself killed?"

Marina closed some of the distance between them. At the last moment, she stopped and maintained a buffer of space. "Every day carries a chance of death, but I don't plan on dying anytime soon. I wouldn't want to deny you my company."

Reed laughed. "Can't have that. Don't know how I ever managed without you." Marina wished she could see his smile in the dark.

"You keep thinking like that, and this partnership's going to work out just fine for us both. Night, Sheriff." Marina let her harpy burst out of her and she was up in the air before Reed could reply. She trusted the darkness to hide her flight from town as she sped into the sky. The night wind rolled over her, and Marina let thoughts of Reed go as she flew home.

CHAPTER 9

Mount Baldy had earned its name by being a collection of rocky crags, caves, and barren ground with few plants to cover its pockmarks. The gravel surface and lack of vegetation on Baldy made tracking animals across its face hard, but not impossible. Marina's back ached from crunching along the rock-strewn surface, doubled over with her nose to the ground. After two days, she had tracked the lion to a large cave on the north side of the mountain. She had yet to see the beast. From the tracks, it was either the largest mountain lion in existence or it was indeed an African lion, as advertised. Marina was hopeful it would return in the next day or two. There was enough spoor and other evidence to suggest the lion had made this location a semi-permanent place to rest.

The sun inched towards the jagged horizon, and Marina considered her options for waiting. She moved upwind, where she could keep an eye on the mouth of the cave and not give away her presence. In her harpy form, she was able to perch in a tree for hours, or an entire day if need be. There were no trees here sturdy enough to hold her considerable bulk. She stayed in her mortal form and looked around. She settled for squeezing into a depression in the rocks that shielded her from view, kept the sun out of her eyes, and allowed her to watch the cave.

Waiting was the worst part of a hunt. She was excellent at tracking and finding the best vantage point for an ambush, but waiting for the right time required all of the patience she possessed, which was not much. She settled into her crevice and dug a strip of dried venison out of her pack. The smoky taste of the meat hushed the insistence of her belly. The peace of the mountains and her solitude after days surrounded by the press of humanity swept over her like a warm blanket. Tension drained from her shoulders as the heat of the rocks at her back leeched into her bones.

It had been quite a while since she had felt this relaxed. Reed's ability to debate her with a mixture of intellect and heat was intoxicating. It was this heady feeling Reed created in her that worried her more than the chimeras, sphinxes, or lions. Keeping herself slightly irritated at him was easier than thinking of him in…other ways. Marina shoved the trail of those thoughts aside roughly.

A speck of red caught Marina's eye. A ladybug sporting six spots was journeying over her thigh. Marina placed her finger in front of it. The whisper of its feet crawled over her hand. The weather was turning. This ladybug was the last spot of summer she would probably see for months. Marina gently nudged it until the bug crawled off her hand and onto the rock. She continued to watch it as it made its way to the top of the rock, opened its outer covering to reveal the soft wings below, and flew off.

The dusk gave way to the swift darkness of the mountains. The lion did not appear. The night was cool and filled with the sounds of animals conducting their nightly business. She sat in her hiding place and dozed.

Marina's eyes snapped open. She blinked, letting her eyes adjust to the night. Her muscles were stiff from sleeping in the crevice, and she tightened each one in turn to wake up. The moon was close to the west, but the east was not yet losing its darkness. Dawn was still a ways off. There was a chuffing noise near the mouth of the cave. Marina followed the sound and saw him.

She had no comparison, having never been to the continent of Africa or any of the traveling shows that included such creatures in Europe. The lion was huge. Not as large as a harpy, but it would dwarf the native cougar as if it were a barn cat. Unfortunately for the lion, Marina's harpy was much larger than either cat, and she had claws of her own.

Careful not to dislodge any rocks as she stood, Marina reached inside the core of herself, the place where she kept her harpy, barely contained and dangerous. The change was like the coolest water on a hot day, welcome and pure. Marina breathed deep and her harpy senses drew in the bouquet of the mountain night. It was a good night for hunting.

Marina called on her speed, spread her tan and brown wings, and lifted off. If the lion heard the flapping of her wings, he did not have time to register it before she was crashing into him. Marina sunk the razor-sharp talons on her feet into the lion's side, hoping they would dig deep enough to reach his heart or at least slow him down.

The lion's roar broke the quiet night, and the smell of its blood poured over Marina as she ground her talons in as far as they could go. She wrapped her wing around the back of the lion's neck and pierced its neck with her needle sharp claws. The warm, sticky blood ran through her fingers. Marina barely missed having her face ripped open by its snapping jaws. She ripped with her talons and felt them scrape bone.

Two things happened simultaneously. The enraged roar of the lion crashed into her, and the sense of other pushed against Marina like a physical force. As odd as an African lion was in the Rocky Mountains, this was no lion. The thing whose blood was staining her feathers was a Remnant. Marina pulled back her claws and struggled to move away.

"I've made a mistake," Marina croaked. She might enjoy a good hunt, but she was not a murderer.

The lion's only response was another ear splitting roar. It reached back with a paw the size of her head and swiped her off his back. Her head cracked on a rock as she fell, and white spots appeared in the corners of her vision. She shook her head, trying to clear her vision, and the weight of the giant cat landed on her chest. The air in her lungs whooshed out and she struggled to pull it back in.

Marina felt the flesh of her shoulder give way under its teeth and immediately understood the gravity of the situation. Nothing survives having its throat ripped open. She healed more quickly in her harpy form, but she had to keep its mouth from her neck. Dead was dead. The jaws on her shoulder locked tight. The pain of the lion's grip reverberated down her arms to the ends of her talons. She had to get far enough to get away from its teeth so she could try to talk to the creature. It was a Remnant, and that meant it could reason.

Marina wrapped one set of claws around the lion's neck and squeezed. With her free hand, Marina tried to gain some leverage on the ground. Her hand slipped in a puddle of blood. Her body fell back onto the ground. She could barely move her lungs enough to draw air as the weight of the lion pressed her into the rocky ground. Marina pulled her feet up and dug her talons into the belly of the lion. It did not even flinch. If she was going to live to tell anyone about this tomorrow, she had to think fast.

Marina put both her hands in the wrecked mess that was the lion's throat and felt for its windpipe. Her claws, slick with blood, slid off it a few times before she could press her clawed fingers firmly around it. The lion's breathing acquired a whistle as it struggled to breathe through the restricted air space. Marina shifted and held the lion as close as she could, pressing her body against it so that the lion could not use its own claws on her.

"Now, listen. I came here under the impression you were just a lion. I apologize. I'm going to let go nice and easy and we can back away and this can be over." Marina did not want to die, nor did she want to kill another Remnant. Killing animals for sport was one thing. Killing a person or a Remnant without cause was entirely another.

Marina released her claws and the lion's breathing eased. She put her hand flat on the ground. The lion's jaw was still wrapped around her shoulder, but the tension lessened. Marina braced herself to scoot out from underneath the lion the moment it moved off her chest.

The lion's head moved back so that it could look Marina firmly in the face. A calculating predator looked back at her from golden eyes. It reared back and slammed its head into her own. Marina heard the crack of their skulls dimly under the crash of pain between her eyes. Nausea crashed over her and spots danced on the edges of her vision. She felt the lion grab one of her taloned feet between his teeth. Her heart beat in her ears and throbbed in her temples as the beast began to drag her away. Marina knew she could not let it take her anywhere.

Marina made her body go limp, and she took deep breaths, waiting for the pain in her head to recede. The lion was dragging her by walking her backwards into the cave. Marina gathered her weight and pulled her power into herself. In a burst of speed, she lunged at the lion's neck. Her fingers sought purchase on the windpipe once again. Unlike the first time, she did not allow mercy to hold her power in check. She pushed violence and fear out from her essence in never-ending waves.

The lion shifted and tried to struggle against her body by pushing its claws into her chest and legs. Marina used her talons to hold the lion close. She could not allow it room to move those claws or it would rip her to shreds. Her own claws were numb and slippery. She pushed harder until no air moved in the pipe underneath them. She tried to rip through the lion's neck, but could not tear the essential pipe from its owner. Marina kept her grip, squeezing and praying to the gods for what seemed like hours.

Her wings started to shake with effort the moment before the lion's body shuddered and fell limp in her arms. Marina did not move, despite her screaming muscles, for a span of minutes—until she was sure the lion was well and truly dead. She peeled her fingers out of the pulp of the lion's throat and kicked off the carcass with her taloned feet. Marina stood, her feathers awash in blood, aching, and looked at the sun peeking cheerily over the horizon.

She tore her eyes from the gold and red of the sunrise and looked at the bloody body of the Remnant at her feet. It looked like a lion and smelled like a lion, but this was a man, and she had killed him. She'd no choice. Marina knew he would have killed her. Regardless, the weight of its death was like a grinding stone on her head. She would take the body to a safe place and then go to town to get help.

She hopped onto the body, dug her claws in, and spread her wings to lift off. Pain shot up her left wing and it refused to lift more than halfway. Her shoulder bore teeth marks from the lion. Marina looked down at her chest and stomach for the first time and registered long gouge marks. They were much too deep. The loss of blood caught up to her, and she swayed until she fell.

The rocks and gravel dug into her back. Her feathers had protected her from being damaged in the fall. She lay on the ground, considering her options. There was no way she could move the body. At this rate, she was worried about getting into town at all. Town was the closest place, and the only option, but she had to do one thing first.

She lay on the ground and stared into the sky. If she could not take the body herself and give it a proper burial, she needed to look around the cave it had been living in and try to find out who it was. If she could find something that had belonged to the lion, she could notify its family or something.

Distantly, she recognized that it was entirely possible that someone might have to give *her* a proper burial before this day was over. Marina knew her wounds were deep. Harpies healed faster than mortals, but she was not invincible. If she stayed here for a spell, she hoped her wing would heal enough for her to fly into town. It was the only plan she had. Knowing it would help, Marina changed into her mortal form and then back into a harpy again. Changing forms did not magically fix everything, but it accelerated healing. Changing would not keep her from losing too much blood or dying of a mortal wound, however.

It was midday before Marina had enough strength to sit up. She was no longer bleeding. Tentatively, she stood and stretched her wings as far as they would go. Pain radiated out from her left wing, and it hung lower than it should. The lion must have broken it or bruised the joint badly. Marina could not tell what hurt worse. The wounds in her stomach and chest were still angry and raw, but the edges had begun to heal and no longer gaped as much. Marina sighed.

She hopped on her harpy legs in an unsteady manner towards the mouth of the cave. Her left wing trailed on the ground. Marina leaned against the opening of the cave and tried to catch her breath. Black spots swam before her eyes, and she closed them. It was a long time before she could move again.

The cave was shallow, only about ten feet deep. The remains of a fire and the carcass of a deer were the only things in the cave. There was no pack and no bedroll, nothing to indicate that a person had been living here. He must have spent all his time as a lion. The search of his space had exhausted her, and she had nothing to show for it. It was time to go. She had to try to get to town and let Doc look at her.

Marina knelt by the body of the lion and ran a hand down its flank. It was useless to feel guilt over his death; he would have killed her had he gotten the chance. Still, a prick of unease went through her. She gathered what strength she had and took off, carrying her guilt with her.

The flight took much longer than it should have. Marina stopped twice to rest. When she landed on the outside of town, her legs buckled under her. She changed back into her mortal form and lay on the ground, catching her breath. With a heave, she stood on swaying feet and staggered to the depot. It occurred to her halfway there that she should go straight to Doc.

She did not think she could make it all the way down Main Street. Lack of food, water, significant loss of blood, and what healing she had done had sapped her of strength.

Iris's blue eyes were the first thing Marina saw when she pushed open the door of the depot. Iris met her gaze over Reed's shoulder and Marina relaxed. She had made it far enough. Relief flowed over the pain. She closed the door and leaned her back against it in an effort to keep her feet. She slid down the door and cheered a little when she kept her feet, barely.

"Gods, Marina, you stink. What did you do, wrestle a skunk and then bathe in its blood?" Dora's calm tone registered in her ear as her sister grabbed her arm to steady her.

Reed turned and was in front of her in a heartbeat. He ran shaking hands down her arms and over her waist. She flinched. Everything hurt, but she thought there was no way she looked as bad as his reaction implied.

She managed to smile and felt the blood on her face crack as it pulled on her skin. "Can't be as bad as all that. I'm still breathing aren't I?"

"You're hurt. Sit down." Reed pulled her to a stool. Marina went without argument.

Iris brushed hair back from Marina's forehead. A lock of it was stuck to her skin. "How badly are you hurt?"

"Nothing that won't heal in a couple days. Some bite wounds and some punctures. Maybe a scratch on my stomach. I didn't want to look too close. I'm not bleeding anymore; besides, most of it's not mine. I think." Marina tried to laugh but the pain flared out from everywhere at once. She tried to be still. Everything was fuzzy.

"Dora, go get Doc." Iris had barely finished before Dora was running out the door.

Marina swayed on the stool and Reed caught her. He scooped her up, one hand under her shoulders and another under her legs. "Where can I lay her down?"

"She has a bed upstairs. This way." Iris led the way with quick steps.

Marina curled a hand around the nape of Reed's neck as he carried her up the stairs. She felt like she was floating. His skin was warm. "I can walk."

"Not today, you can't. Idiot woman," he muttered.

"You smell good."

"What?" he hissed in her ear. Marina did not realize she had said that out loud. She must have lost more blood than she thought. She closed her eyes and pretended to be tired. She did not have to try hard.

The bed was soft when Reed laid her down. With a gentle slowness, he eased his arm from under her head. The weight of the bed shifted as he sat next to her. Marina opened her eyes to look at him and found him staring at her. Tight, white lines rimmed his mouth. The room spun uncomfortably, and Marina closed her eyes.

Iris brought in a wet cloth and a basin. She began cleaning some of the blood from Marina's face. The water was cool and helped center her.

"I need to look at your wounds," Iris said. Marina nodded and braced herself.

Iris slowly pulled Marina's shirt out of the waist of her pants and revealed long, half-inch deep claw marks running the length of her torso. If this was healing, it had been much worse on the mountain. It was a wonder she had not had to fly with a hand holding her innards in place. Reed's mouth almost disappeared, and his body was tight.

"My poor bird. You already changed once?" Iris asked. Marina nodded again. "You'll live, but Doc is going to have to clean them up."

"Don't call in Doc too soon. Reed has murder in his eyes. If you don't mind, let him finish me off and then call Doc. Gods, this hurts." Marina's voice was strong despite her injuries.

"The lion got close enough to the mark. No need to make it worse. I'll save the tongue lashing for later." Reed made the effort to smile. He touched her hair, then repeated the gesture.

She lifted her hand and laid it on his leg. "I told you I didn't need help with the lion."

Reed put his hand over hers and squeezed it painfully. "Christ, woman. Why can't you ever listen?"

"What happened to saving the lecture for later? I didn't need the help. It was a touch harder to kill the damn thing than I thought it would be, though. I swear I punctured its heart with my claws, and I damn near ripped out its throat, but the damn thing wouldn't die." Marina felt her lip tremble. "It wasn't a lion. It was a Remnant. I killed him, or her, or it."

Iris's hand stilled. "You slit the lion's throat and it was still alive? You're sure it was a Remnant?"

Marina licked her lips. "Yes. I had to strangle it. It took a while, hence all the injuries."

Iris had not moved.

"Care to share what is going on in that head of yours, Iris?" Reed asked.

"The Nemean lion in the myths, the one slain by Hercules, was strangled. It was said to have been impenetrable to arrows and weapons. I need to do some research and do some thinking. Why did it try to kill you if you knew what it was?"

Marina closed her eyes. "I tried to stop the fight once I knew, but it kept attacking me. I didn't want to kill it, him, whatever it was, but it had my shoulder in its teeth and wouldn't let go." She opened her eyes and her companions were both staring at her with sympathy, and in Reed's case, frustration. "I didn't have a choice."

Dora came in with the doctor, and Reed stood. He gave Marina's hand another squeeze. "You owe me a story that includes the meanest lion in creation because if a tiny lion can do this, I'll start believing you aren't the big, bad harpy you claim to be. Do what Doc says. I'll wait outside."

She returned the squeeze. "Thanks. You owe me a drink for being wrong about the lion. I'm still alive."

"Not sure this counts. Heal quick. I owe you a drink." He did not move to go.

Doc shifted his weight. "Sheriff, if you'll leave us, I can see what the damage is."

Reed looked sheepish. He ran a hand over her hair again. He walked stiffly to the door and turned to look at her before leaving. His eyes burned into her for a heartbeat, and then he was gone.

The Doc poked at her a bit and muttered under his breath about foolish harpies, but Marina ignored him. The tiredness pulled her under and over in waves. A sharp pain in her gut wrenched her eyes open.

"Sorry," Doc said and continued cleaning one of the gashes on her belly. "I am going to bind these instead of suture them. It's a miracle you're alive if they were worse than this. I think your body will close them up on their own in a couple days. You'll need to remain in bed as much as possible for a few days though. No more lion hunting." Doc patted an uninjured spot on her leg.

"I wanted to go after an elephant next." Marina laughed at her own joke then regretted it as fire washed through her belly. Dora scowled over Dr. Williams's shoulder.

"I'm not jesting. I know how you like to do as you please, but if you don't allow these to heal, they could become infected. Even a harpy would have some trouble with an infection of the blood." Doc put away the distilled alcohol in his bag and piled the dirty rags together. "For once, do as you are told, and allow yourself to heal."

"Yes, sir."

He handed her a cup. "Drink this. It'll help you rest." Marina gulped the bitter tea and handed the empty cup back.

Doc left and Marina heard his light steps on the stairs. In their wake, Marina heard heavy steps, taking the stairs two at a time. The door opened, and Reed hesitated on the threshold. "Can I come in?"

"Come on in," Dora said. "Dr. Williams gave her something to help her sleep, so don't stay too long." Dora patted Marina's foot. She glided out of the room.

"Doc says I have to stay in bed, but I'll be up for that drink tomorrow." Marina did not intend to stay in bed long.

"Like hell you will. He said you are to take it easy for a few days. You'll do as the man says if I have to tie you to the bed myself."

"I'll be perfectly fine tomorrow. I'm not an invalid." She could feel what was left of her blood pounding through her head. It was easier to be angry at Reed than to think about what had happened up on the mountain.

She saw the anger, bright and hot, flash through him. "No. You only just managed not to get your guts spilled out by a lion who's harder to kill than a fool harpy with no brains in her beautiful head. You'll do as the doctor said and take it easy."

"Did you just say I was beautiful?"

His face turned an uneven shade of red. "Don't change the subject."

Whatever Doc had given her was starting to turn her brain to cotton. She held on to the anger to focus. Marina struggled to find words that made sense. "Fine. You've no right to tell me what to do."

"I'll tell you what to do if I damn well please." Reed placed his hands on the bed and leaned over her. "Stop acting like a child looking for the next treat. Act like an adult, be responsible, and stop tearing off around the territory trying to get yourself killed."

"I didn't die, and I could care less what pleases you. You've no right to make any demands of me." Marina pushed herself back into the pillows, leaning back as far as she could. His face was still close enough that she could feel his breath on her cheek. Marina's eyes dropped to his mouth, tight with anger, and she knew she had made a mistake. Something other than anger curled in her belly.

Reed drew in a breath of air and stepped away from the bed. Frustration and heat had replaced the anger in his eyes. He turned from her and leaned a hand against the door frame. "You're right, Sparrow. I've no right to ask anything of you."

He left the room and did not look back.

CHAPTER 10

Reed had departed like his feet were on fire, and Marina did not see him for days. He did not stop by the depot, even once, to see how she was recovering. Even though she'd spent the first few days in bed, she knew he had not stopped by, because she'd asked Iris. It should not have rankled her, but it did. Every day she was a little snappier, and every day the room she was resting in seemed a foot smaller.

Iris took pity on her and let her come downstairs on the fourth day. As the doctor predicted, the gouges from the lion's claws had faded into white lines surrounded by the green and yellow of healing bruises. Marina was sore as she moved gingerly down the stairs, but still happy to be up and about. Iris had helped her wash and dry her hair, and so she sat on her usual stool at the counter feeling quite like herself for the first time in days.

"I need to go take care of the body of the lion. I tried to bring it back, but I had already lost too much blood and couldn't carry it." A wash of guilt washed over her and Marina ruthlessly squashed it out.

"Petra and Dora took care of it already. Burned it." Iris tapped her quill against her lips. "I've started making a list of the incidents around the valley." Iris pulled a sheet of paper from a leather folder. "So far, I have Katherine's disappearance, the chimera, and the Nemean Lion."

"We're just listing things in the last few weeks, right, because if we go back any further that list of yours is going to get real long, real quick." Marina held her hand out for the list. Each item on the list included a date, location, and a few other notes. "You didn't include the sphinx."

Iris took the paper back. "If I included every new Remnant family moving into the area, the list would be useless. We both know being a Remnant doesn't mean anything."

"Pearl's brother is a piece of work."

"Agreed, but being unpleasant doesn't equal evil. You, my bird, are less than pleasant quite often and yet you manage to be a useful member of society."

Marina put her hands over her heart. "If you think I'm a good citizen, I need to try harder at being a reprobate. You wound my heart, truly you do. "

"Can't wound what you don't have." Iris delivered the words without a twitch of a smile.

"Now I'm mortally wounded. I think it's a sign I need to stop taking advantage of your hospitality. You're obviously tired of my company."

Iris smiled then. "You can stay as long as you'd like. I enjoy having you, even if all your pacing and energy puts me on edge after four days."

"Pacing? You kept me in bed for three of those four days."

"Yes, and you made me pay for every hour of every one of them."

Marina left her stool and wrapped her arms around Iris. "Don't be annoyed with me. You're the only one who really loves me." Her voice contained a pleading note in it that she hated.

Iris pulled back from her embrace and placed her hands on Marina's cheek. "Your sisters love you and Reed is fond of you."

Marina snorted. She was a violent creature, and the sooner he came to terms with that, the better. It was just as well. "He likes having me as backup. Otherwise, I think he would be glad to see the end of me."

Iris's mouth twitched. "I'm not so sure."

Marina needed to change the subject from Reed before she told Iris his absence felt more like abandonment. "What are you doing with the list?" Marina went back to her stool.

"I'm trying to find references to the lion and the chimera to see if any of them were connected with the disappearance of women. In the old myths, there are some accounts of women disappearing in the Nemean Lion's territory, but nothing conclusive. It doesn't explain the chimera."

"It could just all be coincidence."

"Few things in Turning Creek end up being pure coincidence."

"True. And it has made life here so interesting." Marina rubbed her hands together and felt her face break into her first real smile in days.

"I hate it when you get that look in your eye."

"What look?"

"Like the next catastrophic event is the most fervent desire of your heart."

She grinned wider. "Who says it's not? After being cooped up for days, a little excitement in any form would be welcome."

Iris rummaged around and shoved a book into her hands. "Really, Marina, you are ridiculous sometimes."

"Yes, but I'm never boring."

"Shut your flapping mouth and get to work."

Iris used research to keep Marina inside the depot for another day, but at the end of the second day of flipping through volumes with cracking spines and worm-eaten pages she was ready to scream. Marina slammed the book she had been reading, an account of some sailors who'd claimed they'd found the end of the world. "I'm going to Vine's."

Iris placed a finger on the page in front of her and looked up. "Why?"

Marina could think of at least a dozen reasons. "If I don't get out of here, I'm going to turn violent and do some actual damage. I'll be useful. I'll go ask around, see if anyone has heard or seen anything else strange going on, you know, besides the usual."

"I'm sure the fact that Vine has a brand new batch of his fine hootch out this week has nothing to do with it."

Marina would strangle another lion for a drink—a regular one this time, though. "Nothing at all to do with it, but I might have to sample it to see how it compares to the last batch." Marina rubbed her hands together and licked her lips.

Iris did not try to keep her there or tell her why she should not be going to a saloon days after being mauled by a lion, and Marina loved her for it. She felt Reed had tried too hard to get her to conform to his idea of how he wanted her to behave. A sharp anger rose just thinking about their last argument. He still had not been to the depot. Her anger was replaced swiftly by disappointment, and she swallowed it down.

Whenever she fought with the other harpies, Iris would nag them until one, both, or all of them apologized. They always made up after a day or two. Iris would not allow it to go longer and, secretly, Marina's heart was sore until they patched things up.

Marina walked into Vine's Saloon and left thoughts of Reed out in the dusty street. There was the usual crowd who came here every afternoon. Andy Johnson sat in the darkest corner, accompanied by two men Marina did not recognize, lamenting the loss of his wife. He looked a few pounds lighter. He probably drank more than he ate now that no one was at home cooking for him. There were some miners and one gentleman better dressed than the others in a vest and coat. By the back door, two women sat with their backs to the wall, facing the door.

Atlanta and Cyrene, Remnants of fabled huntresses. Both possessed loud mouths and questionable reputations. Their posture and expression left no doubt to anyone in the room that the two buckskin-clad, heavily armed women were dangerous. Marina sauntered up to their table, wishing she'd thought to bring more than one knife to the bar.

"I thought we told you two never to come back."

Atlanta lifted her mug and took a steady sip of ale. "We heard there were lions in the area. Thought it'd be nice to visit an old hunting ground."

Marina placed her palms on the table and leaned over the table towards Atlanta. "You hurt my friend." She'd seen the damage they had done to Simon when Dora and Petra had brought him home.

Cyrene spoke up. "If we'd known he was under your protection, we never would've imposed."

Marina hissed. "Everything in this valley and the surrounding mountains is under my protection. You'd do well to remember that." Marina straightened and dug in her pocket. She threw the leather disk on the table. "Know that this time, I have official backing to do whatever the hells I want to your sorry hides."

Atlanta picked up the disk and burst into laughter. The unguarded quality of it took years off her face. "Sweet mercy, please tell me that thing is real."

"It is," Marina said.

"Vine. We need a round of your new batch so we can toast to the new deputy," Atlanta called. She turned to Marina. "Join us for a drink."

Marina shrugged. "I've never been one to turn down a drink. It's no feathers off my back if you pay for my drink before I beat you to a pulp." Marina angled a chair so she could just see the door out of the corner of her eyes. She kept most of her attention on Atlanta.

"Afternoon to you, Miss Marina. I heard you had an interesting hunt the other day." Vine placed three glasses of golden whiskey in front of them. Marina picked up the glass and took a sip. It was smooth and smoky. The color of it reminded her of Reed's eyes when he laughed at her. Marina shoved the thought, along with its accompanying pang of longing, deep.

Marina took a sip. "Vine, you've outdone yourself. This is delicious." Trustworthy or not, Vine knew how to run a saloon and keep his customers plied with drink.

"Thank you for the compliment. You ladies let me know if you require more." He hesitated only briefly on the word ladies and Marina shared a smile with Atlanta.

Daniel Vine left them, and Marina sipped her whiskey in silence. Atlanta was unruffled by her reticence. Cyrene shifted in her seat and cast side glances at Atlanta. Marina allowed her harpy to look out through her eyes, letting Cyrene feel the full effect of her gaze. The huntress gulped her whiskey and held her hands tightly in her lap.

Atlanta scowled at Marina. "Leave her alone. We're not going to harm anyone here. Stop acting like you'd like nothing better than to rip our heads off."

Marina let her teeth get pointy. "Who says I don't?"

Cyrene scooted back in her chair. Atlanta rolled her eyes at her companion. "Grow a backbone. She's not going to kill you in the middle of town."

Marina cocked an eyebrow. "I won't?"

Atlanta pierced Marina with a gaze of remorseless violence. "No, you won't."

Despite her better judgment, Marina admired Atlanta. "You hunted in my territory. You hurt my friend. He's a good man with a family." Marina remembered well the terror on Beth's face when Simon had been taken.

Atlanta cocked her head to one side. A slow grin spread over her face. "Would you like retribution, harpy?"

Excitement lit in her belly. "By the gods, yes I would." Marina cracked her knuckles and rubbed her hands together. This was going to be worlds better than doing research at the depot.

"Excellent." Atlanta waved over Vine. "Two more rounds, I think."

Marina grinned. "One for now and one for after I mop the floor with you two."

"You've the timing of the drinks down correctly, but we'll see about the mopping." Cyrene sat straight in her chair.

Vine looked nervously between the three Remnants. "I don't want trouble in here."

Marina turned innocent eyes to him. "I'm never trouble."

Vine snorted. "Just do it outside and try not to break anything."

Marina clinked her glass against Atlanta's and Cyrene's. "To settling old scores." They drained their glasses.

"Just so we're clear. After this, we're free to hunt here," Atlanta said.

"No people. No Remnants. Animals only," Marina replied. "And if I win, you have to apologize to Simon and Beth Kramer while the bruises I give you are still showing."

"Deal," the huntresses said in unison.

Marina led the way to the back biergarten area. "One more thing. No weapons, and I promise to stay in this form. I don't want to have an unfair advantage." She hesitated. "I did get injured recently, but I think it'll just make this a bit more interesting."

Atlanta laughed. "This is going to be fun."

Energy and power spiked through her, and Marina strode across the clearing in the back garden. Marina turned to find Atlanta directly behind her. Marina pushed her aside with her shoulder and attacked Cyrene, whom she'd judged to be the weak link. Marina used a burst of speed to drive a fist into Cyrene's face. She'd promised not to change, but she had not promised not to use her other skills to her advantage.

Cyrene reeled back, spouting blood from her broken nose. Atlanta dove at Marina from the side, and the two grappled together for some time, rolling and twisting on the ground. Cyrene managed to land a few well-aimed punches while Marina was occupied with Atlanta. The last one was well placed. Pain from her middle spiraled out, and Marina lost the ability to breathe. The deepest of the gashes on her belly had barely healed. Marina went down on her knees. Perhaps this had not been a bright idea.

Marina hung her head low and waited for the next attack. When it came, she grabbed Cyrene's foot before it could connect with her head and flipped the huntress on to her back. Marina planted her fist in Cyrene's temple and the huntress was out. Marina turned to Atlanta.

"It's just us now, harpy," Atlanta smiled.

Marina smiled back. "I almost hate to tell you this, but this is the most fun I've had in days."

Atlanta chuckled. "You and I are cut from the same cloth. It's a shame I'm going to have to beat you so soundly. I rather think we'd make excellent friends."

Marina's fist hit Atlanta's breadbasket the moment her speech ended. "I agree. I think I'd like you as a friend. Let's go hunting sometime."

Atlanta recovered and used her leg to swipe Marina's from under her. Marina fell with a thud on her back and the air whooshed out of her lungs. Atlanta sat on top of her and wrapped her fingers around Marina's neck. Marina scrabbled at the hands holding her windpipe. She knew Atlanta was not squeezing hard enough to kill her, but she was squeezing hard enough to make her pass out.

"What in the hell is going on out here?" Reed's voice cut through the spots in her vision. Atlanta's weight was yanked off her. Reed had the huntress by both arms. "Do I need to arrest you for attempted murder?"

Atlanta jerked her head towards Marina. "I had her permission to beat the pulp out of her."

Marina sat up and rubbed her neck. "That was not the deal. I was supposed to beat you to a pulp." The two women grinned at each other.

Reed shook Atlanta. "I know who you are. Leave town now. The other harpies are in town. If they hear you've come to visit, they won't spare you a second thought before they rip your heads from your bodies." Reed released her.

Atlanta bowed to the sheriff, then offered Marina a hand up. Marina took it and groaned. Atlanta bowed to her. "Mistress Harpy. You're a worthy opponent. I do hope you will hunt with us someday. I swear by the River Styx that we will refrain from hunting in this region unless accompanied by you or one of your sisters."

Marina inclined her head. "Your oath is acknowledged. I still want you to give that apology."   Atlanta nodded. "It will be done, as I agreed."

Marina let her smile break free. "Thank you for the entertainment."

Atlanta hauled Cyrene up. Her head lolled back and forth. "It was our pleasure."

Reed waited until the two huntresses were gone to round on Marina. "Dammit, Marina. You've barely recovered from a lion attack and you're starting a brawl."

Marina laughed. She could not keep it from escaping, even though it burned her stomach to do it. He was so angry, and all she could think was how free she felt. Every nerve ending was tingling with power and pleasure from the fight. "I owed them a good fight after what they did to Simon. At least we came out here where there is less stuff to break. Gods, that was fun." Marina rubbed a sore spot on her jaw.

A tightness formed in Reed's face. "You're a deputy now, Marina. Act like it sometimes. You've responsibilities. Here," Reed shoved her badge into her hand, "you left this on the table." He turned around and walked into the saloon and out the front door.

Marina stood and ran her tongue over her teeth. One of them wiggled when she touched it. The steady beat of pain from her middle told her she had re-bruised some of her abdomen. She could feel the coolness of blood as it dried at the corner of her mouth. Reed was angry at her, but there was a calmness in her soul. This was what she was, a violent thing who loved to fight. She would not apologize for it, nor would she be made to feel guilty.

Marina walked into the saloon and picked up the last glass on the table they had abandoned. Marina drained her glass and slammed it on the table with a sense of satisfaction. She waved at Vine on the way out and left with the warmth of whiskey on her tongue.

The flickering light of a lamp shone through the window of Reed's apartment. Marina hesitated but then kept walking. She would mend that fence later. The whiskey in her belly propelled her through the cool air and into the warmth of the depot. Her two sister harpies and Iris sat around the back table and turned to greet her when she entered.

"The reprobate has returned." Petra raised a glass of the whiskey Iris kept hidden behind the counter.

"Look who's talking. How come I wasn't invited to this party? I just gave the huntresses some new bruises. Vine's new batch is excellent, in case you were wondering." Marina took the empty chair and poured herself a glass.

"Atlanta and Cyrene are in town?" Dora asked. Petra become very still.

"Yes, but let's just say I've come to an understanding with them. They won't be causing any trouble in our valley." Marina poured herself a glass. "And since I won the fight, they're going to apologize to Simon and Beth."

Petra gave her an appraising look. "You don't look like the person who won the fight."

Marina swished the whiskey over a sore spot on the inside of her cheek. "Well, I would've regained the upper hand, if I hadn't been interrupted by a certain sheriff." Dora and Petra shared a look. Marina clinked her glass against theirs. "I'm here now. What're we talking about?"

A wicked grin broke out on Petra's face. She could not keep the glee from her eyes. "Dora and Iris were discussing how you should join the Aspen Jubilee Committee this year, you being a deputy and all."

Marina choked and the whiskey went down the pipe meant for air. She coughed and sputtered through the burning in her eyes, throat, and nose. Every year Turning Creek held a festival when the aspens turned in the fall to celebrate the harvest before the bleak winter set in. It was a time to gather, eat, and dance. Even people from over the mountains came. No one in Turning Creek missed it. The celebration was organized by the merchants, leaders, and matriarchs of the town. Marina always went, as there was drinking after all. The idea of joining the respectable committee curdled the whiskey in her belly.

"You know, I've never quite seen you go that shade before. You should relax. It's just a town committee." Petra's grin was so wide it almost touched her ears.

Marina clenched her fist and considered how many punches she could get in before Dora and Iris broke them up. "No way in any circle of hell will I be on the Jubilee Committee."

Iris rolled her eyes. Marina noticed she was doing that more often.

Marina pointed a finger at her. "If you keep making that face at me, your eyes will fall out of your head because I will scratch them out myself." Marina refilled her cup. She was going to need it.

"You're the most childish woman I've ever met." Iris crossed her arms and glared.

Marina glared back at her. "Gods, you sound like Reed. Well, there's your problem. I'm not a mortal woman. I am a harpy of violence and vengeance. I don't serve on committees and discuss what kinds of flowers to put onto the table arrangements or what kind of pies to have at the bake sale."

Petra poked Marina's arm. "It won't be that bad. Reed is on the committee too."

The slow burn of anger flashed hot. Marina grabbed Petra's finger and pulled it back towards Petra's wrist. Petra stood and used her other hand to punch Marina squarely in the gut. The new pain in the sensitive tissue was enough to double her over. Marina released Petra's hand and tried to tell her lungs to breathe again.

"Enough, for Hera's sake! Who would have thought you two still had the ability to act like children? Petra, you're not helping. You're a married woman now. Try to occasionally act like it. Go make some tea upstairs." Dora's voice was an octave lower than normal. Petra obeyed without a word. They always obeyed Dora when she turned her harpy on them because she rarely did it. Marina followed Petra with her eyes and thought about the best way to swipe her feet out from under her when she returned. The tea tray would make a satisfying crash.

Iris shoved a finger in Marina's face. "You, relax and stop making a list of ways to get back at Petra. She's just irritating you to see you squirm. For once, use some self-control and ignore her." Marina breathed deep, violence ringing in her blood. "Fine. I'll behave, but I don't want to be on the committee." Marina breathed again, stuffing the anger away.

"I thought it might be good for you, but you obviously have forgotten how to act like a civilized human being. Forget I asked. Since you're the deputy, some of the townspeople asked if you would. They like you, only Hades knows why, and they wanted you to be involved. I should have just told them you'd rather be obnoxious and irritating. Including you was their way of thanking you for serving the town." Iris drained her cup and plunked it with thud onto the table.

Remorse was bitter in her mouth. It was not a tender emotion that Marina felt often. "I'll go to the Jubilee and I promise to stay all night, but I absolutely will not be on the committee."

Iris looked pleased, and Marina got the feeling it was the concession she had wanted all along. Damn Messenger with the nosy ability to know what they were going to do before they agreed to anything. Marina finished her drink in silence.

"I'm going to hold you to that," Iris said.

Petra clomped down the stairs minutes later carrying a tray laden with a teapot, cups, and a plate of crowd-arounds, rolls filled with meat and cabbage. "Tuck in ladies. We're going flying tonight, and you'll need the energy to keep up with me."

***

The moon hung large, filling the clear sky with light. Fall was well on its way, and the air was cold without the bite it would gain in a month. The stars twinkled and the harpies danced around a golden-winged Messenger.

Marina had seen Iris's wings often and still the reality of their beauty stole her breath away every time. Even in the moonlight, the golden wings shimmered and emitted a light all their own. Marina loved to watch the joy on Iris's face when she flew. It was love, wonder, and excitement mingled together.

Marina dove and grabbed Iris's ankle, causing The Messenger to drop a few feet in the air before righting herself. "Careful there. I hear there are vicious monsters in this area," Marina snickered as she dived away.

"You forgot to mention ugly." Iris did a complex series of turns, and before Marina could follow her movement, a weight landed between her wings. Iris giggled and dashed away as Marina struggled to right herself.

"Gods, you weigh a ton in those wings." Marina regained her altitude and looped around, showing off her shining tan and white feathers. "I know you're not referring to this lovely body when you use the word ugly. Look at my beautiful feathers, my terrible talons, and my delightful claws."

Marina flew next to Iris and swiped her face with her tail feathers.

"You're so vain. We all know Dora is the prettiest and I'm the scariest." Petra made a dive and landed on Marina's head. "You're just a loudmouth."

In flight with her sisters, an anxiety she did not know she had been carrying the past week was leeched from her bones. In her harpy form, her emotions were always more raw, and tonight they sparkled within her, the good and ill mingled together. Fierce joy in her chosen family surged through her. There was a certainty in her bones that her sisters would always be with her.

Petra's harpy was an uninterrupted inkblot against the sky. On nights when the moon's light was dim, Petra was near impossible to see. Tonight, her darkness in the bright moonlight gave her away. Marina sailed over Petra and lined up the maneuver Iris had executed on her earlier. Dora swooped down and flew on Marina's side, her white chest feathers glowing silver in the moonlight. Marina gestured silently and together they dropped down on their prey.

The guttural screech forced from Petra as two harpies fell on her from above was the sweetest of birdsong to Marina's ears. Their laughter added background music to the curses issuing forth from Petra. It was, by all measurements, a perfect night.

CHAPTER 11

Marina was back in her spot on Reed's porch, watching the sun rise over the town, when the door opened. The impact of standing in his presence after a few days' absence was like a blow. His smell, masculine and fresh, assaulted her. Marina clenched her hand to keep herself from touching him. She focused on her irritation over his lack of concern for her and his obvious disgust at her behavior at Vine's.

Reed paused with the door half open, the steam from his coffee curling over him. His eyes devoured her. Marina was predator enough to know what promises that look held. He blinked and the intent was gone. Without a word, he handed her his cup of coffee and went back inside. She let the bitter liquid and the morning chill chase away the heat in her blood. Marina was thankful to be able to collect herself before Reed returned.

He came back with another cup and leaned against the railing, drinking and watching her. "You seem to be doing fine."

Anger curled around the coffee in her belly. "I am. Thanks for checking in on me." She kept her words civil and took a sip of coffee.

To her surprise, his face flushed and he looked away. She should have been pleased. Reed shifted his weight. "I should have visited. I wasn't sure you'd want to see me."

It was not exactly the apology she wanted. "Apology accepted."

"I'm still sore at you for starting a drunken brawl. You can't do that on a whim anymore." His face was hard.

"I'm not apologizing," she said though clenched teeth. Her anger beat at her temples. "For the record, I wasn't drunk. They had it coming."

"I know they did, and while I don't always agree, I know Remnants have their own form of justice. I wish you'd apologize. I know you won't, so I'm going to drop it." His shoulders relaxed. "Heard you turned down an invitation to be on the Jubilee Committee."

"Word travels too damn fast in this town," Marina muttered into her cup.

"I told them they were fools to ask you. Simon insisted."

"I'd be of no use to them. I did promise Iris I would stay for the entire celebration this year, so there's that."

"I recall you spent most of the time at Vine's booth last year, sampling the pumpkin ale."

Large social gatherings were not her favorite thing, and drinking took the edge off her nerves. It did not hurt that Vine's pumpkin ale was delicious. "I recall that you spent the entire night dancing with every woman in town, including old Mrs. Habner. I thought she would have a heart episode when you led her around the floor." Unlike her, Reed thrived when surrounded by people.

He shrugged. "A gentleman should never let a lady sit alone when there's dancing happening. Ladies like to dance. I've never seen you dance at one of the town festivals."

"Like you said, ladies like to dance. I'm not a lady." Marina swept her hand over herself and pointed to her pants.

"You're rough around the edges, but surely you can dance."

"Not a step. I've never tried. No man has ever dared to ask me." Marina let her teeth grow pointy and flashed them at Reed.

He executed a couple of slow blinks and then broke into a boyish grin. "Doesn't work on me, Sparrow."

"It should." Marina crossed her arms over her chest.

"Dance with me at the Jubilee. Just once."

"I will if you'll stop calling me Sparrow."

Reed looked as if he was considering it. "No deal, but I'll pretend to be scared next time you act like a mean harpy."

"I am a mean harpy. Fine, I'll dance, but only once. Since I promised Iris to stay the entire time, I have to do something else besides drink. My tolerance is high, but not even I can drink that much of Vine's ale and remain standing."

Reed bowed. "You truly are a paragon of womanhood."

Marina threw her empty cup at his head. To her annoyance, he caught it, again. "Just once I wish something I threw at you would hit the mark."

"Have to be faster than me."

"I'll wait until your back is turned."

"You fight dirty." Reed gave her a look of mock surprise.

Marina was happier than she had been in days. She had not realized what a weight Reed's absence had been. Laughter, clean and pure, bubbled out. "Always."

Reed laughed with her and something broke within her. His laugh was rich and deep and danced over her. The emotion took her along and

dropped her in a place she did not recognize. She was losing her mind for
sure.

Reed sobered. "You were torn up bad. You seem to be moving all
right. Have you been back to see Doc?"

"I'm all healed up on the outside, though I'll have some nice scars for a
while. Care to see?" She tugged at her shirt.

Reed waved at her. "No need. But you're fine?"

"You sound like I almost died."

The lines appeared around his mouth that indicated he was getting
irritated with her. "You did almost die."

Marina put a hand on his arm. "I'm mostly healed. I'll admit my fight
with Atlanta caused some extra damage. I still feel bruised on the inside.
Doc said I should be right as rain soon enough. Harpies heal fast."

"Too bad your healing ability doesn't work on your fool head."

Marina smiled. "Your life would be boring without me."

"Quiet doesn't mean boring." Reed sighed. "My life is never quiet
anymore."

"You're welcome."

***

Later on that day, the two of them stood in Reed's office. "It's time to
make some visits to the outlying homesteads. With winter coming, I want
to put eyes on everyone I can so I know if they're set for the season. We
also need a census for the Territory Committee." Reed smoothed a map of
the region over the desk in his office. "It'll be nice not to have to make the
visits myself this go 'round."

Although Turning Creek was a small town, many people lived in the
mountains and outlying area. The people relied on the town for supplies
and for assistance in emergencies, and when the snow was high, travel into
town was limited. Two or three times a year, Reed systematically visited
every home he could to check on the residents. In this way, he was able to
get help for struggling families and let them know they were connected to
the town through him.

Marina watched his face while he made a copy of the map for her to
take on her rounds. She almost missed what he was saying to her. "You
can't fly on your rounds. Take a horse."

"Spoil sport." The task would take days on horseback.

He ignored her comment. "I've marked which families I know are
Remnants. If you find people setting up house and it's not on the map,
make note of it. No policing land usage. Just want a handle on where
people are and if they need anything." He handed her the finished map and
corresponding list. "I'll stay gone until all my rounds are done. We'll meet
up here when we finish. We'll need to make a copy of the maps for Iris. She
and Thomas have a knack for finding people even when they're not on a

87

map, but I try to make their jobs easier when I can."

The door to the office opened, and Lily Hughes walked through the door.

"I hope I'm not interrupting." Mrs. Hughes voice was always more of an alto than Marina expected.

"Not at all, Mrs. Hughes. What can we do for you this fine day?" Reed ushered her in and offered her a chair.

"Actually, I'm here to talk to Miss Marina about the Aspen Jubilee Committee."

Reed smothered a smile, and Marina sent a glare his way. She turned a neutral face to their visitor. "What about the Jubilee Committee?"

"I'd like you to reconsider joining us. All the leaders of the town are involved. Many people respect your opinions."

Marina made a rude noise. "I thought people in this town were smarter than that."

Mrs. Hughes pointed a finger at Marina. "I know you are a lot of bluster. You care about the people here, and they know it. We know you fought for us on Atlas's Peak and that you protect us now with Sheriff Brant. It's just the committee's way of recognizing your contribution. If you want to turn it down fine, but don't be rude about it." Something dangerous moved behind Mrs. Hughes eyes and Marina felt her harpy take notice.

Marina heard Reed start to laugh and then cough in an unconvincing way. Marina said, "I'm not going to start a fight. I can see I've made you mad." Reed's smile vanished as his mortal senses caught up with the power leaking into the room from the two Remnants.

Mrs. Hughes blushed. "I apologize. I would never try to mesmerize you. I just think you don't give yourself enough credit, and nothing irritates me more than someone who can't take a compliment and move on."

Marina fidgeted in her chair. "Styx, that's not what I meant. I'm not good at," Marina waved her hands around helplessly, "organizing and planning. I'm better at rushing in half-cocked and kicking in heads."

Mrs. Hughes patted Marina's knee. "I know, dear, but sometimes we all have to learn new things."

Marina huffed. "Is there something I can do for the Jubilee Committee that does not require flowers, food, or people?"

Mrs. Hughes laughed. "How about I let you off the hook this year and next year you promise to organize some sort of race through town? The entry fee can raise money for the school or go to help pay for improvements."

"I think if I don't take the offer, you'll find another job I'd like less. I accept." Marina shook Mrs. Hughes's hand.

After Lily Hughes had left, Reed rolled up her copy of the map and handed it to her. She was going to cover the north part of the valley, and he would take the south side.

Marina took the map and tucked it into her satchel. She turned to leave, but Reed called her back. "Don't be a mean harpy unless absolutely necessary. We want people to like us."

She gave him a mock salute. "Yes, sir. I'll just be myself."

Reed groaned. "That's precisely what I'm afraid of." She laughed her way out of the door.

***

It took a week of hard riding, but Marina checked in on every family on her list and added five more who had moved into the area over the summer. At night, she flew close to the ground and scouted the area she would cover the next day. Every day dawned clear and bright. The mountains vibrated with life, and Marina enjoyed the peace that always settled on her when she was alone in them. She arrived back in town pleased with her thoroughness and ready to share her findings with Reed.

The mountains were a glorious riot of red and orange in the late afternoon when Marina tied her horse up behind Reed's office and apartment. She heard someone walking upstairs, so she headed up, yelling as she went. "Reed, I'm back. I found some new families and you'd be proud of me. I was nice, even polite, you might say. You can listen to me talk while you buy me a drink at Vine's. I'm dying for a drink."

Marina reached the landing and almost ran into—not Reed, but an auburn-haired woman in an apron holding a bowl and a spoon. Marina backpedaled so quickly she almost toppled down the stairs.

"Reed's not here." The woman, who was a head shorter than Marina, blocked her entrance to the living area.

Possessiveness flared like fire within Marina as her harpy rolled within her. The woman looked self-assured in this place that belonged to Reed. Marina's fist clenched by her side. She should find out who the woman was before she did anything rash.

A small voice cut through the haze of red in Marina's mind. "Who's here?" A young boy walked out of the bedroom, trailed by another boy a few inches taller than he was. The younger boy had the same whiskey eyes as Reed. The older one looked like a younger version of Reed, down to the straight nose and stubborn chin, though his eyes were a normal shade of brown.

The air in the room turned to molasses. Marina's gaze swung from the woman and back at the boys. The family resemblance was unmistakable. Reed had never mentioned having a family, but he had been in Turning Creek for some time and had never shown a spark of interest in any of the women who got up the nerve to fawn over him. He was one of the most eligible men in town, and yet he'd never married or even appeared interested in anyone. Perhaps he had never shown any interest because he

89

was already attached. Marina stood, unable to make any of her thoughts string together into words.

The slamming of the back door shook Marina out of the spiral of her own thoughts. "Marina, I saw your horse. Where are you?" His voice cut through her, and she stepped off the landing as he came up. His eyes moved from Marina to the woman and her boys. Shock permeated his face. "Claire? What're you doing here?" Joy washed over his features, and he swept the woman into a tight embrace.

Marina, forgotten, escaped down the stairs, blocking out the loud and happy reunion. She felt foolish in a way she never had before and her head pounded with it. Her fingers fumbled with the knot on her horse's reins.

She considered where to go. Home was far away, and she was exhausted after days in the saddle. Iris was close, but Marina did not want to talk to anyone. If she scowled enough, Iris would leave her alone until tomorrow. She did not think she would have trouble scowling.

Marina pulled the horse and walked in the direction of the depot. The sound of heavy boots behind her alerted her that she would not be alone long.

Reed's hand on her arm stopped her. "Marina, wait. Why'd you leave?"

"I didn't want to interrupt the reunion." Her stomach twisted.

"Come back. I want to introduce you." He pulled the reins from her hand and turned.

Marina grabbed the reins back. "It's been a long day. We can make introductions tomorrow." She pasted a smile on her face.

Reed rubbed the back of his neck. "I got the sense you're mad at me for something, something serious, not like usual. I've no idea what. Let me make it up to you. Claire's cooking is almost as good as Mother's was, and she's heard all about you. Please stay for dinner."

A memory clicked in Marina's mind. She had delivered a letter to Reed from his sister named Claire. She had two small boys who took their looks strongly from the Brant side of the family tree. Marina laughed. Gods, if she had any brains left in her harpy head, she would flee as fast as her wings would carry her.

She took a shaky breath. "I'll come, and I'm not mad at you, but you do owe me a drink."

"I do. You won't let me forget it." Reed grabbed her hand and dragged her back to his house and up the stairs.

Now that Marina could focus on her, Claire was a pretty woman with kind brown eyes. "I'm sorry if we startled you before. We didn't tell Reed we were coming. I didn't want him, or anyone else in the family, to try to talk me out of it, so I just came. I wanted a fresh start without a slew of lectures."

Marina knocked about for the proper response. "I'm sorry about your husband."

"Thank you, Miss Marina."

Marina chuckled. "Hardly anyone calls me that, and especially not friends. Just Marina is fine."

Claire smiled, and it turned her from pretty to almost beautiful. "Then you must call me Claire. Reed has written some outlandish stories to us that included you. I'm interested to know how much he has exaggerated."

Marina grinned and waggled her eyebrows at the two boys who were staring at her with mouths open and eyes wide. Her clothes were dusty from travel, and she had a gun, a knife, and her sword visible. "I assure you, the stories are all true as long as he said I saved the day and he cowered like a little boy."

Reed snorted rather loudly. "Humility is not your best trait."

"Thank the gods. It's not yours either." Marina chuckled.

"At least I'm willing to listen to others before going half-cocked into the mountains after lions." Reed stepped up to her until his boots touched hers. He took up all her space, and she only had to lift her head a fraction to glare into his face.

Marina grinned. "I missed you too."

There was a tug on her arm and she stepped out of the circle of heat from Reed's body. The youngest boy, the one with eyes the same color as Reed's, was looking at them both.

Reed knelt down. "Marina, this is Stephen." He motioned to the older boy, who stepped forward. "This strapping lad, who seems to have grown a foot since last I saw him, is Jonah."

Marina shook each of their hands. "Pleased to meet you."

Stephen pointed at the handle sticking out from between her shoulder blades. "Is that a real sword?"

Marina winked at the boy. "It definitely is. I have more weapons on me than the ones you can see. You can never be too prepared for trouble."

Stephen considered her answer. "How come you don't have on a dress?"

Reed's bellowed laughter filled the room. "Stephen, that is an excellent question." Two pairs of whiskey eyes turned to regard her. "Marina, how come you never wear a dress like a normal woman?"

Marina was certain Reed had not confided in his family that his town was half-populated with Remnants. They might have been a touch more concerned for his sanity. "I'm not normal."

Reed took his time sweeping his eyes up and down her figure. "Sometimes, I wish you'd pretend."

Claire's eyes had gone round watching the exchange. At Reed's jibe her eyebrows drew down. "Reed Brant. That was a horrible thing to say."

His words would have hurt her feelings, if she had feelings to hurt, but she knew he did not mean anything by them. Not really. She shrugged and brushed a speck of dirt off her shirt. "I thought women wore dresses to please men. I've never had a reason to wear a dress."

Claire laughed. "Marina, I think you and I are going to be excellent friends."

Marina dragged her eyes from Reed and focused on Claire. "On what do you base your prediction after knowing me for so short a time?"

"Anyone who can keep my brother on his toes and make him look like he's ready to spit nails is a friend of mine. Saves me the trouble of irritating him myself."

Marina put her arm around Claire's shoulders. "I do believe you're right. We're going to be great friends. Making Reed spit nails is one of the many things I excel at doing."

Reed groaned. "I'm in deep trouble."

CHAPTER 12

Moving slowly so as not to spill the coffee cups he held, Reed stepped out into the cold morning. Marina turned from the warmth of the sunrise and greeted him. He handed her the extra cup and brushed his fingers against hers in the transfer. Marina's fingers tingled and she concentrated on the scent of the coffee. Reed watched her with eyes half closed. His expression was unreadable.

"How are Claire and the boys settling in?"

It had been a week since Claire had shown up on Reed's doorstep. "I think it's time I found a bigger place to live."

Marina chuckled and she saw his hand clench around his cup. "Tired of being a family man already?"

"Of course not. I want a family, someday. Eventually, I'll find someone who'll put up with me every day for the rest of my life, and we'll have the kind of home I grew up in: loud, boisterous, and full."

Something sharp wedged in her middle. Reed's vision sounded nice, for him. "Do you have a plan?"

"First, I'll need a wife. Then we'll have to, well, the rest of it is what you might call of a private nature." He barely managed a straight face.

Marina laughed full and deep. "You can keep that between you and the future unfortunate Mrs. Brant. Poor woman. If the children are all as stubborn as you, she'll be plagued enough to get into Charon's boat of her own free will. I meant, do you have a plan to move out of your office and into an actual house, for a start. Claire and the boys can't live above the jail forever."

"There're some nice properties near town. Close enough that walking would be an easy distance. I was thinking of looking at them with Claire today. She's got some money saved. I can give her what she lacks. With some help from some of the other men, we can have a decent house up before the first snow. Claire and the boys can live there. I'll expand in the spring to include enough room for me. I've lived upstairs here for a long time. One more season won't kill me."

"You've given this a lot of thought."

"Not everyone charges in without thinking, like you," he added. His jab won him an eye roll. "Can you take Iris copies of the new territory maps today?"

"Sure thing, boss." Marina handed him her empty cup. "Will you meet me at Vine's when you're done with Claire?"

"Are you buying?"

"Depends."

"On what?"

"On if you let me beat you at cards."

"It's more fun if you let me win sometimes," he said.

"For you, maybe."

"Don't know why I spend time with you." Reed ran a hand over his neck.

"Let me know if you figure it out."

The door behind Reed burst open. "Miss Marina, will you teach me how to throw knives today? We heard there's a contest at the Jubilee. Uncle Reed says you're the best he's ever seen." Jonah, who was the ripe age of seven, already worshiped Marina. The feeling was mutual.

Reed laid a hand on Jonah's shoulder. "One thing you need to know about Miss Marina is that compliments go right to her head."

"Please, Jonah, go on. What else does Uncle Reed say about me?" Marina knelt down and brought her face level with his.

"He also said you're the best tracker in the region, and you have a vicious right hook because no man expects a woman as pretty as you to hit so hard."

Reed snorted. Marina threw back her head with laughter. She ruffled Jonah's hair. "He said I hit hard, did he? Your uncle is a smart man sometimes. I'll have to tell you some stories about him to even up the odds. If your mom says it's all right, I'll teach you and Stephen how to throw a knife this morning while your mom and Uncle Reed go buy some land. If you can hit the target four times out of five, I'll teach you how to hide knives so no one can find them. If you get really good, we'll have Henry make you a set of your own."

Jonah's eyes crinkled with glee. "Thanks, Miss Marina. I'm going to tell Mom." The boy flew back through the door.

Reed laid a hand on Marina's arm. "Thank you. Jonah's been quiet since Will died, and he likes you. That's the biggest smile I've seen on his face since he got here."

Marina gave his hand a squeeze. "I am rather fond of him as well."

Reed covered her hand with his, and Marina felt a gravitational pull into him. She had to fight to maintain the sliver of air between them. "The boys both love you, and seeing them smile has eased some of the grief Claire carries," Reed said. He continued to speak but did not move away from her. "Will was her childhood sweetheart. They begged our parents to let them marry early. The boys give her a reason to wade through each day, and you're part of the reason the boys already feel at home here. That means more to me than you'll ever know."

He looked at her for a long time and did not release her. Marina started to feel trapped. "What?"

"There's something I can't work out about you." His eyes traveled over her face, and she felt their movement like a brand.

"What's that?"

"You revel in being a monster, and yet you make friends with every kid you meet."

His observation made her feel exposed. Marina drew in a deep breath. "My mother called the village children nestlings, and she taught me to protect the innocent. Kids accept what they see and don't question motives too often. They're simple and I like them for it."

Marina withdrew her hands. "Go look at the land. I'm going home tonight, but I'll be back tomorrow. There's a storm coming."

"How do you know there's a storm coming?"

Marina winked at him. "I can't tell you all my secrets, Sheriff."

"That's not sporting of you." Reed leaned a fraction closer to her. She did not move away. "What would you demand as payment if I really wanted to know?"

She rubbed her chin in an exaggerated effort, more to keep her hands busy than anything else. "Go hunting with me next time I go."

He leaned back and took his time considering the offer. "That is a fine offer. When was the last time a regular person got invited to go hunting with a harpy?"

"Never."

Reed leaned close. "Deal. Now, how do you know a storm is coming?"

Marina swatted his arm and pointed up. "Easy. Clouds are rolling in."

Reed chuckled. "I should've known better than to challenge you when you've got that look in your eye."

"What look is that?"

"Like I'm about to hand over a bottle of your favorite whiskey, no strings attached." Reed's face beamed at her.

"Let that be a warning to you then not to take me up on a bet when I offer it." Marina laughed at him.

Reed and Claire left, and Marina went back to the depot to get all the knives she had stored with Iris. When she laid them out behind Reed's office, she had the set of three bone-handled ones she carried on a daily basis, two pairs, and her sword. She knew the boys were too small to attempt anything with the sword, but she thought it would be fun to show them what was possible, once they gained some skill and size. If they were going to live here permanently, Marina wanted them to be able to defend themselves.

Marina set a board against a tree and tacked a piece of paper to it. She walked back to where the boys were standing. She knelt in the dirt and looked them both in the eyes.

"What I'm about to teach you is important, but hard. Holding a knife and stabbing something is easy. Throwing one and making it go where you want is hard. It'll take practice. You can't get frustrated. You have to keep trying. Knowing how to throw a knife is a great way to defend yourself when the attacker is bigger than you and you don't want them too close. Remember, though, once you throw it, it's gone. Have a backup plan."

Marina pulled a knife from her boot, twirled, and threw the knife. It quivered in the middle of the paper. "Plus, throwing them is just plain old fun." The boys grinned.

"Stephen, I'm going to let Jonah go first, because he's older." She handed him a knife from the matched pair. "I want you to hold on to this knife and get used to the feel of it in your palm. Mind the pointy end, though." She winked at him.

"Yes, ma'am." Jonah's eyes shone when he took the knife from her. Marina picked up the three matched knives and gave one to Jonah. "Now, feel how it fits right in your hand? Do you feel how the weight is distributed? This set of three was the first set my mother gave me when she taught me how to throw knives." They were the first gift her mother had ever given her. She had been younger than Stephen.

Jonah tested the weight of the knife. "The blade feels heavier than the handle."

"That is an excellent observation. I usually wear my knives and have to draw them quickly before I can throw them. A knife with a heavy blade is thrown handle first. Like this."

Marina held the handle lightly between her thumb and fingers and flicked her wrist out slowly to show Stephen and Jonah the motion.

"Now you show me how to hold it," she said.

Marina adjusted his grip and then walked him through throwing the knife. She stood back while he made his first attempt. It amused her to see the same lines of concentration bracketing his eyes and mouth that Reed so often wore. Jonah's first throws bounced harmlessly off the wood or sailed past it altogether. He did not get frustrated, though, and continued to try until he finally sunk a knife into the side of the plank.

"Excellent job." Marina grinned at him and ruffled his hair. "Do it again."

Jonah hit the target, well away from the paper, five more times before Marina let him take a break. She took Stephen by the hand and walked through the same procedure with the smaller boy. Stephen hit it on his second try. His smile was angelic.

"Well, kid, you might win that knife contest at the Jubilee this year if you keep up that progress. I'd better start practicing."

Each boy threw four more rounds before Marina called it quits for the day. There were groans and protests. "Now listen, Olympus wasn't built in a day, you know. You have to practice over time. Whenever Reed isn't working me too hard and you have all your chores done, we can practice. If you get good enough, we'll see about getting some of your own. Deal?" Jonah and Stephen shook hands with her to seal the deal.

"That made me thirsty. Your mom said there's lemonade for us inside." Marina turned to get it.

"I'll get for us." Jonah stood and went inside.

The trio sat in the sun and drank lemonade. Marina knew she was going to have to get moving soon and get that map to Iris. She looked at the boys, relaxed and happy like puppies.

Jonah finished his drink and set it aside. "Thanks again, Miss Marina."

"Just call me Marina, Jonah. We're friends, aren't we?"

Jonah colored a little. "Yes, ma'am. Marina, I mean."

"That's better. And it was my pleasure."

"Have you ever known anyone who died?" Jonah asked, after a brief silence.

Marina thought of the death she had seen in her long life and of the lives she had taken, some of them last year during the fight with Zeus. "I have."

"My father died."

"I know. Death has a kind of weight to it. It's hard to shake once you see it."

Jonah nodded. "I miss him. Sometimes I forget what he looked like." His eyes were worried.

Marina's heart clenched. "I know that's hard, but what matters most is that you know he loved you and that he taught you what he could while he lived. Tell me something you remember that he told you."

Again, the small nod. "He always said the best things a man can do are to seek justice, show mercy, and be humble before God. It's from the book of Micah in the Bible."

Marina understood the part about justice. "Your father sounds like he was a smart man. He sounds a lot like your uncle."

Stephen snorted. "Mom says Uncle Reed is more stubborn than any man she's ever known."

Marina laughed. "She's right." Marina turned back to Jonah. "What matters, is that you remember your father as a person, not what he looked like. He'd rather you grow in justice and mercy than know what color of hair he had."

Jonah considered her words, then spoke. "Thanks, Marina. I'm glad we came here. Mom smiles more, and I like living with Uncle Reed."

Marina put her arms around both sets of small shoulders. "I'm glad you two are here too. No one else wants to throw knives and drink lemonade with me." She squeezed them tight and put off her errand for a few more moments in the sunshine.

***

The next day, Marina woke up with a riot of birds singing to the morning. The upper ridge of the sun shone above the peaks. The storm had indeed been fierce, and Marina had been unable to resist flying through the driving rain and wind. She was still exhausted after last night's escapade, even with a few hours' sleep in her own bed under her belt. If she did not get moving, she would never make it to Reed's in time for coffee. She threw on some clothes and flew to town in record time. When she changed from her harpy form to her mortal one, she realized she had forgotten to braid or tie back her hair. It was fluffed out in a mess around her head. She ran her hands through it in an effort to keep down the worst of the curls.

When she walked onto the porch, Reed was waiting for her. She took her cup. Reed fisted his left hand by his side and clenched his mug tightly.

"Helluva storm last night." His voice sounded a bit strained.

"It was." Marina flashed him a wicked grin.

A line creased the space between Reed's eyes. "What'd you do?"

"Why do you think I did something?" She batted innocent eyes at him.

"You have the same look of a cat who licked the cream without getting caught."

"I went flying." Marina enjoyed the way Reed's eyes bulged out.

"In that storm? You could've been struck by lightning."

"But I wasn't. You grump worse than a man twice your age."

"When I'm twice my age, you'll still be acting like child in nappies. We'll make the rounds in town today. Make sure no one had any damage from the storm."

"I'll take Henry, Vine's, and the depot. You get the rest." Marina tucked some of her hair behind her ear.

"You've only picked the places you prefer or that will give you a drink. Why don't you just take that whole side of the street and I'll do this side?"

Marina did not have an argument for that, he was right. Marina shrugged.

He rolled his eyes. "Fine, I'll take that side and the houses behind. You take this side."

"I want to talk to Henry about making me some swords and some knives for the boys. Do you think Claire will mind?"

Reed rubbed his jaw. "If you teach them not to skewer themselves, she'll probably not mind much. She likes you, but I've yet to figure out why."

"I want Vine's."

"No. I'll take Vine's. If you go there, I won't see you again until dark." Reed took her cup. Marina pouted. "Stop with that pout. Looks ridiculous on you. I'll meet you at the depot later."

Marina was able to talk to everyone except Mr. Hughes, who had been out when she stopped by. She made a note to swing back by before the end of the day. Marina finished checking on everyone just after noon and made her way to the depot.

After a storm like the one the previous night, people needed to see and be seen by the people they cared about and lived with. Everyone was in the depot checking in on friends. Marina waved to Iris, who was talking to Claire at the counter. Marina stood on her toes to see who had been lucky enough to snag one of the back two tables. Petra's black and grey head was bent close to Dora's auburn head.

Marina turned her head back towards the counter. "Claire, come over to the back when you're done." Claire nodded.

Marina flopped onto a chair. "Got any tea left in that pot?" She grabbed the last sandwich off the plate. Petra scowled at her. "It's packed in here today."

"Everyone's here to check on their neighbors after the storm." Dora poured a cup of tea for Marina then reached into the pocket of her skirt. She unscrewed the pewter flask and added a healthy portion of whiskey to the tea. Dora handed the cup over with a smile.

"Like that already today is it?" Marina let the tea and whiskey warm her belly. "Reed and I made the rounds in town, though it seems I beat him, despite having Simon on my list. There were some shingles off a few buildings, but nothing serious. How did you two weather the storm?"

"James had the herd in a sheltered pasture already. We lost a couple trees, but nothing major. The boys and James didn't need me for cleanup, and I wanted to fly over the valley. I went to Dora's first and we flew into town together."

"How come you didn't come get me?" Marina tried not to sound left out.

"Keep your feathers down. We knew Reed would need you here," Dora said. "We still stopped by, but you were gone."

"I went flying too," Marina said. They laughed together.

Dora's eyes moved to something behind her shoulder, and Marina swiveled to find Claire standing behind her. "Claire, please, sit down."

Marina pointed to the last empty chair. "Would you like some tea?" Claire nodded and Marina poured another cup. She held her hand out to Dora, who balked. "Hand it over. She's not a ninny." Dora gave up the flask, and Claire's eyebrows went up into her hairline as she watched Marina doctor her tea.

Claire took a sip and sighed. "Thank you, Marina. It was just what I didn't know I needed."

"Claire, these virtuous ladies are my sisters, Petra Lloyd and Dora Aello. This is Claire MacKenzie, Reed's sister." Introductions made, they settled back and relaxed.

Claire looked at Marina with a puzzled face. "How are you recovering? I've seen you twice recently, and you seem fine. But the way Reed was talking, it sounded like you were one foot in the grave."

"Reed underestimates me. I'm doing fine. Hardly a scar to show for all the kerfuffle." Marina tried to look reassuring. Other than some white scars on her belly, she was good as new.

Petra fixed her brown eyes on Claire. "What brings you to Turning Creek, Claire?"

There was pain in her eyes, but it was replaced with determination. "My husband, Will, died last year. I was surrounded by my family, and they were very helpful and sympathetic. Too helpful. I could not stay there in the house Will had built for us. I needed to start over and build a new life. Reed has said such lovely things about the mountains here." Claire searched her teacup for words. "Will and I grew up together. It's hard to learn to live without someone once they are so much a part of what and who you are and everything reminds you of them."

Marina's heart pinched painfully as she thought of what Turning Creek would be like without the other harpies, Iris, or Reed. She met Petra's eyes, then Dora's, and saw empathy under their silence. Their family was everything.

Claire looked up and smiled weakly. "Sorry. I should've warned you. I get maudlin when I drink."

Petra reached across the table and laid a hand on Claire's arm. "I'm sorry for your loss. This is a wonderful place. I hope you're able to find some new memories to lay alongside your old ones when they do not trouble you so much."

Marina looked at Petra with something between astonishment and awe. "Married life has turned you into a sage."

Petra's eyes turned serious when they turned to Marina. "I know now what it means to love and to lose. It's not an easy thing to look at that and decide to come back with courage." Marina could see the haunted memories Petra carried from the months she had thought James dead and lost to her in her sister's face. They finished the first pot of tea and then skipped the tea and just sipped whiskey from the teacups.

"Did you lose someone too, Petra?" Claire asked.

Petra turned back to Claire with a smile. "Almost, but he wasn't dead after all like I thought, and he loved me." Petra smiled the secret smile of a woman well contented. "I'm a very lucky woman."

Marina wanted to change the subject and said the first thing that came into her mind. "It was such a nice night last night that I went flying. It was marvelous."

Claire looked confused. "I think I've had too much to drink. Did you say flying?"

Marina knew seconds before his warm hand rested on her shoulder that Reed stood behind her. The heat from his hand blazed through her shirt, and she fought the urge to squirm. She rubbed her hands on her legs. "About time you got here. I've been done for hours."

He leaned over and took the cup from her hands. He downed the contents and coughed. "That's not tea." The women at the table burst into laughter. He leaned over Marina to sniff Claire's cup. "Sparrow, I believe you're a bad influence on my sister." Reed snatched the cup out of Claire's hand and drained the contents of that cup too.

"That was mine." Claire snatched the glass back and refilled it from the bottle they had stashed under the table.

"I didn't know you drank." Reed glared at Claire, then Marina in turn.

"I've never had whiskey, and Marina was kind enough to share with me." Claire took a dainty sip.

Marina laughed. "Welcome to the world, Claire." The two women clinked their cups together.

Reed ignored Marina and Claire and turned to the other two women at the table. "Afternoon, ladies. I trust the two of you have added some sense to the conversation back here."

"I'm not sure about sense, but Marina was about to tell us about fly..." Petra choked off the word and clamped her mouth shut.

"Fly fishing?" Dora suggested.

Marina rolled her eyes at her sisters and grinned up at Reed. Some of her hair, still unbound, fell in her face, and she swiped it away. His hand was still on her shoulder and it convulsed.

"I went fly fishing in the storm last night," Marina said, still looking directly at him. She gave the word fishing extra emphasis.

"That sounds dangerous." Claire frowned. "The storm was terrible."

"But the views were beautiful," Marina said. Reed's hand was tight on her shoulder.

"I bet the fishing was superb. I want to join you next time." Petra added a push to the word fishing. Dora was laughing into her cup. Reed groaned.

"Would James let you go?" Marina asked.

Something dark flashed in Petra's eyes. "He doesn't control when I want to go fishing."

A look of confusion crossed Claire's face, but she wiped it away with a smile. "I've never been fishing at night, much less during a storm. I'd like to go sometime."

All three of the harpies broke into wild laughter. Claire looked confused again. "What did I say? I do really want to go fishing." The harpies laughed louder. Dora snorted and they all collapsed again.

"Ignore them. They've lost their minds or they're drunk. Or both." Reed crossed his arms and glared at Marina. Her shoulder was cold where his hand had been.

"You're just jealous. You wish you could go fishing too." Marina poked him with her finger when she said fishing, and the laughter started up again.

"Sparrow, you've lost your ever-loving mind." Reed turned around to walk back towards the front. "I've got to talk to Iris about the papers we are drafting for the Territory Committee."

Marina stopped him with her voice. "I'm not a songbird, Sheriff. I'm much scarier."

"Not at the moment." Reed delivered the parting shot over his shoulder as he walked over to the counter to talk to Iris.

Marina laughed at his retreating form. Over the hilarity at the table, Marina heard someone yelling.

"Sheriff Brant?" a voice yelled above the crowd. Marina put down her glass, the laughter gone from her lips. Paul Hughes stood in the doorway. The normally immaculate Mr. Hughes's hair stood on end, as if he had been pulling it.

"Over here." Reed waved him over. The conversation in the depot had quieted down with Mr. Hughes's arrival. Marina left the table and joined Reed at the counter.

"Thank the Lord I found you. Lily is missing. I woke up this morning, and she was gone. I thought she had gone out for something, but she never came back. I've been searching and waiting all day, but she's just gone. She wouldn't leave us. Something has happened to her." His voice broke over the last words. Iris made her way around the counter. "Thomas, run upstairs and get Mr. Hughes some tea." Thomas ran to obey. She pulled L.A. off a stool and led Mr. Hughes to it.

A sick feeling settled in Marina's gut. Hughes was right. Lily was devoted to her husband and two girls. Unlike Katherine Johnson, Lily would never leave without word. The room around them stilled, listening.

Reed's voice was commanding in the silence. "I need some men to go on a search with me." Every man in the depot indicated they would go.

"Meet at the sheriff's office in twenty minutes. We'll split up the area to search efficiently." Men scattered, going outside to ready their horses or get more friends for the search.

Reed put a hand on Hughes's shoulder. "We'll find her. Bring the girls when we meet in twenty minutes, and they can stay with Claire and the boys."

Hughes's lip trembled but he shook himself. "Thanks, Sheriff." Mr. Hughes left to collect his children.

The only people left were the three harpies, Iris, and Claire. "Claire?" Reed asked.

Claire walked towards the door and answered, "Of course. Be safe. I'll keep coffee going in the office and the kids upstairs while you search."

As soon as the door closed behind her, Reed turned to Marina and the other harpies. "I need you two," he pointed towards Dora and Petra, "in the air. Try not to be seen. Marina, I need you on the ground. Start at Hughes shop and work your way out. If any of you find anything, report back to me. I'll be leading teams of men sweeping out from the town."

Marina rubbed her hands together, pleased with the prospect of having something to do to help find Mrs. Hughes. "Searching is all well and good, but we aren't going to find a darn thing. If she disappeared any time during the storm, all traces of her have been washed away."

Reed wiped a hand over his face. "I know that, but we have to try. It's possible she left and something happened after the storm. That's why I want Dora and Petra flying. Traces around the town might be gone, but maybe we'll get lucky farther out."

"What about me?" Iris asked.

"Stay here. I'll tell everyone to rally back here after dark, which is too damn soon." Iris nodded.

The four of them left the depot and walked towards Reed's office. A crowd of men had already gathered on his porch.

"What do you think happened to her?" Dora asked Reed.

"I hope it's as simple as she hurt herself and couldn't make it back from wherever she went. I pray to God it's not something worse. There are plenty of things in this place worse than a sprained ankle or a broken bone. On that happy note, get Doc and have him meet us too. We might need him." Dora increased her speed and went to fetch Lee.

Marina left Reed as he was splitting up men into teams in the front of the office and went out the back door. If there was any evidence to find on Main Street, it had been trampled long ago. She wanted to start in the back of the row of buildings. Hughes said Lily had disappeared sometime during the night. She could have gotten up to get water, use the privy, check on her kids during the storm, or anything. The why did not matter so much as what happened after that.

Marina started at the lintel of the back door of the tailor shop. There was a tidy flower garden and trees in a yard behind the building. In increasing half circles, Marina walked from side to side, looking for a sign, no matter how inconsequential. Unfortunately, the rain and wind the night before had been ferocious. All Marina found within the town limits were smooth, muddied ground and plants beaten down by the rainfall.

She increased the size of her circles and went into the woods, traveling down each path. She stopped when there was not enough light to see by. The sun had long since disappeared over the ridge of mountains on the west side of the valley. The days were getting shorter and colder. While she welcomed the cooling of the air and the changing of the seasons, she would have liked a little more daylight today.

Marina had not intersected any of the other search teams for a couple of hours, and, deeming it safe, she shifted and flew farther out from the town in low circles. Her vision was better at night as a harpy, though not as good as a nocturnal animal's would be. She searched for another hour before heading back to town.

Tiredness and frustration gnawed at her. Marina threw caution to the wind and flew almost into the yard behind the depot. No one used the back door of the depot except the harpies when they wanted to go in and out of town without being noticed. Reed sat outside on the single bench beside the back door. His body was slumped against the building. It was too dark for Marina to tell if his eyes were closed.

She landed and shifted in the same breath and walked on two mortal legs until she stood beside Reed.

"I should yell at you for flying right into town, but I can't muster up the effort to care overmuch. I know you were looking for Mrs. Hughes, so I can't be sore at you." He slid down on the bench. "Come. Sit. I can see you've had about as much luck as we did."

Marina sat close enough that her entire left side was flush against his. Instant heat radiated from every point of contact. "I found nothing. There are two more spots I want to check in the morning, but the damn storm washed away anything that would've been useful. I went out farther than I thought possible, and there was just…nothing. It's like she flew away, and we both know she couldn't have done that."

"Dammit. Could something carry her off?"

"I already thought of that. A Remnant that big would've been spotted by someone. I mean the valley is big, but it's not that big. If there's something capable of that, it won't stay hidden for long."

"I can't help but feel the recent influx of scarier-than-normal Remnants is related."

Marina looked for answers in the stars. There was nothing. "Not that he's trustworthy, but the chimera promised to behave, so I'd like to hope he's not responsible. I killed the lion and looked around his den. If there was anything else, Remnant or otherwise with him, there were no signs of it. None of the other groups found anything?"

"No." Reed sighed and the sound tore at Marina.

"What do we do next?"

"We try again tomorrow. We have to. Hughes deserves our best effort, even if we aren't going to find anything." Reed leaned over and put his head in his hands.

The urge to touch him was overwhelming, and Marina stopped fighting it. She ran her hand down his back and then she repeated the movement. She could feel the heat of his skin and the slow breath he drew in and out. "You're doing the best you can. Stop beating yourself up. You have a big heart, Sheriff Brant."

"And you act like you have none, Sparrow."

Marina shifted in her seat and kept her hand in the middle of Reed's bowed back, unwilling to break the contact. "I am what I am. Stop baiting me to make yourself feel better. I feel sorry for Hughes too. The people and Remnants in this valley are mine, or ours I guess, to protect. We have to find out what happened to Lily Hughes, but for tonight, we have to rest. However, if it was one of my sisters or you, I'd be sick with fear. I wouldn't sleep. I'd tear the mountains apart until I found something, anything." Her voice dropped into its low register, threatening an enemy unseen.

Reed went still under her hand. "You'd worry over me?"

Marina chuckled and patted his back. "Of course. You still owe me a drink. That and if anything happened to you, they'd probably make me be sheriff. I don't want your job. I'd have to stop getting into fights and fleecing men out of their money over cards."

Reed laughed low in his chest and her hand vibrated with it. "Seems I always owe you a drink." He shifted and opened his eyes to look at her.

Even in the dark, she could see the amber glint of his eyes. It was Marina's turn to be very still. "It's been a long day. We should both get some sleep."

Reed let out a long sigh. "You're right. My legs aren't too keen on moving at the moment, though."

Marina stood and offered him her hand. "C'mon, Sheriff."

His hand gripped hers with firm determination. She pulled him up and then stood, looking at him, unsure what to do with him now that he was so close. Marina squeezed his hand and let it go.

Reed pressed the hand she had dropped into his thigh. "I'll stay 'til you go in."

Marina cocked her head at him. "Do you think something will snatch me in the few feet it is to the door?"

His teeth flashed white in the darkness. "Nothing is that stupid, but it'll take me that long to convince my body to get moving."

Marina could have touched him again. "Goodnight, Reed." She turned and walked into the depot.

"Night, Sparrow." His voice traveled with her as she walked up the stairs. She took the feel of it to bed with her and went to sleep with a smile on her face.

CHAPTER 13

In the end, all the searching was in vain. Two days after Lily had disappeared, Reed had to tell Hughes his wife was gone and likely not coming back. They had left a broken man and two crying children in the tailor shop. The women in town had kept them supplied with food and had taken turns taking the girls for a few hours. After a few days, Hughes lost the red rims around his eyes, but despair followed in his wake. Marina had done a sweep of the valley every day for a week, though she never came back with anything new.

In the mornings, Reed had started working on the house he was building for Claire and the boys. After coffee this particular morning, he had tasked her with looking at their maps of the region and planning a methodical search for anything. Marina marked the disappearance sites on one of the maps. Even though they had found no evidence, she estimated how far she thought someone could get on horseback or flying with a woman in tow and drew a circle around each site. A growing feeling that she was missing a piece of the puzzle grated on her nerves. Each day that passed without change, Marina grew more snappy, and she snarled at the slightest provocation.

Marina was still staring at the map, hoping for answers, when Reed came home through the back door. His hair was wet from a dunking in the pump outside. "I'll be right back."

He went upstairs, and Marina listened to him moving around. She rolled up the extra maps and shoved them onto the shelf behind the table. She left the one with her markings on the table.

Reed came back dressed in clean clothes and carrying a plate of sliced meat and cheese. He held out the plate to her first. Marina took two pieces each of meat and cheese. Reed put the plate down and leaned over the map.

"These circles seem big," he said.

"It's about as far as I figured I could carry something the size of a woman if I had to." Marina joined him at the table. They both remained standing.

Marina's frustration and anger rolled anew the longer they stared at the map. She finished chewing her last bite of food and pulled the knife out of her belt. She held the grip and flipped it absently as she started pacing away from the table. She walked back, looked at the map, and turned again. Every time she got close enough to the map to read it, Marina felt her harpy rise to the surface a bit more, until anger was pouring off her.

Reed stopped moving his finger over the map and started watching her. "What're you doing?"

"Trying to figure out why none of this makes sense. What in the hells have you been doing? I was here making a plan, like you asked, while you went off to play carpenter." Even in her anger, Marina wanted to snatch those words back as soon as she'd spoken them.

Reed's temper broke. "You're just upset because we've found nothing. Not a scrap of a clue as to what in the hell is happening in our valley. You're worthless in this rage. Get out of here and go fight or kill something until you're in a better mood." He went back to the list he was making of places Marina had looked over the last week.

Marina stopped flipping the knife in her hand and stared at him open mouthed. "Go kill something?"

"Yes. Isn't that what you do when you're this crabby?"

"I'm sorry you're no longer enjoying my company," Marina snapped.

"A pit viper wouldn't enjoy your company in your present state."

Marina hissed in response to his comment, and Reed laughed, which only made her anger boil hotter. Marina slid the knife into her boot and walked over to look at the map on the table. She stopped just short of touching him. Marina could hear him grinding his teeth.

"You shouldn't grind your teeth, you know. You'll have nothing but nubs, and then you won't be able to eat all that fine food Widow Finch sends over." Marina traced the creek that ran through the valley with her finger.

"You'll kill me with your sunny disposition long before I'm old enough to grind them down to nothing."

Her anger dissipated. It was Marina's turn to laugh. "Sheriff Brant, I do believe you are starting to like me." Marina turned her attention back to the map. "These are the areas we searched for Lily and these," she traced another circle, "are where we looked for Katherine. Do you think the two disappearances are related? The two areas are not even remotely close."

Reed rubbed his hand over his neck. "Can't say for sure. There are some similarities. Both women disappeared during a storm."

"Making them hard to track." Marina frowned.

"Exactly. Both were married."

"Though only one happily." Marina started pacing to and from the table.

"Both were Remnants," he added.

"You think that matters?" Marina paused in her walking and then resumed.

"I don't know. But two women are missing with no blood and no way to track them. It's unlikely they both decided to try out a different life and leave in the middle of a storm."

"If they were kidnapped, where would someone take them, and why?" Marina leaned over the map so far her nose almost touched the table, as if proximity would give her answers.

"If I knew the answers to those two questions, we'd not be having this conversation." Reed let out a puff of frustrated air. Katherine's disappearance had not concerned them much. She had obviously been in an unhappy situation with many causes to leave, but Lily Hughes was another story. She was a good mother and a devoted wife with an equally devoted husband.

Marina paused halfway back to the table. "Hells, I can't believe I didn't think of this before."

Reed's focus crystallized in an instant. "What?"

"There's someone, or rather someones, in the valley right now who have a history of taking people."

Reed considered it. "True, but Atlanta swore not to hunt without permission."

Marina snorted. "Atlanta also promised never to show her sorry hide in the valley the first time we caught her. She didn't keep that vow too well. They're sneaky enough to try it."

Reed tapped the map. "They've the skills to pull it off. If one of them waited somewhere else with horses farther out while the other one snatched the women, they might could pull it off. The real question is why hunt the women and why do it here, when they know it would cause trouble?"

Marina's anger from before found a target, and she pulled it to her like a welcome flame. "Why do hunters hunt anything? For the thrill of the chase and feel of blood when you take down your kill. They've made a mistake by hunting here in my valley. Again."

Reed coked an eyebrow at her. "Like I said before, you like to kill things when you're restless. Maybe Atlanta and Cyrene have the same problem you do."

"I will go visit the huntresses and see what they have to say for themselves." Marina felt her blood quicken.

"Do you know where they are?"

"Iris does. They left word with her when they were in town. She's refused to tell us up until now, asking that the huntresses be given another chance. I think their chances are out."

Reed left the table and walked over to her. He put a hand on her arm. At his touch, her anger stilled. "I'm not telling. I'm asking this time. Please take Dora or Petra with you. I won't ask to go. You're faster without me, but please don't go alone."

Marina grinned and a feral glint flashed in her eyes. "Don't worry. I'd never deprive my sisters of a chance to seek revenge when a promise has been broken."

Marina made a move to go. Reed's hand on her arm tightened and she stopped. "Don't kill 'em before they answer your questions."

Marina laughed. "I just want to talk and cause them some pain. How much depends on how fast they spill what they know. I'll be back before the night's out."

***

"I don't think either of the huntresses had anything to do with Katherine or Lily going missing." Iris crossed her arms over her chest and tried to stare down Marina.

"That particular look only works on someone smaller and less scary than me, especially today. Where are they?"

"If I tell you, promise you will ask some questions first."

"I promise."

"Like you mean it."

Marina sighed. "By the River Styx, I promise to ask questions before I remove some of their vital organs."

Iris's eyes turned a steely blue. "I'll hold you to that promise."

"I know, Messenger. Where are they?" Marina's impatience leaked out of her voice.

"Over Cascade Pass in an old hunting cabin in the Southern Valley."

Marina was out the back door and in the sky in moments. Cascade Pass led to the valley that was southeast of Turning Creek. It was small and rocky and did not hold much besides scrub brush and deer. It was also remote enough that if the huntresses were keeping captives, there would be no neighbors to notice anything strange.

Marina went for Petra first. She swooped down and landed on the porch in front of the house. She did not bother to change forms. Petra opened the door, took one look at the fury in Marina's face, and turned back inside to yell at James. She returned moments later and they both launched into the sky.

"What are we hunting?" Petra called over the wind. "Styx, slow down. I can't fly as fast as you."

Marina slowed her wing beats by half. "Not a what. A who. I'd rather only tell the story once. Let's get Dora."

Dora was in her garden and saw them coming. She changed and joined them in the air. "I can feel your anger. What happened?"

Marina altered their flight direction to take them directly over Pikus Peak and into the Southern Valley. "The huntresses are hunting in our land again without permission."

Petra hissed. "They made the promise."

"Not just hunting," Dora said. "You're too angry for it to be that alone."

"I think they might have taken Katherine and Lily." The words brought Marina's anger rolling through her like thunder.

The sky got a little darker and Petra said, "They will die if it is true."

"Do you have a good reason to believe it was them?" Dora asked.

"They had access, and we know they're not above it. It's a hunch," Marina admitted. "Iris made me promise, made me swear, to ask them questions before killing them."

Petra bared her teeth. "'Is anyone home?' and 'Can I come in and rip out your throat?' are questions."

Marina laughed and it was not a sound of amusement. This was the version of her sisters that she loved best and understood above all others. The version that was all violence and rage and purpose.

Once they were over Pikus Peak, they found a small cabin with a tightly angled roof, almost reaching down to the valley floor. There was no sign of the huntresses on the ground. That did not mean they were not home.

"I'll speak first," Dora said. "I don't trust you two to keep your claws to yourself."

They landed and the door opened. The greeting on Cyrene's face died as she took in the fury that swirled around her visitors.

Atlanta shouldered past Cyrene. "Why are you three here in such a lather?"

"Have you been hunting in our valley?" Dora asked.

"We swore to you that we wouldn't without permission." Cyrene moved to stand next to Atlanta.

The sky above them darkened again. Marina felt the cold of it touch her soul. Petra took a step closer to Atlanta. "There are some strange things happening in the valley. Do you know anything about them?"

Atlanta glanced nervously at the sky. "No, we don't."

Marina's anger broke into something resembling euphoria, and she leapt onto Atlanta, pushing her onto her back. "Liar." Marina put her mouth full of pointed teeth into Atlanta's face and wrapped a clawed hand around her neck. She heard Dora and Petra pull Cyrene away so she could not interfere. "I know you're lying about something. Tell me what you're hiding." Marina pushed all her fury and power into the words that were a command Atlanta was not strong enough to disobey.

"We hunted a bear last week, but that's it. I swear by the River Styx. I swear. Just a bear." Atlanta's face had gone pale.

Marina could sense the truth in her words, but the huntress was still hiding something. Marina hissed at Atlanta and pushed one claw into her skin, deep enough to draw blood. "What else are you not telling us?"

Marina saw Atlanta's eyes dart to Cyrene. Dora squeezed Cyrene's arm hard enough to bruise. "What are you hiding?"

"We don't know anything about missing women," Cyrene whimpered.

The air around Petra turned dark, and she moved until she was in Cyrene's face. "We never mentioned any women."

Cyrene's face turned a shade of green. Atlanta squirmed under Marina in desperation. "Leave her alone. For Hera's sake, we don't know anything. We traded with a German couple on the mountain over for some supplies two days ago. Word travels fast when people are missing. We thought it'd be better to lay low here for a few days to avoid this kind of misunderstanding."

The harpies exchanged glances. Petra wrapped her claws around Cyrene's neck until they circled the delicate flesh. "People who run are often guilty. I don't trust either of you." Petra closed the circle of her fingers until Cyrene's breath wheezed in and out of her windpipe.

Atlanta took her eyes off Cyrene and pleaded with Marina. "I swear we have nothing to do with those women. We don't want trouble from you. Please, leave her alone."

Marina swallowed some of her anger. "I think you're telling the truth, but you're also lying about something. I can taste the deceit in your words."

"All Remnants have secrets they don't share. You three know that better than most, I think. How many of the mortals of Turning Creek know what it is that guards them?" Atlanta's look had turned calculating.

Marina chuckled and eased her hand off Atlanta's neck. "Gods, you have backbone to try to blackmail us. You make it hard to know if I should hate you or buy you a drink. You couldn't expose us without exposing yourself."

Atlanta relaxed under Marina. "True, but my natural form looks mortal. Yours is something any sane person would run from, screaming."

Petra eased back from Cyrene. "Are we letting them go?"

"I think we have to, for now." Dora's voice was mournful.

Marina got off Atlanta and then held out a hand to help her up. Atlanta touched her neck, felt the blood there, then gave Marina a feral smile. Marina bared her teeth at the huntress, but she did not pull back her hand. Atlanta took it in a firm grip and Marina hauled her to her feet. Atlanta went straight to Cyrene, and the two threw their arms around each other's waists.

The harpies moved until they stood shoulder to shoulder, a wall of feathers, talons, and violence. Petra spoke for them. "We're tired of having to handle you this way. You'd do well to keep to this valley for some time. I'm tired of your lies."

Atlanta's face turned stony. "We were trying to stay on our side of the pass. You three are the ones who flew over unannounced."

Dora made a chopping motion in the air. "Enough. We agree to come in softer next time if you agree to follow the rules and stop hunting in our valley."

"Can we come into town for supplies?" Cyrene asked.

"Yes," Marina answered without waiting on the other two. "But you will let us know when you are there. No more sneaking about. I still don't trust you. I'll drink with you, but I don't trust you."

"Agreed," Atlanta and Cyrene chimed together.

"Hopefully, it will be quite a long time before I see you again," Petra said.

Marina did not need to look back at Atlanta and Cyrene to know they watched the harpies for a long time after they flew off. The setting sun painted the peaks of the range in orange and red. The cool air over her feathers and face calmed Marina. Iris and Reed would be pleased that they had not killed anyone, but they still did not have answers. The lack of knowledge burned in Marina and fed her frustration until even flight could not calm her nerves.

CHAPTER 14

Reed was waiting for her on his back porch when she got back to town. He was braced against the railing, watching the painted colors of the sky.

"You're alive, then."

"I am."

"Are Atlanta and Cyrene as lucky?"

Marina sighed and walked up the wooden steps to stand beside him. "They might have gotten roughed up a bit, but they are alive."

Reed put a hand on his heart and said with sarcasm, "Sparrow, you followed directions."

Marina snorted. "Don't get used to it."

"You look relaxed but not pleased," he observed.

"They said they don't know anything about Katherine or Lily." Marina put both hands on the railing and leaned over it.

Reed shifted to face her. "You don't believe them."

"No, I don't. They're lying about something, but telling enough truth that we could not untangle truth from half-truth. I think we should keep an eye on them for now. It's been a long day. I'm going to crash at the depot. We can decide on a course of action tomorrow." Marina walked back down the steps of the porch.

"Thank you," Reed said to her back.

Marina swirled around. "For what?"

"For doing as I asked. And for coming back in one piece."

Marina gave him a twitch of a smile. "Don't get used to it."

He chuckled and Marina felt it on her skin. "Wouldn't dream of it."

***

It was after noon, and Marina and Reed were devising the best strategy going forward. It was hard to make any decisions when they had so little to go on.

Marina straightened and leaned a hip on the table. "We might have to make our rounds again to the people in the valley, but ask different questions this time."

"You think someone will just admit to having two women holed up somewhere?"

Marina got a feral gleam in her eyes. "No, but I could persuade some of them to talk. I'd probably know if they were lying, and it is possible someone saw something, but didn't know what it was. All Remnants have some sort of disguising mechanism, and most mortals are blissfully ignorant about Remnants."

"I occasionally wish I was still ignorant." Reed laid his list aside and studied the map.

"Who says you're not?" Marina delivered the line with an almost straight face.

Reed looked up at her. "I'll ignore the last jab. I don't think scaring half the valley will get us the results we need."

Marina let her harpy show through her eyes. Reed hesitated, as though considering stepping away from her. He leaned forward instead and a thrill went through her.

"Fear can be a tool," she said.

"It's a tool with unpredictable consequences." Reed met her eyes and refused to look away until the violence faded from them.

Marina broke the contact and ran a hand through her hair. "You're right, but sometimes it's entertaining."

"I don't agree with your idea of entertainment."

"I wouldn't hurt anyone, just, you know, look scary." Marina flashed a pointy-toothed grin at him. It was her favorite way to prove she was something other.

"Being scary can do plenty of damage. Fear does not beget trust. Let's do it my way first. Starting tomorrow, we'll just do a few visits a day, together. Nothing to draw too much attention."

"You're in charge. We still have the rest of today to get through. Want to practice throwing knives out back? We can bet on it and make things interesting." Marina bent over to retrieve one of the knives she had stashed in her boot. She palmed it and held it out to him.

Doctor Williams showed up before Marina got the chance to show Reed his lack of skills with a knife. His hair was in disarray, and there were deep grooves under his eyes.

"Pardon me for saying, but you look like hell, Doc." Reed gestured to an empty chair.

"I don't look half as bad as I feel." Doc sat with a sigh in a chair.

"Marina, go get the man a drink."

Marina dashed up the stairs and returned in record time with three glasses and a bottle. She poured Doc's first.

Doc ran a hand over his face. "I had a couple come in last night, the German couple, Gerlich, who settled near the Lady." The Lady, as everyone called the mountain, was Lady's Favor, a tall peak that soared over her sisters in the south. "Both of them were badly burned, and they brought with them an unbelievable story."

A sinking feeling filled her belly and tangled with the growing knowledge that a hunt was coming. "I visited Atlanta and Cyrene yesterday. They said they traded with the Gerlichs three days ago."

Reed shared a glance with Marina that said he was hopeful they were about to finally learn something useful. Reed prodded. "Go on, Doc. We seem to only get the crazy stuff around here. One of these days, I'll even get used to it."

"Their burns weren't caused by fire. They looked more like a chemical burn I saw in medical school. The husband was covered in them and in excruciating pain. Despite his injuries, he managed to get him and his wife, who had fewer injuries, into town."

"Did they say how the burns happened?"

"They were clearing some brush around a spring on their property when a serpent snatched Mrs. Gerlich from the bank and tried to drag her under the water. Mr. Gerlich jumped in to save his wife but another serpent came out of the spring and spit a burning substance on him. He succeeded in getting the first serpent to let him go, but not before another two serpents came and spit more of the burning material on him. He wounded one or two of them enough to make them drop his wife. He took his wife back to their house and washed off the venom, which had continued to burn through their skin, got in their wagon, and came to town. They got here after dark last night."

"You're telling me a small spring up on The Lady has four acid-spitting snakes in it. Even for this town, this is above what I expect to handle on any given day." Reed stood and looked out the front window at Main Street.

"That's what I'm saying." Doc poured himself another drink.

"Are the Gerlichs still alive?" Marina asked.

"Yes, though they are less pretty than they used to be." Doc finished his drink and stood.

"I'd like to go ask them some questions. Marina, I think you're going to get your hunt today after all. I want you to come with me when I talk to the Gerlichs, but after that, we may want some of the other harpies to join us."

Marina put her hands on her hips. "One harpy isn't enough for you?"

"Sparrow, you're more than any man can handle, but even you aren't fast enough for four acid-spitting snakes at once."

"Such little faith you have in me. Let's go."

Reed grabbed his hat from the pegs by the door and they followed the doctor down the street to his office.

Doc paused before opening the door. "Try not to appear shocked by their injuries. They're still in shock themselves, and I don't want them more upset than they already are."

The back room of Doc's office contained four beds where patients could stay while they recovered from more serious injuries and illnesses. Reed went to the first occupied bed and knelt beside the sleeping man. Marina hovered by the door, appalled by what she saw. Half of the man's face looked like red, melted wax. Most of his body was covered in large patches of melted, burned flesh. The woman only had burns on her arms and neck. Both slept peacefully.

"I dosed them with large amounts of laudanum. I'll need to keep them asleep as much as possible for a few days until their burns begin to heal. I can wake them enough for you to ask a couple questions of each of them, but nothing more. I've already used most of my power reserves to heal them, but I think I can manage to keep them awake and relatively pain free for a few minutes."

It was a miracle the couple would recover at all, but Marina and Reed knew Doctor Williams had some tricks up his sleeve. "If they're dosed, how're you going to wake them?" Reed asked.

Doc's smile was full of secrets. "There are many benefits to being a follower of Asclepius." He reached down and placed two fingers on the temple of Mr. Gerlich. The man's eyes fluttered open. "Heinrich, can you hear me?"

Mr. Gerlich's eyes flicked open but closed halfway again. "Yes," came the rasping reply.

Reed spoke in an even clear voice. "What attacked you?"

"Green snakes. In the spring. Tried to take Prudence. She is all right?"

Reed's voice turned soothing. "She's going to be just fine. Doc here got you both all fixed up. Did you notice anything about the snakes?"

Mr. Gerlich did not answer for the span of three breaths, and Marina thought he had gone back to sleep when he spoke. His mouth moved, and Reed leaned forward to catch the whisper. "Sounds crazy, but I swear they were smart. You could see them thinking. Coordinating. It was unnatural." Doc Williams removed his fingers from the man's head, and Mr. Gerlich went back to breathing the deep, even breaths of a sleeper.

Doc was a shade paler than before and gripped the side of the bed as he straightened. Reed rocked back on his heels, thinking. Marina's mind worked quickly. "The snakes were trying to take the woman. They probably only harmed Mr. Gerlich because he intervened. Mrs. Gerlich was injured in the fight, but not, I think, on purpose.

"Do either of you know what could've done this kind of damage?" Reed waved at the Gerlichs.

Marina shrugged. "Some kind of water snake? Dragon? I honestly have no idea. Iris is always the one who answers those kinds of questions. The acid, though. That's...different."

"Are the Gerlichs Remnants by any chance?" Reed asked.

Doc rubbed a hand over his eyes and swayed on his feet. He sat on an empty bed. "I believe they both are, but I do not know of what. Marina, do you know?"

The men swiveled to face her. "I don't know any more than the Doc. You think it's related to Lily Hughes and Katherine Johnson?"

"Just thinking out loud is all. Collecting information. You should get some rest, Doc."

The doctor was already reclining back onto an empty bed. "I think I will."

"Let me know if they take a turn for the worse," Reed said.

"Send word of what you find in the spring." Doc closed his eyes and was asleep moments later. Marina left the room with Reed behind her.

He closed the door with care. He spoke in a hushed voice. "We'd best go see Iris and see what she can tell us about the serpent."

When they walked by the mercantile, Pearl Nasso came out of the door with her arms full of bags.

Reed walked forward. "Let me give you a hand there."

Pearl stiffened until she saw Marina standing behind Reed. "Sure. Thanks for the help." She allowed him to take some of the bags from her.

"Pearl, this is Sheriff Brant. Reed, this is Pearl Nasso. I've mentioned her." Marina followed them as Pearl led them to two horses tied in front of Simon's.

"Nice to meet you. How's your family settling in?" Reed asked.

Pearl stuffed some of her bags into the large saddlebags slung over one of the horses. "Good, I think. Since we got here so close to the fall, we're trying to make sure we're stored up for winter. We know it'll be harsher here than back east."

Reed handed her a large sack, which Pearl strapped to the top. "Marina and I check on residents during the winter. If your family has need of something then, we'll do what we can do help."

Pearl stopped lashing down the bag she held and looked at Reed with unfiltered astonishment. "That's unexpected. Thank you. I'll let my folks know. Sheriff, I have one more package inside. Will you bring it out for me?"

Reed tipped his hat and walked inside the mercantile. Marina looked around the street. "Did you come into town alone?"

"I did."

"Don't do it again."

Pearl looked up at Marina with fury building in her face. Marina put her hand on Pearl's arm. "Calm down, kitten. I know, you know, and just about any Remnant you come across will know you're not something to sneak up on. The mortals that live with us, though, they don't know that. All they see is a bitty girl all alone. That makes good men worry and bad men get ideas. Sometimes to blend in, you have to make concessions. People here expect a young woman your age to have an escort. Bring one next time."

Pearl's anger deflated. "Thank you. My family can be suffocating at times. I just wanted some time alone, and the ride into town is nice."

Marina smiled. "I understand that, believe me."

Reed came back out carrying a large sack of beans. He slung it up on top of the baggage horse and tied it down. "You're all set. Anything else you need in town?"

"No. It was a pleasure to meet you, Sheriff, and to see you again, Marina. Thanks for the advice." Pearl swung up onto the saddled horse.

Reed stopped her. "Be careful traveling home. We've had some trouble. You'd do better to have one of your brothers or your father come with you next time."

Pearl's gaze sharpened and the sphinx flashed in her eyes. "What kind of trouble?"

"Two women are missing, and a couple was attacked yesterday. Keep your eyes open and don't go anywhere alone," Marina said.

Pearl nodded and led her horses south down Main Street.

Reed watched her go. "She's an interesting young lady."

"She'll be a force to reckon with when she's older." Marina moved to stand next to Reed.

"I think she's a force already, just hides it better than some. Let's get moving. We've got to see what we're up against."

Dora was with Iris when they reached the depot. Marina said, "I'm going upstairs to get my sword. You fill Iris in on what's happened."

Marina bounded up the stairs. She went to the chest in the spare room and lifted her short sword, which was covered in a soft leather scabbard. She slipped the harness and scabbard on and settled the weapon between her shoulder blades. The sound of the steel coming free sang of the hunt, and her blood ran thick in her veins. She was ready.

Marina came down the stairs, and Reed eyed the handle sticking out over her shoulders. "Being a harpy isn't scary enough?"

Iris looked up at his question. "Do you think Marina is scary?"

Reed hesitated. Marina could see him weighing his answer. "I think she goes out of her way to remind me she's a monster. There's no doubt I wouldn't want to be on the other side of her talons, but I also know she has a soft spot for kids and would die for those she considers her family. Everything in consideration, I'd have to say she could kill me in a flash, but no, she doesn't scare me."

The honesty of his speech touched Marina. "Don't press your luck. I might kill you one of these days if you annoy me enough."

Dora's clear gaze focused on Reed. "Few people would look past the monster to see the rest." Marina looked back and forth between Dora and Reed. This conversation was too serious for her liking.

Reed shrugged. "Don't make sense to only see part of a picture when it's the sum of the whole that matters."

Iris's eyebrows went up in a question she did not voice. She cleared her throat and said, "Tell me what you can about what Heinrich Gerlich said to you and how he looked."

"They'll live. Doc worked a miracle on them. He said he'll need to keep them asleep for a few days. They looked melted. Mr. Gerlich said there were at least four snakes. They spit venom, and it continued to burn until he washed it off. They did not fight back until Mr. Gerlich tried to keep them from taking his wife. Doc said the Gerlichs are Remnants, but he doesn't know of what. Do you?"

Iris tapped a finger on the scroll in front of her. "Mr. Gerlich is a wood nymph. Mrs. Gerlich has said a few things that lead me to believe she may be a Remnant of Medea. Do you think it matters?"

"Who is Medea?" Reed asked.

Iris ran her hand over the book in front of her. "A woman who could wield magic and herbs. Why would it matter what she is?"

"Maybe it doesn't. I don't know. I'll let you know when I do. Any ideas about the snakes?" Marina asked.

Dora flipped a page and pointed to a picture. "This is a Ladon."

Marina leaned around Reed to see the page. Even after years of time to fade, the drawing was crisp and monstrous. It was drawn standing next to a man, which it easily dwarfed. The creature itself looked reptilian, with scales, a long tail, and wings. It could have been a dragon except it had had ten fire-breathing heads sporting mouths filled with jagged teeth.

Marina felt the tension in the man beside her. "That looks like it might be more trouble than it's worth," he said. Marina thought it looked like a challenge.

"The only problem is that it doesn't spit acid." Dora flipped a few more pages. "This little beauty, though, does."

The second picture was no improvement on the first. Another reptilian body, but no wings. Marina counted five, six, seven, eight, nine. Nine heads.

Reed rubbed the back of his neck. "Please give me some good news."

Iris ran her small hands over the page. "It's called a Lernean Hydra. It lives in water and spews venom at people as a defense mechanism."

Reed rubbed the back of his neck and sighed. "Sounds lovely. How do we kill it? I'd normally try to talk to it first, but it's already almost killed two people, maybe more. If it was a wild animal, I wouldn't even question the need. I need to know, though, is there a person under those scales?"

"Will it matter to you if there is?" Marina searched his face.

Reed's eyes moved from the picture to her face. "I'll regret what we have to do more, though it won't change the course of things."

"If it's a hydra, and I think it is, then yes, there's a person under those scales, but that doesn't mean it's a good person under there." There was sadness in her voice, which told Reed that Iris understood the conflict he was having.

Reed sighed. "I took this job to keep people safe. Never thought it'd be easy. This is the task I've been given, God help me. It's just a bit messier than I anticipated."

Marina nudged him with her elbow. "Good thing you're taking me along then. This is more my style."

"And what is that?" he asked.

"Kill first and clean off the blood later." Dora's voice held no condemnation. She was stating truth.

Marina smirked. "Gets the job done."

Reed scowled. "I want to know why it attacked the Gerlichs. What if it's behind the other disappearances?"

Marina shot back, "Sorry, Sheriff, but I may not be able to sweet talk it into answering your questions if I'm busy keeping it from melting your face off."

Reed ground his teeth. "Sweet talking is not your strong suit on any given day. I can't just kill it without at least attempting to get some answers. Do you think for once you could just try to have some prudence?"

Marina turned towards him. "Fine," she spat. "I'll ask it all your stupid questions after it kills you and eats you for dinner. I'll be sure to have 'He died prudently' etched on your tombstone."

Iris stepped behind Marina and put her hand on Marina's back. "Be still, my bird. You can't solve all your problems with blood. Words can cut as well. You should welcome the challenge to create an opportunity to talk during a fight. Perhaps you and the sheriff can both win this argument."

Marina relaxed but did not step away from Reed. She was tall, but he still towered over her, and she had to crane her neck to look at him from this close. "Fine. But if it makes one wrong move, I'm separating all nine of its heads from its body."

"Fine. If it eats me, you have my permission to slay it and dance on its ashes." His face was inches from hers, and her body rose to sudden awareness of just how close he was. Something flashed in his eyes. He took one step back from her and turned to Dora and Iris. "Is there anything we should know?"

Iris moved back around the counter and grabbed another book off a stack. She flipped through the pages. "In some myths, hydra can regrow their heads. I think to be safe, you'll need to attack the main body and deal with the heads last."

"Attack the body while we are getting spit on with acid poison. Sounds like my idea of fun." Marina rubbed her hands together.

Reed turned to Marina. "Woman, you need to reassess your idea of fun."

<h1 style="text-align:center">CHAPTER 15</h1>

The smell of aging cheese and fresh milk mingled in the warm air of the building where James and Petra made cheese. They were dragging long-handled raking tools through thickened milk. Petra was laughing, her golden brown face shining with joy. Petra had always been haunted by the violent nature of her harpy, but since marrying James, she seemed at peace with herself. More than peaceful, Marina recognized, extraordinarily happy.

"This is domestic." Marina leaned against the door frame and crossed her legs at the ankles.

"Good afternoon, Marina. To what do we owe this unexpected visit?" James never stopped moving across the vat of curds, cutting them in the precise size necessary.

"We're going on a hunt. I came to ask Petra to join us."

Petra and her husband shared a look that held an entire conversation. Petra asked, "What kind of hunt and who's we?

Marina stifled the urge to be irritated. She was happy for Petra, but there was a time when Petra would not even have cared to ask. "Reed, Dora, you, and me. We think there may be a Lernean Hydra in a spring on The Lady."

James straightened, a line marring his forehead. "A many-headed water snake that spits venom?" Even before meeting Petra, James had amassed a collection of old Greek texts in his search for the lost myth of Zeus.

"That's the one. It should be a barrel of laughs," Marina said.

Petra lifted her tool from the curds and dropped it into a rinsing basin. "Styx and fire, Marina. That does not sound like a pleasant way to spend the afternoon."

"Good, because we won't actually be looking for it until tomorrow morning. Today, we are going travel as close as we can and make camp." Marina waggled her eyebrows at Petra, who rolled her eyes.

Petra sighed. "I suppose you lot are going whether I join or not."

"You'd be right, though we have a higher probability of being more dead without you."

James leaned over to adjust the heat under the vat of curds. "Harpies. Why can't you ever come visit with benign news like what Widow Finch served for dinner last night?"

Marina tapped her chin in mock thought. "She served shepherd's pie, which was terrible, because she let Shelly do most of the baking, and it got over salted. I know you worry about Petra when she comes with us, but she is much scarier than I am. We need her."

Petra smiled wide. "You think I'm scarier than you?"

"Of course not. I'm just trying to put James at ease." Marina let her harpy flash behind her eyes. Petra flashed her teeth at Marina. Both women laughed.

James ground his teeth. "Of all the fools to get caught up with a harpy, why did it have to be me?"

Petra leaned over and planted a kiss on James's lips. "I couldn't resist your proper English manners."

James caught the back of Petra's head and returned the kiss with enthusiasm. Marina looked away, an odd twisting pinch in her chest. Most days, Marina thought her sister was off her rocker for marrying a mortal, but she could see how it would be nice to have someone to come home to and laugh with at the end of the day. Marina cleared her throat. Petra and James broke apart. A loopy smile adorned Petra's face.

Marina replaced the small seed of jealousy with irritation. "We're losing daylight. Are you coming?"

Petra tilted her head at James, a question evident in her expression. "Go on, but come back to me in one piece." James kissed her again on the cheek.

Marina left before she had to witness any more marital bliss. "Reed and Dora are waiting by the barn. We'll saddle your horse while you get your weapons."

"I'm all the weapon I need, but I'll take the rifle, for looks." Petra gave Marina a push out the door. "I've got to go pack a few things."

The ride through the valley was spectacular. Nothing was as beautiful as a mountain valley in the throes of fall. The golden leaves of the aspens declared Mother Nature's intention to replace the green splendor of summer with the white austerity of winter. Birds darted into the long grass in front of them, swooping down to snatch unsuspecting insects. Slow clouds rolled in a blue sky, Marina was on a hunt with her sisters, and the one man she would choose to have at her back in a fight rode in front of her. It was wonderful.

The Gerlich farm was situated in an aspen grove above the floor of the valley. The leaves whispered to them as they rode their horses up the path to the deserted house. The sun was touching the tops of the mountains on their right. Once the sun dipped below the peaks, it would get dark and cold quickly.

Reed pulled his horse to a stop. "Marina, do a sweep. See if we have any unexpected company by the house."

Marina hopped off her horse and changed. Her muscles lost their soreness from riding the instant she let her harpy free. She stretched her wings as far as they would go, flexing her clawed hands. Reed was watching her with a shuttered expression. She winked at him and launched herself into the sky.

Riding through the aspens was one thing. Flying over the valley took her breath away. Before finding her sisters and settling in Turning Creek, Marina had bounced around Europe, then Quebec. There was no other place that settled her soul like this valley. This was her territory, her heart. With a start, she realized how content she was in her role as deputy, patrolling the place she felt was her own.

Two circuits confirmed that there was nothing on the land around the house but some neglected livestock. Marina dropped down ahead of the group on the path. She stayed in her harpy form. "All's clear. I can see the spring. It's about an hour's walk up the mountain."

Reed nodded. "Good. We'll sleep tonight at the Gerlich's cabin, care for the animals, and then go hunting in the morning."

Marina took back to the air and flew to the cabin, trusting her horse to follow the others. The orange light of the sun made the mountains glow red, and Marina could not pass up the opportunity. She flew up and executed a series of twists, rolls, and loops. She angled for Reed and dropped in a dead fall over him. He pulled down low over the mane of his horse. At the last minute, she changed her trajectory, grabbed his hat off his head, and ruffled his hair with her other hand.

She looped a few more times and then landed with a bow. She held the wide-brimmed hat out to Reed after he dismounted. "Your hat, Sir Sheriff." Petra laughed and Dora clapped.

Reed wiped a finger down his temple where a small trickle of blood flowed. "You got me with your claws." The laughter in his words took the sternness out of his expression.

Marina moved closer to him and peered down at his head. In her harpy form, she was at least a foot taller than most people and she liked making Reed, who normally was the tallest man in the room, feel momentarily small. "It's just a scratch. I could've taken off your whole head."

Reed laughed at her. "If my head was missing, I wouldn't be around for you to torture anymore."

She would miss him if he were not around. It struck her that he could hurt her, if only through his absence. She was fast becoming enamored of the way his laughter made his eyes wrinkle at the corners. She searched for ways to make him laugh so she could drink in his expression when he did. A pain wound itself around her heart. "One of these days, you might make me mad enough to fight you."

Reed's smile did not falter. "I'm not stupid enough to pick a fight with a harpy."

Petra took the horses' leads and led them towards the paddock next to the barn. "Stick around long enough, and Marina will give you a reason. She's infuriating."

Before Marina could come up with a witty retort, Dora interrupted. "If you three are done, we only have about an hour before full dark and a lot of work to do." Leave it to Dora to refocus them before a real fight started.

The Gerlichs raised beef cattle and had some assorted domestic livestock. The sky was littered with stars before they had finished caring for the farm. It was too late to cook a meal, so they warmed slices of bread and cheese by the fire. Dora made a salad from some greens growing in the garden behind the house. They sat around a square table barely large enough for the four of them. Marina's elbow kept bumping into Reed's as she ate. She admitted to herself that she did not mind the contact in the least.

The cabin was large enough to have a separate bedroom in the back of the main room and a loft covering half of the main room, for the children the Gerlichs probably hoped to have one day. Marina had climbed up the ladder before dinner and discovered a store of dry goods and chests of winter clothes. The loft, like the rest of the house, was dust free and organized. Marina thought she needed a visit from Prudence Gerlich. Her house was twice as small and contained three times the dirt.

Petra cleaned off the table after dinner. "I've been up since early this morning. Robert wasn't feeling great, so I helped with the morning milking. Tomorrow's going to be a long day. I'm turning in."

Marina rinsed out the last cup Petra handed her. "The bed in the back room looked fairly big. I think the three of us can sleep comfortably enough."

Reed rubbed a hand over his face. "I'll take the loft. I brought a bedroll."

Petra picked up her bag from against the wall and walked to the back room. "Goodnight all."

Dora smoothed her skirts as she stood. "I'm going to turn in too. Goodnight Reed. Marina, I'll save the far end of the bed for you and make sure Petra leaves you some space."

"I appreciate it." Marina settled back into a chair by the fire. She motioned to the empty chair opposite of hers. "I'm not tired yet. Want to keep me company?"

Reed sat with a sigh and closed his eyes. "I'd never refuse a lady."

Marina felt herself smile. "When are you ever going to learn that I'm no lady?"

Reed did not open his eyes when he replied, "I suppose when you beat me over the head with it."

She used the opportunity to look at him in the firelight. His broad shoulders filled the chair, and his legs were straight out and crossed in front of him. He looked relaxed, but Marina knew he was still alert. The lines of worry he carried everywhere bracketed his eyes and punctuated the space between them.

He cared for the people of Turning Creek with a deep and abiding emotion Marina would label love, for lack of a better word. It was responsibility tangled with compassion and a need to protect. She understood most of it, but compassion felt beyond her grasp most days.

"Sparrow, I know you're watching me. What's rattling around in your head?"

"You know I hate it when you call me that."

His eyes did open then, and Marina had to blink to look away. "So you say, but you haven't punched me for it yet. You didn't answer my question."

"Day's not over and I haven't punched a single thing. As for my thoughts, they're nothing worth sharing." Marina rubbed her hands on her thighs, not knowing what to do with them.

Reed leaned forward and put his elbows on his knees. "How bad do you think it's going to be tomorrow?"

"On a scale from chimera to Nimean lion?" Marina mirrored Reed's posture.

"On whatever scale you choose to follow."

Marina shrugged. "Could be more than we can handle or the hydra could never show. It might have moved on by now."

"I doubt our luck will be that good. We'll have trouble tomorrow, no matter how many prayers we say tonight."

Marina leaned back into her chair. "Prayers never do any good." The gods had abandoned the Remnants and left them to survive or not in a world where they were rarely remembered. Turning Creek had changed that for the Remnants. It was one reason, among many, that Marina wanted to help guard what her town had become. A refuge.

"I don't know about that. Prayer works for me occasionally." Reed got up from his chair and rummaged through his saddlebag. He waved a small bottle in the air in triumph. Marina returned his grin.

"I know you have beliefs, but I never pictured you as a praying man." Marina took the offered bottle and pulled the cork from the opening. The whiskey left a pleasant burning trail down her throat and settled in her belly.

"Guess you don't know me as well as you think." Reed winked at her as he took the bottle. Marina watched his throat move as he drank. Everything he did seared itself into her pores. "My father was the judge in our town, but he also had a degree in theology and was the preacher on Sundays. It was an interesting mix. My mother, though, she was the one who made us memorize scripture and taught us to read from the family Bible. Father taught us reverence, and mother taught us love." Reed passed the bottle back to Marina.

She drank again and considered her next questions. "Do you still hold on to the faith of your family?"

He cocked his head and blinked. "Why wouldn't I?"

"How can you? After all the stuff you've seen and learned? There are monsters and Remnants from myths running through your town."

He took the bottle back from her and held it without drinking. He was silent for a long time. "I did ask myself that at first, but what is faith if it's not tested? In the end, I figured if everything I've seen is true, why not a loving God as well? If there can be evil, why not its opposite? Why not a humble king with grace, love, and mercy? I can't very well believe in monsters and not believe in the thing more powerful than them."

His answer, like the man, was many sided and complicated. If she spent every day in his company for the rest of her life, she would always find something new to discover.

"You amaze and delight me."

She did not realize she had voiced her thoughts until his head snapped up at her words. Marina felt heat flame over her face.

A knowing gleam entered Reed's eyes. "Those are fine words from you."

Marina licked her lips and stalled for time with her silence. Everything rushing into her head had no business being voiced. Desire swirled through her blood, and she choked it down. It was not her time. She was not ready, and this was not a man she could have and leave without rending what she had come to cherish. She cared for him too much and he deserved to have the family he wanted. Her heart beat painfully.

Marina stood and Reed mirrored her movement, putting his body inches from her. She cleared her throat. "I should go to bed."

Reed tensed, then he stepped back, giving her room to walk around him. "Goodnight."

Marina clenched her hands as she walked past to keep them from grabbing the front of his shirt. "Goodnight."

"Sweet dreams, Sparrow." His voice trailed after her and wrapped itself around every nerve she possessed.

As promised, Dora had left her enough room in the bed. Marina slid beside her sisters and sighed as her head sank into the pillow. As comfortable as she was, surrounded by those she loved best, her mind was filled with heat and a longing she was getting tired of keeping contained.

Sleep was a long time in coming.

CHAPTER 16

Dora rose first and fried up some eggs for breakfast that they had collected the previous day. She added chives, and roasted potatoes by the fire. It was a filling and delicious way to start a day that promised to be interesting. They cleaned up and checked their weapons and gear.

Marina followed Reed up the mountain and tried to keep her mind focused on the task ahead of them. The tension under her skin from the night before was a scratch on her back she could not quite reach. Killing the hydra would ease some of the tension in her bones. Marina laced her fingers together and inverted them to crack her knuckles. Reed turned at the sound, which was loud in the quiet forest. She shrugged with a grin.

Reed stopped before they reached the glen with the spring. "I've been thinking," he said in a low voice. "Marina was right. The hydra didn't mean to hurt Mrs. Gerlich. I think it injured her after Mr. Gerlich attacked it to free his wife. I want one of you to walk alone by the spring. Let's see if we can draw it out."

Marina wished she would have thought of it first. "Which one of us should it be?"

A pained expression passed over Reed's face but it was replaced by what Marina had come to think of as his sheriff face. It was a blank expression he used when he needed to get a job done without letting anyone to know what he thought about the job itself. "Out of my choices, I'd say you, Marina. Dora looks less threatening, but I know how you fight and trust you to get yourself out if things go south."

Marina wanted the job and was glad she did not have to argue to get it. She rubbed her hands together, the thrill of the hunt already rushing through her blood. It sang to her and beat a pleasant rhythm in her head. She smiled and knew her harpy teeth were showing.

Reed put a firm hand on her shoulder. "Don't forget. We need to ask it questions if we can. I want to know if it has anything to do with the other disappearances."

"I'll try, but I can't make promises."

"Please, Marina."

Marina reached up and squeezed his hand. "Whatever you say, Sheriff."

"Somehow, I don't think that was an agreement."

Petra snickered behind them. Marina twisted to look at her. "If things do go south, bring the dark, and don't hold back on his account." Marina jerked a finger towards Reed.

"I would never let a little thing like a hydra hurt my sister." Petra gave her a feral grin and Marina saw the harpy swirling behind the depths of Petra's deep brown eyes.

"You two enjoy this more than you should," Reed muttered.

Marina winked. "I did promise you a hunt. This is how we hunt. Life's no fun if you can't scare anything."

"Or kill it," Petra added.

"Or make it bleed," Dora said.

Reed rounded on Dora in surprise. "You too? I rely on you to be the sane one."

Dora smiled and Marina saw Dora's otherness move across her face. "We all have our vices."

Marina unstrapped the sword on her back and handed it to Reed. "Here, I can't change back and forth with this on."

Reed took it with a question on his face. He cleared his throat. "You seem to have no problem keeping your clothes."

Marina shrugged. "Too much bulk, remember. It doesn't translate. Weapons, bags, and such get left behind. I want it, just in case."

Reed looked at the other two women, who he noticed were not carrying the weapons they had yesterday. "What do I do with it?"

"If it won't bother you, wear it. That way I can reach it if I need to."

Determination replaced the curiosity on Reed's face as he swung the sword sheath over his shoulders. Marina stepped around him and adjusted the tightness until the blade fell between his shoulder blades. She ran a hand down the scabbard, letting her fingers play over his back. Reed stiffened in response, but said nothing.

Marina walked around and looked at him from the front. She kept her hand on him as she walked, unwilling to break contact. The sword was a mark that said, "This too is mine," and she thought she enjoyed that more than she should. "It looks nice on you, but don't draw it. If I need it, I'll get it."

Reed nodded stiffly. "Get going."

Marina gave them a salute and walked alone towards the spring. The sun shone merrily on the clear pool sitting in a ring of aspens. The tranquility of the scene belied the purpose of her presence. The sound of her footsteps, quiet as they were, still seemed loud in the morning air. She stopped on the edge of the pool. Small ripples ran over the surface originating from the spring that fed it and ending where the pool spilled over into a thin stream running down the mountain. The entire pool itself was not more than twenty feet by thirty feet. It was impossible to tell the depth of the dark green water. Most mountain pools contained clear water, and Marina interpreted the lack of clarity as an indication that not all was right here. Marina thought their group would likely get their wish and see a hydra this fine fall day.

Marina stopped on the edge of the stream and mentally catalogued all of the places she had hidden her knives as she had dressed that morning. She would have preferred to go into the situation armed with her sword, but she was supposed to appear helpless—or at least approachable. What she really needed, she thought, was a pair of short swords she could keep in cross sheaths across her shoulders. When she was done with this, she would talk to Henry about making her something special.

Marina knelt by the pool, keeping her hand near the top of her boot where her best throwing knife was hidden. The moment before the surface of the pool broke, goose flesh sprouted across her skin. She tensed as one green head, then two more, rose out of the water. Marina's harpy raged to be let out. She kept her instincts caged and waited to see what the monster would do. She had given Reed her word that she would try to talk to it, and so she did not draw her knives.

"Good morning. Nice day for a swim." Marina used her least-threatening voice.

The hydra looked at her with three pairs of eyes. Marina looked into their black depths and felt her thoughts unravel. All she could see was blackness. In the back of her mind, she screamed and raged, but her body was trapped by the gaze of the hydra. Iris had not warned them about this. A few more moments and even her efforts to reach a weapon receded until all she could think about was blackness and water.

There was a pressure around her waist, and the part of her still aware knew it was the coil of the hydra squeezing her. Marina felt the cool kiss of the water on her skin. She should be furious and fighting, but she could not remember why. Darkness closed over her. It was peaceful in the darkness.

A jolt of fire ripped through her and the pressure on her middle eased. Marina sucked in a breath of air, but it was not air that filled her lungs. Ice water filled her lungs. She was drowning. Desperation clawed at her as she kicked, hoping she was moving towards the surface of the pool.

The moment her head breached the surface of the water, she inhaled the air greedily and then coughed. There were harpy screeches ringing in her ears, and Reed was yelling her name. She shook her head to rid the rest of the hydra's hypnosis from her mind and struggled to get her feet underneath her. Her left boot found purchase. Marina used the leverage to launch herself up from the water.

Marina let her harpy flow over her, and she pumped her wings to gain altitude over the pool. "I guess that was hydra for, 'Good morning, I'm going to eat you for breakfast'," she screeched. "Let's see who eats who."

She called over her shoulder as she flew, "Don't look into the eyes. They have some kind of hypnotic power."

She turned when she was high enough and surveyed the scene. The sun had been sucked from the area, and a flash of dark energy, like lightning, struck one of the heads of the serpent. The jolt she felt in the water must have been the hydra getting hit by Petra's darkness. She couldn't think of another reason for the beast to release her. Dora dodged two spitting heads, and Reed was sneaking up on the hydra from the rear, ax in hand. All were still fighting and uninjured from what she could see.

Her observations took less than a breath. Marina could see the place on the hydra's body where all the heads conjoined, just under the water. With Iris's instructions ringing in her mind, Marina dove. She needed to separate the body from the heads. A scream tore through her throat as she dove. The dance of the hunt pounded through her blood. It was euphoric.

Her talons found their mark and sunk deep into the flesh of the hydra's back. Two of the heads whipped around, spitting venom as they came. Marina dodged one spray but she felt the heat of another make contact with her shoulder. One of the heads came within range of her claws, and Marina raked them over the hydra's eyes. It screamed in pain, and two more heads focused on her. Now there were four pairs of beady eyes watching her, and four mouths trying to land sprays of venom on her. The heat in her shoulder was increasing. Marina tore through another of the hydra's eyes. If it could not see her, it could not spit so often at her. Styx, her shoulder hurt.

Marina released the hydra and pumped her wings to gain altitude fast. Looking for another opening, she circled overhead. Only two of the heads remained fixed on her. Dora and Petra each had one reptilian face focused on them. They were diving and taking out the eyes as Marina had done. The hydra had not noticed Reed's approach.

A large portion of the tail had flopped up on the bank during the hydra's struggle with Marina. Marina saw Reed's intent before he took action, and she dove. The fool was going to get himself killed. Unlike the harpies, Reed did not heal easily. He died as easily as the next mortal man.

Reed swung and left a gaping hole in the wake of the ax. The hydra howled in a voice devoid of anything mortal. Marina landed on the head nearest to Reed, who continued to hack away without a care for his own fool head. She dug her talons in deep right behind its eyes. Marina sunk her teeth into the cool flesh of the serpent head. Her mouth filled with a mixture of warm blood and foul tasting poison. Marina ripped in opposite directions with her teeth and talons, and the hydra's head separated from its body with a wet, tearing sound. She cackled as she dropped the severed head in the pool. The noise of the splash was drowned out by the screeching of the hydra.

Her pleasure over her triumph was short lived. Almost immediately, two more heads, grotesque and wrinkled, emerged from the ruined neck of the hydra. Bile rose in her throat, but determination pushed it down. She only had moments until the new heads were functional. Marina looked around.

Reed had taken advantage of the hydra's preoccupation with her and was advancing on the body of the monster. He had waded waist deep into the spring. Marina could see he would never get enough leverage immersed in water to chop into the body and hit something vital. Iris had been right, of course. They needed to destroy the body first. Talons and teeth were all well and good, but Marina needed a sword to reach the heart of the beast occupying the spring.

Marina calculated how fast she could fly to Reed, gain some altitude, and change back into her mortal form. She would need both accuracy and speed after she was in her mortal form.

"I need some time," Marina called to Petra and Dora. They redoubled their efforts, darting in between the heads and scratching whenever they got close.

Marina flew low and swooped over Reed. He saw her coming and stopped his forward motion. She pulled the sword free. The sound of it was lost beneath a roar of one of the hydra's heads and Petra's laughter.

Marina flew straight up until she was above where she thought the heart would be underneath all the heads and scales. With a battle cry, she dove headlong towards the place on the hydra where its far-right neck met its body. A breath before she slammed into it, she threw the sword into the air, changed forms, pulled her sword from the air with her right hand, and gripped the hydra's neck with her free arm.

Her momentum carried her around to the front of the monster. With another cry, this one let loose from her mortal throat, Marina plunged her sword between the ribs of the hydra until the hilt prevented it from going deeper. The body of the hydra flexed with shock and pain as the sword rendered its heart useless.

The hydra carried Marina with it as it plunged into the pool. Marina scrambled to keep from getting crushed under the weight of its chest, but the water was over her head in moments. Her feet could not move her away quick enough. The weight of the hydra and the pounding of her own ears echoed thunderously in her blood. The thrill of the kill was fading as she floundered, pinned under the water between the body and the muddy bottom of the spring. The need to breathe became a screaming tattoo in her head. Almost drowning two times in one day was two times too many.

Black spots appeared in her vision, and Marina stopped struggling. Her shoulder ached where the acid had burned her. It occurred to her that she could actually die. The thought was a new one. Even with the lion, she had known she would somehow come out alive. She never had considered her own mortality with any seriousness. She was not ready to die. She wanted the thrill of the hunt back to replace this maudlin emotion drowning her as sure as the water was killing her now.

The weight of the hydra lifted, and Marina struggled with what energy she had left. The hilt of her sword knocked her in the head. She tried to grab for it, but her hands would not obey her. Strong hands gripped her under her arms and hauled her from the water. They laid her on the bank of the spring and Marina saw sky and three concerned faces. The faces babbled at her. Marina took deep gulps of air and her senses slowly returned to her.

"I need to sit up," she croaked. Reed's arm went around her shoulders, easing her up. She shook the water out of her ears and kept breathing. Gods, the air tasted wonderful. Her lungs still burned.

Reed was kneeling in the rocks and sand beside her. "Are you all right?" His hands ran down her legs, her arms, and then checked her ribs. "Nothing's broken."

"My sword's till in the hydra. I want it back. Before we leave. Styx, that was amazing," Marina gasped between gut stretching breaths. It still felt blissful to breathe.

"Nothing's broken except her brain. You almost died, Sparrow. You're worried about a damn sword?" Reed put his hands on her shoulders and shook her.

Marina winced. "Careful. Acid burns, there. It's a nice sword."

Reed looked abashed. "Sorry. Are they bad?"

"I'm not sure. I was busy trying to drown myself." Marina started to lie back down. Reed's arm moved across her shoulders and eased her down. "I'm tired. Are you all alright?"

"I'll do. That was some fierce flying," he said.

"A compliment and no lecture? Are you sure you didn't get whacked in the head?" Marina smiled at her own joke.

Petra patted her uninjured shoulder. "You earned a rest. We're all fine. You took the brunt of the injuries and the risk. We'll figure out what to do with this mess and wake you when it's time to go. Do you think you can change and fly in a bit?"

"Of course. Takes more than a bitty little water snake to stop me from flying." Marina closed her eyes then opened them back up. Reed was still kneeling beside her. It took an effort but she reached up a hand and put it on his leg. "I'm sorry we didn't get a chance to ask it questions. Now we won't know if it was responsible for sure."

Reed put his hand over hers and squeezed. "I'd rather have you alive than have a polite conversation with a hydra."

Marina felt Dora's small hand smoothing back her hair. "Sleep for a bit. You'll feel better." Marina closed her eyes and slept.

***

She woke up to darkness and the smell of roasting meat. Marina stretched and found her shoulder was no longer sore. Her head was no longer pounding and demanding rest. In fact, she felt refreshed. Experimentally, she sat up and looked around.

The glow of a large bonfire lit a clearing about three hundred yards from where she lay. She saw the silhouettes of Dora and Petra as they walked in front of the fire, stoking it with sticks and sending sparks into the air. Marina did not see Reed. She stood on steady legs and walked towards the orange glow of the fire.

The fire burned from a pit in the ground. Once it burned down, the pit would make it easier to cover what was left of the remains with dirt. Marina stopped when the heat of the large fire was a gentle touch on her skin. She searched the areas lit by the fire and found Reed, leaning against a tree, watching her. Marina held his gaze for a moment then smiled and walked around the fire pit to him.

Reed did not move as she approached. Marina did not stop walking until she was standing almost flush with him. The heat coming off his body rivaled the fire in the cool autumn air. Marina dug her shoulder into the trunk of the tree and faced Reed. He kept his body facing the fire, but turned his head to face her. His breath tickled her face when he spoke.

"Feeling better?"

Marina relaxed and allowed her body to enjoy the contact. "Wonderful, if I am telling the truth. Like I slept in past breakfast and woke to a day of leisure."

Reed smiled. "Not like you slayed a dragon and almost drowned, twice."

Marina grinned back. "I had help."

Reed snorted. "Not much."

"I'd certainly be dead by now if I'd come alone."

Reed straightened and pulled away from her. Marina felt the urge to curl back into him. "Wait. I need to note this day. Marina Ocypete admitted she needs help to kill monsters and that she's not immortal. I'll tell Iris to note it in the history she keeps."

"I heard that too. Dora and I dragged that carcass off your body. You

136

owe us a drink or something." Petra chuckled from the other side of the fire.

Marina laughed. "Harpy, I'll buy you a drink." She turned back to Reed. "We live for three hundred years, not forever. Everyone has to die. I'd rather die with a sword in my hand or my claws around someone's neck than asleep in a bed."

Reed reached down and grabbed something. The smooth hilt of her sword was pressed into her palm. Reed's fingers smoothed over hers and Marina caught her breath. "I pulled this out of the hydra before we burned it." He took his hands off hers and planted his shoulder blades back into the trunk of the tree.

Marina slid the blade and the sheath back between her shoulders. "Thank you. Not just for this," she gestured towards the blade, "but for dragging me out of the water and guarding my back today."

Reed's eyes did not waver from her face. "You're my partner. You're damn good at being a deputy, minus your acidic tongue. I'd hate to have to replace you."

Marina relaxed back into him. "No one would ever be able to put up with you like I do. Besides, no one else is as scary as I am."

Marina felt Reed's body shake with a silent laughter. "No one else makes me laugh like you, Sparrow. Don't ever die on me."

Marina let a slow smile break over her face. "I wouldn't dream of it."

CHAPTER 17

The fire burned all night. They took turns watching the blaze to make sure it did not spread to the grass and trees. Marina used the hours of her watch to relive the hunt. In spite of the burns and almost drowning, it had been a damn fine hunt. Thinking of the feel of the hydra under her claws made Marina's blood race again. The firelight warmed her already-heated face, and she gripped the stick in her hand until her knuckles were white. This feeling was why she did not want to settle down to have her own daughter. Marina loved the violence of her life. She thrived in her place at the top of the predatory mountain.

Marina looked at the shape that was Reed sleeping on the ground, near enough to the fire to be warm, but far enough to be safe from the sparks. He was a fine man to look at, but down that path lurked trouble of a kind she did not think she wanted. He was important to her, she could admit that to herself, and he had become a part of what she considered to be her family. She would protect his back and fight with him whenever he called, and that was where it would end. It was where she needed it to end.

When it was time to wake Reed to take his shift, Marina sat next to him for a long time and watched him sleep. With an exasperated sigh, she placed a firm hand on his shoulder and squeezed. He rolled over, awake and alert, eyes wide in the dark.

"It's your turn," she said.

Reed sat up and ran his hands through his hair before reaching for his hat. "I'm getting too old to be sleeping on the ground. Puts too many cricks in my bones."

Marina snorted. "You're far from being old." She stood and offered him her hand. It was warm in hers, and she pulled him up to a standing position.

"Thanks. Dawn is still a couple hours off. Sleep while you can. I'll keep watch. Use my blanket if you need."

Marina sank down, tiredness pushing her into the ground. She had not realized how tired she was until her butt hit the ground. "I think I will. I'm suddenly feeling too tired to get my own blanket." She rolled over on her stomach and placed her head on her crossed arms.

"Sleep tight," Reed said before walking away. Marina fell asleep quickly, surrounded by the one smell she could not banish from her thoughts.

Dawn did come too soon, and Marina woke stiff on the cold ground. The fire was down to nothing but hot ash and coals. The sky matched the color of the ash in the pit. There was a storm brewing, and it would be upon them before the end of the day.

"Good morning." Petra handed her a cup of coffee. Marina hummed in thanks. "We've got to finish this and get moving. There's a storm coming."

Marina sipped the black coffee and let it remove the cobwebs from her brain. She looked around the clearing. Dora was shoveling dirt into the pit to cover the coals.

Petra gave Marina a pointed look. "Reed went to get the horses so we could leave from here."

"I didn't ask," Marina ground out.

Petra chuckled. "You didn't have to."

Marina scowled into her coffee. "I don't want to talk about it."

Petra smirked. "Suit yourself, you stubborn harpy. Take my advice and stop resisting."

"I don't know what you're talking about," Marina muttered.

Reed came into the clearing, riding his horse and leading the three others. He tied them to a tree then removed a folding shovel from his saddle. He nodded to Marina then joined Dora in her work.

"I didn't know you packed a shovel." Marina said, kicking dirt with the side of her boot as best as she could in an effort to help.

Reed winked at her. "You squirrel away knives and pointy things. I carry tools. Everyone has a purpose, Sparrow."

Marina stopped kicking and stared at him open-mouthed. He so easily poked at the places she ignored. He was too canny for his own good. "And what, in the name of the gods, is my purpose, oh great Oracle?"

Reed paused between shovels of dirt. "You're a weapon and a very good one, just as I am. We have different methods, but our purpose is the same. We fight because others can't. Someone has to shed blood so others can have peace." He went back to shoveling dirt.

Marina watched his efficient movements. Violence was a part of who she was, and she enjoyed it. She had belittled the gift by not giving it the credit it was due. Her ancestors had understood what the violence meant.

They had stood against the tyrant, Zeus, and led a rebellion for all the people under the shadow of Mount Olympus. They had shed blood so that all the Remnants could be free from tyranny. Marina's face heated. She had served a similar purpose in defense of the home and the people she loved.

Marina turned and stalked off into the woods, angry at herself. Reed called her name. She kept walking into the trees. When she had walked far enough that she no longer heard the scrape of the shovel, she leaned her forehead against a tree. *I should not have forgotten*, she thought. She knew that violence must always serve a purpose or it ran the risk of becoming vulgar. Reed's words had pulled her from the precipice of that vulgarity as surely as if he had tied a rope to her waist.

She was a violent monster, but her violence was not without purpose. She had been reveling in her nature for its sake alone, afraid it would drown her otherwise. What she had not realized was that the violence was a tool, like her knives, that she could use to defend her home and the people she loved. Turning Creek was hers, and it would have the defense of her blood and her weapons until the day she died.

When her spirit was calm, she walked back and joined the others.

Dora and Petra gave her questioning glances, but it was Reed who voiced the question. "Everything evened out?" Marina nodded and helped them finish covering the pit without talking.

"What next?" Marina asked.

Petra crossed her arms. "I checked the pond where the hydra had been. It had to have been deep to hide the body of that thing, but when I looked at it this morning, it was nothing but a shallow watering hole. I could've walked across it without it going up to my waist."

"Could the spring have operated on the same principles as you three when you change?" At their questioning looks, Reed cleared his throat and fumbled forward. "Your clothes disappear when you change. Could the spring have changed into a larger lake under the same kind of magic then back when the hydra was killed?"

Petra shrugged. "It's possible. Hells, anything is possible."

"There were no signs of either woman around the pond or in the woods. I checked," Dora added.

Marina swallowed uneasily. "Do you think it ate them?"

Reed shifted his weight. "An unpleasant way to go. I want to believe the hydra was the culprit. We don't know for sure. Don't say anything to Mr. Hughes or Andy. Best we should bide some time and see if things settle down."

They all agreed. The small party mounted and left the remains of the hydra buried in the earth. When they reached the base of Lady's Favor, Dora split from them and went east, towards Silvercliff. Petra continued on with them until the edge of town, where she continued on to her farm.

As predicted, the wind was picking up and the rumble of thunder bounced over the mountains. Reed cast an eye to the sky. "You staying in town tonight? That storm might come on fast."

Marina shook her head. "I'm going to grab some things I left at Iris's and head to Folly. After sleeping on the ground twice in the last twenty-four hours, I want my own bed. Storm be damned. I'll leave my horse and fly if I need to."

Reed's brow creased. "I suppose I'd waste breath trying to tell you not to fly right into the lightning."

Marina shot him a grin. "You'd be right."

Reed's sigh was loud for effect. "I'm going to check in with Doc and see how the Gerlichs are doing. I'll fill you in. Will I see you tomorrow?"

"Probably. I've got nothing else better to do."

"I'm flattered."

"You should be."

Reed moved his horse closer to hers. "When you left the fire earlier and stalked off, did I say something I should apologize for?"

"No, though I should apologize for going off." Marina paused. "In the ancient times, when Zeus still ruled from Olympus, the harpies were his tools, used to torment souls to repentance. They were called the Hounds of Zeus. The original four harpies reclaimed their violence in defense of others who were weaker and suffered under Zeus's rule."

Reed interrupted her. "There're three harpies in this valley. Should I be expecting more?"

"The four harpies led the rebellion and paid the cost for their treason with one of their own." Marina stopped her horse behind the depot. "You have a way of seeing me. Today, you reminded me of something I'd forgotten. My violence serves a purpose. Thank you for that. I needed the reminder more than you'll know." Marina got off her horse and tied her to the post there.

Reed swung off and walked around to where she stood. He paused and tilted his head, then broke into a broad grin. "You're getting old on me, Sparrow. How old are you again? A hundred and some change?"

Marina crossed her arms. "You know very well I'm a very sprightly sixty-two. Why?"

Reed reached out and touched her in the middle of her forehead. Marina jolted at the brush of his fingers. "I remember Petra getting soft when she got them too. No wonder you're being thankful. You've a grey hair. Right here." His fingers burned a trail around her face and tucked the curl behind her ears.

There was a loud buzzing in her ears. "I have to go." Marina ignored the shocked look on Reed's face and turned around. Her harpy was clamoring for her to go back. For the second time that day, she walked into the trees and did not look back or pay heed to the voice calling her name. She did not try to think past the words he had said. Marina walked far enough away and then let her harpy go.

The wind in her face was full of the smell of the coming storm. She pushed the last moments with Reed from her mind and lost herself to flying. The night was coming on fast, hearkened along by the clouds. Lightning sizzled to the side of her, and she felt the answering thunder in her bones. She landed in her yard the moment the sky opened and let forth the rain.

Dripping, Marina walked into her dark house. It took a few tries to light a candle with her wet hands and the shaking flint. She took the candle, the shaking of her hand barely noticeable now, and walked to the only mirror she owned. Marina put the candle on the dresser and leaned into the reflective surface of the mirror. There, in the middle of her brown, sodden curls was one iron-grey hair.

All of her protestations about Reed had been fool's gold. She could now put a name to the burgeoning feeling growing within her. It was love. Marina gripped the hair firmly and yanked it out by the root.

CHAPTER 18

Overnight, the wind shook her windows and pounded on the roof with small, angry fists. Exhaustion helped her sleep through the worst of the storm's raging, though it did pull her out of troubled dreams one or twice. Marina woke rested in body. Her spirit, however, beat against her head like the rain from the night before. Her brows ached with the pressure. Marina rubbed her temples.

She needed some advice. Out of her two sister harpies, Petra was in the best position to give her advice in her current situation, but Marina was uncertain she could take any of the ribbing that was sure to accompany whatever Petra would say. Dora had the calmness Marina needed. The pressure in her head eased a little, and Marina knew she had made the right decision.

Dora opened the door to her cabin on Marina's second knock. She peered hard into Marina's face and waved her in. "I just made tea. You missed breakfast, but there is still some bread for toast if you're hungry."

"Just tea is good." Marina plunked herself down into a chair at the table. Dora placed a teacup ringed in blue flowers on the table in front of Marina. She pulled a bottle off the shelf and splashed a good amount of whiskey into the tea.

Marina cocked an eyebrow at her. "Bit early for that. Didn't even know you had that bottle."

Dora pushed the cork back into the mouth of the bottle and left it in the middle of the table. "I hide it when you and Petra come over. You look like you need something more fortifying with your tea this morning." Dora poured herself a cup of tea, minus the whiskey, and joined Marina at the table.

Marina patted the flask in her trousers. "I brought my own, but I'll happily deprive you of yours."

Marina sipped her tea in silence, aware of Dora's eyes on her. The whiskey curled in her belly with a pleasant warmth. When her cup was empty, Dora refilled it with tea from the pot. Dora gestured towards the bottle and Marina shook her head.

"Why are you here, Marina? I can see by the look of you that something is wrong."

Marina rubbed the warm cup in her hands. "Avoidance tactics."

"Why are you avoiding Reed?" Dora's voice held a note of disapproval.

"I never said it was him." Marina crossed her arms over her chest.

"You wouldn't avoid anyone else, you'd just go have it out with them. You two seemed fine, well, as near as fine as you two ever do with each other, when I left yesterday. Did something happen on the way home?"

Marina made a noise in her throat between a laugh and a snort. She reached for the whiskey bottle and poured it into her half-full teacup. Dora did not push for more information. She waited for Marina to be ready. This quiet patience was why Marina had come here instead of seeking out Petra. Dora let her tell the story at her own pace, without beating it out of her.

Marina took a deep breath and said the words she had been dreading all day. "Reed found a grey hair on my head yesterday when we got back to town. I didn't tell him what it means. I couldn't think. I flew home and then," Marina gathered her strength and said fiercely, "I pulled it out."

Marina's hands were clutched hard around the teacup. Dora wrapped her own small hands over hers. The touch comforted Marina. Dora ran her eyes over Marina's hairline. "It's back this morning. Did you know?"

"Yes." Marina's reply was a whisper. To her dismay, her lip trembled.

Dora squeezed her hands harder. "No, Marina. Don't cry. Don't you see how wonderful this is? Anyone with two eyes can see he cares for you too."

Marina yanked her hands from the cup and slapped the table. "That's the problem. Why in the inner circle of hell does this have to be hard? We're friends, good friends. I trust him as much as I trust you, Petra, and Iris. I trust him beside me in a fight, and I've defended him with my blood. I've never had that with anyone else other than my sisters, and especially not a mortal man." Marina paused, her face twisted with pain.

"I can't ask him to father my daughter. I'd never risk losing his friendship for that. I want him in my life. If he was my mate, I would have to leave the valley after I conceived. Gods help me, I don't want to go."

"Then don't, you idiot." Dora's anger was palpable. "Do you think Petra's going to leave James when she gets pregnant?"

Marina shrugged, and Dora punched her in the arm. She rubbed the spot and glared at Dora. A trickle of irritation wove through the uncertainty in her chest. She was better equipped to handle irritation and anger, and she embraced its appearance.

"Listen. The damage is already done. The grey hair indicates a loss of your immortality, but we still don't know for certain what that means. Only time will tell. Don't waste what time you do have, either way. You love him. It doesn't matter what happens from here on out. Have a daughter by him or not, as you choose. It won't change the truth of this." Dora jabbed a finger into Marina's scalp where the offending hair had reappeared this morning.

Marina sat with the words moving over her. Dora made it seem simple. Perhaps it was this easy. Marina would lose her long life now, regardless of whether her love was returned. She could have a daughter by any mate she chose and keep her daughter by her side without fear because her immortality was already lost.

The whiskey mixed with the revelations, and it made her head float a little. "Do you think he might be willing...?" Marina was unable to finish the sentence.

Dora smiled. "I do think."

Marina leaned back in her chair. She gave her mind free rein to follow some of the ideas she had kept locked down tight for weeks. A loud pounding on the door broke into her thoughts.

"This certainly is a day for visitors." Dora got up and opened the door.

Reed stood on the threshold, disheveled and dusty. "Have you seen..." He looked past Dora and stopped when his eyes found Marina. "Thank God. I've been looking for you all morning."

Marina stood. "How did you find me?"

Reed strode into the house and wrapped Marina in a rib-crunching embrace. He took a deep breath and his body relaxed around hers. Her body, in contrast, flared up at the contact. He broke the embrace but kept his hands on her shoulders. "You left like there was a demon on your tail last night. I'm never going to mention a lady's age ever again. Never. Then, the storm came. I know we killed the hydra, but there is the possibility we were wrong. When you didn't show for coffee this morning, I went to your house. You were gone. I started to worry in earnest." His hands tightened on her arms. "I went to the depot next to see if you'd changed your mind and gone back there. Iris didn't seem overly concerned about your absence. She told me you'd be here. She seemed certain. Couldn't drop the worry, though."

Marina pictured Reed coming out with two mugs and finding an empty porch and her heart twisted. Marina laid a hand over Reed's right hand on her shoulder. "I came over to Dora's this morning to talk. I needed to get out. I'm sorry I worried you."

Marina felt his arm flex under her touch then relax. "No harm done, Sparrow. You just took a few years off my hide, but you seem to do that for sport most days. I'm glad I've found you."

Lines still bracketed his mouth. "There's something else," she said. It was not a question. A sick feeling was brewing in her belly.

Reed's hands squeezed her shoulders. "Atlanta and Cyrene were attacked in their camp last night during the storm. Cyrene rode over the pass as quickly as she could. Whoever or whatever it was took Atlanta."

"Why would they take Atlanta and not Cyrene?" Dora asked. Marina still held on to Reed's hand and was loathe to let it go. His hands remained on her shoulders. "That is an excellent question," she said. "I'd hoped we had seen the last of this trouble."

"We all did." Reed's hands dug into her shoulders hard enough to make her wince. "When we find the bastards, we'll ask them why, polite like, before we show them what we think of their behavior."

Marina's lips curled upward. She liked the violent side of Reed. She couldn't help but believe she was a good influence on him.

CHAPTER 19

Marina stopped Reed before he walked into the depot. "I'm sorry I ran off yesterday, and I'm sorry if you lost any sleep worrying about me."

Reed's smile washed over her. "Nothing to forgive. I should've known better than to lose any sleep over you. Any monster that seeks out a fight with you is a monster not long for this world."

"Stop flattering me. You'll make me blush." Marina gave him a saucy grin.

"I'd like to know what makes a harpy blush." Reed cocked an eyebrow at her.

"Careful what you wish for, Sheriff." She turned and walked into the depot before he had a chance to retort. She did love getting the last word.

Cyrene sat in the back of the depot, nursing a cup of tea and talking to Iris. She had bruising on her jaw and a swelling on the back of her head. Her face held a pinched look, conveying her lingering pain and lack of sleep. Relief was evident on Cyrene's face when she saw them walk through the door.

Iris was sitting in a chair beside Cyrene. She glanced up at them, and then her eyes whipped back to Marina and up to her hairline. Iris stood and started to open her mouth, but Marina shook her head curtly. Iris clamped her mouth shut, and Marina tucked the offending hair behind her ear. She sighed inwardly and thought of the conversation she was going to have to have with Iris in short order.

Marina sat down beside the huntress. Reed stood, a strong comforting presence at her back. "Tell us what happened. Everything you remember." The loss of Atlanta made Marina's anger burn brightly. It was past time for this to stop.

Cyrene's voice was strong as she told her story. "The storm picked up quick. When there was a pause, Atlanta went to check the horses. She wanted to be sure the storm hadn't damaged the small lean-to where they stay. She loves those damn horses as much as she loves me." The ghost of a smile touched her lips.

"The rain started coming down again, and she'd not returned. I got worried after a while and thought maybe something had happened to the horses, so I went out to see what was keeping her. I looked everywhere, but she wasn't in the lean-to or the yard. I was soaked to the bone. Sweet Olympus, that storm was awful. The rain was pelting down. I was standing by the horses, who were there just where they should be, and yelling for Atlanta when something hit me from behind."

Marina's focus snapped onto Cyrene. "You said something, not someone."

Cyrene nodded. "Right before I was hit, I could feel it. A Remnant, something strong, but before I could turn, I was hit over the head. I came to, laying in the rain, with this." Cyrene touched her jaw. "Bastards hit me while I was down. I owe somebody my fist in their face."

Marina's blood rose at the words. Those were the sort of sentiments she understood best. "We'll do our best to see that you get to return the favor. If I don't rip them to shreds first."

Reed spoke. "Why take Atlanta and not you?"

Cyrene shrugged.

Marina had been considering that issue. "Maybe they could only carry one of you out of there. If it was one Remnant working alone, they wouldn't have been able to carry out two bound or unconscious women without a cart or some horses. We haven't found any evidence at any of the other sites of horses or a cart. It means that whoever or whatever took Atlanta, and probably the others, carried them off."

Reed made a noise of disgust. "Never find a damn thing, thanks to the rain. They sure know how to time things." He tapped a finger on the back Marina's chair. "Is it possible that we're dealing with a Remnant that can control the weather? We seem to be getting more than our fair share of storms this season."

All heads turned towards Iris. "I'll have to look. It's possible. Anything is possible, really," she said.

"Well, that's helpful at least." Reed pushed off the chair and paced to the door and back.

Marina understood his frustration. With each disappearance, they seemed to know less and less, and her anger grew in turn. "I'll go look today and see if there is anything the storm hasn't managed to wash away."

"I want to go with you," Reed said.

Marina twisted in her chair to face him. "I know you do, but we only have half the day left, and there's no way you can ride a horse that far and be back by night. I can fly there, look around, and come back after dark. It's faster if I go alone."

Reed ground his teeth together. A look a resignation entered his eyes, and Marina knew she had won. "Take Dora or Petra with you."

"I don't want to spend the time to go and get them." Marina stood.

Reed rubbed his hand over the back of his neck. "Fine. I'll follow on horseback and check the road and trails for any signs of movement farther out. You look at the area around the cabin. All the other women disappeared on this side of the mountains. It's possible whoever it was had to transport Atlanta over the pass and travel through the south side of the Turning Creek valley there. If it was late enough in the storm, there could be evidence of their passing through."

It was a good plan. Marina placed a hand on Cyrene's shoulder. "We'll be back tonight. Stay with Iris, but be careful. She has that look in her eye. She's going to make you do research all day. Take my advice and plead a headache from injuries."

Cyrene gave her a weak smile. "Thank you, all of you. I know Atlanta and I are not always your favorite people, but we've always known we could trust the people here. It means a lot."

"One thing I need to know first." Marina tightened her hand on Cyrene's shoulder. "When we visited last time and had our little chat, I was certain you were hiding something. What was it?"

Cyrene pressed her palms against her thighs. "We were hunting the hydra. That's why we went to see the Gerlichs. We needed a reason to be on their property."

Reed bent over and put his face in front of Cyrene. "You knew that thing was there? You didn't think to warn those people? Do you know what they look like now? They almost died." Rage shook his voice. Marina's harpy rolled within her in approval.

Cyrene pushed back in her chair to get away from him. "We didn't know it would attack them. Why would it?"

Reed's voice was stony. "Doesn't change what the right thing to do was."

Marina leaned forward. "You gave your oath. You swore on the River Styx that you'd no longer hunt in my valley. You planned to break that vow the moment you made it. How can we trust anything you say?"

Cyrene covered her face with her hands and cried. "I'm sorry. Will you still look for Atlanta?"

Marina looked at Reed. He nodded. She said, "Yes, but I can't promise not to beat her to a pulp before I return her to you." Marina changed her voice, letting it deepen and fill with menace. She let her power, filled with violence and blood, leak into the room. "After that, we're going to have a serious chat about what it means to break a vow to a harpy."

Cyrene nodded.

Reed grabbed Marina's arm and broke the spell of violence she had woven around the huntress. "It's time to go."

Marina followed him, but she left some of the violence linger.

Iris's voice stopped them. "When you two get back, we need to talk about the Territory Committee. They want to come see Turning Creek for themselves." She paused. "Be safe. Both of you."

Reed nodded. "Yes ma'am."

Marina flew ahead. It was one of those clear days that come after a storm. The sky was a piercing blue, and the air was crisp, as though the rain had washed the whole world clean. On any other day, it would have been a beautiful day to fly and enjoy the sun on her feathers. Marina clenched her pointed teeth together and angled down into the valley on the other side of Cascade Pass between Pikus Peak and Lady's Favor.

The valley on this side of the mountains was smaller and had less open space than the valley to the north, where Turning Creek sat. Marina located the cabin from the air. She did not want to land and add her own footprints to the soft ground. She circled low, letting the tops of the trees tickle her talons. She kept her circuit tight, searching for a sign of any disturbance. Methodically, she opened her search area. Wider and wider she flew, looking for a sign, some direction to indicate what had happened to Atlanta.

Marina tried to envision what would be able to get the drop on the cunning huntress, and a shiver ran through her. Marina knew picking a fight with Atlanta was something you did before you got your face bashed in. Anything strong enough and crafty enough to bag one of the huntresses was not something Marina wanted to meet on a dark and stormy night.

The thought hardened her resolve. She repeated her low circles and found nothing. Marina landed in the yard in front of the cabin and walked the area on foot. This search proved as fruitless as the overhead search had been. Marina looked at the sun. She had maybe one hour of good daylight left and then another hour while the sun set before it got too dark to see. She needed to leave time to meet up with Reed.

There were three paths leading away from the cabin. Marina chose the one that went northwest, towards Turning Creek, first and followed it on foot. The pines were bright green and the patches of aspens sparkled gold in the afternoon sun. Marina found nothing down the trail but some fat squirrels and a deer. The other two were just as empty. Marina changed back into her harpy form and turned east to meet Reed.

She knew from the set of his shoulders that his search had been as productive as hers. She swooped down on silent wings, beating them slowly to avoid moving the air, and plucked his hat off his head. Reed grabbed at his head and swore, before looking up.

Marina cackled as she flapped away. Reed laughed. "Sparrow, you scared another ten years off my life. You're lucky I didn't shoot you. Hope you aren't making a habit of that trick. At least you're getting better at it. Didn't scratch me up that time."

Marina flew back in close. Reed's horse sidestepped and Marina followed the movement. While the horse was getting used to having the harpies near, it still did not like having a deadly predator at its back. Marina could hardly blame the poor beast. Marina placed Reed's hat back on his head. He adjusted it.

"I searched the cabin and most of the valley around it. Nothing." It was hard for Marina to fly low enough to talk to Reed while maintaining enough altitude to keep her wings off the ground. Her claws scrapped the ground twice and she growled in frustration.

"I came up with nothing. Rode down all the trails leading into this valley from the pass. If they came this way, the storm covered their tracks," he said. He eyed her. "Could we be dealing with something that can fly?"

Marina flew back in close to reply. "It would have to be at least as big as I am to be able to carry that much weight for any length of time without setting down somewhere. I can carry a deer for a few miles, but even I can't stay in the air for long without some kind of break. They could've dragged those women on foot and we wouldn't know with the rain the way it was."

Reed kept riding and did not reply. Marina flew around him and felt his eyes on her. They were getting close to town, and she was flying low. "I'm going to gain some altitude to fly in. I'll meet you at the depot."

Marina did not wait for his acknowledgement. She flew straight up into the cloudless sky, tinged orange by the setting sun. She took her time flying back, knowing that Reed's horse could only travel at a fraction of her speed. The mountains burned orange and red. The beauty of her valley calmed the frustrations of the day, though a kernel of anger seemed nestled permanently under her breastbone.

By the time she'd landed in the woods behind the depot, she had marshaled her spirit enough to give Cyrene the bad news. Cyrene took it well enough, though Marina saw a glint of steel in her eyes. Marina knew the cause of the look. If one of the other harpies were missing, or Iris, or Reed, she would not rest until she had turned over every rock and bush in the territory. Cyrene would not give up either. Iris offered the huntress a bed at the depot for as long as she wanted it.

It was full dark when Reed walked through the door of the depot. The jaunty bell announcing his entrance was at odds with the grim expression on his face. Marina gave him a cup of tea. He peered into the cup and wrinkled his nose. "Sorry," she said, "we're surrounded by tea drinkers here. It's what we got for now. This'll make it better." She pulled her flask from her pocket and poured a finger of whiskey into his glass.

"Thanks." Reed drained the tea in two gulps. "Where's Cyrene?"

Marina pointed up the stairs. "Asleep. Her head was still aching, and

Doc told her to get some rest for now. You hungry?"

Reed shook his head. "I ate some on the ride. I'll grab something more when I get home. Claire usually saves something for me."

"It must be nice to have someone to come home to who will cook for you." A small spike of jealousy flared, and Marina squashed it with guilt. She liked Claire.

Reed hesitated. "It is. Don't mind the company either. I've been away from my family for a long time now. It's nice to have one of them close again. Missed them more than I'd thought."

A light step on the stair sounded, and Marina turned to see Iris, her golden hair spilling over a green shawl wrapped on her shoulders. Reed stood as she joined them. Iris waved him back down.

She rounded the counter and sat on a stool. "I take it you found nothing as well." Reed shook his head.

Marina slapped a hand on the counter. "Hells, I'm tired of not finding a damn thing. We need some answers so I can have something to kill."

Iris sighed. "We have learned some things."

"The women all disappear at night." Reed ticked off a finger. "There are never signs of a struggle." He closed another finger towards his palm. "No blood, nothing."

Marina rubbed her hand over the counter. "No blood, so they aren't killed where they are taken at least."

"No scuffle, so they are pulled away quickly," Reed added.

"You both forgot one important thing. They all disappeared during a storm, so there is nothing to find. Even if they had struggled." Iris rubbed a hand over her eyes.

Marina tapped a finger on the counter. "They were all Remnants."

"I just don't get the why of the problem. The why might tell us the how." Reed rubbed the back of his neck.

Marina clenched her hands into fists. Her nails grew pointy as her anger boiled over. "This is getting out of hand. I care less about the why and how and more about the who I can poke my claws into." Her voice dropped an octave.

Reed ran a hand down her back. "Easy there, Sparrow. We'll find someone for you to pummel soon enough."

Iris sighed and pulled a letter from one of the top pigeonholes. "This letter came yesterday. It's from the Territory Committee. They're going to be here in less than a week, just days after the Jubilee. They've requested that all three of us be present to meet them."

Reed nodded knowingly, and Marina's brain latched onto what Iris had said. "All three of us?"

"Yes. We're the only three who hold any kind of office, so they've requested all of us. Is that a problem?"

Marina pressed her lips together. "No, I just didn't think they'd want to see me. I didn't take this job for the responsibility of it. I just needed something to do."

Reed's mouth turned down. "Well, it is a responsibility. It's not fun and games."

Marina's tone hardened. "I know that now, but I'm not a politician. I don't want to have to play nice with some strangers. You know better than anyone I'm not good at playing nice."

"Iris is better with words than either of us. I suspect she'll do most of the talking. They'll only want to talk to us to see how well we're keeping the peace and maintaining order. Not all mountain towns have a semblance of order." Reed turned a questioning face to Iris.

"You're likely right, but the committee may not want a woman to be the representative of the town," Iris said.

Reed harrumphed. "Any man that doesn't think a woman has the power and intellect to be in charge is a man who's never met a woman like you two or my own mother. She was a general with a light touch when it was needed." His face softened.

Iris was fiddling with some of the papers on the counter. "There's something else you haven't told us," Marina said, watching her movements.

Iris nodded. "I didn't want to bother you, but there is something else." Iris pulled a map out from underneath the papers. "I've had some people over the past couple weeks come in with stories."

Reed fixed Iris with an eagle sharp gaze. "Stories regarding what exactly?"

Iris disappeared under the counter and came up with the green leather-bound book. "A ladon."

Reed rubbed his face. "Which is what again? Dora mentioned it before the hydra. Please don't tell me it's another acid spitting snake."

Marina rubbed her hands together. "I think it's something better than an acid spitting snake." Reed shot her a disgusted look.

Iris flipped open the book and turned it around to face them. Marina already had an idea of what it would be, and her heart sped up to see she was right. Reed leaned low over the page. His breathing was loud in the quiet of the room. Marina could feel the anger boiling within him. Her anger had never left her. Now, it was joined in her blood with a hunger for the hunt.

Reed was just angry.

Reed's hand came down hard on the book. "For the love of all that's holy, are you telling me there is a damn dragon in my valley?"

Iris cleared her throat and pulled the book protectively away from Reed. "A ladon could be mistaken for a dragon, and it has, actually, in many myths. I believe that's where the stories of dragons originated from in the old days."

Reed got up from his stool and walked over to the opposite wall and kicked it. Marina wanted to do more than kick the wall; she wanted to feel the blood of a dragon running through her claws. If she could not find what was taking Remnants in the valley, the ladon was an acceptable secondary target.

Reed came back over and stood next to Marina, radiating tightly controlled fury. "Is it behind the disappearances?" He spoke through clenched teeth.

Iris released a breath. "There's no way to tell. The sightings do not line up with any of the women who are missing or the storms. I just thought with all the other things happening in the valley, you should both know. It may not be related at all."

Reed snorted. Marina looked at him. "Not all monsters are bad, Sheriff." She flashed pointed teeth at him, angling for a release of his anger. She could feel her own uncurling to meet his, and she needed to tamp down her rising need to hunt. Tonight was not the night to head out.

Reed sat down and put his head in his hands. "I know, Sparrow, but sometimes, I wish there were a few less to keep track of."

CHAPTER 20

The next day, Marina prepared for battle. It would be easier if it were a battle she could fight with claws or a sword. Neither one of those things would help her today. She planned her arrival to coincide with Reed's daily circuit around town.

Now, Marina stood before the back door of the sheriff's office. There was still time to walk away, and no one but Iris would know she had not gone through with it. "Styx, I must be out of my mind." Marina opened the door and went up the stairs. With each boot fall on the steps, Marina thought of reasons to forget her quest and go have a drink instead. She got the landing and pulled what courage she had together.

Claire was bustling around, her arms full of clothes, when Marina found her. "Reed is gone already. Didn't you see him this morning?"

Marina cleared her throat. "Yes, I saw him. I wanted to talk with you. Alone."

Claire raised an eyebrow at her. It was a look that mirrored the one Reed often leveled her way, and Marina almost laughed despite the nervous rolling of her belly.

"Is something wrong?" Claire asked.

Marina rubbed her hands on her pant legs. "No, but I've a request I wanted to make in private."

"Let me put these down." Claire disappeared for a moment into the bedroom. When she came out, she motioned Marina to the table. "What can I do for you?"

"Reed said you're making women's dresses to earn money." Marina steeled herself. "Can you make me a dress in time for the Jubilee on Saturday? I can pay whatever you ask for. I could ask Mr. Hughes, but since Lily is gone, he's not much for making dresses. I've never owned a dress, and I thought maybe now was a good time to start." Marina bit her lip to keep herself from rambling on.

Marina had expected some kind of trepidation or more questions, but Claire was all business. "I think you would look lovely in a strong color, like blue or even red. With your hair, you could pull off a red easy."

Marina ran a hand over her hips. "These curves in a red dress might give the wrong impression."

Claire smiled. "Right enough, but you should show them off a bit more. You're lovely."

Marina shrugged. "I've never cared much one way or the other. I like pants. It's hard to cause trouble in a skirt." She tapped a finger on her thigh. "Well, the kind of trouble I prefer."

Claire laughed. "There are other kinds of trouble, and they can be just as fun."

"That's awful scandalous talk," Marina said.

"All the best talk is."

"I see snappy comebacks run in the family."

"There were so many of us, you had to be quick to the punch or someone would beat you to it."

Marina cast her eyes down. "One more thing. I want the dress to be a secret. From Reed, I mean. I don't want him to know about it."

To her relief, Claire did not comment, but smiled in a quiet way. "Come. Let me show you some patterns. I think I can have something done in time. It will be our secret."

A couple of hours later, Marina was rethinking what had seemed like a brilliant idea. She had thought looking at patterns would mean she would show Claire what she liked and that would be it. Claire had gone directly from that to cutting fabric, and Marina now stood with the beginnings of a dress pinned to her.

She must have sighed aloud, again, because Claire said, "Relax. I just want to pin this last piece into place, and then you can get out of this and change. I'll need you to come back tomorrow or the next day and try it on again."

Marina groaned. "I'm rethinking this plan. I'm not the dress-wearing type for a reason."

"There." Claire stood up and helped Marina take the pinned fabric off without dislodging any of the pins. "You're an unconventional woman to be sure. You're just what Reed needs in his life."

Marina paused as she buttoned her shirt. She felt her face heat and wondered for the thousandth time if she was making a mistake. "I can say with certainty Reed wants conventional." He'd said it often enough. A normal life, a normal wife, and a house full of kids. All things she could not give him. This dress had not been a good idea.

Her dismay must have shown on her face. Claire put a hand on her arm and waited to speak until Marina's eyes met hers. "I said needs, not wants. Those are two different things."

The truth of what Marina was almost came out of her mouth. She bit down on her tongue and buttoned her shirt.

Marina liked Claire MacKenzie, but she did not know how she would react to the truth. Claire had all but given Marina her approval to pursue Reed. Marina wondered how fast she would retract that approval if she knew she was sewing a dress for a monster.

***

Marina successfully avoided any long talks with Iris in the days before the Jubilee. It turned out, however, that not being on the committee did not keep you from being conscripted into service. Marina was pressed into duty hanging banners, fixing boards in the boardwalk, and constructing booths for food, drinks, and wares.

The day before the Jubilee, Claire delivered a large, wrapped, brown package to the depot. Marina led her up to the spare room and closed the door.

Claire put the package on the bed and started peeling back the layers. "You didn't ask for them, but I included some stockings and underthings that I thought you'd need."

Marina opened her mouth like a fish and closed it while she watched Claire placing two cream-colored stockings with lace around the top on the bed, followed by a simple chemise and garters. It had been hard enough to convince herself that the dress was a good idea. She had not even considered what went underneath the dress.

Claire pulled the dress up from the package and shook it out. The soft cotton fabric cascaded out in a swirl, a deep red that bordered on maroon. Claire hung it from two empty pegs on the wall. She pointed to some ribbing on the bodice. "I put some extra support here because I figured you'd refuse to wear a corset if I asked."

Marina laughed then, and the tight feeling in her chest released. "Thanks. I think the dress is probably all I can contend with in one evening."

The dress was better than Marina had imagined. It was pretty without being fussy. The deep red was offset with blue piping around the bodice and skirt. The cut was simple, not too low or high, and the sleeves were fitted with tiny buttons from the elbow down.

Claire glanced at her from the side of her eyes and continued to fluff out the dress. "What kind of a place did you grow up in where you were allowed to wear something else besides skirts?"

Telling the truth was tempting. Marina walked over to the dress and ran a finger over the material and settled for a portion of the truth. "I grew up in Athens, Greece, in a secluded but influential household. My mother

157

allowed me to wear whatever I pleased."

Claire paused in her work and straightened to look at Marina. "Athens is a long way from Colorado."

"It is."

Claire did not pry. "Will there be someone here to help you dress? Even if you were used to a dress, you'd need help with the laces on the back and the buttons on the sleeves."

"Iris will help me." Marina fingered the knife at her belt.

Claire's eyes followed her movement. "I almost forgot. I thought you might want to have access to a weapon, should you need it. Most ladies' skirts have deep pockets for little things. I'm always finding bits of twigs and leaves in mine thanks to the boys. I thought a smaller pocket, instead of the usual larger one, would work better for a knife." Claire lifted the right side of the skirt and revealed the small pocket near the waist.

Marina beamed. "It's perfect."

"I made one more alteration." Claire lifted the dress and flipped it around to display a slightly larger pocket that ran along the back of the dress, underneath the laces. "It's not big enough for your sword, but a large knife will fit."

"How did you know?" Marina grabbed Claire and squeezed her tight. "I don't know how to thank you."

"It's my pleasure. You've made our settling in here easier than it could've been, and I know from things Reed says that you've gotten him out of some tight spots. For that alone, I would've made this. You've been a good friend to me. Put it to good use."

"Oh, I think that won't be a problem." Marina chuckled. Claire hugged Marina again and left the room.

Marina sat on her bed and looked at the dress hanging from the pegs for a long time. There was a soft knock on the door.

"Marina, are you in there?" Iris asked.

"Are you alone?"

"Yes."

Marina stood and smoothed her hands over her thighs. "Then, yes, I'm here. Come in."

"You've been avoiding me for days," Iris said as she entered the room. Her words died down to a whisper when she saw the dress hanging against the wall.

Marina shifted her weight and watched warily as Iris fingered the material and ran a hand down the skirt. Each silent moment increased the pressure in Marina's chest. "Well?"

"It will look marvelous on you. This color suits you perfectly. I assume this is what Claire brought by earlier." Iris turned from the dress and hugged Marina.

The tightness in her chest eased. "I'm glad you approve. I'll admit, it might be the worst idea I've ever had, and I've had some really horrendous ideas."

Iris ran her fingers over Marina's curls, smoothing over the cluster of grey there. "Do the dress and you avoiding me have anything to do with this?"

Marina puffed out her cheeks in a sigh. "Yes."

Iris laughed and cupped Marina's cheek. "My bird, you look like you're headed for the gallows. You've chosen well."

The tightness came back into her chest. "He wants things I'm not sure I can give and other things I know I can't. Maybe I should just stick with what I know."

Iris tilted her head. "And what is it that you think you know?"

"I'm a weapon." Marina sliced through the air with her hand. "A monster with a purpose." Marina's legs were weak, and she sat on the bed. "I never considered I could be anything else. What if I can't be anything but violence and blood?" The words, once spoken, wound around her soul and choked her.

Iris sat beside her and wrapped her arm around Marina's shoulders. "My poor bird." Iris put her hand on Marina's cheek and turned her face. "Do you not understand that you're not bound by your nature alone? Your violence will always be part of you, but it's only one part of a whole. You have the capacity to be many things. What those are is entirely up to you."

Marina's chest opened up and was filled with the possibility of hope. Marina rested her forehead on Iris's shoulder. "I don't even know what my life would look like if I allowed myself to be something else."

"Tackle one thing at a time, like how to walk in a dress without killing yourself."

Marina looked up and smiled. "I was more concerned with where to hide my knives, but Claire solved that problem for me." Marina rose from the bed and showed Iris the special pockets.

Iris's laugh was full of joyful bells. "That's the harpy I love. Get some rest. It's going to be exhausting shocking the town when you come to the Jubilee in that."

CHAPTER 21

The day of the Jubilee dawned bright and clear. The town of Turning
Creek was full of industrious people who threw themselves into the joy of a
day off with the same energy they invested into their toil. The mood of the
town had continued to sober after Atlanta had disappeared. Marina thought
the distraction of the festival was just what the townspeople needed.
Thoughts of her own plans for the festival made her giddy with anxiety.

She helped set up all day, and in the early afternoon, she excused
herself and went back to the depot to get ready. To her dismay, putting on a
dress required more effort and even more underthings than Claire had
provided. Iris had loaned her the required amount of petticoats and helped
her tie the laces in the back and button the arms.

Marina gave herself an honest appraisal in the mirror in Iris's room
while Iris finished fluffing and patting her hair. Iris had deftly twisted some
of her curls away from her face, leaving half of her hair down. The
bouncing curls falling down her back gave her a look of innocence. Marina
would never admit it out loud, but the dress did look nice on her. The
simple cut of red cotton fell over her curves with grace.

Marina slapped Iris's hand away from fluffing her skirt one more time.
"Stop fussing. I look fine. Don't I?"

Iris smiled. "You look amazing."

Marina reached around Iris and picked up the two knives she had laid
on the quilt. The cool weight of them released the tension building at the
base of her neck. Marina slipped one into the hidden pocket at her waist
and slid the other down her spine. She rolled her shoulders, testing the
placement.

Iris frowned. "It's a town festival. What could you possibly need them
for?"

Marina pulled the knife at her waist out and flipped it in her hand before replacing it. "You never know. I feel naked without them."

Iris gave her a shove towards the door. "Get going. I'll be right behind you."

With one last plea to the gods, she left the depot and walked towards the end of Main Street, where the booths, bonfire, and dance floor had been set up. Petra and James were standing near a table full of food. Marina headed in their direction first.

James and Petra turned when they saw her coming. Petra was rendered speechless. James recovered more quickly. He bowed over her hand. "You are the second most beautiful woman here tonight, Marina." Normally, Petra would have preened, but she was still staring at Marina.

"Harpy got your tongue?" Marina stuck her tongue out at Petra and got the result she wanted.

Petra laughed loud enough to draw eyes in their direction. "I'd bet the farm James is the only man in attendance who thinks you aren't the most beautiful thing here." Petra's eyes ran over Marina's hairline, and her eyes widened a fraction. Marina knew Iris had tried to conceal the grey streak, but enough of it peeked through. Marina shook her head, her eyes pleading for silence.

Petra grabbed her hand and squeezed it hard enough to grind the bones together. Petra's own grey hair shone silver in the setting sun. "It's not so bad, you know." Her eyes swept to James and softened. Her sister's happiness eased some of the tension fighting through Marina. "We'll see. The day's still young, and I have plenty of time to muck things up."

Robert Mullins joined their circle and whistled. "Miss Marina, that color suits you. Does this mean you won't be entering the knife-throwing contest this year?" There was real hope in his voice.

Marina squashed the hopeful look with her laugh. "Afraid not, my boy. I can't let you win. Wouldn't be good for my reputation. I have my knives handy and sharpened, ready to show you, again, how it's done."

Robert looked her up and down. Marina twirled to give him a better view. "If you don't mind my asking, ma'am, where are you hiding your knives in that getup?"

Marina winked. "Wouldn't you like to know?"

Petra guffawed. "Come along, Robert. You should just start resigning yourself now to losing. Marina is better with a knife, and with words, than you."

"She cuts with both equally. Always be wary of a lady who wields a knife and her words with abandon." Reed had come up behind Marina without her knowing. His voice moved over her and heat crept up her neck. She steadied herself before turning. His reaction was better than she could have hoped.

His throat worked as he swallowed. He opened his mouth once but closed it. She began to get worried. He finally asked, "Where *do* you have room for knives in that dress?"

Marina laughed. "A lady does not share her secrets."

"Thought we established already that you're no lady." The retort came easily.

Marina exhaled. If he was going to treat her the same as always, she could relax. "Tonight, I'm pretending. I'll share one secret, though." She lifted the hem of her skirt high enough to let the toes of her usual scuffed boots show. "Iris tried to get me to wear some fancier shoes, but my knives wouldn't fit in them after they were buttoned. I told her no one would see my shoes anyway."

Iris walked up in time to see Marina heft her skirt. "Marina." Iris's tone was full of censure. "You're hopeless."

"True. No one seeing you in a dress will think to look at your shoes," Reed said. Marina grinned wickedly at the compliment.

Marina canted closer to Reed. "Besides my boots, I have a couple other knives hidden as well. Thanks to Claire."

Reed's face shone with laughter. He held out his arm to Marina. "Sparrow, may I escort you to Vine's booth for a drink?"

"Finally, a man who knows how to treat a lady. I'm dying of thirst and you owe me a drink, anyway." Marina slipped her hand into the crook of his arm. He pulled her closer than was necessary, and Marina's harpy somersaulted with pleasure. This was going to be a highly entertaining night.

"It seems to me that I always owe you a drink," Reed said.

"You're learning." Marina squeezed his arm.

Daniel Vine's booth was twice as big as the year before. He wore a traditional laurel circlet around his brow.

Marina narrowed her eyes at him. "No maenads or satyrs tonight, or you'll be in a world of hurt."

Daniel Vine inclined his head to Marina. "You know I was under duress, as were we all."

"You seemed under less duress than the rest of us." Marina took a sip of the ale Reed handed her. It was malty, with a hint of pumpkin, perfect for the Aspen Jubilee. It was hard to hate someone who made such good ale.

"I've apologized already." Vine's eyes grew hard.

"I'm not the forgiving kind, but if you keep making ale and stay out of trouble, we'll call things square." Marina took another pull from her mug. "I wish I could hate you, but this is delicious."

"Who knew the way into the heart of a woman was through good ale and whiskey." Vine's smile did not reach his eyes.

"Oh, I could've told you that. She'll do anything for a good drink."

Reed winked at Vine.

It was Marina's turn to scowl. "Not anything."

Reed laughed and Marina turned her back on him to look at the rest of the town enjoying the fading warmth of the afternoon sun. The steady pulse of heat from the man next to her both raised her excitement and sent pings of contentment through her. Reed led them through the crowd and past the booths.

Widow Finch had a booth selling slices of cake, crowd-arounds, and cider. The booth with items for the raffle was run by Simon and Beth. Children ran between the legs of adults and chased each other down the street. Families who lived in the farther reaches of the valley would be camped on the outskirts of town until tomorrow. After dark, the bonfire would be lit, and everyone would have enough food and drink in them to keep off the evening chill.

Marina and Reed stood next to one of the barrels that served as outdoor tables. They were greeted by a steady flow of people. Marina received her fair share of compliments regarding her dress. Reed glared menacingly after each comment, and most men took the hint and left. Only one was persistent.

L.A. brought Marina a small glass of whiskey. "A token for your beauty."

Marina took the glass. "To a man who knows how to win my heart." They clinked the glasses together and sipped. Reed rolled his eyes beside her, and Marina ignored him. L.A. smiled at the sheriff.

"What does L.A. stand for anyway?" Marina asked.

"Llewellyn Alexander. My mother was fond of the Welsh stories from her youth. My father thought it was too long and called me L.A. Only my mother ever called me Llewellyn." L.A. lifted his almost empty glass. "To our mothers." Marina did not feel so charitable about hers, but she toasted just the same.

Marina saw a family walk into the Jubilee. She straightened and followed their movements, her instincts on high alert. Marina counted heads. Pearl was accompanied by her brother Claude, an older couple she assumed were the parents, and three other men Marina assumed were the rest of the Nasso brood.

Reed noticed her attention and followed her eyes. "Looks like we're going to meet the rest of the Nasso family tonight." He looked relaxed, but Marina approved of the wary look in his eye.

"They've a right to be here, but they still have to behave. Something about Claude makes me want to rip his eyes out," Marina growled. Her fingers curled around her glass.

Reed closed a tight hand over her arm. "Sparrow. No fights tonight. Be a shame to ruin that dress."

Marina relaxed with effort, but she kept her eyes fixed on Claude. "You're right. Claire worked hard to sew something that would look decent on me." Reed pressed his lips together in a tight line and said nothing. Marina pulled his hand. "Let's go introduce ourselves and be friendly."

Marina did not release Reed's hand as she made a beeline for Pearl and her family. He gave her fingers a squeeze then dropped them when they reached the Nassos in front of the auction table, laden with quilts, pies, wooden furniture, a set of new tools, and a gleaming new saddle. Reed stepped beside Marina and relaxed into the posture he used to survey the street in the mornings. Marina calmed the riled harpy inside herself and adopted Reed's posture.

While she smiled in greeting, she sent small tendrils of power out as a warning. "Pearl, will you introduce us to your family?"

Pearl smiled in genuine warmth. "I'd be glad to. This is my father and mother, Tyler and Edna Nasso. Father, I told you about meeting Marina."

"Nice to meet you, Sheriff Brant and Miss Ocypete." Mr. Nasso's handshake was ordinary. Marina tried to send tendrils of power to feel him out. He was definitely a Remnant, but she could not sense anything else. He let go of her hand quickly.

Reed shook hands with Mr. Nasso. "Welcome to Turning Creek," he said. "I'm sorry I've not been out to welcome you properly. We've had some trouble in town."

Mr. Nasso leveled serious eyes at them. "We heard some women were missing. We came here because it is said to be a safe place."

Marina thought of Katherine, Lily, and Atlanta, all missing with no indication of where they had gone. She cleared her throat and looked Mr. Nasso in the eye. "Turning Creek is a good place. We will find out what's going on. If you see anything suspicious, we'd be much obliged if you'd let us know."

Mr. Nasso nodded. "I'm not so much worried about my boys. But Pearl, she's our only daughter, and we treasure her."

Mrs. Nasso, who had been silent, wrapped an arm around her daughter. She was browned from working in the sun, and her face was etched with lines earned from a hard life.

Reed waved a hand at the other Nasso men. "I've not met your sons yet."

Mr. Nasso pointed to Claude. "Claude is the oldest, then Olen, Billy, and Chris."

Marina shook hands with everyone but Claude. However strong they were, they hid it as well as their father. Marina still felt Pearl's power over them, a steady beat against her inner sense. Marina sized up the four brothers. They all had some shade of straight brown hair and a husky build that seemed to come more from working outdoors than anything else. Only

Claude seemed to wiggle beneath her skin and make her uneasy. He stepped closer to her and quirked his lips in a smile that looked like a smirk. Marina clenched her hand and reminded herself that he had done nothing wrong.

Marina turned to Pearl. "Want to have a drink with me?"

Reed, who had continued to stand next to Marina, leaned over and spoke into her ear just loud enough to be heard, but soft enough that her toes curled in her boots. "Go easy on her, Sparrow. She's just a kid."

Marina turned to reply and found her face very close to his. "I was going to get her something else besides ale. Vine sells other things besides alcohol. I think," she added.

Pearl smiled and stepped away from her family. "May I?"

Mrs. Nasso made a shooing motion with her hand. "Go on. I know you can't go far, and we'll be able to see you."

Pearl threaded her arm through Marina's and pulled her to the booth with the largest crowd. Marina elbowed her way to the front and waved to Vine.

Pearl, her cheeks red and eyes shining, turned to Marina. "What should we have?"

Marina patted Pearl on the shoulder. "Stick with me, kitten, and I'll show you everything you never wanted to know." Marina turned to Vine. "Two lemonades."

Pearl deflated. Marina laughed in her face. "Have faith."

Marina took the two cups and took Pearl to an empty table. "Your first lesson is this: always accept a drink when offered, but be prepared and bring your own." Marina bent over, lifted her skirt a few inches, and pulled her flask from her boot. "I don't normally carry my flask in my boot, mind you, but this dress doesn't have many hiding places." Marina topped off their drinks with whiskey. "Don't tell your father. Or Reed, for that matter. I'm trying to stay on his good side tonight."

Pearl accepted the cup Marina offered and took a tentative sip. A slow smile spread over her face. "This is good. Burns a bit. But good."

Reed had moved on from the Nassos and was talking to Beth Kramer. Marina felt a prickle on her neck and swept the crowd. Claude Nasso lounged against a table on the other side of the street. Marina glared at him and sipped her lemonade.

"Your brother doesn't like me," she said.

Pearl followed her gaze, saw Claude, and rolled her eyes. "I think he does like you, actually. He likes getting under people's skin."

Marina grunted. "I get under people's skin, but I'm fun and entertaining. No offense meant, but your brother gets under my skin in a way that makes me want to punch his face."

Pearl's laugh was youthful. "He makes me feel that way too."

Marina doubted it was exactly the same. "Reed was right when he warned your father. Something is going on around town. Be careful. Stay inside at night."

Something deadly moved in Pearl's eyes. "I can take care of myself. My family can be over-protective."

Marina tipped her cup in the direction of Iris, Henry, and Dora, who were talking at a nearby table. "The problem with family is they always think they know better than you and can boss you around. Doesn't make them wrong."

"I'm not a child in need of protection without an opinion to call her own." Pearl crossed her arms over her chest.

Marina rubbed her right hand over her hidden knife. "Slow down there. I'm on your side. I know you can defend yourself, and you will be something to behold in a few years, but whoever or whatever is behind the disappearances is crafty or strong or both. They took Atlanta, a huntress, someone who'd never go down without a fight. Be safe."

Pearl took a drink and cocked her head at Marina. "You're worried about me?"

Marina sighed. "Yes. Don't put too much stock in your abilities. You're young yet, and you've a lot to learn about the world."

"That woman, Atlanta, she was your friend?"

"Yes." It was not the answer Marina thought she would give, but she found the words to be true. She liked the huntress and admired her, even if she continually lied through her teeth. "I consider Lily Hughes, one of the other missing women, as a friend as well. She was, is, a kind soul."

Pearl's smile faded. "I'm sorry about your friends."

Marina clinked her cup against Pearl's. "Me too. A toast to finding them, then. May they be safe." Marina drained what was left of her drink.

"What will happen if you find the people responsible?"

Marina's answer was cut off by Simon's booming voice. "Knife throwing competition starts in five minutes. Entry fee is two dollars for new books for the school. Knife competition in five minutes. Come try your luck against Deputy Marina, reigning champion."

Marina rubbed her hands together. "About time. Must be hard for everyone else, waiting around to lose to me." She winked at Pearl, who laughed at her bravado.

Marina parted ways with Pearl and went over to the range that had been set up for the knife throwing. Marina looked over the competition. There was no one she was worried about, really. There were eight participants, all men except for her. This year, the prize was a set of wooden-handled knives donated by Henry. Marina wanted them. They were light, balanced for throwing, and her palms itched thinking about them.

Marina won her first round easy enough and watched Robert as he dispatched his opponent. He was on the opposite side of the bracket from her, so they would both need to win the next round to face each other. The targets were moved from fifteen to twenty feet for the second round.

Marina was paired up next with Olen Nasso for the second round. Marina shook his hand before they started. It was petty, but when he took her hand, she squeezed it hard and let her power leak from her. His only reaction was to smile. It softened his face and made him look like an overgrown boy.

"I'm sorry we're meeting again under these circumstances," Marina said.

Olen, poor man, looked genuinely confused. "Why is that?"

"I'm going to beat you soundly, and that is hardly the way one goes about making new friends." Marina tapped her knife against her thigh. "In hindsight, though, I think I tend to make many new friends that way. Maybe there's hope for you after all. You do seem more pleasant than your brother, Claude."

Olen blushed. "I'll take that as the compliment it was meant to be."

"In the spirit of friendship, why don't you go first?" Marina gestured towards the target, a painted board.

Olen accepted her offer, but his good mood evaporated as he realized he was no match for the harpy. Marina beat him with ease. He left with a murmur and melted into the crowd. Marina turned and watched Robert dispatch his opponent as well. Marina joined him at his target as the judges moved the last two targets back to thirty feet for the last round.

"You've been practicing since last year." Marina patted Robert on the shoulder. "I might have to try harder this year to beat you."

"Miss Marina, can't you at least pretend like I might win?" The pleading look in his eyes was too much.

Marina laughed. "Sorry."

Robert stepped aside. "Ladies first."

Marina rolled her shoulders. "You'll be sorry you offered." She threw her first knife and it thunked into the center circle of her target.

Robert concentrated and let his own knife fly. It landed in the center of his target. A cheer went up from the crowd. "I think it's time you got knocked down a peg. Can't have you be the best fighter, drinker, card player, and knife thrower. You make us all look bad, Ms. Marina."

They each had one more knife to throw. "You forgot, I'm excellent with a sword too." Marina took two steps back, tested the balance of her knife, and let it fly. It landed with a satisfying thunk in the center, next to the other knife. Robert groaned. He straightened, took aim and released his knife. It dug in just to the right of center. The crowd erupted.

Marina put an arm around Robert's shoulders. "Keep practicing. There's always next year. I'll buy you a drink, if it'll ease your feelings."

Robert held out his hand and Marina shook it. "I'll take you up on that, ma'am."

Henry walked over and bowed in front of Marina. He held out two matched knives. "Congratulations, Ms. Marina."

Marina took the knives. They were smooth, warm, and fit her palm perfectly. "Henry, did you make these just for me?"

Henry shrugged, and Marina saw a smile tug at his mouth. "No one throws a knife like you."

Marina flipped one of the knives in her hand. "Would you mind terribly if I gave them away to someone worthy?" Marina knew two little boys who'd love them.

"As the lady wishes." Henry bowed again. Marina laughed and hugged him. He stiffened and then wrapped his large arms around her and squeezed the air out of her lungs. He gave her two soft leather sheaths before he left.

Marina looked around the crowd. She found Claire standing next to Reed. She walked over to where they stood. Reed's eyes burned into her the entire way.

Claire tugged at Marina's hand and turned her in a circle. "It looks even better on you than it did yesterday."

"It's all in the hand of the artist." Marina winked at Claire. "Are Jonah and Stephen around?"

Two eager faces came running towards them, both speaking in a rush. "That was amazing."

"I'm going to practice every day until I can do that."

Marina wanted to kneel down in the dirt to talk to the boys and then thought better of it. She squatted down, careful to keep her skirt modestly tucked over her legs. She looked the boys in the eyes. "Have you been practicing?" They nodded. "Do you two think you're old enough for your own knives?"

"Yes." The boys bounced with joy.

"No." Reed crossed his arms.

"Don't mind your uncle. Henry made these special for people with smaller hands. I think they'll be perfect for the two of you." She held the knives, handle out, to the boys.

"Wait." Reed dug in his pocket and gave each boy a coin. "You pay for a knife so it knows its owner and won't cut you. Give the coins to Marina as payment for the blades and thank her."

Jonah put the warm coin in her palm. "Thank you, Marina. This is the best present I've ever gotten."

Stephen mirrored his brother. "Me too."

"It's my pleasure. But boys, remember one thing. If you ever hurt yourselves or someone else with them because you weren't being careful, your Uncle Reed will have my hide. I'd hate to beat him up on your account." She gave them a wink. "We'll practice soon."

"Yes, ma'am." They chorused. Marina helped them strap the knives to their belts and the brothers ran off. Jonah turned around and ran back. Marina leaned back over to see what he needed and was almost pulled over when his small, strong arms wrapped around her neck. She hugged the small bundle of joyful boy. He gave her a gap-toothed grin and ran back into the crowd.

Claire put her hands on her hips and turned to Marina. "I think Jonah is working on a serious case of hero worship."

Marina's heart felt melted. "I guess this dress had the effect I wanted after all." She laughed and Claire joined her.

"That was a nice thing you did, Sparrow." Reed's eyes rested on her. "Those boys feel at home here, and you've a lot to do with it."

"What can I say? I have a soft spot for the men in the Brant family." Marina delivered the comment without embellishment.

Reed stilled for a beat then showered her with an unabashed grin. "We can be charming when the prize is worth the effort."

"Come on, flatterer. I owe another man a drink. Might as well buy you one too." Marina pulled him over to Vine's booth. His palm was rough against hers, and she reveled in the warmth of him. They joined Robert and Adam at a table once their drinks were in hand.

The sound of a fiddle warming up floated over the crowd. The music would start soon. The first flames from the bonfire were licking up the dry logs across from the area cleared for dancing.

"It'll be a shame if you got all dressed up in that and don't dance." Reed took the mug Marina handed him.

Robert took his with thanks. "I'd like a dance, Ms. Marina, if you'll allow it."

"I won't." Reed growled. Marina choked on her drink.

Robert shrugged. "Thanks for the drink, ma'am." He went off in search of easier and less guarded feminine company.

Marina elbowed Reed in the side, causing him to slosh some of his beer. "Watch the drink, woman."

"You should be nicer to Robert. He's just a kid."

"He's a grown man and shouldn't be looking at you the way he was."

"My age quadruples his. He's a baby." Marina laughed again and let the comment slide. Jealous Reed was hilariously funny.

Marina fanned herself with her hand. Despite the cool air, she was hot under all the layers of her dress and underthings.

"Do you know how warm stockings are?" Marina asked.

Reed sucked in the pumpkin ale he had been drinking and coughed until his eyes watered. "Christ, Marina. Ladies don't mention stockings in public." He took a few deep breaths.

Marina was delighted to see a tinge of red creeping up Reed's neck, and her eyes sparkled with mischief. The hand not holding his mug was clenched against his leg.

He grabbed her mug and put them both on the barrel next to them. "Come dance with me."

"I wasn't finished with that," Marina protested.

"You are now." Reed grabbed her hand and pulled her towards the dancing area.

His hand was firm and warm, and Marina had wanted to be right where she was all night. The fiddle was peeling out a fast-paced reel when they joined the line of dancers. It was a simple matter to follow the steps of the couples in front of her, and the movements repeated on the chorus. By the third chorus, Marina was adding her own turns and skips to the steps. Reed caught her doing it and laughed, full throated and free in a way that sailed over the music. Marina promised herself to wear a dress more often if only it would elicit that laugh from him again.

Whenever they came together, Reed gave her hand a squeeze. By the third song, Marina thought her skin might burn off from the fire he was casting her way. She was definitely wearing this dress again. There were questions she still did not have the answers to, but it was too nice a night to open up that box. Tonight, she wanted to enjoy the company of a man she desired and bask in his gaze. Tomorrow, she would sort out the challenges.

The song ended and Reed bent his head to Marina's ear. "Walk with me." The words traveled up her spine. She nodded and let him lead her through the crowd. He led her down the street and opened the door of his office. He motioned her inside. The door closed and the gaiety of the crowd was muffled by the wooden barrier.

"I don't think a lady would have followed you here." Marina could see the outline of his face and felt rather than saw him smile.

He was beside her in one long stride. "It's a good thing you aren't a lady."

Reed closed the last bit of distance between them. His lips were warm and gentle for a moment. Then his hands went into her hair, and his kiss became a scorching brand. Marina fisted her hands in his shirt and pulled him closer, giving him as much as he was giving her. He stepped back, pulling her along with him, until his back was to the door. She used the leverage to press into him. He deepened the kiss, and Marina forgot about everything else.

Reed broke contact and pulled back to search her face. Her blood beat in time to his ragged breathing. She leaned forward, put her face in his neck, and breathed deeply. The smell of leather, oil, and the essence that was Reed flooded through her already overloaded senses. Her body melted into his. She drew in another deep breath through her nose then kissed the hollow at the base of his neck.

"Are you smelling me? Is that a harpy thing?" he asked.

Marina pulled his head down and kissed him until the only thing holding her up was his hands around her bottom. "Yes, I was smelling you. No, it's not a harpy thing. Styx, I've wanted to do that for months."

"Sparrow, if I knew a good whiff was all you needed to kiss me like that and get weak kneed, I would've let you do that months ago." Reed chuckled, more vibration than sound, and Marina buried her face into his chest in an effort to soak up the sensation.

He tilted her face up and kissed her forehead, her eyelids, and her checks, ending with a brush across her lips. His hands were not idle. They found the lacings on her dress and deftly opened the top few to give his hands room to move.

His hands stilled when he found the knife hilt along her spine. Reed rested his head on her shoulder, his body shaking with laughter.

"Never underestimate a harpy." Reed placed a careful kiss on her exposed neck.

He continued loosening her laces. His hand dipped into the bodice of her dress. The rough palms of his hands sliding over her sensitive skin was a delight. Marina hummed with pleasure.

Reed frowned. "You're not wearing a corset."

Marina pushed against his hand in protest of his stillness. "I was hoping the dress and stockings would be concession enough to my gender. Besides, it would've gotten in the way of this." She moved his hand over her skin again and laughed.

"You'll be the death of me," he said as he left a trail of kisses along her collarbone before claiming her mouth again.

Reed's hands slowed in their ministrations, and Marina made a sound of protest. "You're right. A lady wouldn't have followed me in here." His voice was hoarse.

"We have already talked about this. Hush and kiss me again."

Reed laughed. "Demanding already, are we?" He did not kiss her again. His hands, so sure and firm on her breasts a minute before, pulled the bodice of her dress together and started tightening the laces by feel.

Marina slapped his hands away. "Stop."

Even in the dim light, Marina could see the determined set of his features. He pulled the top tight and laced it. He cradled her face in his hands and pressed his lips to hers. "Marina, I want more than this from you."

Her mouth was dry and she blinked at him. For the first time in her life, she was well and truly scared and she could not think of a thing to say. She was not prepared for this conversation that had no answers.

Reed swept her hair back from her face. "I'll not take advantage of you this way, though later tonight I expect I'll be lying in bed, alone, and cursing my sense of morality."

"I'm cursing your sense of morality now." Marina pulled him down and Reed allowed her unfettered access. She kissed him in a heated tangle and pulled his shirt out of the waist of his trousers. She ran her hands over his chest and pinched his nipples hard enough to make him wince, in a fit of spite for lacing up her dress. He flipped their bodies and pressed her between the hard surface of the door at her back and the harder planes of his body in the front.

He pulled back eventually and used one arm to keep her at arm's length. He ran his other shaking hand through his hair. "What do you want from me?"

Marina stepped back. "What kind of question is that?"

"Answer the question." Reed dropped his hands and took a step back.

The air between them was charged. Marina gave him the only thing she could, honesty. "I don't know. I know I want you to kiss me again, and I'd like to see what else we can come up with to do here in the dark. Beyond that, I'm not sure. Being with you gives me the simultaneous feeling of being grounded and drowning at the same time. It scares me." She paused and licked her swollen lips. "Nothing scares me."

Reed's shoulders squared. "I want to kiss you and do things to you a lady should never discuss, but I want a hell of a lot more than that."

A weight dropped in her stomach. "I know." Her voice was a whisper. "I can't give you what you want. I can't give you domesticity and a house full of children. It's not even possible." Reed was a man born to be the head of a large, rowdy family. She was cursed to be the mother of one.

Reed closed the distance between them, and Marina almost sighed with relief at the renewed contact. He wrapped his arms around her and rested his chin on her head. "I won't deny that's what I've always wanted. I just never knew who I wanted it with."

"It can't be me." The words choked her.

Reed's arms wrapped tight and then he eased his embrace to place his lips firmly on hers once more. The kiss was long enough to leave her blood singing but not enough to give the fire inside her what it wanted. "We'll see, Sparrow. I think this conversation will hold. It might do us both good to put a night's sleep behind us before we finish it. If I'm being honest, there's not much blood left in my brain at the moment. I'm not sure I can make any reasonable choices just now."

"You seem fairly reasonable to me at the moment. Too much so." Even to her ears she sounded petulant.

"Let's go back to the Jubilee before we're missed. Lady or no, I don't want to start any rumors about you and your wanton behavior," Reed said.

Marina nodded, but leaned in and inhaled his scent once more. She wanted to take it away with her as a balm for the disappointment billowing inside her. She could not think of a single reason he would accept for changing his mind and staying inside, so she followed him willingly into the chill of the night.

CHAPTER 22

Marina woke in the room above the depot with frustration still rolling in her belly. She flipped over and punched the pillow, imagining Reed's face. There was only one thing Marina could think of to do with her feelings over how the evening of the Jubilee had ended. Go hunting. She did not want company. She wanted—no, she needed—to be alone, and there was only one thing she wanted to hunt. The ladon. If it existed.

Marina took the map Iris had made from the depot and planned her route. The places where the creature had been spotted made a circle around the valley. She decided to start at the northern-most point, the Neal farm, and wanted to work her way around. All the sightings were reported to Iris from Remnants, so Marina felt no misgivings about showing up in her full harpy at the Neal farm.

The flight across the valley gave her time to box up her feelings about the Jubilee. While the kisses were as scorching as she could have wanted, the conversation afterwards had brought home all the reasons that Reed was not the man she should choose. Marina did not think she was ready for respectability. She wanted to see where her feelings for Reed would take her, but she knew emotions could not change reality. She could have one daughter. Reed wanted a family, a large, respectable family. Marina could not supply either of those things for him.

The Neal homestead came into view, and Marina shoved the unresolved situation with Reed away. She landed in the yard and waited to change into her mortal form until the moment Mr. Neal and two of his sons poured out of the door. They got a good look at the monster in their yard before she changed. Of course, her mortal form was armed to the teeth, so in either form, she was dangerous. Mr. Neal carried a gun loosely at his side. Marina used a trickle of her power to feel out the three of them. They were all Remnants, but not powerful. The eldest Neal stiffened at the intrusion.

"Good morning, Mistress Harpy. What can we do for you this fine day?" His tone was casual, but Marina knew what the undercurrent in his tone meant. It said, "This is my farm and I expect you to be civil on it even if you can rip me to shreds."

"I'm here on official business, more or less. I'm not here to cause trouble." She smiled in what she hoped was a non-threatening way. "Iris passed along some information to me. She said you and one of your boys saw something on your land a couple weeks ago. I'd like to talk to you about that."

Mr. Neal relaxed and nodded. "Sure thing." He turned to the shortest boy. "Go fetch Martin and bring him here." The boy ran off. "Can I offer you some coffee? The pot is still hot."

Marina nodded. She had missed having coffee with Reed this morning. Missed was not the right word. She had deliberately skipped that part of her morning routine because she was deliberately avoiding Reed. Mr. Neal disappeared inside and returned with a steaming cup of dark coffee. Marina sniffed it. It smelled burnt, and she sipped it cautiously. It tasted terrible. She drank it anyway. She would rather be here than on Reed's porch, regardless of the bad coffee.

"I saw your knife throwing at the Jubilee yesterday. You have a fine hand, girl." She had never in her life been called girl. She sipped the coffee and decided she couldn't care less.

"Thank you, Mr. Neal," Marina said. The remaining boy was staring at her. "Do you have a question for me?"

"Is it true that you killed a Nemean Lion and a hydra?"

"Joseph." Mr. Neal's voice was sharp.

Marina waved him off. "No, the boy's fine." She placed one knee on the ground. "I did do both those things. I didn't listen to my friend and went alone to hunt the lion. I wrestled him for what seemed like hours. He tore up my belly, and I almost didn't make it home. I thought my guts would spill out for sure." Joseph's eyes were like saucers. "I remembered the lesson, and next time I took my friends with me to hunt. We went looking for a hydra. We worked together and none of us were hurt too badly, even though the hydra spit poison and had *nine* heads."

"What are you hunting today?" the boy asked.

Marina leaned closer to the boy. He had freckles and clear green eyes. "A ladon, but you probably know it as a dragon."

Joseph cocked his head and looked around the yard behind Marina. "You're by yourself."

Marina winked. "I don't learn lessons well."

Joseph glanced at his father and then leaned in close to Marina. She moved closer still. "I could go with you. I've been practicing with a gun. Pa says I'm getting better."

Marina kept her face straight and nodded as though she was considering it. "That's a fine offer, it is, but I'm not going to do any actual hunting today. This is more of a scouting mission. I'm gathering information for a later day. Tell you what. It would be a great help to me if you would keep an eye out for anything strange around here. There's been some trouble, and we aren't sure what to do about it yet. If you see anything unusual, send a message to me at the depot. Miss Iris will see that I get it."

Joseph nodded. "Yes, ma'am. I will."

Mr. Neal put his hand on his son's shoulder. "Run along now. Your mother is in the back garden. She'll be needing help with the weeds." Joseph ran off, then reappeared from around the corner to wave goodbye. Marina laughed and returned the wave.

"That was uncommonly kind. Thank you," Mr. Neal said.

Marina smiled. "It's no problem. I like kids. He seems like a good boy."

Mr. Neal's other two sons joined them. Mr. Neal made introductions. "Andrew, my oldest here, and I were in the southern pasture, mending a fence when we saw the creature."

"Will you show me the place where you saw it?"

"Follow me."

The fence was a quarter of a mile from the house. Marina turned in a circle, trying to find something important about the area. She did not know anything about a ladon other than what Iris had said the other day. If she had been smart, she would have stayed in town and done some research with Iris first, but being in town meant being near Reed. Her thoughts tangled at the thought of Reed. She shoved everything but the task before her aside.

Mr. Neal pointed. "It was over there in that clump of aspen and brush. It was long, like a snake, but had legs and what looked like wings. It was at least as tall as a grown man."

Marina walked over to the place Mr. Neal indicated. It was not more than one hundred yards from the new section of fence. Two weeks had passed by since it had been spotted, and it was unlikely there was any evidence of the ladon. Marina still looked. Nothing in the small place revealed any secrets. She crouched down to see what was visible from this vantage point. There had to be a reason the ladon had chosen this spot.

"Who saw it first?" Marina asked.

"I did. I was picking up a fence post to hand to Pa, and it moved, just the smallest bit. It was enough. I saw it and it saw me." Andrew kicked a clump of dirt.

Marina rubbed her hands over her thighs and thought. "What color was it?"

"It was light brown with darker spots down its back, like a gopher snake. I never would have seen it, but I think we startled it, and that's when it moved."

Marina turned her body so her left side was facing east. "Was it facing the way I'm standing right now?"

Mr. Neal and Andrew both nodded.

Marina kept her body turned in the right direction and took inventory of all she could see. There was the rest of the pasture with a smattering of cows munching tall grass. The side of the Neal's house was visible through the trees lining the pasture. There was one more thing plainly visible from this angle. Mrs. Neal held a large weed in her hand and was displaying it to Joseph. They bent over together and disappeared from view. In another moment, Mrs. Neal stood up and paused next to her son before moving on with her gathering basket.

"Mr. Neal, I need to ask you a question of a personal nature." Iris had the family listed as Remnants, but either of the Neals could fall under that description. After talking with them, she knew all the males in this household were some flavor of Remnant. Marina had never seen Mrs. Neal except in a crowd and never close enough to know if Mrs. Neal was a Remnant herself. An idea had begun to form in the back of her mind. She wanted to be wrong.

"You can ask, but I may not answer."

"Fair enough." Marina looked back at the garden. Mrs. Neal was plainly visible as she stopped and picked tomatoes and peppers. "Is your wife a Remnant, or do you and your boys have their gift from your line only?"

Andrew opened his mouth, but Mr. Neal silenced his son with a curt look. "My wife is a Remnant."

"I need to ask you one more thing. What line is your wife descended from?"

"Why do you want to know?" Mr. Neal shifted warily.

Marina could compel him into telling her. She knew he was not powerful enough to resist her, but she waited, hoping to undo him with patience.

She was only able to wait a few beats, then asked, "If you don't want to tell me what line she is descended from, would you instead be willing to tell me if your wife was from a powerful or dangerous line?"

Mr. Neal coughed. "Just what in the circles of hell is that supposed to mean?"

Marina backpedaled. "That was worded poorly."

"I'll say," Andrew said. Both Marina and his father leveled him with sharp glares.

"What I mean to ask," Marina said through clenched teeth, "is not if she is a threat, but if can she change into some kind of monster." Mr. Neal looked furious at her use of that word. This was going worse than horrible. If she did not get it under control, Mr. Neal looked ready to come to blows, and, for once, Marina was not in the mood to fight. "A monster, like me. Something that would scare a mortal child at night, or does she have the ability to do something powerful?"

Mr. Neal looked at Marina and then shaded his eyes to better see his wife. She was laughing at something Joseph was saying. He turned his attention back to Marina. "She's a Remnant of the Manticore. My family line comes from a simple mountain ash dryad, a meliai in the old myths. My father always said I'd married above my station."

A manticore was a creature with a lion's body, a scorpion's tail, and the wings of a bat. Mr. Neal had most definitely married into a higher class of Remnant. Unfortunately, it also meant that Marina's hunch was right. Someone was hunting powerful Remnant women. Marina just did not know why.

"I think the ladon sat here for the purpose of watching your wife."

Mr. Neal clenched his jaw. "There's rumors that all the women who have been taken are Remnants. Is that true?"

"They are, and you should keep your wife close for a spell. Don't let her go anywhere unarmed if she does have to be by herself. I would suggest making sure one of the older boys is with her whenever it is impossible for you to be."

"I will do as you say, of course, without question." Mr. Neal's eyes hardened with resolve, his earlier anger at her gaffe forgotten.

Marina was glad she did not have to convince him of the danger. "I'm not saying the creature will be back, but if she were mine, I'd not take the chance."

Mr. Neal nodded. "I appreciate the advice."

"I meant what I said to Joseph. If you see it again or anything at all out of the ordinary, send word to The Messenger. She will make sure I receive it and I will come to your aid." Marina hoped invoking Iris's title would give her words the weight they needed.

"Yes, ma'am."

Marina shook Mr. Neal's hand and nodded in farewell to Andrew before leaving the small homestead.

Marina's next stop was a farm at the base of Silvercliff that was situated south of the Twins. Silvercliff was Dora's mountain, and Marina considered going to see her to enlist her help, but she was not ready to answer the questions she knew Dora would have for her. Dora would ask about Reed, why they had disappeared last night at the Jubilee, and why she had emerged from Reed's office with a chip the size of a mountain on her shoulder. Marina did not have answers for any of those questions, so she went about her business alone.

By the time she landed in front of the modest log cabin at the base of Silvercliff, Marina had done her best to banish Reed from her mind – again. A willowy woman with mouse brown hair answered her knock. Her eyes widened when she saw Marina in her mortal form on her threshold. Marina knew without asking that the woman was a Remnant, and a strong one.

Marina shook hands with the woman. "We've never been formally introduced. I'm Marina Ocypete, deputy in Turning Creek. I'm just here to ask you some questions. Do you have time to talk, Mrs. Eisler?"

"Please, call me Caroline. I do have time. Would you like to stay for tea?" Her broad English accent told Marina she was from the countryside, perhaps an immigrated farmer.

"That would be lovely." Marina would have preferred coffee, but tea would be fine, especially if there were biscuits.

Caroline offered her meat and cheese scones, which crumbled to perfection in Marina's mouth. "These are wonderful. My hands are better suited for things other than cooking. I could never make anything close to these scones."

Caroline beamed with pleasure. The door opened and a man on the other side of one too many of his wife's scones joined them. "George, this is Miss Ocypete, the deputy from town. She's here to talk to us."

He moved into the room and kissed his wife first then shook hands with Marina. "Pleasure to meet you, Missus." His accent also marked him as British. He sat down and Caroline poured him tea and gave him a plate of two scones and a tartlet.

"Call me Marina, please." Marina felt him out and was not surprised to find that he too was a Remnant.

George ate his first scone in two bites. "What do you want to know?"

"How long have you lived in the valley?"

Husband and wife shared a look across the table. George answered. "We felt Zeus's call last year, and by the time the call had faded, we were already well into our journey. We hadn't left that much behind. We were tenant farmers back in England." He reached out and squeezed his wife's hand between his beefy fingers. "We figured we'd take the opportunity to start fresh."

It was a common story in the valley. "Iris, The Messenger, told me you saw something a week ago on your property. Can you tell me what it was?"

George polished off the tartlet in one bite and chewed before speaking. "We were clearing one of our fields to plant next spring. Caroline was with me. I saw something out of the corner of my eye, and when I turned, it fled into the bushes."

Marina was on its trail. The excitement of the hunt entered her blood in trickles, but it was enough to make her palms itch to change into claws. Her tension was too high today. Marina took a deep breath to steady herself. She noticed Caroline had gone still, watching her with wary eyes. She must have been sending out power without realizing it. Marina adjusted the woman's ability level up a notch. "Sorry. Can you describe it to me?"

The creature George described was the same one who had been spying on Mrs. Neal in her garden. Marina would bet the ladon had been here to watch Caroline Eisler. The pattern in the hunt was unmistakable. "Caroline, may I ask you a personal question?"

George stiffened beside his wife, and Caroline nodded.

"Who are you descended from?"

Caroline smiled and her canines grew to points. "I'm a Remnant of Laelaps."

Marina felt a trickle of Caroline's power fill the room. Laelaps was a mythical hound, created by Zeus, who never failed to catch its prey. "It's nice to meet you, Remnant of Laelaps. If you like hunting," Caroline's eyes grew hungry and the urge to hunt hit Marina like a blow, "my sisters and I would love for you to join us sometime."

The wildness took over Caroline's eyes. "I would love to."

The monsters at the table grinned knowingly at each other. Thoughts of the chase and of warm flesh between her talons made Marina shiver. And there would be a hunt, and it was coming soon, because there was a ladon hunting Remnants in her territory and that would not do.

George cleared his throat. He had sunk back in his chair, trying to appear smaller. Whatever he was, Marina thought, he was prey more than predator. Marina forced her harpy out of her eyes and turned to George. "Can you show me the place where you saw the thing?"

"It's in the northwest corner of our land. We can take you there."

"Do you know what it is we saw?" Caroline asked.

"Iris thinks it's a ladon, like a dragon."

"Do you know why it was here?" she asked.

"I can't say for certain, but if I were you, I wouldn't go anywhere alone or unarmed for a while. I think something is hunting Remnant women."

The Eislers nodded. Caroline stood and cleared away the plates. George gathered the cups and placed them on the sideboard. He laid a hand on his wife and rubbed the small of her back. Marina looked down at her hands, unwilling to intrude.

George broke away from his wife. "Let's go, then."

The field was a good twenty minutes from the farmhouse. The skeletons of stumps and boulders dotted the southern edge of the clearing. The rest of the field was bare and ready for planting in the spring. Marina thought of the work it had taken to clear a field for planting and thanked the gods she was not a farmer.

George led her to a thick stand of aspens and scrub brush. The ladon, with its brown and spotted scales, would have been near invisible behind it. Marina walked a circuit around the stand. On the side opposite from the field, there was a gap in the bushes. She walked through it, doubled over to avoid whacking her head on the branches above. The leaves pulled at her hair and shirt, and she slapped the branches away with annoyance.

The center of the stand opened up. There was enough room for Marina to crouch down and turn in any direction. Through the screen of branches, she had a clear view of George and Caroline Eisler standing on the other side of the bushes. She could see the entire field from where she crouched.

An insect buzzed in her ear and she batted it away. Marina rubbed her knees and thought. If she were hunting Caroline Eisler, she would have sat here and watched for a few days, waiting for an opportunity. The ladon had not made a move on either Mrs. Neal or Caroline, which meant the ladon had not found the right opportunity. Marina suspected the right opportunity was a storm to cover up whatever the ladon was doing with the women.

By the time Marina and the Eislers had walked back to their farmhouse, the sun had dipped below the peaks of the western mountains. Marina took her leave of the couple and flew into the air. Home was on the opposite side of the valley. A flight would clear her head, but she did not want to go home. Dora was closer and, despite her earlier wish to avoid her sister, Marina flew up the side of Silvercliff towards the comfort she knew Dora would offer. With a sudden urgency, Marina wanted very much to go flying with her sisters.

Dora was in her herb garden when Marina landed behind her house. Dora's hands were black with dirt, and there was a smudge on her cheek. She greeted Marina with a smile. Marina's blood was still up from the conversation with Caroline and the flight. Dora's smile widened, and Marina saw awareness shift in her eyes.

Marina did not bother changing. "Want to go flying?"

Dora stood and wiped her hands on her skirt. "Let's eat first before we get the others."

The moon was high in the night sky by the time Marina, Iris, and Dora landed in the yard on the Lloyd ranch.

"Should I go in like this?" Marina hopped around on her harpy legs.

Dora cackled. "If you do, make sure to wake up James first and see how high he jumps."

"Gods, help me. Dora, I usually count on you for some gravity. Don't encourage Marina. I'll go wake Petra. You two crows stay out here." Iris tucked her golden wings close to her body and went into the house.

Before Petra had known James well, she had spent nights chasing his dairy cows into a lather. Marina wondered if they could get away with chasing the cows tonight. Petra had said they made a satisfying bellowing noise when they were chased over the valley, and Marina needed the satisfaction of scaring something tonight.

Iris emerged from the house and opened her wings the moment she was through the door. Petra was on her heels and bouncing with excitement. "Good evening, sisters. Are we hunting or flying?"

Dora deferred to Marina. "Flying." The call to hunt was strong, but Marina wanted to give her energy a less violent outlet for once.

Petra changed and spread her wings, stretching them out and over her head. "James said to stay away from the cows."

"Spoilsport," Marina grumbled.

Petra laughed. "He is, but I don't want to herd up the cows tomorrow either, so if you do decide to chase my cows, I'll have your tail feathers."

Marina flashed her teeth at Petra. "You'll have to catch me first, old lady." She shot into the air. Marina was faster than either Dora or Petra, but she heard Petra screech as her sister accepted the challenge and chased after her.

Marina flew as straight up as she was able, then leveled off and flew east towards the Twins. She thought she had lost Petra until something large hit her in the back. She felt Petra's talons brush the muscles between her shoulders without breaking the skin as Petra pushed off and flew away, cackling.

"I taught you that move." Marina flapped her wings in rapid succession to steady her flight and looked around. Dora was just behind her, and the golden gleam of Iris's wings gave The Messenger's location away to her right.

Petra had knocked her close to the ground. Marina scanned it, searching for movement that would give away the hiding location for something small, scared, and furry. Her hunt did not last long, and she rose in triumph with a fat opossum dripping the last of its life to the ground below. Opossums were not great to eat, but Marina had a different plan for this kill.

Marina flew beside Petra and continued beside her without speaking. Without warning, Marina moved the limp body of the opossum from her talons to the claw on the end of her wing. She lost altitude immediately and threw the bloody body. It smacked Petra in the face with a soft splat. Petra let loose a hideous screech as she flapped and tried to grab at what had hit her. She tumbled towards the ground in a mess of feathers and furious harpy.

Moments before she would have crashed into the ground, Petra righted herself and landed on the body of the opossum. Marina was laughing so hard she tumbled to the ground and rolled in the dirt, unable to breathe. Dora and Iris dropped to the earth beside the two cackling harpies.

"What is wrong with you two?"

"'Possum," Marina wheezed, and Petra collapsed again in gales of laughter.

Iris shook her head. "'Possum?"

Petra waved the bloody carcass in Iris's face. Marina hiccupped with laughter. Petra said, "I think its dead."

"Gods, you two have lost your minds." Iris smiled at them like errant children.

The weight Marina had been carrying slipped away with her laughter. She loved her sisters and Iris. If nothing else, she had this, and this was enough for her to be content.

"I have an idea. Let's go." Petra launched back into the sky.

"Why do I get the feeling this is not an idea I'll like?" Iris spread her wings and followed the three harpies.

"Iris, you be the referee," Petra called then threw the bloody carcass at Dora, who caught it midair.

"Marina," Dora called and threw the dead opossum as high in the air as she could.

Marina flipped through the air, diving and snatching the opossum before it hit the ground. In one smooth movement, she tossed it back to Petra.

"I declare you all out of bounds." Iris laughed at them and stayed out of the fray.

The harpies played opossum-ball until the sliver of moon hung high in the sky, and Marina's earlier tension dissipated into the dark raucousness of the night.

CHAPTER 23

The next day, Marina flew to the location of the most recent sighting in the southern part of the valley by Lady's Favor. This report had come from Reggie Miller, who had seen the original chimera weeks ago. He had stopped to water his horse in the river that flowed from the Lady down into the valley on his way to town. *Poor Reggie,* Marina thought, *he probably thinks he is going crazy.*

Marina started upstream, almost to the Gerlich farm, and followed the river down into the valley. She flew the circuit three times and found nothing. There were no other farms in the vicinity. The ladon had most likely been traveling through the area to somewhere else, possibly to the Eisler's farm to the northeast.

Marina landed beside the river and changed into her mortal form. The water of the river was ice cold and quenched her parched throat. She drank her fill and sat on a sun-warmed rock. With the sun on her face, Marina closed her eyes and made a mental list of what she knew.

All of the sightings of monsters and disappearances had occurred in the south and southeast part of the valley except for one. Katherine Johnson had vanished from her home on Jolly's Folly in the north corner of the valley. Marina had killed the Nemean Lion on Baldy, which hunched in the southwest corner. The lion had been in the right region of the valley, but Marina did not think it was connected to the ladon or the chimera. The lion had been dead before Lily or Atlanta had been taken and before the Gerlichs had been attacked.

In the past two months, Marina had, for one reason or another, hunted or searched every mountain in the area except one. Shaker's Way was directly south of Turning Creek. The wide base of the mountain culminated in a jagged peak that reached higher than its fellows to the right or left. It also happened to be where the Nasso family lived. Marina thought it was time she paid the Nassos a visit at their house.

The Nasso homestead sat just below the tree line on the mountain. It was at a higher altitude than most families would have chosen. The family had not been here long, but they had been industrious with their time. The fields surrounding the house had been terraced off for spring planting. A full-sized barn sat behind the house. Marina spotted two men working in a clearing far from the house. There was no other movement.

The moment Marina's talons dug into the yard in front of the house, a mastiff launched itself off the porch, barking and dripping saliva. Marina held her ground. She bared her teeth at the dog and hissed, which was usually enough to make anything cower. The hackles of the dog stood up as it crouched down and growled in a low rumble.

Marina did not move, but she stayed with teeth bared. If she moved first, the dog would launch itself at her, and so she stayed and maintained eye contact. Another dog, even larger than the first one, came around the corner of the house, alerted by the noise. Marina swept her eyes between the two mutts. If they charged, she would fly up. She did not think she could fight both dogs and come out uninjured.

The door of the house opened, and Marina flicked her eyes in that direction to see who had joined them. It was Mrs. Nasso. Marina kept her eyes on the dogs and waited to see what the woman would do.

"That's enough, you two mutts." The dogs backed down and went to stand beside the woman. The first dog continued to growl from behind her skirt.

"What do you want?" Mrs. Nasso's voice matched the hardened steel color of her hair.

Marina had been prepared to be neighborly. The woman's demeanor vaporized Marina's desire to have a friendly chat, and she did not change into her mortal form. She was more vulnerable in that form, and her senses cautioned her; the two dogs were not the only predators nearby. "I was in the area and wanted to check in on things."

"We don't need coddling, girl. We can take care of ourselves."

Mr. Neal had called her girl with affection. This woman used it as an insult, and the challenge in the words brought the violence in her blood to a head. Mrs. Nasso had been quiet at the Jubilee. Her confrontational reaction to Marina's appearance ticked Marina's suspicions up a notch.

Marina ruffled her wings. "I'm here to ask questions only. I'd appreciate it if you remained civil."

"What's going on, Mother?" Pearl stepped out of the house onto the porch. The larger dog moved to stand in front of the girl. She pushed him out of the way with her knee and continued to walk towards Marina. The dog growled and snapped at her heels. Pearl smacked the dog across the nose. It shook itself and backed off.

Marina's earlier assessment of the young sphinx had been right. She would be powerful when she was full grown. "Good day to you, Pearl. I was just having a friendly chat with your mother."

Pearl cast a frown over her shoulder at her mother. "I'm sorry for the lack of welcome. We aren't used to visitors."

"So I see." Marina stared down the mastiff hovering behind Pearl.

"Would you like something to drink?" Pearl asked.

"The deputy was just leaving." Mrs. Nasso put her hands on her hips. One of the dogs started growling again.

"I think it's best if I don't stay long, but thank you for your kind offer." Marina paused to hiss at the smaller mastiff. "I want to ask your family some questions, and then I'll be on my way."

"Of course. I'd be happy to talk with you," Pearl said. The mother harrumphed and stomped back into the house. Pearl turned to face the dogs. "Go inside with mother." The smaller, tan mastiff obeyed. The large, dark one stopped in the open doorway and sat down.

Marina raised the feathers of her neck. "If you prefer, I'll change and we can talk, but I don't trust your dogs to behave if I change into my mortal form."

Pearl nodded. "Excuse me." She turned and stomped up the stairs to the porch. Using her knees, she shoved the mastiff back into the doorway and slammed the door in its face.

Marina heard the dog scratching the door from the inside. She laughed and changed, her voice going from broken glass to human woman in a flash. "Thank you."

Pearl blushed. "I'm sorry about my family. What questions do you have?"

Marina told her about the ladon sightings, the hydra, the Nemean Lion, and the chimera. "You're a strong, young Remnant. I'm concerned the recent sightings have something to do with the missing women in the valley. Have you or anyone else in your family seen or heard anything?"

As Pearl listened to Marina's explanation, a line appeared between her eyes. She frowned and twisted her skirt between her fingers. "Things have been quiet here. Father says this is the best land he's ever seen. Nothing unusual has been around here that I know of." Her eyes darted towards the barn standing next to the house.

Marina's senses went into overdrive. The girl was nervous. Marina let her own power flow from her and into her words. "Have you seen any of the creatures I mentioned?"

Pearl blinked and opened her mouth, and then she pressed her lips together. Marina could almost see the cloak of power surround the sphinx as she fought off the compulsion in Marina's words. "No, I've not seen anything out of the ordinary."

Marina straightened and started wrapping her own power around her in thick waves. She felt the violence and call to blood rush through her. She let it come with joy, and she let Pearl see all of it in her eyes. "I know you're lying."

Pearl met her stare head on. "You asked for an answer to your questions, and I gave one to you. I'm sorry it was not the answer you wanted." The girl ran her hands over her skirt and for a moment she looked like a young girl.

Marina dropped her voice and flashed her teeth in menace. "I was hoping for the truth."

Pearl looked at the barn again, deliberately. "I'm sorry, Marina. I like you, but I've told you all I can. Everything is fine here."

All she can, Marina thought. *Not all she knows.* It was not an admission, but the girl was seeking to be honest while still concealing the truth. There was a reason why the girl would or could not tell Marina the truth. Perhaps the girl herself was in some kind of trouble. If the trouble was dire, Marina thought Pearl would ask for help now. Marina swept her eyes over the yard, not lingering on the barn, but trying to remember as many details as possible. She wanted to get into that barn.

Marina backed down. "I understand." Marina flicked her eyes to the house and back, giving Pearl a pointed look. "I like you too, Pearl. I hope this means we can talk again sometime."

Pearl smiled until a dimple appeared in one check. "I'd like that."

Marina looked at the house again. "Why don't you stop into the depot or the sheriff's office next time you're in town and we can have a chat, just the two of us. Come as soon as you can."

"That sounds good. Thank you for understanding."

Marina changed and spread her wings. "Thank you for your honesty. If you need anything, you will find help easily enough. For a while, don't go anywhere alone or unarmed."

Pearl waved goodbye and walked into the house. There was no doubt the girl knew something and had been trying to tell her something while assuring her all was well. Marina could only hope she would find the time and courage to confess what she knew while it would still do them some good. Marina did not think Pearl was in any danger. The sphinx could look after herself, regardless of the strange dynamics of her family.

It was time for Marina to share what she had discovered. Marina flew straight north towards Turning Creek and the man she had been avoiding for two days.

CHAPTER 24

Marina flew to the edge of town and ate the ground up in quick steps after she changed. She passed by the depot without pausing. Simon waved at her from the front window of the mercantile. She returned the greeting but did not stop. She focused on her purpose and shoved her thoughts about the night of the Jubilee aside.

"Reed," she called as she opened the door. His desk was empty. Marina took the stairs two at a time and almost collided with Claire. "Sorry, I'm looking for Reed."

"He's not here. I think he's at the depot with Iris. He's been looking for you since the Jubilee."

Marina turned to go back down the stairs. Claire's hand on her shoulder stopped her forward momentum. "Wait, Marina. What happened that night?"

Memories washed over Marina. Memories she had been forcing into a small, hidden place. Reed's body flush against hers. The feel of his hands on her body. The way the sound of his laugh made her toes curl in. Marina knew her face was turning red. "Nothing happened."

Claire crossed her arms over her chest. "You're lying. He's been like a bear in a trap the last two days, snapping and growling at everyone. Something happened, and I think that something was you."

Fury rose its head, and Marina sought to pull it back. Claire was not the person she should skewer with her anger. She could not keep it from her words though. "It doesn't matter what the something was now."

Claire stepped closer to her and ran a hand over the curls framing her face. "Where did this grey come from? Don't tell me my brother scared you so much your hair turned grey?"

Claire said the words lightly. They landed like lead ore in Marina's gut and churned there. "You were wrong about what he needs. It'll never be me." Marina fled down the stairs before Claire could stop her again.

She sought to pull her fury under control before she reached the depot. Anger was a familiar friend she understood. It was all the other emotion pounding through her that she did not comprehend well. Marina knew she was in no state to see Reed, but she had to tell him about what she had discovered and learned while retracing the ladon's movements.

Iris and Reed looked up when she opened the door to the depot with more force than was strictly necessary.

"There you are. I was hoping you'd come to town today." Iris was nonplussed by the anger radiating off her. "We were just talking about you."

Reed's gaze focused in on her. "Where've you been?"

"Playing 'possum," Marina snapped. Iris laughed and Reed deflated in confusion. Marina took a breath to steady her nerves. She stood beside Reed at the counter, keeping a space between them. "You were talking about me? Should I be worried or flattered?"

Reed shifted his weight. His eyes searched her face and hesitated on her hairline. "A bit of both, maybe. We can talk later after you tell me where you've been."

Marina smoothed her hair behind her ear, knowing that the grey was more visible. Her frustration bloomed. "I was checking the places in the valley that Iris said the ladon had been sighted. I think I found something."

Reed tensed. "What?"

Marina revealed what she had found on the Neals' farm. She laid out her theory that something was taking the women because they were powerful Remnants. None of the people taken or attacked had been minor Remnants with little or no power, and none of them had been mortals.

"What do they want the women for?" Reed rubbed his neck with his hand.

Marina shook her head. "I haven't worked that part out yet. There's something else, though." Marina told them about her strange welcome at the Nasso farm and her conversation with Pearl. "I think she knows something and wants to tell us."

"You don't think she's in any danger, do you?" Iris asked.

Marina tapped a finger on the counter. "I don't think so. She is capable of taking care of herself and her family will certainly protect her from whatever is in the hills. Unless they are the monster in the hills."

Reed turned his attention back to the papers on the counter. Marina looked down at them for the first time. There were maps of the town, lists of businesses, and the census papers she and Reed had drawn up after their rounds a month ago.

"The Territory Committee will be here tomorrow. I need you to be here when they arrive." Reed angled his body so he faced her instead of the counter.

"I want to go keep an eye on the Nasso place. Something's going on there. I want to know what it is." Marina moved her body to mirror Reed's.

"That can wait, Marina. The committee's visit is important for the town. They expect you to be here." The vein in his forehead was jumping. He was annoyed with her. *Good,* she thought.

"The Nassos are hiding something or Pearl knows something. It might be related. I think we need to go now. Women are disappearing." The fury was back and Marina was losing her grip on it.

"You think I don't know that? That I don't lay awake at night and wonder how the hell I'm going to protect my town from an enemy I can't find, don't understand, and against which I'm powerless? Just because the Nassos' dogs barked at you and Pearl lied does not mean they're doing anything wrong. They could be guilty of nothing more than wanting to keep a mine on their land a secret."

"Well, last time someone tried to keep a mine a secret in this valley, that turned out jolly for everyone."

"Dammit, Marina, that's not what I meant."

"I know what you meant. You don't trust me. Something is wrong, Reed. I know it. I want to go stake out their property." Marina inched into his space.

Reed did not back down and his voice went up in volume. "And I want you here. For the love of all that's holy, could you, for once in your miserable life, just put someone else first and be useful instead of chasing every shiny thing you see? The Nassos can wait. I don't want to ruin months of work for the Territory Committee because you have a damn hunch."

Iris waved a hand at them. "You both need to calm down."

Marina glared at Iris. "Stay out of this," she hissed. Marina felt her teeth grow pointy and knew it was her harpy looking out of her eyes. She turned her predatory gaze on Reed, who met her stare without blinking. If she were not so furious with him, she would have taken a moment to appreciate his backbone.

"I'm going to the Nasso farm with or without you."

"One day, Marina. That's all I'm asking. Wait one damn day, and then we can go hunt whatever you want. You're sore about the Jubilee, and you're taking it out on me now."

White-hot anger burned through her. "You're right. I am angry about the Jubilee, but I'm also mad that you aren't listening to me. We need to go. Today."

"No, we don't. It can wait. Please, Marina. Give me a single day. I don't want you to go alone."

"You have no right to order me around. I'm going, and you can go burn in the inner circle of hell. By the Styx, I hope you rot there." Marina heard Iris gasp at her use of the oath. She could see nothing but the red haze of her fury.

"Fine. Go chase your damn monsters in the mountains. I hope they rip you to shreds." His voice was low with bitterness and anger.

Marina sucked in a breath and found she could not speak. She dared a look at Iris before she left. Her face was pale and her blue eyes were large and filled with pain. Marina stomped out of the depot, barely reaching the edge of Main Street before she released her harpy. With a furious yell, she beat the wind with her wings and flew home.

Marina's fury gave her speed an extra boost. She saw the roof of her cabin appear before the heat of the argument had left her. She did not want to start the hunt on the Nassos' land rippling with fury, so she kept flying. She flew through Newlywed's Pass, around Atlas's Peak, and back around to Jolly's Folly.

The smell of pine and cedar was strong on the cool wind. By the time she landed in her own yard, the crisp night air had given her argument with Reed time to settle in her mind. It was not, she realized, a new argument between them. He was right that she did not like to listen. He was wrong about the most crucial point, the one that had dug into her heart and bled her dry during her flight.

The cabin was dark and smelled musty. She had been away too often. After this business with the Nassos was concluded, Marina would turn in her badge and resign as deputy. She was tired of trying to be something she was not. She was good at being a monster, she thought, but she tangled up everything else. Marina lit a candle and walked over to her small mirror. Her lips thinned when she saw her reflection.

There were too many to pull out now. A swath of silver hair swept from the middle of her forehead and back into her brown curls. She had never imagined that Reed held her and her motivations in such contempt. He thought she was a selfish monster bent only on her own desire for violence. While he was not completely wrong, as she was a monster who loved violence, she was also a harpy who loved her family and her town above all things. Gods help her, she loved him too. It was too late to change his feelings or hers. It was not too late to do what she knew was right.

Marina packed her satchel with enough food for three days. After that, she would forage something or come home. She put knives in her boots, strapped the sword on her back, and put an extra dagger in her belt. She found her gun and some extra ammunition and threw that in the bag. Guns were too loud for what she intended, however, she would be nothing if not prepared. Marina took her heavier duster from its peg. It would be cold, and she was planning on sleeping outside for the next few days.

Her beaten leather badge lay on the table where she had dropped it after coming in from her flight. Its worn surface was dark in the candlelight. Marina could just make out the words 'Turning Creek, Colorado Territory' on it. Before she could change her mind, she slipped it into her pocket, blew a puff of air on the candle, and went out to hunt.

***

The moon gave off enough light for Marina to get a good view of the Nasso land as she circled the house and outlying area. She passed over multiple times, looking for movement and the right place to sit and watch without being seen. There was no movement on the ground below, except for a family of rabbits startled by her flight overhead. Marina found just the place to sit on her sixth circuit over the property. A jumble of boulders and pines perched up the mountain from the Nasso house that could give her cover from three directions and a clear view of the house and the barn. At the moment, it was downwind of the house. She hoped it stayed that way or else the dogs would be on her. Marina flew down to the spot, changed into her mortal form, and settled in for a long night and day.

Marina dozed until sunrise, then kept a watchful eye on the house and its inhabitants. She had chosen well. She saw Pearl and her mother come out, feed the chickens, and work in the kitchen garden behind the house. Once during the day, Pearl took a basket of something into the barn. The sphinx came out a short time later with the basket still slung over her arm. She could have been gathering eggs or doing any number of chores. Marina still made a note to take a peek into the barn once night fell.

The males of the Nasso family were noticeably absent most of the day. Mr. Nasso, Claude, Billy, Chris, and the tan dog from her previous visit had left the house after breakfast. The sun was past its zenith, but it was not too close to the mountain peaks. Marina thought, from the men's heading, they had gone to the outlying field with the terraces. If she was careful, she could circle around the field and take a gander at the Nasso men.

There were five men working in the field when she approached downwind. Mr. Nasso and Claude were chopping a stump. Olen, Billy, and Chris were using a horse to remove boulders. Marina saw no trace of the tan mastiff. Her eyes swung back to the trio with the horse and boulders. She had seen four men this morning, but there were five in the field. Olen was leading the horse, and Marina gave his shaggy, tan-colored hair a closer look. Olen had not been with the other men this morning. Something else had left the house with them.

"Oh, hells." Marina muttered. She had little doubt Olen was the mastiff from her previous visit. She would bet one of the men before her was also the dark-colored mastiff. Marina racked her memory and tried to think what myth involved a large dog. She could only think of Cerberus, the three-headed dog who guarded the underworld. None of the dogs she had seen on the farm had more than one head. Of course, generations of

192

interbreeding with mortals did tend to lessen the power and manifestation of some Remnant lines. *If one of the Nasso brothers is Cerberus, what are the others?* Marina wondered.

A twinge of regret twisted her middle. Perhaps Reed had been right, though he had been a jerk about it. She was outnumbered and should not have come alone. Marina backed out of her cover with care and made a wide circle to go back to her perch by the house and barn. She would stay one more night, then, if nothing happened, she would go back into town. She huddled in her hiding spot and waited.

Pearl meandered up the hill towards Marina's hiding place. If the girl got too close, she would be able to sense Marina's presence. Pearl bent over to pick a flower and twirled it between her fingers. She sat on the ground, not fifty feet from Marina, and drew her knees up to chest. Marina scarcely breathed.

The only explanation Marina could muster was that Pearl was too young to be overly cautious. Pearl never looked her way. The young sphinx's back curled away from the harpy, exposed and vulnerable. The girl needed to learn awareness. If Marina had meant her harm, she could have killed Pearl before the sphinx even knew what she was about.

"Pearl. Dinner's ready. Go get Father and the boys." Mrs. Nasso's voice carried up the mountain. Pearl sighed, brushed off her skirt, and went to fetch her father and brothers.

Something savory accompanied by the yeasty smell of bread wafted up to where Marina sat wedged between the rocks. Marina ate her stale bread and apple and tried to imagine it was chicken dumplings or beef stew with rolls. Night fell and Marina settled in for another cold and uneventful night. The lights in the cabin winked off, and Marina found herself dozing off.

She woke with a jolt. The hairs on her arm were standing on end and her senses were screaming. She was being stalked. She hunched deeper into the cleft between the rocks and pulled her essence in tightly, trying to hide.

"I wondered when I would see you again, darlin'." The male voice cut through the night with menace. Marina's lips curled at the sound of Claude's voice.

Marina pulled the leather disk from her pocket and wedged it into the rock before standing up. She prayed to the gods she would be the one to retrieve it after she broke Claude's neck. If something did happen to her, Petra or Dora would find it. Marina wanted to think Reed would come looking for her, but she did not think he would forgive her harsh words anytime soon.

Marina let her power leak from her in waves. She did not want to go wherever Claude wanted to take her, and she wanted him to know she would not go without a fight. Marina pulled a knife from her boot and stood. The bulk of Claude Nasso stood less than ten feet from her hiding place. He was joined by Billy.

"I was just passing through and stopped to get a few hours' sleep. I hope it's not a problem." Marina stood and stretched, flashing the knife in the light of the moon. No sense in hiding the fact she was armed and willing to fight.

"If it's a place of sleep you wanted, I would have invited you into my bed." Claude's hands shifted to his hips and one hand rested lightly on the gun there.

Marina took a guess as to which brother was the dark-colored mastiff. "You'll pardon me if I say no. I'm not in the habit of sleeping with mutts."

That got a chuckle. "I don't think you're in a position to be picky, little harpy." A crunch of leaves broke the quiet behind her.

Marina looked back and saw the other two brothers behind her. She cursed her foolishness. Claude had distracted her while his brothers surrounded her. Four strong predators. With a start, she realized one of them she had felt before. Now that there were fewer people around, she could sense his familiar presence. The chimera. Claude and Billy in front with Olen and Chris, the chimera, behind her. The odds were not horrible, but she might come out of the fight looking worse than normal.

Marina let her harpy show in her voice. "A lady can always be picky. I see you've brought backup. Afraid of me?" Her teeth elongated to points. The anger of the previous day rose up and she wanted nothing more than to sink her teeth into the neck of Claude Nasso.

Claude's laugh had an edge to it that danced up Marina's skin like ants. "Not afraid, but prepared. We Nassos have survived by our wits, and we have emerged as the most powerful Remnant family of the age."

Marina twirled her knives. "I hear words coming out of your mouth, but the only ones I understand are the ones that sound like you're making excuses instead of fighting."

Marina considered her options. If she changed and flew away, Claude was standing close and would likely have enough time to draw his gun and shoot her. She was fast and could take a chance that he was a terrible shot, but she'd rather not gamble on that. Claude wanted her alive, not dead. He may not shoot at all. Marina thought she could throw her knife before he had time to draw his gun and aim at her. That would leave her with two knives, a sword, and her wits. They would be on her before she could draw any of her remaining weapons.

Marina sensed the other two moving in. If she were going to act, it would have to be now. Marina flipped the knife to her left hand and drew her sword with the right. The sound it made coming out of the scabbard bolstered her resolve.

Claude laughed again. "Little harpy, those knives won't do you a bit of good."

"We'll see how useless you think they are when I am removing your head from your body." Marina checked. The two brothers behind her had not come any closer.

"That ain't gonna happen," Claude said.

Marina tightened her grip on the hilt and bunched her muscles, ready to spring. "What makes you think that?"

"Because Olen has perfect aim and he's got a rock."

Something large hit her temple, and she dropped onto all fours on the ground. Grey spots floated in front of her eyes. Marina shook her head. The movement caused one of her arms to crumple underneath her weight, and her face crashed into the rocky ground. Her knife and sword clattered from her hands. She tried to move her arms, but everything was grey in her vision. She had to change and fly away.

"Not so fast, little harpy. We don't want you to fly the coop."

"Too bad for you, I've an exceedingly thick skull," Marina rasped.

"I'm counting on it." Marina was lying on her side. Her vision cleared enough to see the boot coming for her head. Her body did not obey her orders to move. The boot came slowly, like it was happening to someone else. Marina yelled at herself to move but nothing worked. She heard the crack of the boot as it hit her head. A blinding flash of pain was truncated by a black release.

<h1 style="text-align:center">CHAPTER 25</h1>

The copper smell of blood mixed with the pervasive odor of damp earth. There was a constant throbbing in her temple that echoed the rhythm of her heart. Marina shifted and heard the clank of metal. Her wrists were heavy.

In a rush, she remembered Claude's boot and sat up. Stars filled her vision, and her stomach did a flip. She lay back and moaned. She lifted a hand to feel the throbbing epicenter on her head and something cold and heavy hit her in the face. Marina cracked open an eye and saw nothing but blackness. She used her fingers to feel the heavy metal on her wrists. There was a matching circle on her neck.

"Hades hounds, I'm going to kill them. They put me in *chains*." Marina yelled the last word, and her head throbbed in protest. Her anger almost rode over the pain, almost.

There was a feminine chuckle to her left. "Hello, harpy. Always ready to kill something. Welcome to the party."

Marina spoke without moving. "Atlanta, please tell me you have a brilliant plan for escape, now that I'm here to back you up."

"Please tell me you brought a drink with you. Those idiots think I can live on water and milk alone."

The alto of the huntress's voice calmed the running tempo of Marina's heart. "How long was I passed out?" The blow to her head might have killed a mortal. Marina's head would be fine in a few hours. If she could change into her harpy form, she could speed up the process.

"Couple hours, though it's hard to judge time down here."

Marina took a deep breath, and the pain in her head lessened enough for her to sit up. She lifted a hand to touch her head again and the chain jerked her other arm. She said a nasty word under her breath.

"If it makes you feel any better, they only chained my hands after I tried to poke Olen's eyes out with my fingers. Yours, they did right away. They must think you're dangerous." Marina could hear the smile in Atlanta's voice.

Without opening her eyes, Marina reached down to see if they had confiscated the knives in her boots, her hands met the end of pant leg and her socks before meeting a manacle on her right foot. "Hells, they took my boots and chained my leg." Marina had expected the knives to be gone, but not her boots.

Marina opened her eyes and strained to find any sliver of light by which to see. Marina sniffed the air again. "Are we underground?"

"From the smell, I think we're below the barn," Atlanta said.

Marina sniffed again and detected the warm smell of hay, manure, and animals. She remembered Pearl going into the barn with a basket. "I think you're right." Marina heard a cough from her right. "Who else is down here?"

"Lily Hughes. How's your head? Atlanta said it looked awful when they brought you in."

The list she had been staring at for weeks swam before her eyes. "I heal fast. I'll be good as new in a couple hours. Is Katherine Johnson here as well?"

"I am," came the reply from farther to her left.

The darkness was so thick the voices and sounds seemed to float from nowhere before reaching her ears. It made her feel off kilter.

"I hate being right," Marina mumbled. For a brief instance, she wished Reed were here to bask in her genius while she gloated. Of course, he had also been right about her not coming alone. Again. "Have they said why they have put us here?" A quiet sob came from Lily's direction. A finger of fear and rage trickled down Marina's spine.

Katherine answered. "We're brood mares. They want us to bear powerful Remnant children to restore the glory of their family from the times of Olympus."

Some of Claude's words came back to her. Marina asked, "Just who are the Nassos, anyway?"

"Tyler and Edna Nasso are the Remnants of Typhon and Echidna. In the old myths, Echidna bore seven monstrous children, just like the charming Mrs. Edna Nasso." Atlanta shifted, and Marina heard her chains clink together.

"Thanks for putting down two of them, by the by. They were frothing at the mouth after you and the others killed Logan, the hydra. I heard you also killed the Nemean Lion. His name was Frank," Katherine said.

With a twist, Marina wished Iris were here. "I'm not sure I remember what monsters Typhon and Echidna created. Anyone up on their myths?"

Katherine answered. "We are now. Orthus, the two-headed hound; the

Sphinx; the Nemean Lion; Cerberus, the three-headed guard dog to Hades; the Ladon; the Lernean Hydra; and the Chimera. Olen is the hound. Frank was the lion. Pearl is the sphinx. Claude is Cerberus. Billy is the ladon. You killed Logan the hydra. Chris is the chimera."

"Styx and fire," Marina breathed. Gods, her head ached.

"That about sums up my feelings as well," Atlanta quipped.

"Why do they need us if they already have a brood of monster children?" Marina drew her knees up to her face. Even though she could not see them, their proximity gave her some comfort.

"They believe the gods have blessed them as the reincarnation of the original myths of their name and it's their duty to sire children upon the most powerful Remnants they can find to continue their lines." Katherine's voice held the enthusiasm of a child recalling memorized material.

Marina cleared her throat. "You sound well informed."

A snort sounded in the dark. "Olen likes me the best, and he likes to talk, after. About himself mostly. He thinks I'm going to see the light and decide to stay with him after I produce the wanted child." There was little hurt or bitterness in her voice, and Marina wondered what Andy Johnson had done to make his wife so disconnected from her feelings.

"Oh, I doubt they plan on keeping us around once we've produced the children they want. We're too much trouble." Atlanta was smiling. Marina could hear it.

"So they want to rape us until we get pregnant, steal our babies, and then kill us." Marina thought if she'd wanted to start her own family of monsters, it was not the worst plan ever. It was, however, a monstrously evil plan.

"That sums it up. Lucky us," Katherine said.

Lily sobbed. "How can you three joke like that?"

"I expect if we didn't, we'd start screaming and not stop," Marina said in a gentle tone. "What did they do?" she asked the dark.

Lily cried her heartbreak into the room. Atlanta spoke. "They beat her at first to keep her eyes sealed. Wouldn't do to let her mesmerize her way out of her cell. Eventually, they decided to keep her eyes covered. Edna was afraid the repeated beatings would permanently damage Lily's eyes. She wanted to be able to use Lily's Medusa ability if the need arose."

"Like I would ever do anything for those...bastards." Lily's voice was thick but strong. "It's not the mask I hate. It's the other thing. I love my husband. How can I go back to him after this? What if I go back carrying a child? What if I never go back at all?"

"You'll get back. We all will. Reed and the other harpies will find us." Marina lifted her head and found the throbbing had receded.

"How do you know? I've been here two months or so. Lily about a month. Atlanta a week or more. It's hard to keep track. How come you never found us before this?" Katherine asked.

"They were clever. They took each of you during a storm so there was no trail to follow. We didn't know what we were looking for. I told Reed and Iris I was coming here. They'll look here first. They'll find us." Marina wondered how long Reed would fume after she missed the meeting with the Territory Committee before coming to look for her. How long after that until thought to look here? Two days? A week? That assumed they did not believe she went off hunting elsewhere in a snit and let her be with her anger.

"You don't sound sure of a rescue," Atlanta observed.

"Well, I may have left in a bit of a cloud of anger. They may not come looking for me right away," Marina admitted.

"Wonderful. I'm going to rot below the boards of a barn because one harpy could not keep her emotions to herself." Marina heard Atlanta pacing as she spoke.

Marina thought of her grey hair. The huntress was more right than she knew. "They'll come. They just may not be quick about it." Her sisters would find her.

"Did they hurt Cyrene, when they took me?" Atlanta asked with hesitation.

"They whacked her over the head, but nothing serious. She was more distraught over you than the bump on her head."

Atlanta sighed into the dark. "She's strong, but Cyrene's heart is softer than mine. She keeps me grounded. I was worried they had hurt her."

Marina thought of Reed and how he'd demanded her to think beyond her instincts. "I know what you mean. She stayed at the depot for a few days with Iris, who loves nothing better than someone else to mother hen."

"Good. She'll be safe there." Atlanta yawned.

The muffled sound of a cock's crow reached them. "I think I'm going to sleep while I'm able. Goodnight, ladies. And Atlanta." Marina lay down in the pile of hay in her cell.

"I'm glad you're here, you molting bird," came Atlanta's reply as Marina drifted into a troubled sleep.

A light woke Marina. There was a single candle on the top of a set of stairs leading out of the cellar. She stretched as far as her chains allowed and shook her limbs to regain feeling in her hands, which had gone numb. She blinked and got her first look at the room where they were being held.

The cage she was in was not more than six feet by six feet. The bars were metal and placed close together. The manacle on her ankle was attached to the back set of bars. There were four other cages, each identical to hers. One of them was empty. The cages were separated by four or five feet of space. Marina stood and reached out to test the distance. The chain on her ankle stopped her before she could press her face to the bars. The heavy tread of boots on the wooden steps told Marina it was not Pearl coming to visit.

"Just the person I wanted to wake up to," Marina said as Claude sauntered up to her cage.

"Little harpy, you can spit words at me all you want, but it won't change the fact that you're mine now. I've wanted you from the moment I saw you." Claude dug in his pocket and pulled out a key. It opened the lock on the door of her cage.

It would be an easy thing to overpower a single man as a harpy and make a break for it, but she could not get out of the manacles. The light had given Marina enough time to see the glyphs on the surface of the metal. These chains were made to remain in place regardless of what form she took. Usually when she changed, whatever she was wearing disappeared. She was no expert, but she had a feeling if she changed into her harpy, the chains would still be there, only she would be in considerably more pain; the manacles were made for mortal limbs and not harpy ones. It was also unlikely the key Claude was holding unlocked the manacles.

The door to the cage opened with the slightest creak. Marina stood near the door, as far as the chain allowed. Claude stepped into the space and it seemed to shrink by half. Marina kept her eyes steady on his as he moved forward. He grabbed at the chain between her two hands, twisted them together, and held them fast between his own. Marina could not move her feet or her hands. For the first time, she felt trapped.

Marina loosened control on her harpy and let her anger leak out from her pores. Claude leaned forward and she held herself stiff. He put his nose to her throat and sniffed, long and deep. He repeated the gesture. "Delicious. You smell like rage and power."

A shiver ran down her spine and bile rose in her throat. Claude's action was a sinister shadow to her behavior with Reed the night of the Jubilee. Claude chuckled and his breath was like acid on her skin. She jerked her hands in his. He almost lost his balance in surprise. Marina tried to take advantage of his shock by kicking him in the balls. She forgot she was chained by one leg and ended up in a heap on the floor.

Claude released her hands and stepped out of the cage. "It's going to be fun to break you. I have your smell now. You're as good as mine. You won't be fertile for another week at least, though we could always practice a bit, if you like."

"That's disgusting. How do you even know that?"

"I'm a mutt, remember? Dogs have a remarkable sense of smell."

She thought she might throw up. Marina wanted very badly to punch him in the face and break his nose. "If you behave and offer your daughter willingly to the family, I'll ask mother to spare you. I think we'd get on well together, once you see the benefits of joining us."

Marina flashed her teeth at Claude. "You're not monster enough for me."

He growled at her, the sound getting deeper as it went on. He flashed elongated canines at Marina and spoke, his voice barely mortal. "Little harpy, you're exactly the monster I've always wanted."

He turned, walked up the stairs, and grabbed the candle on his way out. The trap door closed behind him. The darkness he left behind in Marina's mind was as dark as the prison in which she was trapped.

CHAPTER 26

It was impossible to tell how much time had passed before the trap door opened again. This time, a lighter tread and a skirt heralded a female visitor. A faded blue dress and thin frame came into view. Edna held a lamp in one hand and the large basket Pearl had carried the day before in the other.

"Good afternoon, ladies. I hope you're all feeling well." The cheery greeting belonged in a front parlor, not a cellar smelling of dirt and imprisonment. This friendly version of Mrs. Nasso was at odds with the confrontational woman Marina had met the other day.

Edna lit a twist of paper from her lantern and used it to light two more in different corners of the room. Marina blinked as her eyes adjusted to the intrusion of light. The smells coming from the basket were delightful. Marina had not eaten for hours, and her stomach reminded her forcefully of that fact. Marina did not move from her position in the corner of her cell.

The older woman went to Katherine first. "Here you are, my dear. I know you must be getting hungrier these days, so I brought you something special." From the basket she produced a lemon tart and a jug of tea. She handed the food items through the bars. Katherine blushed a bright red and did not look at the other women when she mumbled her thanks. "I also brought you extra provisions to tide you over until Pearl comes tomorrow." Understanding hit Marina at once. It was followed by a churning of disgust in her belly. Katherine had been here the longest and was already carrying a child sired by one of the Nasso brothers.

Edna gave Lily and Atlanta smaller bundles, speaking to each of them kindly. She stopped before Marina's cage with an assessing eye. Marina kept her face passive and the reins tight on the boil of anger in her blood. Edna laid a bundle of food on the ground just inside the bars of her cage. Marina did not move towards the food.

The woman sat and smoothed her skirt out around her ankles. "You know, I've always admired the harpies for the role they played in bringing down Olympus. Your lines have always had backbone. We heard about how you defeated Zeus again last year. The stories are impressive."

"I assure you, impressing you was not our goal." Marina adopted Edna's casual tone.

The imitation of a smile moved her lips. "Of course not. Nonetheless, the word is out. There's a valley in Colorado Territory where harpies keep the peace and Remnants can be safe. We'd been looking for a place to settle and grow our family. We also needed exceptional candidates to mother the finest generation of monsters since the first brood born to the Remnant of my name. We wanted you, above all the others, so we came. What a prize it will be to have one of the only daughters born to this generation of harpies and to have her be a Nasso."

Marina's rage surged from her, causing Edna to lean back. Marina's voice was low and cut the heavy air. "No one in your family will ever lay hands on a harpy daughter as long as I have air to breathe. They are not commodities to be created and owned." Marina's hands curled as she imagined her claws sinking into the beating heart of the woman before her.

Edna closed her eyes, a slow grin growing on her wrinkled face. "Your power is strong and raw, but you misunderstand my intent. I do not think your daughter to be a commodity. She will be cherished as my own daughter Pearl is cherished. She will know the history of her line and the glory of the warriors who came before her. With us, she'll have a large family who will love and protect her and teach her what it means to be a monster among monsters."

Marina hissed at the woman, "She'll have a family, and it won't include you. The other harpies will not stop looking for me. They'll come for me and kill you."

Edna laughed. "Oh, they may come, but by then it'll be too late. Claude tells me you are a week at most away from being fertile. He has a very good sense of smell. You know how dogs are." She laughed and Marina shivered. "They haven't figured out where the other women were after all this time. We'll stay long enough for you each to give birth, and then we'll leave with your children. It's too bad you aren't more cooperative like Katherine. I'll be sorry to kill you when we go. You could have been useful."

"It would be hard to be of use to you after I rip out your heart with my claws." Marina widened her mouth and touched her tongue to an incisor until it drew blood. "Your blood will taste like fine wine."

Edna stood and brushed off her skirt. "That is exactly the kind of usefulness I mean. I pray to the gods your daughter is half the harpy you are."

"You'll never know. By the Styx, I swear you will die in this valley by a harpy's hand. If it's not mine, my sisters will avenge me, and I will wait for your spirit by the boatman, where I will hound you until the eternal sands run out." Marina let a wave of fury follow her oath, and the hairs on her arms floated up with her power.

For the first time since Edna had come into the cellar, she shifted her eyes to the floor and her face paled. She cleared her throat. "I'll leave the small lamp on, for Katherine's sake. It's got enough oil for a couple hours. Enough time for you to eat." Edna took a lamp and the basket with her when she left. She did not look at Marina again.

The trap door closed with a bang, and Marina put her head on her knees and fought to control the waves of emotion warring within her. Rape she would have endured. There was no way in any circle of hell she would allow Claude or any of the Nasso brothers to sire her only daughter. If Claude was right, and she would be fertile in days, she had to get out of the cellar before that happened.

Marina knew with certainty something she had avoided for months. There was only one man she wanted to father her daughter. She did not know how she would get free, but she had some words to say to Reed Brant when she did. For weeks, she had piled excuses up onto a teetering pile to hide behind. Marina loved Reed, gods help her, and the rest they could negotiate as they went along if he still wanted her after all the things they had said to each when they parted. She could give him a large family full of her harpy sisters and their daughters and Iris. It would not be the traditional family he had dreamed of, but perhaps it would be enough.

The lamp was starting to flicker before Marina got a handle on the volcano of emotions she had released. Katherine nibbled on the tart Edna had left her. Marina stood. "I'm getting out of here and I'm taking you all with me."

"Do you really think the others will come for you? For us?" Lily's voice held a trickle of hope.

Marina's hand went to where her knife usually sat on her hip. She clenched her fist. "They'll come. They know I was coming here. The only question is when. By the gods, I hope it's soon."

The lamp burned down to nothing, and they were left again in inky blackness. Marina tried to sleep. She was disconcerted, not knowing if her eyes were closed or not because the light never changed. Asleep or awake, she played out scenarios of how she could get out of the cellar. In all her dreams, she managed to taste Claude's blood. It was not always before he had accomplished his deed. Even if she killed him in the cage, she still would be chained. She raged, asleep or awake, and bided her time.

The next visit they received was from Pearl, bringing them food. The visit was spaced far enough from her mother's that Marina guessed another day had passed. Marina tried to engage her in conversation.

"Pearl, you're a powerful Remnant on your own. I know you don't think this is right. Get word to one of the other harpies or Sheriff Brant. They'll come for us, and you can be free from your family. You can start over, here if you'd like, or elsewhere. We can give you enough money and provisions to go anywhere you want."

Pearl did not answer or acknowledge the plea and left without speaking.

When she returned a second time, after perhaps another day, Marina did not speak to her. Pearl placed a small bundle of food on the floor of Marina's cell. "Mother said you'd try to persuade me. She knows you can influence people and that I am the weakest link in the family, she says. They've allowed me this job to give me the opportunity to prove my loyalty."

"You're not weak, Pearl. You have a right to make your own choices. We always have a choice." Marina resisted the urge to embellish her words with power. Pearl would have to be persuaded by her own conscience.

The young sphinx lifted her chin. "They may not be perfect, but they're my family. I know you don't understand our ways, but we'll raise your daughter in the old ways. She will know her history, and she will be loved."

Marina lunged to the end of her chains and allowed her harpy's anger to fill the room. "You'll never have the chance to meet her. Your line will be snuffed out by the rage in my talons, and I will dance on the ashes of your bones. My line will continue on to tell the story of the family of monsters who dared to think themselves equal to the task of bringing a harpy to heel."

Pearl swallowed convulsively, grabbed the lamp, and fled from the room. Marina's laughter sounded like broken glass and chased the sphinx up the stairs. The women ate in a darkness enhanced only by the residual power in the room from Marina's outburst. Marina flexed her hand and hoped she would feel blood dripping from her claws before long. She had a running list of candidates who would appease her bloodlust to greater or lesser degrees.

Marina shifted, and the metal of the manacles scraped the raw skin on her wrists. She untucked her shirt and ripped off strips from the bottom to wind around her wrists. She ripped another strip and tied it around her neck. She tucked her pant leg under the manacle on her leg. The bindings eased the discomfort enough that Marina dozed.

Two sets of boots on the stairs informed Marina and the others they had some gentleman callers. A lamp in the hand of the first revealed

Claude's leering face. This was followed by Olen's eager countenance. The latter made a beeline for Katherine.

He reached a hand through the bars. Katherine hesitated for a moment, then placed her hand in his. "How are you today? I'm sorry I couldn't come the last couple days. Father doesn't want me coming down here every day. He says I'll get too attached."

"Already too late for that," Claude mumbled.

Olen shot his brother a look and dropped the volume of his voice. Katherine had to lean forward to hear him. Marina realized Katherine's chains were longer and allowed her to reach to the door of her cage. Marina shifted her gaze to the other dangerous monster in the room.

Claude leaned against the bars of her cell and looked her over. "I see the dark and the cage have not quelled your spirit." He smiled, a look full of malevolent promise, and, for a moment, Marina doubted she would get out of this intact.

The moment passed. She lifted her chin. "You're not monster enough to scare me."

Claude laughed. "I can smell your fear under the spice of your anger. The fear is small, but there. I can't wait to taste it up close."

"Burn in hells," Marina spat.

Claude ignored her and pulled some canvas from a pile under the stairs. Horror bloomed in her chest when Claude attached the canvas to one wall of her cell. He returned to the pile and brought another canvas over. When he was done, her cage was blocked from view from the rest of the cellar.

A giggle escaped Marina's lips. Claude was shy about his business. She heaved in air and sought to calm herself. She needed her wits about her and going crazy as a lemming would not get her out of this place. Claude pulled back the curtain over the door and twisted the key in the lock.

Marina moved back against the wall. No matter what happened, she was not going to make this easy on him. He might get what he wanted from her. However, he would pay for it in blood. His. Marina pushed everything but her rage to the bottom of the well of her soul. Only her rage would assist her in the next few minutes.

Claude sniffed the air of her cell. "You're perfect, you know. I've never smelled anything like you."

"Smelling me is the only thing you're going to get to do." Marina let her harpy loose in her voice. While the chains kept her from changing completely, she could elongate her claws once Claude got close enough. She needed the element of surprise on her side.

Claude took a step closer. "This doesn't have to be difficult, you know. If you cooperate, you might even find you like it."

Marina snorted. "I doubt it."

Claude's smile sent a chill down Marina's skin. "I don't care one way or the other. I'll like it fine whether you fight like a harpy as I take you or like a mortal woman. Either way, today, tomorrow, or the next day, you'll be carrying my child."

"I'll rip your balls from your body and stuff them down your throat if you try." Marina kept her hands by her side and let her fingernails grow long. The murmured voices of Katherine and Olen could be heard through the heavy canvas. Marina knew it did not matter who heard what went on down here. If she did not get free before Claude laid hands on her, no amount of screaming would change the outcome. She would not allow this monster to sire her daughter.

Claude laughed. "You have fire in you. I've dreamed of this for a long time."

"Funny. I haven't." Marina's fingers hardened into claws, and she waited.

Claude moved his hands and revealed the rope he held. "Like I said, either way, I'm taking what I want." He moved closer and reached for the chain linking her hands together. The moment before his eyes dropped, Marina pushed her power into speed and raked her claws over Claude's face and down his chest.

He screamed in pain. The coppery smell and warmth of the blood on her hands released the anger in her own veins. She missed his eyes on the first pass and raised her hands for a second try. Claude tried to grab the chain between her hands. Blood was in his eyes and his hands were slippery with it. His grab redirected Marina's blow from his eyes, and her claws opened up his scalp.

"Claude, are you all right?" Olen yelled, inches from the canvas covering the door.

Claude retreated and put his back to the door of the cell, out of Marina's reach. "I'm fine. Just a lover's quarrel." Marina hissed at him. Claude wiped blood from his eyes. "Nothing I can't handle. Why don't you give me some privacy to do what needs to be done?"

Olen shuffled his feet in the dirt floor of the cellar. "I don't think leaving you alone in there is a good idea."

"I didn't ask for your opinion. Give me twenty minutes. If she manages to kill me, then I deserved to die. If you don't leave, I'll tell father about your visits down here to the scylla." Claude waited until Olen's footsteps went up the stairs and the trap door closed. Claude entwined his fingers and cracked his knuckles. "Now, darlin', where were we?"

"I believe I was about to serve you your balls for dinner," Marina said.

"And I believe I was about to show you what it means to be my bitch."

This time when he approached, he was ready for her attack and he grabbed the chains between her hands and yanked her forward. The forward motion propelled Marina face first into the dirt floor. Claude wrapped the rope around the chain and tied it to the bars on the door, immobilizing Marina face down on the floor. She tried kicking, but with one leg chained to the wall it was ineffective.

Marina stilled and gathered her strength. She was not going to give in. She sucked in a breath too fast and dirt went into her lungs. She coughed convulsively. Claude used the coughing fit to turn her over on to her back. His big hands unbuttoned her pants and removed them from her body. They hung on the chain attached to her ankle. The air was cool, and goose pimples rose up on her skin. He grunted when her free leg landed a solid blow to his chest. Marina's leg was mostly talons, and she added to the strips of blood blooming underneath his tattered shirt. His response was to sit on her unfettered leg.

Real fear crawled over her. *This must be what a rabbit feels like when it knows it is being watched by a hawk and there is no escape*, she thought. There was nowhere to run. She could only face what was coming and deal with the consequences later. Claude had neutralized her talons and her claws, but she was not helpless. She had a full set of sharp teeth at her disposal.

Claude started unbuttoning her shirt. Halfway down, he lost patience and ripped her shirt open. He released the buttons of his own pants next, and, leaving much of his weight on her free leg, he knelt between her legs. Marina tried to shift away as much as she could, but Claude had strung her tight between the back wall and the door. She fixed her eyes on the pulse beating in his throat and waited. She had to wait until just the right moment.

The muffled sound of gunfire sounded from somewhere above ground. Hope flared in Marina, and Claude jerked in dismay. His movement brought certain parts of his anatomy closer to her own exposed body than she preferred. Instead of putting him off, the gunfire, which had continued, galvanized Claude into action. Marina gathered her anger to her and wrapped it around her like armor. She clutched tight to the knowledge that no matter what he did to her, he would be dead by her hand before it was over.

He ran his hands down her body and spread her legs wider. His fingers invaded her, and Marina gasped at the suddenness of the intrusion. Claude leaned over her, put his face to her neck, and drew in a deep breath. He shuddered. Marina did not hesitate. She turned her head and sunk her teeth into the skin over the jugular in Claude's neck.

His blood filled her mouth, and she swallowed as she clamped down. His blood tasted like lust and fear and iron. His fingers jerked out of her, and he brought his hands up to pry her mouth off his neck. His blood made everything slick. He could not find purchase. He shook himself like a dog, and Marina kept her teeth clamped tight. The pulse of his lifeblood slowed.

Marina had never enjoyed the symphony of the kill more. Right before his life went, Marina closed her jaws and ripped the rest of his throat out. His body collapsed on top of hers, and she spit out the meat in her mouth. His naked, lifeless body pressed into hers. The ropes and chains still held her immobile, and Marina had a violent urge to get Claude's body off of hers. She struggled without being able to move him, and she fought the panic warring with the violence coursing through her.

Through the rage and thrill of the kill beating in her own blood, she heard yelling and a pounding of many feet on the stairs. The canvas of her cell was pulled back and she twisted her head to see Reed's face, white and pinched with fury, taking in the horror before him.

Reed shook the door of her cell. "Sparrow, are you hurt? Did he hurt you?" Anguish beat through the rage in his voice. "Where are the keys?"

Marina's anger had kept most of her panic at bay. The look on Reed's face whipped away whatever distance she had achieved from what had almost happened. "None of the blood is mine. He didn't hurt me much. Untie my hands and I'll see if I can get the key to the cell."

Reed's hands shook as he untied the rope. He knelt in the dirt, reached through the bars, and flipped Claude's body off hers. The air chilled the warm blood that coated her body. Marina sat up. With jerky movements, Reed unbuttoned his own shirt and handed it to her. With her hands chained, she could not put the shirt on or properly hold it over her front. She put the now blood-smeared shirt in her lap.

Reed still knelt by the cage door, his shoulders slumped. "I'm sorry. I'm sorry I didn't come with you. I'm sorry I yelled at you. I'm sorry I didn't get here sooner. A few more minutes and I could have prevented him from... "

"Dying? He didn't achieve his purpose in stripping me bare, but I achieved mine." Marina allowed herself to glory in the violence of killing the man who had threatened her and everything she wanted. Marina reached into Claude's right pocket and closed her blood-slicked hand on the key. Her hands shook as she tried it on her wrists. It did not fit into the lock. "Hells. He would still be dead by my hand regardless of when you arrived, but I am glad to see you." She handed Reed the key, now smeared with blood. "This one is only for the door. I think you'll find the key that goes to our chains in Edna Nasso's possession." She licked some of the blood from her lips. Her entire body was starting to feel like it was covered in sticky sugar.

Marina thought he would go back up the stairs and look for the other key. She did not want to be alone with what was left of Claude Nasso. Instead, Reed shoved the key into the lock and came into the cage, still radiating fury. Marina did not know what he would do, confronted with so much blood and violence. Watching her kill a monster with a sword was one thing. Seeing the aftermath of violence in this cage, her naked and covered in blood after ripping out Claude's throat, was another.

He sat down next to her and pulled her into his lap. He folded her legs until they were under her chin and put the shirt over her back and around her front. She was surrounded by him. Her vision swam, and her tears spilled over. Small tremors shook her.

Reed's arms tightened like a vise. The pressure was reassuring. He kissed the top of her head. "Who else is in here? I rushed through without taking stock."

Marina burrowed into him. "All of them. Katherine. Lily. Atlanta."

"Ladies, are you all right?" Reed asked.

"Right as rain now that it looks like our escape is eminent." Atlanta's voice held the relief Marina felt fluttering in her own chest.

Reed bowed his head back down to Marina. "I'm so sorry. This is all my fault. I should have listened to you," he said into her hair. "I'm so sorry."

"It's not your fault. I should have waited as you asked. It was foolish to come alone." Marina breathed deep, and the smell of Reed was enough to begin to banish the worst of her demons.

Reed squeezed her tight. "I should have listened. It killed me to deny you and stay in town when I knew you would go and knew you needed me. I thought if you got into some trouble you would learn your lesson. Marina, please forgive me. I never thought it would be this bad."

"I'll forgive you if you forgive me for all the horrible things I said to you at the depot."

"We both said horrible things."

Marina uncurled enough to look Reed in the face. "Forgiven?"

"Yes. Am I forgiven?" Reed stroked a hand down her back.

"Of course." Marina smiled then. She knew she must look scarier than normal, covered in blood and naked. "I hope you don't make it a habit of holding naked women in your lap." Marina waited a beat. "Unless it's me."

Reed's body relaxed and he pressed his forehead into hers. "Sparrow, next time, I could do without all the blood. If you want to sit in my lap, just ask. No need to go into all these theatrics."

Marina could feel his breath on her face. She brought her hands up to cup his face and then saw the state they were in. She dropped them. "No more theatrics, then." Marina took a steadying breath. "I love you."

Reed kissed her on the lips, but he pulled back quickly. Marina's heart twisted into a restrictive knot. It was not the kiss she expected from a lover. His brown eyes were wide, and Marina closed hers, unable to look at his face. His hand on her cheek stopped her from turning her head down.

"Look at me, Sparrow." Marina reluctantly obeyed. "I love you, just the way you are, teeth, claws, feathers, and especially your heart. But now that you know, I'd rather the first time I kiss you after that declaration not be here, with you covered in blood and in a cell under the ground with a man whose throat you ripped out. Part of me wishes he was still alive so I could do the honors." Reed let out a shaky breath. "This is not how I imagined this conversation going."

Marina gave him a dazzling smile, which he returned. "Am I the scariest thing you've ever seen?" Marina cocked an eyebrow at him.

"Always," he replied.

CHAPTER 27

The sound of boots was loud overhead and they pounded down the stairs at a run. "Sheriff?" Dora's voice was still pitched low. It sounded wonderful.

"Over here," Marina called.

Dora's footsteps paused in the middle of the room as she registered what she saw. "Styx, what was wrong with these people?"

"Glad to see you again, Dora. It's good of you to break up the party. I was getting tired of the view," Atlanta said.

"Over here," Marina prompted. "Behind the canvas."

The heavy canvas was ripped from its moorings. Dora stood, her strawberry blonde hair in a riot over her head and her skin pale against her freckles. "Styx and fire, what in the hells happened in here?" Her eyes raked over naked, blood-covered Marina. "Did he... Are you all right?"

Marina smiled from her perch on Reed's lap. She waved a hand at Claude's body. "This mongrel thought he was going to sire my daughter. I informed him otherwise. This is the key to the cells." Marina elbowed Reed, and he handed Dora the key. "There's another one for the manacles."

"They chained you like animals?" Dora's voice became dangerously low. "If they weren't already dead, I would kill them all. They fought back, but they were no match for two angry harpies and a furious sheriff."

"If Edna Nasso is still alive, ask her where the key is located. She probably has it on her person. She wouldn't have trusted it to any of the men." Marina leaned back into Reed. Her energy, sustained by adrenaline and the kill, was leaching out of her.

"Mrs. Nasso and Pearl are still alive. We were waiting to find you before killing them in case we couldn't find you and needed to ask them questions." Dora went to each cell and unlocked them. "I'll be right back."

Marina turned to Reed. "I know you knew I was coming here, but how did you find me?"

Reed ran a hand down her back over and over, in a steady rhythm. "We had the meeting with the Territory Committee, which went fine, thanks for asking." Marina elbowed him. "I waited a day to go looking for you. I'd half hoped you were just pouting in your cabin. We went there first, but you were gone. We came here next. Petra found the spot she would have used to spy on the Nassos and looked around from there. She thought someone had been dragged from the spot between the rocks up behind the garden."

Marina nodded. "That's where I was. Four of them snuck up on me at once. Cowards."

"I went to talk to the Nassos. They denied seeing you. Dora found your badge wedged into the rock. I knew you'd left it on purpose. Things got ugly from there." Reed kissed the top of her head.

"Define ugly," she pushed.

"You're blood thirsty."

"Always."

"Mr. Nasso fired the first shot. I dove behind their wagon. I thought all I was going to have to contend with was some flying bullets, but the Nasso boys turned into a two-headed dog, the ladon, and our friend the chimera."

"Twice the heads, twice the teeth," Marina said. "Sounds fun."

"Dora plucked the dog up before he could reach me, and Petra took out Mr. Nasso and the ladon, I think. I was too busy fighting the chimera to notice much for a while."

"How did you manage with the chimera? It was slippery last time we saw it." Marina thought of Reed fighting the monster alone, and she dug her fingers into his arm.

"Ease up on my arm, Sparrow, before you leave a bruise. Worried about me?"

"No."

Reed made a sound in the back of his throat that said he did not believe her. "Didn't give the chimera a chance to get close. I know my strengths, and hand-to-hand fighting with a monster twice my size is not one of mine. I'm a crack shot, though. Right between his beady little eyes."

Marina sighed. "You tell the sweetest stories. I wish I could've seen that." They both laughed.

"Lord help me, but I think you are the only woman I could ever love." Reed tightened his grip on her. She was chained to a wall and covered in blood, but everything was going to be all right.

Dora returned, waving a key. "It was on a string around her neck." Dora passed Reed the key and he unlocked the manacles. They fell from her hands and Marina rubbed the raw skin.

Reed unwrapped the cloth she had tied around them. He looked up when Dora moved to Atlanta's cell. "I'd be obliged if you ladies would stick around so we can talk to you before we take you home. Dora, take them all to the front porch. Get them something to drink, eat, or whatever they need. I'm taking Marina to the creek to get cleaned up."

Reed stood and pulled Marina to her feet. Marina put her arms through the sleeves of the shirt and did enough buttons to cover herself. Reed pressed his lips together. "If I thought you'd let me, I'd carry you out of here."

"Good thing you know I don't need you to carry me." Marina bussed him on the cheek. "I'd let you, if you really wanted to." She winked at him and walked out of the cage.

Her first breath of fresh air in days was sweet. Her body took it in greedily, smelling the tapestry of fall with the undertone of blood. There were splashes of blood everywhere, and pools had begun gathering under the bodies.

"Marina," Petra called from the porch. She was in her harpy form, guarding the Nasso women. "You're covered in blood. Dora said you were all right. Are you?"

"Yes. Claude just put his neck too close to my teeth. I'm only in need of a bath. Don't let those two leave. I have words for them." Marina took Reed's hand and walked towards the creek running behind the house.

Reed hesitated by the bank of the creek. "I want to get you some clean clothes from inside. Will you be all right while I'm gone?"

Truthfully, she did not want to be alone. Marina gave him a look that would wither lesser mortals. "I know how to bathe in a creek."

Reed wrapped his arms around her and squeezed. "I may not be all right if I leave you."

Marina's heart melted into something resembling warm taffy. "I don't want you to go, but I do need something to wear. Go. I can't get in too much trouble alone out here. Hurry back, though."

He released her. "Sparrow, you find trouble where ever you go."

"It's my special power." Marina winked and unbuttoned the shirt.

Reed crunched up the path to the house. The shirt was covered in blood and probably beyond redemption. Marina completed its demise and used it as a washcloth. She scrubbed until her skin felt raw in some places. It would have been nice to have soap, even if no amount of soap would erase the feel of Claude's hands on her. She shuddered.

Marina stood on the bank, the chill air drying her skin, when Reed returned carrying brown pants, a faded red shirt, and a cake of soap. He had put his duster on over his bare chest while he was gone. With his eyes carefully averted, he handed the soap to Marina. She took the soap with a shaking hand.

Reed laid the clothes on the bank and turned his back to her. "I saw the soap and thought you might want it."

Marina nodded before realizing he could not see her. "Thank you." She finished washing and stepped out of the water. Marina bent over to pick up the clothes. She did not know who they had belonged to. She did not want to put anything next to her skin that had belonged to Claude. Marina smelled the clothes. They smelled like soap and wood.

Reed put a hand on her shoulder. She jumped.

Shame flooded her. "I didn't mean to get startled."

Reed's hand tightened on her shoulder. "I shouldn't sneak up on you. They're not his. I asked Pearl before I brought them down. They were Olen's." Reed turned his head again to allow her to dress.

Tenderness flooded her, and for the second time today, she saw the world through tears. Marina blinked them away and pulled the clothes on. She was still barefoot and stepped with care around the rocks to stand in front of Reed. Marina placed her palms flat on Reed's bare chest and leaned forward to breathe deep. The smell of comfort overwhelmed her and she melted into him.

"I feel like I need to scrub for a day, but this is as clean as I'm going to be until I can have a proper bath. Will it do for now?"

Reed put his fingers deep into her damp hair and drew her in. It was a tender kiss filled with the promise of many more to come. Marina wished she could stay here the rest of the day to see where they could take this one kiss. Her body was aflame with it, and there were things she needed Reed to erase from her memory.

Marina moved her hands farther into Reed's duster and ran them around his torso, pulling him closer. He deepened the kiss, and Marina pushed back, asking for more. Reed moved his hands over her neck, tracing delicate lines from her face to her collarbone. Marina angled her head to give him better access. Reed groaned and pulled away.

"We still have things to say to each other." He ran a hand over the wide strip of grey hair she now possessed. "This is new. When you came into the depot, there were only a handful."

Marina tried to squirm out of Reed's arms, but he held her fast. She gave up trying to escape. "I acquired the others by the time I got back to my cabin after I left the depot," she said.

Whiskey-colored eyes searched her face. "Iris told me about them. What they mean. That's what we were talking about when you came into the depot that day."

Marina chewed on her bottom lip. This was new territory for her. "So you know."

"I do."

Marina was not sure he did. "I know you want a big family, but I can only have one daughter. I don't want anyone else. I want you. I love you. Would you consider being my mate or husband or whatever, even if you can't have the things you've always wanted?" Marina stilled her body, waiting.

Reed ran a hand over her grey hair. "Aren't I the one typically supposed to ask that?"

Marina let out the breath she had been holding. "Nothing about me is typical."

"And I thank God for it every day. Sparrow, I love you. I do want a big family, but I want you more. You are the thing I've always wanted. I just didn't know it. Besides, I think you're all I'll be able to handle for a while." Reed put his hands on her hips.

Marina relaxed into him again. "Good. I'm not sure I would've taken no for an answer."

"Your stubbornness. I could do without that." His hands gave her a squeeze.

"As you say, kettle." Marina's lips pressed into Reed's. His hands moved to her backside and pulled her up tight against him. Marina had no doubt about how she was affecting him. She could feel every solid inch of him against her very willing body.

He broke their kiss again.

Marina put his face in her hands. "If you keep kissing me like that, only to stop when things are getting really good, you're going to make me start wondering if I'm doing it wrong."

Reed planted a short kiss on her lips. She followed him when he pulled away. "Harpy. We have plenty of time. Iris assured me that even with the probability of a shortened lifespan, you'll likely outlive me. We'd better go deal with the rest of this mess."

Marina stepped back from him. "You're right." She reached up and did two of the buttons on his duster. "So I'm not tempted. Let's go." Reed twined their fingers together, and they walked towards the house.

Pearl and her mother were sitting in chairs on one end of the long porch. Petra stood guard over the sullen pair. Tear tracks stained Pearl's face. Edna's cheeks were dry, and her eyes blazed with hate. Marina was tired of killing today, but Edna could not be allowed to live. Dora was on the other side of the porch, giving water and food to Katherine, Lily, and Atlanta. Marina noted the huntress had already acquired a gun.

Petra pointedly looked at Marina and swept her eyes down to where Marina clasped Reed's hand. Marina shrugged and smiled. Petra laughed, drawing a nasty look from Edna.

"Gods, it's about time. Welcome to the family, Sheriff," Petra said.

Reed nodded his head in acknowledgement. They stopped next to

Petra, and though there was no reason to do so, Reed continued to hold Marina's hand.

"Do you know why they took you and the other women?" he asked.

Marina laid out the Nasso's plan. "They wanted a family of the most powerful monsters they could breed. Unfortunately for them, they forgot that monsters seldom like being caged and almost never cooperate," she concluded.

Petra's hands clenched. "They came to the wrong valley."

Dora had come to stand beside them during the retelling. She spoke to Edna. "You knew we were here, yet you came anyway. We may be the first harpies in centuries that chose to live together in the same region, but we're still creatures of violence. Harpies protect what is theirs, and the people of this valley belong to us."

Edna screamed. "You're all trash. Katherine and Pearl will start our family over. The line of the Nassos will not end, even if you kill me. In another generation, we'll try again to breed the strongest Remnants, and the Nassos will rule this land. Nothing and no one will stop us."

"Stop it, Mother. Just stop. Don't you see what this has cost us? Father is dead. Olen, Claude, Billy, and Chris are all dead. Frank and Logan before that. They've killed them *all*. It's over." Tears retraced the tracks on Pearl's face.

"It'll never be over as long as you and the baby Katherine carries live." Dora, Petra, and Reed swiveled to look at Katherine in horror. Edna continued, "I'll not rest until I see our family returned to a place of honor."

Edna's voice changed as she spoke, the last word becoming a hiss of rage. Her skin turned an unhealthy shade of green, and her body elongated. The ropes binding her slid to the ground as her body became thinner. She lunged at Petra, who dodged the fangs sprouting from Edna's mouth.

A blur of tan fur and wings hit Edna in the side of her snake-shaped head. A full-grown lion with the face of a woman and wings of an eagle pressed the head of the snake into the rocky ground. Without further warning, the sphinx leaned down and bit off her mother's head. The snake's body flopped in reflex and then went still. Pearl shook herself and stretched. She trotted over to Marina and dropped Edna' head at her feet. Marina had been right. The girl had backbone.

Pearl changed back into a lithe mortal girl. "It's over." She told her mother's body. She turned to her rapt audience. "Sheriff Brant, Petra, Marina, and Dora, I'd like to formally apologize for the actions of my family. I would like to request to stay on in the valley on my family's land. I offer my mother's head in payment for the debt owed to the people of the valley."

Reed looked at Marina. She shrugged her shoulders. The other two harpies had similar reactions. He said, "You may stay, but you will submit to regular visits by the harpies to make sure you abide by the rules of the valley. The people and Remnants here are important to us, and we don't take kindly to those who think otherwise."

Pearl nodded. "By the River Styx, I swear to submit to visits and to do no harm unless it is in self-defense."

The tension evaporated from the air. Petra changed into her mortal form. "Would you like help burying your dead?"

Pearl clasped her hands before her. "Yes. If you could help gather them for a pyre, I think that will be enough. I will do the rest."

"Dora and I can stay and help Pearl. Sheriff, you and Marina should take the other women home to their families."

"I don't want to go."

The group turned to look at Katherine. She stood and smoothed the material of her skirt. "I won't go home to Andy. I've had a long time to think about the kind of life I want. Let me leave. Tell my husband I was not here when you rescued the others. Just give me a horse and some supplies, and I'll never step foot in the valley again."

Reed rubbed his neck. "I don't like lying."

Marina turned to Reed. "She's carrying Olen's child. How well do you think Andy will take that bit of news?"

Reed grunted. "With half the liquor in Vine's."

"Exactly."

Reed put his hands up in defeat. "I'll go saddle a horse from the barn."

Marina turned to Dora. "See if you can fill a sack of provisions for her."

While preparations were being made, Marina sat by Katherine on the front step of the porch. "Send word to the depot when you get settled in case you end up needing some help with the child." Katherine nodded. "Thank you, I will. Thank you for looking for us and for not giving up until you found us."

"Stubborn is something I do well," Marina said.

They all stood and watched as Katherine rode away from the Nasso homestead and disappeared under the rattle of the aspens. Dora and Petra went to help Pearl drag the bodies of her family to a clearing away from the house.

Reed hesitated beside Marina. "You were right about the Nassos, and you're probably right about Mrs. Johnson needing to leave the valley."

Marina bowed to him. "Thanks for saying so, Sheriff."

Reed crossed his arms. "Still, coming alone was reckless. If we get married, you'll have to listen to me occasionally."

Marina sidled up next to him and leaned into him, reveling in her ability to do so. "How often is occasionally?" She angled her elbow into his side.

Reed wrapped an arm around her, pinning her to him. "The majority of the time."

Marina smiled. Loving Reed was going to be an adventure. "I can only promise to take it under advisement."

CHAPTER 28

When the path to the southern valley veered off of the path to town, Atlanta reined in her horse.

"This is where I leave. Sheriff, thank you for coming for us."

Reed nodded. "Anytime."

Atlanta turned to Marina. "Harpy, I'd like it if you and your sisters would come hunting with us sometime soon."

"We would be honored to join you." Atlanta turned to go, but Marina spoke before she could leave. "Huntress, I like you, but do not forget that this valley is ours and that we do not always deliver mortal justice."

"As it should be. Don't worry. We'll follow the rules. I owe you a debt now. Until spring." Atlanta gave them a salute and turned her horse south.

Reed, Marina, and Lily watched her ride away until the bend in the trail took her from view. They continued on the road towards town. When the path became wide enough, Marina urged her horse to move faster and pulled up alongside Reed.

"Does it bother you," she asked, "that the Nassos didn't get put through a proper mortal trial?"

Reed was silent. Marina glanced sideways at him and could see him thinking. He stopped his horse. Marina did the same.

Reed's eyes, when they met hers, were fierce. "I thought it would bother me. It shouldn't sit right at all, but when I saw you in that cage, I could have killed them all with my bare hands." Reed reached across the space separating them and grabbed a handful of her hair. "You are mine, God help me."

Marina's harpy soared with the rightness of this man by her side. Her voice was deep when she replied, "And you are mine. Gods help you indeed."

Reed used his grip on her to bring her close enough for their lips to meet. When they broke the kiss, stupid smiles adorned them both. Lily's horse snorted behind them.

"Let's get going. We still have business to attend to today." Reed cast a sympathetic glance back at the rider behind them. Unlike Atlanta, Lily Hughes was less anxious to return home.

The rest of the ride was made in silence. When Turning Creek finally came into view, an overwhelming feeling of love washed over Marina, and she knew something she had only understood on the surface before. This place was her home, but it was more than that. It was the cornerstone of something different. Marina had not just learned to love Reed, she had learned to love this place in a deep, soul-changing way.

For generations, the harpies had lived separate and lonely lives, never putting down deep roots, never building a home, never fostering their relationships with the other harpies, and never reaching for something more than Zeus's curse had allowed. Now, in this place, they were building something new and rewriting their history. Marina's eyes caressed the form of the man riding in front of her. As if he could feel her look, he twisted in the saddle and raised an eyebrow at her. She shook her head and smiled.

They rode around the back of Main Street in an effort to avoid being spotted by the town. Reed wanted Lily to be reunited with her family before the town descended upon them. Reed helped her dismount and held their horses while Marina walked her to the door.

Lily hesitated on the threshold of her house. "What if they don't want me back?" she whispered.

Marina shared a glance with Reed. She took Lily by the shoulders and shook her. "Stop it. That man in there loves you. He was devastated when you disappeared. He will not care one whit what happened while you were gone. He'll just be glad to have you back."

Lily's eyes dropped. "I'll have to tell him about it, eventually."

Marina gave her shoulders a squeeze. "Yes, you will. But not today. Let today be about rejoicing. Face those demons tomorrow, and take comfort in the fact that they're all dead."

A hardness came into Lily's eyes. "Yes. They are all dead."

"There's that scary Medusa I've been waiting to see. Go on then." Marina gave her a nudge. "Do you want us to come in?"

Lily shook her head. "No, I can do this alone." She opened the door and walked back into her life.

Marina hesitated, waiting. After a moment she heard it. The sound of an exclamation and the joyous screeching of children. She turned to Reed and smiled.

He handed her the reins to her horse. "Will you come have dinner with Claire, the boys, and me?"

"I need to go see Iris first. She'll be worried."

"Go talk to Iris, and then bring her and Thomas with you. We're all family and we have a lot to celebrate tonight."

Marina hesitated. She found she was not yet ready to leave. "Do you think we should tell Claire?"

"About us?"

Marina laughed. "Oh, I'm fairly sure she already knows about us. In fact, she'll probably try to take credit for it. I mean about the Remnants. About me."

Reed's arms went around her waist and pulled her close. "Let's tackle that another day, shall we?"

Marina laid a hand on Reed's cheek. "Poor, mortal man. Tired of all the monsters already? I thought you loved me."

Reed dug his fingers into her waist. "Are you going to make my life miserable?"

Marina flashed her teeth at him. "Probably, but I promise it'll be entertaining."

Reed hauled her into a kiss. He pulled back and grinned. "Sparrow, I'm counting on it."

THANK YOU

Thank you for reading the first book in the Turning Creek series.

Would you like to know when the next book is available? You can sign up for my newsletter at www.wanderingeyre.com. On my blog, you will find all kinds of fun information and general shenanigans. Follow me on Twitter @wanderingeyre, or like me on Facebook at https://www.facebook.com/MichelleBouleAuthor.

I appreciate all reviews. They help readers find books and mean the world to authors.

Turning Creek Reading Order
Lightning in the Dark
Storm in the Mountains
Letters in the Snow
Plagues of the Heart
Journey of the Lost

MYTHOLOGY CODEX

This is a list of mythology characters and mythological locations mentioned in the Turning Creek series and a brief description of each. The information in this codex is for the mythology as it relates to this fictional series. As an author, I have taken some liberty with the original myths.

***

Achilles - The original Achilles was fatally wounded by a shot to his heel because this was the source of his power, speed, and strength. Thomas, the Remnant of Achilles, has the gift of speed and delivers mail in Turning Creek.

Aegis - The aegis is the name for the four warriors who make up the Shield of Zeus which is the title for his bodyguards and henchmen. They are Ioke, Alke, Eris, and Phobos.

Alke - Alke is the personification of strength. He is part of the Shield of Zeus and his main weapon is a sword.

Aphrodite - The Greek goddess of love.

Asclepius - A Greek physician who was granted the power over life and death by the gods. Lee Williams is a Remnant of Asclepius and the doctor in Turning Creek.

Atlanta - Atlanta was a famous huntress who made an oath of virginity to the goddess Artemis, but was later tricked into marriage by Aphrodite. Atlanta, named for the first of her name, travels with her companion and partner, Cyrene, in a quest for the next adventure and hunt. (also known as Atalanta in the Greek myths)

Bellerophon - Bellerophon was one of the hundreds of bastard sons of Zeus who spent his life trying to attain acknowledgement and vindication from the gods.

Charon - Charon is the ferryman who took souls across the River Styx on their way to the god Hades in the underworld, sometimes also referred to as Tartarus.

Cerberus - A three headed dog, the son of Echidna and Typhon, who guarded the door to the underworld for Hades.

Chimera - A monster, sired by Echidna and Typhon, whose front and torso is that of a lion and whose bottom half is that of a snake.

Cyrene - Cyrene was a princess and huntress who once wrestled a lion with her bare hands. The current Remnant of Cyrene travels the world with Atlanta in search of the next greatest hunt.

Dionysus - Dionysus, god of the vine, stayed neutral during the battle and Fall of Olympus, making him unpopular with those on both sides. The Remnant of Dionysus, Daniel Vine, owns the saloon in Turning Creek.

Dryad - Similar to a nymph, a dryad is a spirit of the forest, the trees, or other natural phenomenon. This affinity to nature can give them the power to communicate with nature or similar abilities.

Echidna - The original Echidna was called the Mother of All Monsters in the time of the old myths because her children became the nightmares of the Greek era.

Eris - Eris is the personification of strife. He is part of the Shield of Zeus.

Hades - The god and ruler of the underworld.

Harpy - A harpy has the body of a bird of prey and the head of a woman, though their face is more angular in this natural form. They have the ability many Remnants have of taking the form of a mortal when needed. There were four harpies who stood against Zeus in the uprising; Aello, Celaeno, Ocypete, and Podarge. The Remnants of the three surviving harpies lived in isolation from each other, and most of the world, until the current generation.

Hephaestus - Blacksmith to gods, he had the ability to craft weapons of magic and power in his forge, lit by the fires of Olympus. The Remnants of Hephaestus carry some of this original power and are marked with a clubfoot. Henry Foster of Turning Creek is a Remnant of Hephaestus.

Hera - Hera was the wife and queen of Zeus. By the time of the uprising, she had became angry and bitter over Zeus's many affairs and bastard children. She turned a blind eye to the work of the harpies and fled before Olympus fell.

Ioke - Ioke is the personification of onslaught and pursuit. She is part of the Shield of Zeus and her main weapon is the crossbow.

Iris - The original Iris has golden wings, delivered the messages of the gods, and had the gift of prophecy. She shared parentage with the harpies and argued on their behalf often, softening their punishment when Zeus's anger turned against them. The Remnant of Iris, also called The Messenger, is marked with a birthmark of golden wings. The Messenger chronicles the history of the Remnants and the harpies in particular.

Ladon - The Ladon is the serpentine monster child of Typhon and Echidna. Also known as a dragon or a drakon.

Laelaps - A mythical hound, created by Zeus, who never failed to catch its prey

Lernean Hydra - The hydra is another serpentine-like child of Typhon and Echidna. It is a nine headed serpent who occupies bodies of water and spits acidic venom on its victims.

Medea - A powerful and vengeful witch who helped Jason of the Argonauts in many battles and later became his wife, bearing him six children.

Maenads - Maenads are women controlled by Dionysus who turn into raving, mad women. They have been known to tear apart men with their bare hands in their rage.

Manticore - This creature has the head of a woman, the body of a lion, and the tail of a scorpion. It was a meliai, a kind of nymph from the island of Melos.

Medusa - Medusa, in the old myths, was a creature with snakes for hair and eyes who could hypnotize a man. Lily Hughes, the Remnant of Medusa, has the power of persuasion if you look into her eyes.

Mount Olympus - The mountain that was the seat of Zeus and the center of his kingdom during the time of the old myths.

Nemean Lion - The Nemean Lion can only be killed by strangulation. It is one of the monster children of Typhon and Echidna.

Nymph - A nymph is a fairy-like creature with an affinity for nature.

Orthus - Orthus is a two-headed hound and the son of Typhon and Echidna.

Phobos - Phobos is the personification of fear. She is part of the Shield of Zeus.

Satyr - A creature with the lower body of a goat and the upper body of a man. They were creatures of Dionysus and known to harass and sometimes rape women during festivals.

Scylla - Scylla was a sea goddess with a woman's head and torso and the body of a serpent.

Sphinx - The Sphinx had the body of a lion and the head of a woman. It was the offspring of Typhon and Echidna and was known for asking riddles of men and then eating them when they answered incorrectly. The Remnant of the Sphinx is Pearl Nasso.

Styx, River - The River Styx is the body of water that separates the underworld from the living. To swear on the River Styx is to give a binding oath.

Tartarus - Another name for the underworld where souls go to be punished for their bad life choices.

Typhon - Typhon was monstrous being. He had one hundred dragon heads sprouting from his neck, a human torso, and a snake body. He is called the Father of Monsters because he sired the worst of the Greek monsters with his wife, Echidna.

Zeus - The Father of the Gods, Zeus was the tyrannical ruler of Olympus. While heralded as an innovator of culture, he ruled with violence and vengeance and held his kingdom together with blood and war. He was notorious for his hundreds of bastard children. Zeus was unseated in the Fall of Olympus which occurred during the uprising led by the harpies.

ABOUT THE AUTHOR

Michelle Boule has been, at various times, a librarian, a bookstore clerk, an administrative assistant, a wife, a mother, a writer, and a dreamer trying to change the world. She is married to a rocket scientist and has two small boys. She brews her own beer, will read almost anything in book form, loves to cook, bake, go camping, and believes Joss Whedon is a genius. She dislikes steamed zucchini, snow skiing, and running. Unless there are zombies. She would run if there were zombies.